"Mary Jewell is a wonderf
extraordinary circumstanc

"*Mrs Jewell and the Wreck o̶̶̶̶̶̶̶ General Grant* is a superb
novel, highly intelligent and riveting from start to finish."
—Catherine Robertson, *New Zealand Listener*

"Just a fantastic book." —Don Hollander, bookseller

"For adults and young adults alike, this is superb
and poignant reading." —Jessie Neilson, *Kete*

"Dramatic and well paced, it is rich with vivid descriptions
of sea, land and weather, and Cristina Sanders offers insight
into the physical and psychological effects of being stranded
in an inhospitable environment. Historical fiction at its best."
—Judges, Jann Medlicott Acorn Prize for Fiction

"I have recommended this book to a wide variety
of readers and they have all been captivated."
—Caroline Harker, bookseller

"Is this the best historical novel of the year?"
—Steve Braunias, *Newsroom*

"It's intriguing how many ways the novel overlaps with the
way I imagined the story, and humbling in all of the many
ways in which it far exceeds the scope of my own imagination.
Breathtaking." —John McCrystal, author of *Worse Things
Happen at Sea*

"*Jerningham* is an accomplished, vibrant and historically
grounded novel which deserves a big readership."
—Lydia Wevers on *Jerningham*

Mrs Jewell
and the
wreck of the
General Grant

CRISTINA SANDERS

THE CUBA
PRESS

Edited by Mary McCallum.
Cover design and interior layout by Sarah Bolland.
Cover image: *West Entrance, Carnley Harbour, Auckland Isles, NZ*
by F A Sleap, engraver, from a photograph by Mr Dougal,
Invercargill; October 13, 1888; State Library Victoria, Australia.
IAN: 13/10/88/189.

A catalogue record for this book is available from
the National Library of New Zealand.
Kei te pātengi raraunga o Te Puna Mātauranga o Aotearoa
te whakarārangi o tēnei pukapuka.
ISBN 978-1-98-859555-9

Printing by Blue Star, Aotearoa New Zealand.
bluestar.co.nz

Published with the support of

ARTS COUNCIL OF NEW ZEALAND TOI AOTEAROA

THE CUBA PRESS
Level 6, 138 Wakefield Street, Te Aro
Box 9321 Wellington 6141
Aotearoa New Zealand

to Groovy Shirl

who is 100 this year and has never
been shipwrecked (yet)

CREW AND PASSENGERS OF THE GENERAL GRANT WHO SURVIVED THE WRECK

SHIP'S CREW

Bartholomew Brown, first mate, Boston
Cornelius Drew, able seaman, Melbourne
William Ferguson, able seaman, Scotland
Aaron Hayman, ordinary seaman
Joseph Jewell (31), able seaman/miner, Devon
Mary Ann Jewell (22), stewardess, Manchester
David McClelland (60), able seaman/rigger, Glasgow
Peter McNevin, able seaman, Islay
Andrew Morrison, able seaman, Glasgow
William Murdoch Sanguily (18), ordinary seaman, Cuba/Boston
William Newton Scott (26), able seaman/butcher, South Shields

PASSENGERS

Nicholas Allen (28), miner, England
David Ashworth (30), miner, England
Patrick Caughey (34), miner, Newcastle, County Down
James Teer (34), miner, Newcastle, County Down

THE GREAT CIRCLE ROUTE

We boarded the *General Grant* in Melbourne on the third day of May, 1866, with light hearts and heavy steps.

The night past I had spent stitching gold into our clothing—sewing by candlelight with the curtains drawn and my husband watching my hands as though surprised his new wife had such skills. Skills to fold stones into silk bindings hidden between seams and in false pockets in the band of his trousers.

"Are all women so artful?" he asked me. "Or have I married someone extraordinary?"

My grey travelling dress was now over a hundred pounds richer and I had a petticoat worth fifty pounds. I adjusted the hem so it didn't drag. Joseph needed a new belt to keep his heavy trousers up.

We folded everything else we needed for the journey into our travel bags. There was not much: a change of clothing, some toiletries and salts, a pair of warm boots. Slipped in against the seam, a tin whistle.

I gave my husband a present bought from the last of my wages, a small bundle of the Negro tobacco he liked, in a strong waxed pouch that he slung on his belt.

Joseph's brother took us to the docks and right until the end he was on at Joseph to leave something behind, something to invest in the farm, but Joseph said no. We were going home to England and were never coming back.

I was ready to leave Melbourne. I had waited longer than most. Other girls from the hotel had found husbands early and gone to the diggings to live in high hopes and squalor but I'd remained in service: seeing to the ladies, waiting in the dining room, bettering myself by listening and learning the way the ladies conversed, the words they used. Waiting. I had been rewarded with Joseph Jewell. Less than three weeks after he met me he said he would marry me and take me home to his gentle Clovelly in Devonshire, with promises of land and a house of our own. He had the means to provide it.

Joseph was shy and gangly with a wide mouth in an oblong face, and serious eyes I felt I could trust. When he said he would look after me I believed him.

The first time I saw him he was strung out from the mines with his face still shining from the barber, impatient to get on with things. I'd seen it before. Men would come into our dining room and leave their dirty shadows outside, stepping clean as their laundered shirts through the door. I saw in Joseph a man ready for home, wanting a wife to take with him, and there I stood, a modest and diligent girl, waiting. In Clovelly, he told me, there were steep streets washed with misty rain that wound down to a pale, cool sea. I had never imagined a man saying something like that. We married within the month and booked passage home.

Other men from the diggings boarded the *General Grant* with us. Some gave Joseph a sideways look to see him before the mast. They knew of Jewell's Reward, the brothers' lucky claim, and knew we could have afforded a cabin, but I had no argument when Joseph signed on to work his passage, keeping his savings for our new home. I had been assigned some light duties for the cabin ladies, and they called me a stewardess, but that was mainly so I could speak to my husband without breaking ship's rules. We were neither of us used to money and Joseph didn't mind the work. He said sailing was a welcome change after the mines.

We paused on deck to admire the scrubbed planks and coiled ropes and Joseph rubbed his hands together, warming up for the graft ahead. She was a fine ship, the *General Grant*: a three master, 180 foot long and comfortably wide. American.

An older sailor clapped Joseph on the shoulder as he passed by on long shanks, and Joseph turned to take his hand. "McClelland! You're homeward bound? Good to see you."

"Aye, Jewell, and ye."

Behind him came a man I recognised from the hotel and I took Joseph's arm as he passed. It was the little Romeo, Bill Scott. It seemed he had also signed on as a sailor. A few months before he'd been banned from the hotel for first propositioning a housekeeper and then returning the next day to make a similarly lewd suggestion to me. He had a handsome face and a teasing lilt to his voice, but I hadn't misunderstood him. I reported him to Matron and didn't expect to see him again. Now here we were, packed together on the *General Grant* for months. I turned my face away and hoped he wouldn't bother me.

Joseph was sent to sling his hammock in the crew accommodation in the fo'c'sle and I waited on deck, hearing singing coming from their quarters, a Scottish love song I knew well and that the girls had sung to me laughingly the night before I married. I stood by the rail and lifted my head in pleasure, tapping my foot, watching the docks.

Men swarmed like ants with lines of activity and loads carried, grouping and breaking, busy with the excitement of departure. A man with a rope slung over his shoulders came along whistling and gave me a fast look over. His whistle trilled and eyebrows waggled and I dropped my head so he wouldn't see me smiling.

"You won't want for music," I said to Joseph when he came back.

He stepped close and dipped his head to me. "Ah, the music's fine, but I'll miss your tender breathing, my love."

He looked at me as if I were truly his jewel. And my heart sparkled because in truth I was. I had become Mrs Joseph Jewell.

Joseph had a reserved manner with most people, but he had opened his shutters to me. From a distance, and at first, he came across as taciturn, but I saw a shy man waiting to be found. He let me find him. He spoke to me without words, saying: Here. Come in, you. Let's be Mr and Mrs Jewell together. We'll be the Jewells of Clovelly.

I left him to his duties and set myself up below in the women's quarters but immediately felt his loss, which was foolish of me. I had been independent for years and would hardly give up my courage with my name. I unpacked my clothing and stowed my canvas bag, choosing a lower bunk and letting the children swarm across the upper ones while their mothers packed too many belongings into too little space. We were a small group, so the carpenters had reduced the cabin accordingly.

The children buzzed like flies in a jar. Against the bulk-head, the table was already covered with sewing and clothing and dolls. I lifted the lamp from prying fingers and hung it from a higher hook.

On my bunk the mattress was thin and lumpy. I lay down, realising how spoiled I had been by the soft marriage bed of recent weeks. I was glad to have brought a blanket of my own but I thought how much nicer it would be to have Joseph keep me warm.

I closed my eyes and smelled mice.

Three months and we would be in England. I could manage three months.

I went up to watch the passengers arrive while we waited for the afternoon tide. There was a giant of an Irishman called Teer, who helped load the luggage aboard though he was a paying passenger and had no authority. The sailors seemed to like him and humoured his offers of help.

"Mr Teer, if you'd just hold the casks while I lash 'em you'd be doin' a man a great favour." And, "Mr Teer, can you give us a hand stacking the crates there?"

He was agile for a big man, competent with ship work and he obviously enjoyed being part of the activity rather than an observer.

There were Customs men on the quay and women passed them with false smiles before hauling their clumsy skirts over the gangway, their men stumbling along in tip-heavy shoes. The big Irishman lifted their bags as if they held nothing but cotton and sent them aft to the cabins. I smiled at the thought of gold pocketed everywhere. The gangplank was lifted and stowed, and the tugs made fast to pull us from the dock.

Teer stood back when Joseph and the sailors cast off. He thrust his hands deep in his pockets as if afraid they might turn back into the hands of a sailor and reach for the mooring lines.

I tried to catch Joseph's eye, to pass some celebration as we were set adrift from Australia, but he was busy with his work. He climbed aloft with the men, out on the yards above, untying gaskets to drop the sails.

We sailed on a good wind across Port Phillip Bay and picked up a pilot boat to guide us through the heads. Australia fell behind, the southern waters opened out and I felt a great desire to stand at the rail, breathe a lung full of sea air and sing something loud and rousing. The last three years I had lived confined, governed by a no-nonsense matron, bound by hotel rules and walls, tied to service. The fussiness of flower arranging and exactness of linen folded just so, the arrangement of objects on a table and the polishing of silver. The needs of the women I attended. The gossip of the girls.

At sea the world was limited and yet so infinite.

❧

I found my sea-legs fast. From the deck I watched Joseph at his duties, following his activities wistfully as one might watch a handsome actor in a play. His slim frame moved about and above me and if he passed I imagined him pausing to sweep me into his arms. Of course he never did.

I tucked myself behind the mast and if he looked around he caught my smile. I tried to be crossing the deck when he climbed down the shrouds so at least we could touch hands. Close up we exchanged heated glances. I blushed when I thought of him and missed being in his bed. It was an unexpected longing, married such a short time then deprived of something I'd never known before to miss.

Love was surprising.

It was love that had brought me under those sails: the motherless girl from Manchester who had answered an advertisement for hotel maids in Australia, returning home three years later with a husband and a fortune. "An impulsive little miss" Pa had called me when I announced I was leaving home, and I was happy to accept that moniker because my impulsiveness was bringing me to a much better home than I had left. Clovelly. The *Jewells*.

My mam had married on an impulse, too, but hadn't had my luck. Every marriage was a risk; how could she have known her man would turn so grim?

We sailed southeast into painted sunrises as Joseph and the men fixed the many things that needed attention up the masts—chaffed sails, frayed and broken lines. I never feared for him aloft. Joseph's father was a sea captain, carrying trade to Ireland and along the coast. He had taught his sons to climb even before they could run. In the clear blue sky Joseph was handier than any man aboard. There was a grace in the way he swung himself over the futtocks, climbing out along the yards with his gully knife, treacherously sharp, held in his teeth. Sometimes I thought he shouldn't smile at me like that. Not with a knife in his teeth.

It grew cool soon enough as the *General Grant* blew fast down to the sub-Antarctic, following the great south circle route to Cape Horn. Every day the sun diminished and the sky turned paler, looking tired and washed out after the harsh skies of Melbourne. In just a week the Australian warmth drained away completely and a cold came off the sea to numb our hands and faces. I wrapped a rug around myself and stamped my feet on the deck when I went up to see the sky, to see Joseph's hands haul and ease, pulling and giving. Thinking of the callouses growing on his palms.

"That these hands would touch your soft skin ..." he whispered as he passed me, but the men were all about and I was unable to reach out to take those rough hands, feel them hot on my cold body.

Teer and his companions went about the deck in great-coats now, chins wrapped in beards, standing with the confident poise of muscular men. They talked loudly and laughed in clouds. I stayed away from them and when Joseph was off watch I rested below with the women.

The wind, which until then had been blowing from the northwest, swung around, obliging the captain to change our bearing and point to the icy south. On the eighth day out the fog closed in and both Joseph and Bill Scott were posted as lookouts, high up the masts.

"Are you watching for ice?" I asked Joseph, when he came down with his nose dripping and cheeks chaffed wind-raw and red. I was wrapped in my blanket, having no coat warm enough for the wintery cold.

"I've been watching a whale," he said, his face lighting up. "She was near the length of the ship and swam alongside for a while."

My husband, like me, was in awe of God's creatures. He'd been the first to point out the dolphins that dived and swam under our bow wave, and we'd laughed as they jumped high in groups of three or four. I'd only seen whales from a distance and was disappointed to have missed seeing one close. Looking into a whale's eye, I'd been told, was the best of luck.

"Wish I'd had a harpoon," said Joseph.

He reached out and tucked in a corner of the blanket at my shoulder and rubbed my arms with his hands. It made us both warmer.

"But no, we're not looking for ice, my lovely, not yet. There are islands away to the south, though we'll pass well clear of them."

I was called to help in the cabins, extra hands for Mrs Oat and her four little girls. It was really the job of Mrs Brown, the wife of the first officer. But Mrs Brown lay abed with a spinning head, and I didn't mind spending time with Mrs Oat and her pretty daughters. I brought my tin whistle in the evening and played lullabies for the girls.

"Call me Elizabeth," said Mrs Oat. "And I'll call you Mary. I've got a Mary, too. She's my absolute favourite child." She said this, and the little girls all laughed because it was clear they were all treasured equally and could simply smile at their mother and be called favourite, too.

"But I'm the closest!" said the middle sister, Rosie by cheek and name, elbows out to push her bird-like frame through to her mother's knee.

"Well, that certainly makes you the favouritest of them all," said Mrs Oat.

"And me!" This was little Ada, only three years old but full of her words and now waving a hairbrush at her mother. "It's brush time, Mama."

She clambered up beside her mother, who removed the brush to a high shelf and gave her darling a hug.

"I've got my hair tied up for the night now, lovey. But you'll give me thirty strokes tomorrow? We'll all count—won't we, girls?"

Mary Oat was the oldest with dark shining hair, which I plaited and tied with the ribbons her sisters pulled from bags and baskets. They handed them to me as formally as if we dressed a lady, eyes round with the responsibility.

Mrs Oat, on discovering I was just recently married, quickly descended into women's talk. It took an hour of petty confidences before I pulled the knot of courage from my stomach, where it tangled up the new, odd feelings there.

"Elizabeth," I said, and must have said it in a sombre way because the older woman stopped fussing with the baby and reached over to take my hand. I had already told her I had no mother or siblings and a father who was cold and distant. She would easily guess how unworldly I was.

"How do you know—" I began and then stopped, my tongue unable to push the words further. I'd been married such a short time and was confused with new feelings. There were changes in my body, an awareness. A regular timing missed. Maybe they were merely the awakenings of a man's touch, no more. Pleasures. I didn't have the courage to ask about that.

"How do you know?" I asked again.

"Ah, my dear," she said. And she placed her little baby into my arms, gathered a daughter or two comfortably around her and told me what I needed to know while the little girls listened, slack-jawed.

I waited for the opportunity to tell Joseph.

చ

I didn't see my husband that day, though I went up early—alive with an unfamiliar glow—waiting for Joseph to appear. There are things that a woman says to a man in the course of a life, short phrases with which she changes him. *I will marry you,* I'd said to Joseph—so shyly!—when he came to me for my answer and the girls at the door ran away giggling up the stairs to tell Matron. *I love you* was another, said from the pillow on a breath between kisses. And now this third thing, the natural progression of the first two, the phrase I held like a baby inside of me until I could share it with him, wanting to tell him before he climbed.

My hotel Romeo, Bill Scott, came down the ratlines and passed me as I stepped from the companionway. I gave him a polite nod. I was married now and needn't fear his flirtations. He smiled as if my indifferent face amused him, but was friendly enough.

"Your husband's staying up," he said. "He's been on watch since midnight."

Scott seemed to have dismissed or forgiven our previous encounter in the hotel and now worked closely with Joseph. They were to share the rigging for three months. My unease with him must pass. Perhaps I had misunderstood him and his advances had been a form of homesickness, like so many of the men. I was more unsettled by the fog swirling close in on the ship's railing.

"But he's on the morning watch," I said.

"Aye. We were both called overnight. Captain's doubled the lookouts."

"Why?" I asked, immediately realising it was a stupid question.

"Fog. We don't want to run into the Aucklands. You'll not see your lover today, Mrs Jewell."

"Run into them?"

He laughed, cheeky as a boy. He was teasing. "Nowt to worry about. Captain's just being cautious. We must be well clear by now. "

I stepped past him onto the deck, balancing my weighted petticoats. He turned with me and I felt his eyes on the folds of my dress, my waist. Whether he watched for the weight of stone or flesh I don't know but I stayed my hands from running over the fabric.

The wind had swung back and was blowing strongly norwest again. It should have been good sailing weather but the courses were clewed up and I watched the men out on the t'gallant yards, pulling up the sail, reaching over and down for the gaskets like long-limbed spiders. We were cutting speed. I loved the sea best when the ship was flying along, but the *General Grant* wasn't flying now. She sailed cautiously forward on a surging sea.

From behind came a stamp and a rough voice.

"Get on, you! I'll have no idle hands on my ship." I turned quickly to see Captain Loughlin, but his comments were directed to Scott, who had remained staring at me like a goggle-eyed fish. "Go forward. Mr Brown will find work for a man can't keep his own business."

He took Scott by the shoulder, turned and pushed him away down the deck. Over his shoulder the captain said to me, "You get below. You're distracting my crew."

I shot a last look upward, where the clouds and sails merged and men crawled over the shrouds. Joseph would be higher still, but everything beyond the topsail was now lost in mist.

Reluctantly, I took a last deep breath of cold morning and left the deck.

☙

Mrs Oat didn't need my companionship and Mrs Brown had taken charge of the girls, so I returned to my bunk and slept most of the day. I remembered the feeling from the trip out, the sudden wave of sleepiness that had overcome me during the early weeks at sea, the exhaustion of so much air.

In the mid-afternoon I woke, restless. I had no desire to sit in the dim light with the other women. The mouse smell had been overcome by that of soiled napkins. I was grateful when Mrs Oat sent for me to take her daughter Mary up to feel the wind.

"I'm glad we have the same name," the child told me, as I buttoned her into her warm coat so her pretty face peeked out of the fur trim. I took her hand and we held the rope as we ascended the companionway. "I think it's a lucky name," she said.

"Do you?" I thought about it. I'd known a few Marys. None had been particularly lucky. One decidedly not. But she seemed so convinced by the idea I had to agree.

I tried to shelter her as we came up but she turned to the weather with her small hand on her hat. The fog was still banked up and, running with the wind as we were, we got little impression of the speed we were making. I felt strangely adrift.

"We could be in the clouds," I said.

"It's not very fluffy."

"Clouds aren't fluffy like cotton. They're just wet air. Fog is a cloud that's fallen to earth."

She gave me a sideways look that made me laugh.

"It's true," I said.

Down on the lower deck the families were out. Mary pointed out the Oldfield boys, Frederick and Ernest, engaged in a lesson with a man in a high-buttoned jacket—Reverend Sadra. Mary seemed to know all their names. Next to them was a young girl trying to stand on one leg as the ship rolled.

"Emily is eleven," Mary said. "She's French."

We tried to stand on one leg, too, but found it surprisingly difficult.

"Have you been to England before?" Mary asked me.

"Yes. I was born there."

"I'm going to meet my grandmother. She lives in London. I had two more sisters but they died. Father has stayed behind to make a stone for them. Mother talks about going home but it's not my home. Is there fog there?"

"In London, yes, certainly."

"I don't like fog. Mrs Brown says it might be foggy now until we pass the Cape but I think the sun will be back tomorrow. She's just tired of being at sea but I like it, don't you? I could stay out here forever."

She had such a straightforward manner she made me laugh. I wish I had that courage in speaking, to be so sure of myself.

"Do you know any songs? Do you know 'O Susanna'? If you don't know the words, you could play on your pipe and I could sing."

I imagined Joseph catching me playing the whistle for an audience of sailors, whistling up a storm. But he surely wouldn't object to me singing with the child, at the stern of the ship where the music blew away with the wake.

"*I come from Alabama* ..." I began with my best American twang, and young Mary clapped her hands.

She took up the tune.

"... With my banjo on my knee
I'm goin' to Louisiana
My true love for to see."

We held hands and I twirled her around, her cheerfulness catching me tightly as her little hands.

"It rained all night the day I left
The weather it was dry
The sun so hot I froze to death
Susanna don't you cry!"

Our burst into the chorus was applauded by Mrs Roberts, who had brought her sickly daughter out for the air. The girl stood blinking at Mary.

"Join in, Lizzie," I said, and she did, for a line or two, but my Mary out-sang her for two more verses.

"What about 'The Merry Month of May'?" she asked when we paused.

It wasn't one I knew.

I was aware now of a sailor resting in the rig and another who had paused on deck. He held a rope, but his hands had stopped coiling it.

"Never mind. I'll teach you," said Mary, including the spellbound Lizzie in her offer. "I can tell you like to sing."

"I do, very much, but we must take care not to disturb the sailors."

I wasn't sure what Joseph would think if I made an exhibition of myself on deck. He'd heard me sing out loud in church, of course. He liked to say he'd met my voice first, singing "Just as I Am" from the pew behind him, a hymn that always moved me and that day changed my life. He said he knew then that he would love me before he even turned around. And then he looked at me as if he adored me, though we'd never met.

Singing for Joseph felt intimate, an act of love. I'd sung for him the night we sat up while I stitched gold into our clothing.

But our time on deck was up and the captain sent us below. "We'll sing tomorrow," I told Mary.

"Promise?"

I nodded. "Promise."

I looked after the Oat girls at supper and afterwards accompanied them back to their cabin, where Mrs Oat was fussing with the baby. There was a lamp on, a warm domestic scene. Mary, still slightly pink-cheeked, helped her sisters out of their shoes and into nightdresses. Then they played pat-a-cake on a bunk, amid a tumble of giggles.

"Will you read to my girls, Mary?" asked Mrs Oat. She looked drained and she hadn't been eating. I wondered what it meant in a marriage to give birth to six daughters. Perhaps she still hoped for a son. I loved her pile of girls, inquisitive and cheeky with no man present to discipline them.

She indicated a collection of books behind the rail on a shelf. Read?

"I ..." The bookshelf appeared to offer no books of pictures or nursery songs but thick storybooks with many pages. The children had stopped playing and were looking at me expectantly. "My eyes are tired," I said.

I looked, I knew, well and rested. Bright-eyed, I'd been called, often.

"A story!" cried Rosie and her sisters tumbled over me to pull a book from the shelf, which fell open on the bed with its rows of large wiggling print. "This one!" Little Ada took another book from Mary and held it up.

"No," I said, turning away and feeling the shame creeping up my neck.

I took the baby from Mrs Oat. She was a fat little thing,

with china-white skin, and a strange tuft of pale hair on a bald pate as if the rest had blown away. She fretted in my arms, but I whispered a poem—"Nobody knows this Pilgrim Rose", which I thought might satisfy Rosie—and Mary kissed the baby's toes until she gurgled with a rumble deep in her throat, like a cat's purr.

"She'll grow into a bonny girl with a happy laugh," I said.

Mrs Oat looked over, a book open in her lap. "Do you not read?" she asked gently.

I lowered my face to the baby. "I have my letters," I said. I didn't mean to sound defensive.

"Nothing to be ashamed of."

I was ashamed. I dressed tidily, kept my thick hair neatly braided and held a steady gaze. I could remember poems and songs easily and had learned to use my words well. But I'd only been to school for a year and never learned to read nor write more than my name. I felt I had been caught out, pretending an education I didn't have.

"It'd be nice to read," said Mrs Oat, "don't you think? So when you and Joseph have a family of your own you can read your Bible aloud in the evenings."

This scene I had imagined. Sitting with Joseph in a cottage on the hills of Clovelly. There were babies in the picture. I dreamt of babies as ships just below the horizon, waiting to come into view, to be recognised. Strong boys to help Joseph, and girls, little poppets like Mary, for me to love. I should like to read to them.

It didn't seem right to ask, but Mrs Oat offered.

"I'll be your teacher, Mary Jewell. You're a smart girl, you'll be reading in three months. Writing, too. It will be a fun way to pass the time, don't you think?"

I could write to Matron and have her read my letter to the girls who remained back in my old room, serving and polishing, waiting for their own jewel to set them free.

Show them how life could lift them up and make them as good as anyone. I now had two things to tell Joseph.

☙

I played for the girls, a soft Irish song, and when they fell asleep, Mrs Oat pulled a book she called *Tom Thumb's Picture Stories* from the shelf. It was soft and dog-eared from many little hands, and I looked through the pages to pick out the letters I knew. "S," I said, tracing the letter with my finger, and again, S. "Sailing ship," I guessed. We sat comfortably together, admiring the drawing of a tall ship running on a high sea with the clouds billowing behind. I should have left her to sleep, but she said she wasn't tired and seemed glad of the company.

"Sing me one of your songs, then, Mary," Mrs Oat said when we finally put the book away and I had a head full of letters. "A sailor's song—would you know one? Not bawdy, mind! And not one of those long tiresome ones that drone on and on. Would you have a peaceful one, something soft?"

A peaceful one, a quiet one, a gentle sailor's verse. They flowed in my mind, drifting tunes and words. They started well, sailors' songs, but there was always grief somewhere in the telling. But I came upon one, short and sweet, for when we were through the open sea and once more near land.

> *"Now to her berth the ship draws nigh,*
> *With slacken'd sail she feels the tide;*
> *Stand clear the cable! is the cry—*
> *The anchor's gone, we safely ride,*
> *The watch is set, and thro' the night,*
> *We hear the seaman with delight,*
> *Proclaim—'All's well!' Again—'All's well!'"*

There came a shout, and more shouting, and stamping across the deck above. Mrs Oat, who startled easily, gripped my hand. We heard the muffled calls of the officers and the "two-six-heave!" shouts from the sailors. The creaking of wood.

"They're squaring the yards," I said, a sailor's wife now, and knowing the feel and sounds of the ship, though I hadn't felt the wind change. I wondered if Joseph would go up for middle watch again or stay rolled in his hammock till dawn. I wanted to go back to our nights together. I'd liked our double bed, the talk shared between husband and wife, words dropped safely onto a pillow. If he was off in the morning we could take a turn around the deck together. Perhaps the fog would be gone. I wanted to tell him about the stirring I felt in my belly and what it might mean.

The pitching motion of the last hours changed as we turned with the wind behind us and rode with the swell.

I told Mrs Oat there was nothing to fear, but a minute later Mrs Brown came hurriedly into the cabin. She pushed aside a tumble of children's limbs so she could perch on the girls' berth. That was unusual—she liked her bed and usually shut herself away after dinner. "There's land on the port bow," she said. "Did you hear the shout? It's the Aucklands, Barty says, and jolly glad he is to see them so we know where we are. He's gone up. I can tell you now, he and the captain have been sailing blind these last few days, all fogged up like we are. But they have our position now. They'll put us back on course."

"There's land outside?" asked Mrs Oat. The quickness in her voice matched the sudden speed of my racing heart. I carried in my mind an image as if looking down from a bird's view of our little ship crawling across a vast and empty ocean. There weren't meant to be islands. Hadn't Scott said we were well clear?

"Desolate islands," replied Mrs Brown, and she picked at the skin around her nails. "There used to be a settlement there, but it was abandoned years ago. Nothing to see. We'll be well past by morning."

Mrs Brown didn't leave. It seemed she didn't want to be alone, though she sat quietly. I knew from hotel life that when a chatterer stopped talking it was time to take note. After days untethered on the sea, the thought of land nearby made us all jumpy.

I sat with the book on my lap, letters forgotten, watching the sleeping girls, their breathing so peaceful, soft kittens curled together. Mary lay in the middle with her sisters tucked in around her and on the edge sat Mrs Brown, staring at the wall with round unblinking eyes. We changed course again, no longer running with the wind but rolling across the swell. I saw Mrs Oat's lids drooping but the anxiousness of Mrs Brown kept me awake. I hoped any minute she would stand up, brush down her dress, declare the worry over and return to her cabin so we could all get some rest.

And then came the shout, loud and clear and directly above our heads. There was no mistaking it. "Land on the starboard bow!"

WRECKED

In a moment of absolute quiet I lifted my chin, ears straining. A stillness between one heartbeat and the next as the world paused in disbelief and one thing, the thing that I knew to be true, changed into something different. Something unthinkable.

Starboard bow? Hadn't Mrs Brown said *port*?

Land both port and starboard? How was that possible?

God in heaven, where were we? *Where were we?*

The sudden thudding of boots above signalled the men crossing the deck and there was the captain's voice hammering into the very wood of the ship. "All hands!" he shouted. "Bring her around! Hard on the helm!" The shouting of the men was covered by the squealing of the yards, and the ship lurched with a sickening roll, throwing Mrs Brown to the floor.

I reached out to steady her but found myself shaking her arm. "What does it mean?" I cried. "Why is there land?"

Again we rolled and I wedged my back against the door to lift the heavy woman to sitting. She had a stupid look on her face and was patting her own cheek.

Mrs Oat woke and seized her baby to wrap tightly in her arms, but the baby, indeed all the girls, slept soundly, unconcerned by the proximity of land in the middle of the ocean.

"Barty's there," whispered Mrs Brown, as if her husband was the captain and they were not sailing between islands in a fog at night. "We'll be fine. Trust Barty."

But I couldn't. I knew nothing about her Barty. Why would I trust him? I wanted to find Joseph, who would tell me whether or not I needed to worry, but couldn't think if he was above or below. He should have been with me.

Land?

The rushing of the waves on the hull ceased. The ship sat down in the water. We'd gone from days of open sea to the lee-side of something. The *General Grant* heaved and rolled like a breathing animal.

"We've lost the wind," I said. There were cries from above now, discordant, not the rhythm of command and response but shouting from all quarters, and the unmistakable squealing of the yards pulled one way and another. There was no corresponding drive forward of the ship, instead she reeled from side to side.

"Barty is there," said Mrs Brown again, with her absolute trust that her husband would steer us past danger.

I wanted Joseph. Right then. Before the worst happened. I wanted his calm voice, his steadfastness. Joseph was a sailor and he knew about the sea. He had explained to me about ship sails and winds, drawing diagrams with a stick in the sand at the park. But he had said nothing about islands in fog at night and the fear that comes with a sudden calm.

The shouting continued above and the ship moved in a deep heaving motion. She was alive with sound: taps and scrapings and gurgles from deep below like a household rearranging its furniture, horrible on the ears. Without the sound of wind and waves we echoed like a drum.

I opened the door to the corridor and stepped out to hear above.

"We're drifting!" called a sailor. Not Joseph.

"Current will push us clear." Another, and another again about drifting along the coast.

One voice, above all the others.

"Land dead ahead!"

And then the most dreadful call, a clear voice calling, "Rocks!" And still the thunder of activity through the planks above and the shouts to "Haul!" "Heave!"

"No," cried Mrs Brown, and Elizabeth Oat and I were crying, too. Wailing came from the cabins on either side and men were shouting, doors banging.

I needed Joseph so desperately that I leapt to the door but Mrs Brown held me back, tugging my skirt down. "The men don't need us above," she said. "Trust Barty. Trust the captain."

But I didn't. I couldn't. I felt my throat closing up in that tiny cabin and I pushed her hand off me.

The crash of splitting wood screamed through the *General Grant* like a giant tree ripping apart, magnified through the great cavity of the ship and through the water all around. We were dashed forward across the cabin and the girls thrown on top of us, ripped from their berth and tossed through the air by the hand of some invisible devil, their voices woken and loosed in high wails.

The ship had slammed into a hard mass and a part of her torn away.

ে৯

Mrs Brown, Mrs Oat and I clutched the girls and pushed through the salon, joining passengers fighting up the companionway onto deck; the bold Mary Oat of just hours before suddenly small and fearful and clinging to my neck. I surged forward like the sea. I would not be caught like a fly in a bottle when the water flooded in.

Above, sailors ran past, none Joseph. They weren't

working together to save us. They gripped the rails or leapt onto the rig and seemed, every one, to stare into the black nothingness that surrounded the ship and shout to one another, each with a different demand, and made no attempt at order or to listen for the captain's calls.

"Get below," one shouted, shoving me back towards the hatch, but "Muster stations!" came from another, pulling my sleeve and pointing somewhere mid-ships. "Go forward, get back, find your husbands!" I could make no sense of their commands and could see nothing.

"Aft!" shouted another, more clearly. It was the big man, Mr Teer. "To the aft deck." He stretched out his arms to gather all the passengers into his embrace and herded us away from the danger.

Mid-ships the lamps were lit but they threw scant light into the fog. People poured from the steerage companion-way and followed us back, carrying wrapped bundles, children and blankets. Beneath our feet the deck came and went with no rhythm and we staggered like drunks.

"Jibboom's gone," a sailor shouted to Mrs Brown's Barty, who didn't look at all in control. He was dragging his sailors from the rails and slapping them to attention.

"She's smashed right back to the cathead."

The ship juddered and slipped backwards, away from the rocks that had risen from the middle of the ocean to catch us dead. We made the aft deck and could go no farther. We clutched our people to us as we drifted.

We drifted.

Windless. We waited.

I knew enough to know that there was no steering a ship without wind. We might drift all night until a morning breeze filled the sails to set us free or we might drift forward again, on the tide and the currents, and smash ourselves against the rocks ahead.

Mary Oat buried her face in my neck and I held her fast. Halos draped misty gold around the lanterns; beyond was dense black. We waited, clutching each other, and still we drifted with sickening lurches.

It seemed a long time later that the cry came from up the mast. Was it Joseph, still above? His cry was joined by those all around. Over the stern behind us, where there should have been open sea, there rose a wall of rock, flaring wide, blacker than the night. Driven backwards at speed, gripped by a dark current, we fell down a great swell towards it.

The *General Grant* struck.

I grasped the man next to me and we all went down, thrown to our knees, spilled, rolling over the deck, and Mary fell beneath me with a big woosh of air. I cradled her below the wheel as the man above screamed through the crowd, "Rudder's crushed, Captain! Steering's gone!"

We lifted and fell again. Then the spanker boom hit rock and split, and the slivered shards thrust forward to catch the man through the back of the chest and impaled him, splayed across the wheel.

We pitched forward but there was a cliff face there as well, dead ahead and again the foredeck smashed into unforgiving rock. We were caught side-on to the swell in a narrow cove with the tide pushing us in, crashing back and forth on a surging sea, and the rocks grew tighter and higher overhead until I thought the ship must be crushed and we all squeezed to our deaths. The cliff closed overhead and with a pull and a slide, ship and all, we were sucked into the gaping mouth of a cave.

෴

Joseph was there beside me. I collapsed into his arms. I heard my voice on the air still calling and calling for him and couldn't stop myself. He held me steadily, though in the swaying light of the lanterns his face looked so afraid.

"Back, Mary. Back from the rails." He pulled me so I turned and staggered against the skewered helmsman with his punctured soul and bulging, lifeless eyes. Mary Oat screamed and I covered her eyes and bent over to clutch my stomach as I heaved and heaved my guts onto the deck, heaving the horror away.

The man's face hung backwards on a loose neck, his fantastic grimace staring up into a swinging lamp of looping shadows that stretched his features this way and that as if he was trying to escape from his face.

"Oh God—oh God have mercy!"

Above, the mast scraped across the cave's ceiling, catching in a pocket of rock and jerking the ship like a puppet. We tilted and the wood creaked, pulling and forcing until something must break, and then it came: the splintering crash as the top foremast split, ripping canvas as it fell through a billowing drape of sails and into the water ahead. The ship wallowed and dragged.

A cascade of rocks from above bounced off the deck around us and I pushed Mary into the folds of my skirt, as if a layer of Manchester cotton could save her from the rocks raining down.

But the shock settled and the screaming paused and I raised my head. We shuddered, trapped on slow swells. It seemed miraculous that we were out of the weather and harboured from the sea, that we were contained, somehow, and safe from being dashed to our deaths against the cliffs. I looked up, we all looked up—faces turning, astonished, at the cave's glossy black rocks in flickering lamplight.

We were afloat, still, not listing.

The tide pushed us farther until the ship wedged fast, now with the mainmast scraping above in a crevasse of rock, knocking loose stones and dirt that clattered through the rigging. My mouth sagged and I shivered violently.

"Steady, Mary," said Joseph, his face bent to mine, eyes huge in the eerie light. "I need you to be sensible so I can go to the captain. I need you to calm the women. Deep breath, my girl. Can you do it?"

He couldn't leave me. There was a dead man behind me. I couldn't turn around. Couldn't do anything. Dear God. What did he expect me to do? I hauled in a breath, the air icy and smelling of rock. His arms were steady on my shoulders.

"Mary. Look to the little girl, look to her mother. Help them. I'll be back."

The tall shipmate, Mr McClelland, strode past, hands busy with a long coil of rope. He called to Joseph, "Captain wants depth soundings, port side, Jewell. Let's see what we've got."

And Joseph was gone.

The men swarmed around, cutting lines, pulling and heaving and carrying lamps, calling and shouting, their voices loud in the enclosed space but seeming to achieve nothing in the darkness. Faces swung by on the lamplight but Joseph didn't return. I closed my eyes as men stepped past to pull the helmsman from the shards, but I learned the sound of ripping flesh. When they laid him out on the deck the blood poured from his heart and ran slippery under their feet.

I untangled Mary Oat and brought her to her mother, who lay slumped with the younger girls in the nest of her dress. Despite her burdens Mrs Oat had one hand clasped firmly to Mrs Brown, who was flailing her arms and crying for her husband, throwing her fear around the assembled crowd so it caught and grew.

"Mrs Brown!" I took her arm and slapped her hand. "Your husband is an officer. This will not do." The older lady turned to me, the side of her face a mess of blood. There was mud and gravel in her hair, and a loose, slippery thing on her cheek. I reached up to brush it away but found it was attached to her. Flesh. The inside of her cheek, hanging on papery skin.

Over the crying came the harsh sound of another mast scraping like a fingernail against the rock above and I realised the top mainmast, too, might split and fall. A sailor turned his face aloft and a rock smacked into his eye socket and felled him. He rolled into the darkness. We covered our heads with our arms.

A pair of shiny shoes appeared and a man thrust a baby down at me. I grabbed the child to stop it falling and the man shouted something unintelligible about a blanket and headed for the hatch, his accented voice loud as people were suddenly unnaturally silent, drawing breath perhaps, poised for the next surge, the next rain of debris.

I stared at the bundle in my arms, bewildered as to why this heavy whimpering thing had suddenly become mine. I had to give it back. It was not my responsibility.

"We're safe for the moment," Mr Brown said, a calm voice amongst us, taking his wife's hand, helping her to stand, gentling the frightened woman. He folded the flap of skin back across her cheek and held it in place with steady fingers, placing her hand under his to press on the wound. "We'll wait until daylight and see what's to be done." He took his wife's arm and nudged her forward. "Come on, old thing," he said, and led her off and we followed behind: Mrs Oat with her girls and the cabin passengers, men from steerage gathering their families, tripping over the sails that draped the deck, past the smashed spars. Me with a foreign man's baby.

I fell, twisted, and my nose smashed into skin. A folded face with a wet mouth gaped in a great curdling cry, just one more sound in the wretched night. Boy or girl? An Italian man, I remembered, with his baby daughter. No mention of the mother. Poor baby. I blew and she blinked, startled out of her cry. Poor baby.

Joseph was there again, crouched down before me, hand on my shoulder.

"When the time comes," he said, "I want you first into the boats."

"Oh no, no." I looked past him. Sailors were upturning the ship's boats and dragging them to the side. I couldn't understand this. The *General Grant*, for all her smashed masts, was not sinking. We surely weren't going back out into the wild sea in the little boats?

"We're safe here," I said. But as I spoke there was another rolling surge and a crack in the mast that was now wedged firmly above and straining down on the deck.

"Tide's coming in. The mast will be forced through."

"Through where?" I didn't want to understand. I needed Joseph to tell me.

"It will breach the hull. She'll sink. You be ready, Mary. First in the boats when the call comes. Promise me."

He took my face in his hands, this new husband of mine, his eyes so fierce they hurt. "Promise me, Mary!"

Into a little boat? I couldn't promise that.

"Give the baby back," he said, "right now." And he was gone to join the others: Teer and Bill Scott and Mr McClelland, who together had heaved fallen debris from a quarter boat. They turned it and lowered it into the water.

With a terrible crack, the main top-mast split and swung free, caught in a spiderweb of rigging that tangled into the shrouds below. I scrambled to my feet, clasped the baby and ran for safety.

Below was a riot. Decency had disappeared into a shoving brawl. Bags were upended, possessions strewn as people grabbed and stuffed valuables into purses and pockets.

The Italian man was there, struggling into an oversized coat, a heavy thing with bulging pockets, his fingers unable to bend for golden rings.

"What are you doing?" I cried, but he elbowed me aside and rummaged in his boots, little sacks moving to his pockets, a bulky hat on his head. "Your baby. Sir—your baby!"

He reluctantly took the burden from me and wedged the child precariously on a sloping table. In the corner sat Mrs Brown, keening as the doctor put a stitch in her cheek with a coarse black thread. I stood apart from them all, listening to the calls from above, trying to summon courage, not knowing what to do.

The ship groaned and creaked. I went above.

The first light filtered in, uncovering our tragedy. We were a ship in a stone bottle, rammed hard into the cave end. Grey-faced sailors stood beneath tattered sails. Shredded spars were strewn over the deck but the remaining mainsail stood tall, jammed into the rock. I felt the pressure bearing down and thought of Joseph's prediction that the rising tide would force the mast through the hull.

Once again, we were called to assemble on the aft deck, sombre as Captain Loughlin explained we would climb down into the boats.

"Leave all that," he said, pointing to the bags and bundles of possessions the families tripped over. "Keep calm and hold on to your children." Even as he gave his instructions the sea began working again, waves surging into the cave. The first ship's boat rowed away towards the entrance with three men aboard, hauling a heavy line and anchoring iron. As the craft passed to the outside world it dipped, tipping perilously close to the rock face. Joseph couldn't ask me to get into one of those flimsy boats and go out there, out onto the sea.

"Women forward!" called the captain, and from behind him Joseph shouted my name. It sounded like a betrayal. I couldn't do it. There was a contraption rigged up, a rope and a spar out over the side with the look of the hangman's scaffold. I was pushed to the front of the crowd and peered at the quarter boat down in the water, banging dangerously against the ship's side. The height was too much, the sea too dark. I cringed but there were hands on my shoulders, urging me forward. They wrapped me in a rope and led me to the edge. It happened so quickly I had no chance to step away, to step back and say: *No, not me. Someone else must go first.*

"I can't!" I cried, but it was Joseph there then, fastening the knot around my waist, holding me steady, lifting my foot to stand on the rail, pushing me up onto the scaffold.

"You can, my love," he said. "You must. The others will follow you. We need a leader. Be brave."

The boat was below.

The swelling sea lifted it towards me and I saw Mr McClelland and Mr Brown holding the oars. Teer stood with his arms outstretched for me, and on Joseph's nudge I cried, "God save me!" and jumped.

The boat wasn't there. It sucked back on a wave like a chair pulled from a table. I dropped a long way and hit the sea, plunging down and clamped by a freeze that filled me. The shock of it felt final. An end, like death. And I felt such surprise that it had happened. I never expected to die. It had never happened before. Death happened to other people. But it was here. Now.

Joseph, who I had loved and trusted, had killed me. He had called for me and sent me to my death.

God couldn't mean for me to die. But still I sank, pulled by the weight of my gold-seamed dress.

The downward fall stopped abruptly as the hauling rope jerked taut, punching the air from me. Death came with such pain. Life to death. It wasn't one thing or the other but a process of crossing. I was obliged to feel myself leave, to witness my own death's occurrence, and it was a horrible thing to be alive as one died, to feel the heart stop and the mind freeze and for one breath to go never to be replaced by another.

When the rope pulled I was bashed against the ship neither alive nor dead, dragged head first up against a wall of barnacles.

I sucked in the ocean as I was grabbed from above. Hands hooked into my clothing and manhandled me through the water that wanted to take me down.

As I died I saw Joseph. His hands were under my arms now, pulling, and I wanted him to leave me alone. It was over and he tugged at my corpse. But I had no control over myself, the involuntary thrashing of arms and legs, the death spasm as my mind disappeared into a black dot. I felt a final bashing of my head and the black dot exploded but I hadn't been swept through that point of darkness. I was still on this side of life, gasping against the small boat, scraped the length of my torso and hauled like a fish on a line, past Joseph's face, so long and wet, and flung on board. Strong hands gripped my ankles and hoisted me upside down so water poured from me like a jug. My arms flung wide and I breathed while all around us people fell from the ship into the water. I was laid spluttering across someone's lap and Teer was there with his arms around me. Close. Huge.

"Good girl," he said, "hold on." And he pushed me onto a bench behind him.

I rubbed my eyes, saw Joseph in the water dragging a man by the collar. Teer grabbed both men and hefted them aboard, then turned to catch a man who'd slid down a rope from the ship into the boat. The man scampered past to the stern and kept his face turned away from the ship.

But the women? I lay winded and in pain waiting for the others to go through the trial and land spluttering on the bench with me.

They never came.

Not one woman followed. Not one of the children.

"Come on!" The Irishman's voice filled the cave, roaring like thunder. "Come on—jump!"

I screamed at them, to the dark shadows gathered on deck, "You must! You must!" But I had no breath and my cry didn't carry.

Great bubbles burst from the water as the mast of the *General Grant* split her hull and her body filled, and with decks awash she listed, the upsurge pushing our boat far away. The Italian man rolled to the edge where the gunwales had been smashed clean off, his long legs kicking in the air. I willed him to save himself, my hands twisting the fabric of my dress in fists, but he clenched only his bag and toppled into the water from the ruined deck. He sank, instantly gone, with his gold secure in the pockets of his large coat and his bag clutched to his chest. A bundle wrapped in a shawl rolled from the deck soon after, across the broken planks. His daughter. Emilia. I remembered her name as she hit the water and began to unravel, a pale wrap drifting.

Joseph was on his feet, and in terror and desperation I prayed for him to leap in to save the baby but the heavy hand of Teer pulled him back from the edge.

"No one gets out of this boat!" He shoved Joseph back onto the planks. "You can't save 'em."

Mrs Oat, oh, dear heaven, Mrs Oat and the girls scrambled aboard a long boat as a sailor cut its tether with an axe and I could see her tucking her girls in while she shouted back for her friend. But Mrs Brown clung to the ship's rigging and the long boat drifted away without her.

The captain, climbing the mizzen, lifted his voice over the cries in a command to free the one remaining boat. It was hopeless. It lay smashed under the debris of the fallen masts.

Mrs Brown was abandoned.

Her husband, in command of the quarter boat in which I crouched, saw his wife left behind as men slipped from the deck into the water. He tried to turn us back but Teer and the other men pulled clear as a swell came from below.

All our eyes were on the *General Grant* as she sank and Mrs Brown, the captain and remaining souls fell into the churn and were swallowed.

We were nearly out of the cave when the wave hit and bounced off the end wall. We gripped on. Thirty, perhaps forty people cowered behind us in the long boat. The wave lifted and swamped them. Capsized, there were screams and frenzy and bodies falling.

I saw them drown.

The talkative Mrs Ray and her husband went down fast. Two sailors from Joseph's watch, Dutnold and Collin, tried to catch the Oldfield boys but they sank together in a tangle of young limbs. Mrs Roberts sank before her buoyant babies, and I reached out as if I could scoop them up from that distance. They were three and two and one years old, and they bobbed about in the threshing before they went down. Reverend Sarda stayed with the French family until the end: little Emily with her arms wrapped around his neck, and the baby held aloft as the reverend kicked and kicked while the parents sank fast. Then other desperate hands grabbed at him and they all disappeared beneath the water, God reclaiming his own.

Sucked by a strong pull, we couldn't reach them. Elizabeth Oat held a girl by each arm with the baby around her neck, and I watched my friend and her children sink. Darling Mary struggled for a few moments after her mother went down, her dark hair floating loose on the icy water like a shroud. Mr Brown tried desperately to pull us back to them, and I prayed aloud to God that we might save Mary, just Mary, a sweet child innocent of all things, but the flood hit us then and I fell back off my seat onto the boards.

I didn't see Mary again. I didn't see her drown.

Only three men swam clear of the wreck to join the few on our boat, and when no one else remained above water we rowed out of the cave to join the boat that had waited outside. Fifteen souls floated in two twenty-foot boats out on the turbulent sea and wept and cried and prayed, but it made no difference. Every other person on the *General Grant* died that day.

CASTAWAY

The big Irishman, Teer, shouted to the men to pull the oars and I hugged my arms across my stomach where the rope still bound me tightly. Too tightly. I tugged at the knot with white fingers but my hands were jittery in the cold and I could get no purchase.

We had left babies and children to drown.

Every single child on the ship. Before our eyes they had been swallowed by the black water as we saved ourselves. It felt like the collapse of the world.

The rope strangled my stomach.

I cried out as I fumbled and Teer heard. He paused in his rowing and reached back to slip his hand inside where the knot jammed, pulling it loose so the rope slipped through.

I took in a great breath but immediately coughed a splattering gush of water onto my shoes.

Did I carry a baby still, was it possible?

Had we killed it, Joseph and I together, when the rope cut me in half, before I had even had the chance to tell him that our child existed?

I closed my eyes to the rolling sea and towers of rock. Listened for a heartbeat. Was there someone with me, or was I alone?

With every incoming breath, I believed I held it. I believed there was another spirit within me. I could feel its presence. Perhaps with my body I had saved one child from death.

In a freezing morning mist we rowed clear of the cliffs and looked up at the heights of them, stretching all along the coast in both directions and diving into the fast-running sea. Ominous and bare, inhospitable beyond imagination. The waves hurled against them. The wind was growing.

Mr Brown sat crumpled in the stern, his head in his hands, and Teer rowed us away. I say Teer—though Joseph and the other men were all at the oars and pulling feebly against the tide, it was the Irish giant who hauled us over the swell.

The other boat, with only three men, soon dropped behind, and we waited out on the sea for them to catch us.

"That's my wife!" Joseph shouted over the sound of the wind and the waves, and he crawled across the men to claim me with his arms. I realised we were being split, some men crossing over to balance the boats, and I broke through the ice that was setting my bones to cling to Joseph. Some of the men, looking about after rowing with their backs to me, now realised that they had a woman as cargo. Their faces showed their despair. They were trying to save themselves and a woman was a responsibility more than they could bear. Were they thinking then that my fast death in the freezing water would have been easier for all of us? I stared them down, clenched my teeth to stop them rattling and held on.

❧

We were three days in those boats, in mist and fog and desperation. Perhaps more. Every minute was interminable. We sheltered in the lee of rocks that appeared in the night, the men holding us against the current. In the morning a few of the sailors tried to climb ashore, too late to see the danger. The water fizzed and popped and when it fell off the rock with a great suck the second boat capsized. They righted it fast enough and pushed off, but some supplies— tins of meat and salt pork grabbed from the galley and stuffed into the bilge—fell into the sea. We had already discovered our quarter boat held no food.

Mr Brown cried then, shuddering howls in a low key that fell upon the water as one of the sailors dived through the waves after a sinking piece of wrapped pork. The sailor, a wiry man with a swarthy look, pulled up against our boat and pushed the meat at Mr Brown to hold.

"Here. Your pork. I fish it for you," he said to the grieving mate, but Mr Brown turned away and the meat fell in his lap. He wasn't crying for the lost pork. He was crying for his wife. She had drowned in front of him. He had not saved her. The men were shouting for the lost supplies but Mr Brown was not in the same world.

I had been with her at the end. I, too, had failed Mrs Brown. Had failed all of the women.

I crouched in the boat and blocked my ears to the shouting. My life had capsized into immediate and constant peril, but I was alive, alive! Could I have pulled Mrs Brown by the hand when I jumped and saved her? She had been right beside me on the deck. I recalled vividly the absurd stitch tacked through her downy cheek, a black knot tied hastily by a doctor on a wrecking ship. The stitch was uneven and would leave a terrible scar. As if that was the worst thing that could happen to her. And then Joseph had asked me to set an example and in my fear I had let him down. I hadn't leapt bravely but had fallen into the sea. If I had jumped and landed safely in Mr Teer's arms, would they all have followed me? Might they have been saved?

I couldn't think about what Joseph had done, couldn't begin to understand that moment when he had sent me into the water. I thought I had died when I fell, but God spared me. Brought me back between two heartbeats on a held breath. Why me?

Dear God, of all the women, why me?

The men rowed through the night and next day, and we came through a rocky channel into a sheltered harbour. I was so paralysed with cold my back set unhappily, twisted into the shape of the boat. I needed to change my position, to work my muscles, but couldn't rouse myself. The men took turns pulling the oars and couldn't help me. Even Joseph, after that first day, had collapsed and slept like a dead man next to me for a long, long time. Bill Scott was there, his face close to mine, talking to me. I think he fed me something from a tin, some foul meat, moist and salty, that I licked from his fingers.

The beat of the oars stopped, and a moment later the crunch of gravel rushed beneath us. I opened my eyes. Joseph was calling to me, placing my arms around his neck. In pain I hung from him as he lifted me from the boat and laid me on the stony sand in a world of dreary light. The salt on my clothing chafed terribly against my wet skin, and in that moment the pain of the icy rubbing clothing seemed worse than anything I could bear. The men pulled the two boats up the beach.

I looked around at our pitiful group. The survivors. So few.

える

I peeled myself from the wet sand and sat up with my arms wrapped around my knees. My eyes were thick with salt and I blinked through a haze of tiny flies that circled my head. My fingers ran across cuts dragged down my face, washed clean in seawater, numb. In the pale light, shapes formed into people. They moved and I lost them.

I felt hard and empty as a shell.

I concentrated. Willed breath into my body. Willed my heart to beat. Put my mind to my extremities and raised a finger, tapped a foot. Slowly I turned my head.

I counted fourteen men on the beach. Sailors. Miners.

Some were barefoot and some without shirt or jacket, as if they had been surprised by the disaster, pulled from sleep without time to dress properly, white-chested as gulls.

I didn't know what kind of men they might be. Violent or mad. Ungodly, evil. How could I tell? They had stopped moving now and dropped their hands onto their knees, heads slumped. It looked like relief. As if they had reached the end of their troubles, as if they had arrived somewhere. But there was nothing. In this bleak place I knew our troubles were just beginning. We hadn't arrived anywhere. We were castaways.

Mr Brown, our only officer, stood at the edge of the harbour, disengaged from the others. He watched a wide-winged albatross sweep across the grey sky. His hands hung at his side, empty. He was a big man, but he was made small by the sea.

I swayed with sickness, more than the feeling of being on land after so long rolling. I felt the blood had washed from my body and been replaced by seawater that was freezing my flesh from the inside.

A sailor brought fresh water in a tin to me and I cut my lip on the jagged edge as I gulped it down, so cold it pinched the back of my nose. I hadn't recognised how thirsty I was, how my body had filled up with salt. The little biting things flew in a black cloud around my head.

The sailor's bare feet disappeared and were replaced by Joseph's boots. I was glad he had kept his boots. "Teer has matches," he said. "We're going to light a fire."

"We have nothing to cook."

"We'll get warm for a start."

"The men will want to eat."

"We have a few tins of meat still. And a piece of pork." He crouched beside me, laid his hand on my shoulder. I didn't have the words for the menace that gripped me, the fear of being so exposed. I couldn't make sense of what had happened to us and was frightened of what would happen next. We had nothing but a few morsels and the men were starving.

"And when that's gone? What will they eat tomorrow?" I asked. I looked along the desolate beach and saw stones, grass, trees. Nothing a man could eat. There was no settlement here, no human comfort. God help me, but I was in a dark place. "When they are dying of hunger, will they turn on me?"

Joseph looked shocked. "No one will harm you, Mary!"

The battered men were regrouping, circling, desperation written in their folded bodies. When they were dying, who knew what they would be capable of? Perhaps each one would sooner eat a woman than starve.

Joseph took my frozen hands in both of his, cupping them as if to share a prayer. "I am with you," he said. "These are good men. God will protect us."

But it had been Joseph who had sent me into the sea. And it had been these men, every one of them, who had rowed away from drowning children.

God protect us? I could find no sense of God's purpose in what had happened. He might do anything. *If God ...* I wanted to say, but I bit my tongue. There was no end to thoughts that began *If God ...*

Three days ago, God had drowned his own minister.

We limped across the beach and joined the men who gathered on a spongy lick of turf above the gravelly sand. They dragged driftwood and grass into a pile. Teer pushed it into some sort of order, scrappy bits of bark and twigs on the bottom, a few small branches above, heavier clubs of wood to the side. The sandflies were everywhere and I was too tired to slap them away. They feasted on my skin.

A scuffle broke out, a tall man in good boots pulling at Mr Brown's arm, spinning him around. "The matches!" he shouted. "For God's sake, man! Don't waste them!"

Teer turned with his fists up. I saw Mr Brown throw something onto the ground. Surely not a wasted match. Surely he hadn't spent them all!

"Do we have plenty?" I asked Joseph, but the answer came swiftly on Teer's heavy punch. Mr Brown, caught on the chin, fell to the ground.

"Oh the foolish, foolish man!" I cried. Seeing the stacked wood now my body was ravenous for a flame, heat to melt me and warm my frozen womb. The stupid man had been striking uselessly at the wet wood and a dozen sticks now lay dead at his feet. I wanted to kick Mr Brown as he lay on the ground.

Teer raged. "Where are the rest? Who has my matches?"

Cautiously he struck the few that remained and only once did the grass catch for a second with a sharp flare before dying. Each lost flame took a little bit of me with it.

There was one match remaining. Teer blew on it, and I thought he said a prayer. But he didn't strike it. He stood and put it into his hair where no one could reach it.

"We wait until it is dry," he said, and then he saw me shivering behind Joseph. His face changed, the way a man's expression will change when a woman walks into a room.

"Mrs Jewell—it is Mrs Jewell?" he said, and he held out his hands to me. "My name is James Teer. Come. Sit down."

In this cold wilderness, this place of birds and sea and mist and helplessness, I beheld James Teer. I prayed he was a man strong enough to save us.

With a sweep Teer cleared a seat on a driftwood log, pushed the sailors back as if installing me on a throne. He crouched so our heads were level. Behind the dense tangle of his brows he regarded me. Dark green eyes, uncomfortably close. Beside him Mr Brown sat up, put his hand to his jaw and flinched. I sat warily, shivering. I didn't think Teer would punch me but I didn't know what he might do.

"Mrs Jewell. I will light you a fire, and you will be warm and dry," he said. "And while we are waiting for the fire, Mr Brown will take men and go along the shore and gather shellfish and birds or eggs for our dinner. We will build a hut to keep you sheltered. We will keep a fire burning every day and when a ship passes we will be rescued. We will be rescued."

He was speaking to all of us, but his eyes were on mine, watching for a response. His attention frightened me. He was so close I could see the pits in his cheek, the shadows of childhood pox, and there was a white scar that slid down under his beard, something private, a hidden transgression. Sandflies crawled over his skin. I shuddered violently and my shoulders tucked up around my neck.

James Teer turned to my husband. "Joseph Jewell, keep heart. I pledge to you I will protect your wife. I will use any power I have to keep her safe."

His voice was deep and he spoke with the brogue I knew from childhood, and like with Mam's brothers from County Down I heard an earnestness, as if everything said was for God.

"And I." Joseph's friend Mr McClelland straightened his back and stepped forward beside Teer. He was an older man with an honest face.

"And I." This from Bill Scott.

"Aye, and me." The whistling sailor, he was here.

"And me." There was a ripple around the circle as one

by one, these men lifted their eyes and vowed to keep me safe. Joseph stood with his hand on my shoulder. I felt the pressure deepen. *You see?* I felt through his fingers. *These men won't harm you.*

It was a pledge made to Joseph, but it was a covenant for us all. We would keep each other safe. I wanted to say something but there was nothing these men wanted from me. So I crossed my fingers and made a secret pledge to the unborn child I carried. *I will keep you safe. I will hold you until we are rescued. You will be born in a bed.*

The men went in groups along the shore. I stayed on my log, flexing my brittle fingers, trying to rub my hands together. They felt as though they would break. Something sharp was at my elbow. I pulled my tin whistle from my sleeve, where I had tucked it after playing the last lullaby to Mary Oat. I had the strange sensation, as I gazed at it lying across my palm, that I could bring it to my lips and whistle my life backwards, blow back to the cabin with the girls when we were warm and safe.

Although we had not been safe. We hadn't been safe at all.

Joseph also remained behind, with the swarthy sailor who had dived for the pork. They laid the meat in the creek to soak out the salt.

"It was a good swim you did, Sanguily," said Joseph, "to rescue that pork."

The man was young, shirtless and nut brown, with a shining dark pelt on his chest. He had a moustache that perhaps had curled once and now hung from his lip, stiff with salt. He was fast and jumpy, often touching his chest with the sign of the cross and pressing his fingers together in prayer, his eyes rolling to heaven.

"My pockets have no rocks," he said. "So I float."

He had nothing other than the trousers he wore. A

sailor's gold ring in his ear. Nothing to sink him. Nothing to save him.

In my mind I saw the tilt of the ship's deck and the tumbling bodies, the swift pull downwards as if the devil himself had grabbed their heels. The vision began to grow, but Sanguily clapped his hands and snapped my attention back to him, a wide grin on his face. "But I am born in Cuba. By the sea. All the days we swim. Of all my brothers I am swim champion. And you know," he fixed me with shining brown eyes, "I have my pig."

He pronounced it *peeg*. Pig? Peg? I looked back blankly, for a second dropping my eyes to his leg, but there was no wooden peg leg—tender bare feet showed below his trousers. He rolled his foot to show off his ankle. There, by the heel, was an inked tattoo of an animal. When he walked it trotted with him along the ground. A pig.

He went to collect more wood. I wanted to ask Joseph what the pig meant to a sailor but he looked down at me with unreadable eyes. I thought he might reach out and touch my hair, but his hands hung by his side.

"Where did that come from?" he said, pointing.

"It's Mam's whistle," I said, turning it over. It did seem a strange thing to have pulled from my clothing. "I showed you before. My father gave it to me when I left home."

"Why is it here?" he asked.

I didn't know what answer he wanted. Why were any of us here? It wasn't planned, that we would be here, wrecked and cold on this beach. I hadn't packed the whistle with this in mind. We couldn't eat or burn it. I hadn't realised until then that I'd carried the useless thing.

"Did you play it on the ship?" he asked, and without waiting for an answer he told me to put it away, not to let Sanguily see it, and he turned and followed the Cuban into the forest.

Alone, I brought the whistle up but could feel no touch on my cracked lips nor summon the breath to blow. My fingers, once so lively over the holes, lay loose and flat. All my music had drowned with the Oat girls.

I closed my eyes to make myself breathe and keep my useless body alive. We were wrecked and I had saved a tin whistle. I put it away and it lay like a thin bone tucked against my arm.

Joseph and Sanguily returned with armloads of damp branches, which they spread out to dry in the cold breeze. The sweat on the Cuban's naked chest gleamed for a moment, but his heat quickly disappeared into the cold air.

He went on with his task, slapping himself with his hands—to keep the flies away or to keep warm, I didn't know. When he was out of sight, with fumbling fingers I lifted my skirt and pulled the damp cord of one of my cambric petticoats, the top one, one without extra seams. I struggled to step out of it. When Sanguily came back I turned my face away, but held it out to him, bundled in my hand.

"Please. You must take this."

Joseph stepped forward, "Mary, no," but with the bare-chested man before me he changed his mind and took the bundle from my hand, pressing it on the Cuban. "She is right. You need something with which to cover yourself. You must accept this."

Sanguily looked at me the way a man looks at his mother, and with his big eyes and thick lashes he looked no more than a boy. "Why you do this for me?"

"Please," I told him, "you must take it."

By the time Teer arrived back with a clutch of crabs waving their legs in his hands, the tinder of the fire was almost dry and Sanguily's naked chest was covered by my damp petticoat, a baby's gown through which his head poked. Teer took the match from his hair. The last match. Our last hope.

He struck it with a steady hand. The flame leapt, a delicate orange orb. It shifted to a patch of moss and hesitated, feeling its way around a twig, hissing over a leaf, not alive nor dead. We waited for the intake of breath. A gasp of air from below and the orange burned darker. It ran along a stripe of dry grass. I stood up in the circle of men and we willed the wood to catch, each of us praying, making promises to God of faithfulness and obedience if only the sticks would catch, if only we could have this fire, this most basic comfort. The light gathered in the dark beneath the tinder, spreading in the loose twigs. With a burst the insides caught and a flame shot up into the stack, through the loosely braided branches and into the air.

It was like a birth, another living thing amongst us. Without it I'm sure I would have died that night. The men fed and fed the pyre, and it grew into a monstrous wall of heat and light and I sat in my steaming clothes, sucking the flesh from the legs of crabs, chewing something that had recently grown on a rock, suffering the scalding heat gratefully. A tin of water was heated and passed around and the warmth filled my belly.

After the few scraps of beach-scavenged food were gone we sat in our own silences, not ready, yet, for talk. We needed something before we could go on, a blessing or an acknowledgement of where we were and what had happened. We had no man of God with us, no doctor or gentleman.

We waited for something to bind us together before we disappeared into the darkness.

"Does any man amongst us have a pipe?" Joseph asked and the men tapped their pockets as they might do in a drawing room at home to discover that no, they must have mislaid their pipe somewhere on the way to this place. But Joseph emptied his pouch onto a flat stone and each man took a pinch of the sodden tobacco, rubbed it between his fingers and sprinkled it into the fire, prayers to bless us tumbling out as the leaves burned. I fell asleep lying against Joseph with his arm around me and the last smell of civilisation drifting away into the sky.

⁊

I woke in pain. I was lying with Joseph behind me and the raging fire hot on my face and was gripped by a clenching spasm, my body twisting like a wrung cloth. I pushed up and tried to roll away but my belly contracted and I vomited into the dirt, a mass of bile and mucus, helplessly turning my body inside out, expelling the pain.

There were men sleeping close by. Teer with the snore of rocks tumbling down a mountain, Sanguily on the other side muttering words in a language I didn't understand. Others sat opposite on the windbreak, watching me spit and shudder. They didn't turn away, but after I finished and lay holding my stomach, Bill Scott took the tin of water from a stone beside the fire and brought it across to me.

"Drink this, Mrs Jewell. It's warm and will settle your stomach."

I felt such disgrace, as though the man had witnessed me on the privy and was offering to wipe up the mess. I shook my head at him but felt the nausea coming on again, and my spine seized and broke into a hundred pieces as my empty guts spewed glistening strings of saliva at his feet. Scott laid down the tin, touched me lightly on the arm and stepped away. Joseph slept through. The sickness was a relief. Such mornings had begun before we even left shore, and Mrs Oat had told me it was a sign of a strong baby. It gave me hope.

With my hand shaking, I lifted the tin, gulped the water down and turned back into the fold of Joseph's coat. I could feel my loose hair tumbling out into the vomit but I was already dropping back into a deep sleep.

Later, Mr Brown, bullied out of his apathy by Teer, brought pockets full of limpets from the low tide to throw into the embers, and a fat albatross struck dead with a stone, which Teer cut up and stuffed into the tins to boil. No one said out loud that it was bad luck to kill an albatross, and we all ate it.

Throughout the day the men moved hesitantly around. They looked to Mr Brown as ship's officer for instruction, but with nothing forthcoming from the distressed man they followed the lead of Teer. He had them upturn the boats for shelter, and they dragged twisted branches of a dense wood from the surrounding forest to keep the fire burning through the night.

I stayed on the bank by the fire, my limbs still fixed in the curled shape of the quarter boat. I couldn't unfold myself to stand. At least the smoke from the fire kept the flies away; already my skin was alive with their sharply itching bites.

Mr Brown and Joseph came up the beach with another small bird and a clutch of limpets and we ate a tepid, messy meal, picking half-cooked morsels from the tin. The taste disgusted me and I gagged and spat them out.

"Will we have the pork?" I whispered to Joseph. My voice sounded pitiful and small to my own ears and I hated to be weak when the men were already industrious in our trouble. But my stomach was in knots.

"Tomorrow," he said, laying grass to dry by the fire for our bedding.

This was not the time to tell Joseph I had a baby to nourish, but when I cried pleadingly that I was hungry he shook me off.

"We can't eat it now. We need to soak out the salt."

He must have said something to Teer, because a decision was made to open another tin of meat. Sanguily said he had thrown fifty tins in the smaller boat as the ship sank, and thirty pounds of salted pork, but when the boat capsized on the rock we lost all but nine tins of bouilli and the small piece of pork. Through stupidity. He spoke against a fat sailor called Ferguson, for his mishandling of the craft causing it to tip, and how desperate we would become when these tins were gone. The fat sailor called him a dirty monkey and the men stood there swearing at each other until Teer took his gully knife and pierced the tin.

We emptied it among us, using a fragment of wood for a spoon. The tin went around the group twice. It proved impossible not to watch the amount consumed by the others. We measured with our eyes and we judged.

Of the nine tins saved, we had seven remaining and fifteen hungry people.

A sleety rain fell through the night and if I slept at all it was in black oblivion. When the light came my cheek lay on wet moss. I itched all over. Joseph lay between me and the men, but we were jammed in together under the boats and I found Bill Scott sleeping below me with his arm flung up and resting on my leg. Suddenly anxious for the fire I wriggled away upwards over spongy soil and crawled free.

I found Mr Brown at the fireplace, scratching. The men had rigged up a cover of leafy branches, and he was dry enough and warm by the steadily burning flames. One of the men lay at his feet, not a sailor. He was a miner perhaps, but with good shoes and a warm coat, without the rough look the others wore. His skin looked whiter and softer than mine. In sleep he looked more a dandy than a miner.

Mr Brown turned to me with as gaunt a face as I have ever seen on a man. He seemed surprised to see daylight.

I didn't want to imagine the dark place he had been, sitting alone through the night while his watch-partner slept. He nudged the sleeping man with his foot. "Get to your feet, Allen. No need to rile the Irishman."

Allen opened one eye, muttered and rolled over, flopping back into sleep.

Mr Brown, who had seemed so gentle just the second before, rose fast and struck like a snake. He landed a heavy kick at the buttocks of the sleeping man.

"Get up, you snivelling coward!"

Allen cried out and rolled away, but Mr Brown reached down and grabbed him by his jacket, heaving him up to throw him staggering on sleep-slackened legs across the fireplace. He slapped his hands together, spat at Allen's feet and began to load the fire. I had no idea what the poor man had done to provoke such an outburst and put it down to Mr Brown's deranged state.

But there was something odd about Allen. I remembered his face from the *General Grant*, but couldn't place him. There had been a man, handsome and vain with swept-back hair who had looked similar, a man with a wife and children. Perhaps a brother?

⁊

Joseph went off in the morning and came back exhausted but with news that they had found some huts south along the harbour, possibly the remains of a settlement, long abandoned. Scott, the Cuban and another of the sailors had remained to investigate. Joseph would return and explore farther tomorrow.

I was desperate to be under cover. The cold and wet had climbed inside me. Nights were icy. We had nothing dry to lie on, just bundles of grass steamed warm and damp by the fire.

Teer insisted I lie on his coat and I wrapped it around my dress, but even that massive bulk didn't stop the cold blood running like a river through my body. It rained and everything was sodden. We lay together in a huddle under the boats at night but there was little body warmth to share.

"Are there flies there?" I asked, and Joseph replied that yes, the little biting flies were everywhere.

I climbed reluctantly back into the boat the next day and, like the sailors, I spat before I stepped in. Their superstitions were foolish but I wouldn't be blamed for any misadventure. We carried the precious fire with us—smouldering embers in a tin that Teer fed with moss and breath.

"It's not far, Mrs Jewell," Mr Brown told me, as he and the men set to pulling the oars. "I know the outlay of these islands. We are in Port Ross. We will make camp down the harbour a way, in Sarah's Bosom, until a ship comes. Men have lived here before." Mr Brown had swung his mood again, and he was in charge, decisive and clear with the men and courteous to me. I watched him suspiciously but his sailors were not alarmed by him, as if this man, this steady man, was the one they knew.

The advance party shouted out over the water when they saw us rowing in.

Sanguily—comical with his head poking through my petticoat—came waving to the shore, as if afraid we would row past and leave him freezing. He and his group had collected limpets.

"They are disgusting to eat cold from the sea," he said, and his lip curled down. "We are sick in our stomachs in the night. We want tinned meat. We need food, Mr Brown."

"We save the remaining tins. They are for emergencies."

"This *is* emergency. We're starving, Mr Brown."

"Absolutely not. Call the men, Sanguily, and get in the boat. Where's Scott? He can carry the fire to the hut and get it going. Jewell, you are with me. Mrs Jewell, you will stay by the fire in Scott's care. We'll investigate the rest of the harbour and be back before dark."

Mr Brown helped me ashore and I stumbled on the stones. I wanted to walk upright and strongly and not be a burden to the men, but my legs were feeble and I was bent like a crone. Above us the seagulls swooped and cried.

"I will take the fire," I said, but Mr Brown gave it carefully, the hot tins wrapped in a heavy canvas sack, to Bill Scott, and I was glad because I didn't want the responsibility of keeping the precious pile alight.

Mr Brown put a hand on my arm. "The huts, Mrs Jewell. Please don't expect too much. The settlement has been derelict for a decade."

I looked him straight in the eye. I saw then how much pain he held. In the black space behind my open eyes was the image of his wife falling into the dark water of the cave. She fell over and over again, the stitch across her cheek some gross caricature of a pirate.

I put on my hotel voice. "Mr Brown, I don't think you know, but this voyage is my honeymoon. I expect my husband to have booked the best hut on the island."

For a second I thought I had misjudged him. It took him a long while to smile. But his lip curled up in a tired way and he looked grateful.

"Good girl," he said. "I'll send a bell-boy along with your luggage shortly. Scott! A fire in the lady's room, if you please!"

My shoes were filled with water and the hem of my dress with sand, but I stood unaided. I wanted to reach out to poor Mr Brown and put my arm around his sad shoulders like I would to a child who needed comfort.

"Your wife was very kind to me," I told him. I left them to their explorations along the coast and followed Scott up a path the men had trampled through the tussock.

If I was initially uncomfortable to be left alone with Bill Scott, the feeling didn't last. He focused on his work, laying the embers on the kindling and blowing in a long stream as the flame caught. He didn't neglect me, tried to put me at my ease. He spoke of his home on the River Tyne, his words running together without endings in a soft pitch for a working man. Pa's brickyards had been full of men who dropped their aitches and left their words half finished. My mother had taught me better.

He'd visited Manchester once, he said, and knew the brickworks where my father managed a team. Perhaps he had tried to find work there but he didn't say.

"You don't sound like the women I met there," he said, laying wood on a fire now hot and glowing.

I wasn't sure how he meant this. I didn't want to be reminded of home and had worked hard to leave my Manchester vowels behind. But he seemed to be saying something different.

"What do you mean, Mr Scott?" I said. "What women?"

"I'm sorry," he said quickly. "I meant nothing by it."

He had the surprised amusement east coast people carried in their accent, a grin in his voice that made his words light. There was much about him that seemed childhood-familiar, a version of every boy I ever knew who grew up to work for my father: built to carry bricks and load barges, to run and to fight, the sort of man who lifted his chin when he spoke so he could look down on everyone. He was tough and physical and there was no poetry in him, but God knows he could drag wood and light a fire. Within minutes he had heated a tin of water and laid it on a flat stone for us to sip during the day.

As he worked and I was silent, his chatter died. I wouldn't encourage reminiscences of our past association at the hotel and his pursuit of me before I met Joseph. He needed to understand such things would remain in Melbourne. Those had been days of clean clothing and hot meals served on white dinnerware, of sweet maids who giddied at a flatterer's attentions and cried when he transferred his affections to another.

He gave me twigs to break and wrap into bundles of kindling for a second fire, a flame he carried to an exposed knoll, ready to spread into a high signal when our rescue ship was sighted. Only then, with the fires well established, did he turn his attention to the huts.

It was as well Mr Brown had given me some warning. These were not huts, but the bare bones of nasty rotten hovels. Only one had walls, though the roof had collapsed through the front.

"It's the better of the two. A house with a sea view, Mrs Jewell," said Bill Scott as he wove branches together and stuffed them with the harsh grass that lined the shore.

He showed me how to plait and twist the grass to make a quick twine, but though I was handy enough with dressmaking my fingers were shaking and clumsy. I was tired and nauseous and wanted to lie before the fire and sleep, but I kept at my task.

"How're you gettin' on?" Scott came to the fire and took a sip of the hot water we shared. I showed him my efforts and he was kind—he twisted two of my strands together for a short tie which was, he said, just what he needed. We would learn how to strip flax, he told me, and roll the fibre out to bind into a decent rope.

How long did he intend being here?

"Are you a rope maker, Mr Scott?" Like Joseph, he had taken passage on the *General Grant* as an able seaman. I didn't know what profession he had practised in Melbourne, or before he'd left home.

"That'd be a handy skill, fettling with ropes and the like." He handed more grass strands to me, knotted the end with the start of a plait. "But no—other than a disappointment in the mines, I've been a butcher all me life. Meat's given me a living and I'm handy with the cooking of it. Give us any cut you like and I can turn out a square meal. Pork, beef, mutton. If I had a shoulder of lamb, Mrs Jewell, I'd bake you such a tasty stew, you'd swoon."

The word "stew" had an immediate effect on me, strong as a punch in the stomach. Empty, my belly turned inwards. We'd divided up the pork in the morning, but the tough flesh and salt I had thrown up, with bile, into the boat's bilges as the men rowed. I was famished. The thought of a stew, made from a good cut of meat by an English butcher, turned a word to a smell and a physical sensation. My head was light and I wanted to be sick but my body was nothing but water and I was sinking. I could smell meat. That word. *Stew.* I could feel it in my mouth. Would Bill Scott cook me a stew? A dark meaty stew, with onion and carrots and a thick gravy to be mopped up in brown yeasty bread.

The world drew back, the fire dimmed and I was in another place, a quiet place of peace, breathing deeply, sinking in a rising black fog that came from behind my eyes. I felt nothing.

ల

I was propped on the ground with my legs stretched out in front of me and I rested against a pillow. A smell woke me, so desirable all my senses piled into my mouth and the fluid gushed.

A wooden spoon was before me and I opened my mouth and closed my eyes. A dream of warmth and comfort. I took it. Soft meat. Salty. Rich with flour and lard. I swallowed. I opened my mouth and again the spoon came forward.

Three times I swallowed. I knew the soft pillow behind me breathed and was not my husband and yet I took another mouthful.

Bill Scott took his arms from around me and moved away, leaning me back against the cold log. When I opened my eyes again he was crouched in front of me, making me look at him. A flat stick pulled stew from a steaming tin.

The cold descended fast and I pushed his hand away, gagging deep in my throat.

"What have you done?" I cried, my hand to my neck. The precious tinned meat. We had managed four days. We might have weeks before we were rescued. "The tins are for an emergency," I said. Even to my ears my voice sounded dishonest, flat.

The smell of bouilli was overwhelming and the fire was rosy, and I felt thoroughly warm for the first time since I had fallen off the ship and into the water.

Bill Scott stayed still and looked to where the heat from the tin changed the shape of the air. I watched the gravy drip off the spoon. There was nothing else to see, even as I tried to turn my head away my eyes stayed on the viscous blob on the flat wood. I found my tongue out, licking my lips. I folded it away but my lips still worked, rubbing in against each other.

"It was an emergency," Scott said in a voice so gentle it wrapped its arms around me like a mother. "You were fading. I needed to bring you back. Here. Take another spoonful. There is no shame in it. You're small and fragile and don't have the strength to survive the cold and hunger."

"But the men ..."

"Imagine if your husband returned and found you had died in my care? Not while I'm watching, Mrs Jewell." He brought forward the spoon again. I nudged it away, but he took it in his own mouth and savoured it and I saw the apple in his neck rise and fall as he, too, swallowed the meat. He fed me again and I followed his lead. I ate.

"Not all of it. We must save some for the others," I said. On my tongue the words were thick and slow.

He looked into the tin. We had eaten more than half already. I was dizzy with the feeling of life returning. I could grab the tin and tip it to my mouth, swallowing it like a man would glug beer. Had I been alone, I would have stuck in my tongue and sucked out the contents, licked the meat from the tin. But our eyes met over the spoon and we both pulled back our greed, the moral strength of one drawn from the other. The savage thing that had escaped us was reined in.

Scott wiped the wooden spoon on the lip of the tin so the food dropped down inside. He passed the wood to me to suck and I put it in my mouth, my tongue feeling for salt in the crevices. Carefully, he put the stew by the edge of the fire and laid a flat stone on top.

"The rest for the others."

He sat opposite me, cross-legged like a boy, and the tin sat there, within his reach and I watched his hand and willed it to move. We stayed like that for a long time, with me staring at his hand and him staring at me in my pain and the pressure grew fierce, each daring the other to be the first to move.

I thought of my death. I thought of the deaths of all those who had drowned in the cave. I thought of the death of the baby I carried who would die in the night if it wasn't fed. My eyes were drawn upwards and his were full brown orbs, shining in the firelight, locked onto me. He lifted his eyebrows, waiting for my nod.

I closed my eyes against the pull of him but my head tipped back and I opened my mouth. The smell returned first. I kept my eyes closed as the spoon touched my lips. Afterwards we sat by the fire not talking, spent.

Joseph's party came back well after dark. They didn't see the empty tin. They had rowed to Enderby Island, the land that protected the harbour from the northern ocean, and the big sailors, Ferguson and Morrison, had clubbed two fat seals. Butchered and lying in large blubbery strips on the fire, they almost smothered the flame and the smoke rose and choked us. Mr Brown's party returned and I sat away from the men and the smoke, wrapped in Teer's coat, and fell asleep in the grass. I woke to hear them arguing.

"I'll bring discipline if you're too soft, Brown." The voice deep and Irish. Teer. "We must thrash him for this and send him away. If we have no discipline we will all perish."

"She had collapsed, man!" Bill Scott's voice. "She was pale and lifeless and I couldn't rouse her. We had no food. I couldn't leave her so close to the flame and—"

"Did you eat?"

"One spoonful is all. To encourage her—"

"It doesn't matter if he ate or not! He stole a tin—"

"*Hostia!* To save the woman. *Santo Dios.*" A passionate cry. The Cuban, Sanguily.

"We must have discipline!"

"Banish him!"

"We vowed to protect her. He was feeding her."

"They are all we have."

"Four days, for God's sake."

"Those tins are to save us from starvation. She was not starving. She fainted, that's all. It's not for you to feed her, Scott, the woman can eat cockles like the rest of us." That was the pretty man Allen with the bile in his voice. The one Mr Brown had kicked. I would remember this. He was no friend to me.

"Joseph Jewell, what do you have to say?"

There was quiet for a moment and I lay still and afraid of how my husband would react. He was a man before a jury, answering for the fact that his wife had betrayed them all, tempted by the devil Bill Scott, and fallen.

I had been married only six weeks to Joseph and the thought that I'd broken his trust choked me. Nothing he said would surprise me, I simply didn't know him well enough. Our marriage, until we were wrecked, had suffered no trials. We had come together carefully, with our inexperience and particular habits and no real knowledge of the other apart from the stories we'd told as we walked out through the Melbourne parks and made our choice. In our room, together, the choice had seemed a good one. I had found a calm man, solicitous, neither fiery nor dull. We had come together gently and had become one without shame. I had not seen him roused to anger. Yet every man had a tipping point.

Would it have made a difference if he knew my impulse to eat had been driven by a baby created in those first precious days of marriage?

Joseph had a warm voice, round vowels rolling. But his words were as cold as the frozen ground.

"My wife is a burden on you," he said, and the shame saturated me. I didn't want to be anyone's burden. I opened my eyes so he would see I was listening, but no one was looking at me. *I'm keeping your baby alive,* I wanted to tell him. But if a woman was a burden to these men, how much more was a baby?

Joseph spoke quietly, a man in church, in penance. "Do you think I am unaware of how her frailty weakens us when we are scratching for our very lives? She is my responsibility but I can't save her on my own."

The men shuffled around the fire. Other than Mr Brown, none of the others sailed with wives or children. Mr

McClelland had said he had a wife waiting at home. But the others? What did they know of the frailty of women?

"Mrs Jewell is of honest character," said Joseph, "driven to desperation. If William Scott says he saved my wife's life today, I believe him. I will take the punishment for his actions."

Perhaps what Bill Scott had said was true. Perhaps I would have died if he hadn't revived me. But I tasted again the sweet, soft meat on my tongue and swallowed a dark guilt.

There was more argument then. Teer ignored Joseph and fired hell on Scott. He called him a thief and a liar, said he could smell the food on his breath. There were no words from anyone against Joseph, no call for him to take any blame. After a while they wore themselves out and came to a different mood. They expressed pity. Pity for me, though I heard beneath their words pity for themselves. They had pity that I had been brought here, a woman in a place where only the hardest of men would survive. They would protect me, they pleaded in voices pulled out in indulgence, until eventually even Teer stopped his call to banish Scott. I recognised Mr Brown's voice.

"We will put the matter aside tonight. In the morning, I will decide what is to be done with William Scott."

The men were quiet then, and the fat crackled and spat on the fire. The black smell of burnt seal flesh coiled in the air and settled across the camp and into our clothes and lined my nostrils so I thought I would never be rid of it. It burned away all memories of any other taste and soon it was as though I had never swallowed that tender meat at all.

FIFTEEN SOULS

In the night Teer and another Irishman called Caughey had taken Scott by force and rowed him to a rock in the harbour. He was left there in the rain without food or water, in nothing but the thin clothes he wore. When I discovered this punishment I went to Mr Brown to plead his release, but Mr Brown had lost himself again. He didn't seem to recognise me. He wore the look of a man in a trance. I shook him.

"A man under your care will die, Mr Brown," I said. He held his hand to his head and looked at me with puzzled eyes that reflected the sky. The insects settled on his face, bit his cheeks. He seemed not to notice.

"You must send a boat for him. You are our senior officer. You are in charge and must stop this."

Joseph had walked out with a party to look for seals. Once again, my husband wasn't near at hand when I needed him. I noted this as if keeping score, building a charge that I could later hold against him. Teer was rowing somewhere along the coast. They were gone all day and darkness was close and still Scott remained abandoned on the rock in the harbour for feeding me. The other men all had their backs to me, busy with firewood and building. Only Allen sat idle.

"Mr Allen, you know this banishment was my fault. *I* ate

the meat. You must row out and bring Mr Scott back to the fire. If he stays on that rock he will die."

Allen turned away. I didn't know if he was afraid of Teer or simply had no pity in his soul. The thought that Mr Scott would freeze to death wrenched my soul. We had suffered so many deaths already. Joseph's party returned with nothing for the pot. Hot with anger, I pulled my husband aside and shook his arm.

"You cannot let this happen. Scott was trying to save me. For the love of God!"

"He must be punished, Mary."

"He cannot survive out there."

Joseph had nothing more to say. He was a man of too few words. It seemed his tongue had been loosened only for the brief period when courting had made it necessary. There was something wrong between us, as if he had thrown away the last weeks when we had opened ourselves and begun to trust each other. The taciturn man was back and I didn't know how to reach beyond. He turned away but I kept hold of his arm, wanting to goad him to action.

"You leave him there and his death will be on your conscience," I said, but my passion roused no reaction in my husband. "You are heartless. Just as when you made me jump from the ship, when you knew I would surely drown."

As soon as the words had dropped into the air between us I wanted to pull them back. I expected an immediate reaction from Joseph; he would have been quite in his rights to strike me. I had grown up taking beatings and knew every man had his limit, the taunt which must be shut down with a fist. I had accused Joseph of sending me to my death, and he should surely, brutally, reply. I closed my eyes and waited for the anger that would come fast and hard.

When it didn't, when Joseph just lifted my hand and

dropped it off his arm, I realised that I didn't know this man at all. The Joseph I had imagined I knew had gone. He put me aside as if I was of no account.

Jesus, God, but I needed him on my side. He walked away and my loneliness filled the place where he had been.

It was Mr McClelland who went to the island to bring Scott back. He took Mr Brown with him, leading the stumbling mate past Teer, who glared but didn't stop them. The officer was confused but still held the senior rank. When they returned from the harbour, Scott dropped a small plucked gull onto a stone. An offering. Mr Brown said, "You will leave it now, Teer."

Mr McClelland handed Scott the tin of water and he drank with his head down, his skin tinged blue, as if ice had already formed inside him. The rest of us settled down around the fire and fell asleep listening to him hungrily sucking flesh from a strip of seal one of the sailors had put aside for him. The bird he left for us to share.

☙

We woke, and before anything else we gathered stuff for the fire. I tugged at soft grass that came away easily from the peaty soil, leaving a rotting base. It was springy underfoot, wobbly and unsettling. I was careful where I put my hands. It looked a place where bones might lie. The men brought branches from the forest, most were twisted and heavy but Sanguily dragged in smoother branches with red berries under pale green leaves. The berries rubbed off in my hand and bled between my fingers, stinking.

"Not those," said Teer, kicking the branches aside.

"The blood!" cried Sanguily, flinching from my red hands.

Teer scowled at him. "It's not blood, you fool. It's stink-wood. Useless. Doesn't burn."

It seemed that because of my frail sex there was to be no blame for my weakness, and Bill Scott, his penance paid, was forgiven, though he moved gingerly amongst the men. I worked at Joseph's side. The tension was terrible, but neither of us found words to make amends. He had called me a burden and I had called him heartless and the accusations remained. I could cry but couldn't take back my words.

When the rain stopped, Teer called us and we gathered in our soaking clothing around the fire. My hair swelled in the damp and broke loose from its braids and I tried to tuck it together. It was stupid to fret over my lack of a bonnet, in that remote place with all of us wild animals and with problems like mountains before us, but I felt indecent and on display. I had no shawl and had lost the top button on my dress during the morning's labour. I placed my hand over my collar, pressing the edges together.

Joseph stayed closely by my side.

Teer stood well balanced on his booted feet, arms folded across his wide chest, stamping on the grass to mark his place by the fire. "It's time for some order and a plan," he said. "But first, a man must know who his companions are. So let's be having it, formal like."

He rubbed his beard and looked to the ship's officer to step up, but Mr Brown waved his hand at him. "Passengers first," he said. "Tell us your story, Irishman."

A pause, a gathering of breath. We were still the loosest of groups. It was time to know who was here, who we were, what we added up to. A collection of fifteen wrecked souls to be counted.

℘

"My name's James Teer," the big man began, his words coming through closed teeth as if every word had to be let out of a cage. But with the white light of midday on his face, his beard and brows were less black than the night before. "I've called many places home but my boyhood was in Ireland and my family are fishermen. I washed up in New Zealand as harbour pilot at Hokitika before I went to the mines in Australia." His large hands and broad shoulders were tools or weapons. Who knew how they would be used? "There's work for pilots out of Belfast now and that's where I'm heading. I'm goin' home."

He said this with conviction and despite our helpless circumstances, I believed he would. He could take us all with him. I looked up to catch his eye but he wasn't looking at me.

The next man stood. He was well framed, in height just shy of Teer, with a mess of dirty sand-coloured hair. He had a soft face for a sailor, blue eyes and the beginnings of a beard that speckled gingery on pale skin. "Patrick Caughey," he said. "From Newcastle in County Down, same as our man James here. We left home some years apart but met again in the mines—would you believe it? We grew up on the same street and I travelled halfway around the world to find the big man at my elbow in the diggings."

Caughey had the light behind him, his shoulders back for breath, a man used to an audience for his stories. He took a sip from the tin of bark tea as it passed around the circle. It had been brewed by Mr McClelland and tasted of dirt. He handed it on. "I did the mining with a small share of luck, but I'm a baker by trade and I'm to take over from my father. I'm sorry we've no flour here or I'd bake ye a loaf."

Teer smiled at that. "Perhaps you'll give us a story tonight, Pat," he said, and Caughey nodded.

"Aye, p'rhaps I will."

The next man was narrow-hipped and handsome and moved like a dancer. His coat was thick and smart and his long boots were a soft leather, white-lined with salt. "David Ashworth," he introduced himself. He took each man by the eye, but his gaze slid over me. I sat with my spine curled and could imagine I might slip the attention of a man like Ashworth. "I was born in Lancaster but emigrated to Massachusetts as a child. I've little memory of England." His tone was that of an educated man, a man who could earn a living without dirtying his hands and who was accustomed to good things. "I followed the gold to Victoria for the adventure. A man needs to live a little." He looked around at where his adventure had taken him and some of the smugness fell away.

"What are your family, Mr Ashworth?" asked Teer.

"The family are printers. It's the trade I'll return to." He smiled, a bit nastily. "I put my gold in the bank so it'll be waiting when I get home." Ashworth was one who had saved himself when the long boat capsized. I'd watched Teer haul him in as the water churned around him, a strong swimmer in a heavy coat. He had managed to cross the distance to our boat. Yet he, too, had saved no one. He had swum past drowning children.

Allen was the last man from among the passengers, and Teer had to tell him to stand because the lazy northerner had his head right down into his coat. He mumbled his name, Nicholas Allen, staring at the ground as if he expected to be found wanting by these men. His vanity showed in his stylishly trimmed hair swept back from a wide forehead, but he pushed his fingers through it restlessly now and with no pomade to hold the wave it flopped into his eyes. The beginnings of a beard hardened up the otherwise effeminate sweep of his jaw. In the curve of his cheek a memory came back.

Nicholas Allen was the man that had swung down the rope into the quarter boat and climbed past me, out of the way, face frozen in fear. I wouldn't judge him for that. We had all been terrified as the boat went down.

"I was a miner," he said in a quiet voice, but there was no directness in him and the men around him looked away. Nicholas Allen offered no more than that.

Mr Brown spat in the dirt, but perhaps he was just clearing his mouth.

I watched and listened to the men, noting their manner and the truth in their voices, trying to get the measure of each. In a mass they appeared rough and daunting, but one by one they were just men, going home. They threw glances at me, sideways, first to my boots, my filthy dress and clenched hands, before braving a look upwards to my face. Joseph watched from side to side like a beacon, keeping their eyes, like flies, away from his wife.

The mate stood next, looking more in control of himself. "First Officer Bartholomew Brown, American." He had sailed with the *General Grant* from America and said he had been a sailor all his life. There was a decent ordinariness about the man, so no one turned away as he spoke of his wife, married twenty-two years, the gentlest soul, and now … gone … and he couldn't … he hadn't … she …

It was Mr McClelland who took his arm as the officer reached out and, with touching respect, helped him sit. Mr Brown dropped his quivering jaw into his big hands.

Mr McClelland waited for him to settle before taking a deep steadying breath and squinting around the group. He was a big-boned man without much flesh, and his clothes were thin but neatly patched.

"David McClelland," he said with a nodding bow to the company. "From Glasgow. My wife, Janet—we've been married for forty years—she's expecting me home for good in August. So I'm not planning on staying here too long, I'd hate to let her down."

The men chuckled. I was growing to like Mr McClelland—married forty years and made happy by the mention of his wife.

"We lost our boy five years past in the Clyde and Janet looks after the wains now, the grand-babbies." His voice was breathy and light as if all his ideas were coming out in one long exhale, quietly, so not to disturb the air. "Well, they'll no' be babbies now! The oldest, she's marryin' in September. I'll need to be home for that."

"Your trade?" asked Ashworth.

"We're silk twisters, the McClellands, but when business stalled I took to the shipyards as a rigger and signed on, able seaman. But it's time to go home now—my eyes are failing. I cannae see farther then you," he said, pointing to Teer, unmissable across the circle, whose frown deepened at this admission. Where I saw an intelligent, gentle man, Teer scowled at a blind man near sixty, a burden. "But I can feel with my fingers. I can hear a change in the wind and I can smell snow. I can tell ye there'll be snow falling tomorrow."

We all lifted our heads then and breathed deeply. I smelled unwashed bodies and something putrid from the fire, salt and the tang of the damp forest. Was it possible to smell snow? I prayed he was wrong.

Peter McNevin replaced the older man as speaker. He had poked holes into a boat's sackcloth to make a sleeveless shirt to wear under his jacket and his feet were wrapped in grass, but he still wore his knife on his belt. He told us he was from Islay where every man was a singer.

When he gathered his breath and his foot tapped four times I knew we were in for a song. But when it came—and I was surprised any among us could rouse a tune in our misery—the words appeared haltingly as if a song he had known all his life hadn't caught up with his new situation:

> *"There's meadows in Lanark and mountains in Skye,*
> *And pastures in Hielands and Lowlands forbye;*
> *But there's nae greater luck for the heart so they say*
> *Than to herd the fine cattle in bonny Islay."*

He gave us three verses, the brave man, a yearning in his voice as he sang of his home. I recognised Mr McNevin as the singer of the love song on the day we left Melbourne, but he had not the same voice now he'd been wrecked. I doubted he'd ever get that joy back again.

He sat to an applause that warmed our hands.

"Andrew Morrison. Able seaman." The next sailor was heavy-shouldered and thick-necked, with curly brown hair receding from a baby face, one of the few men in warm clothing. He'd been in the first boat that had escaped the cave and in the confusion not returned, along with his friends William Ferguson, who looked clumsy and fat for a sailor, and Cornelius Drew, who was soft and white-faced.

Drew ducked his head and stuttered his name as he blinked continuously up at Teer. He didn't look like a man of strength and courage. Unlike his two friends, he had lost his coat, shoes and knife, though the three of them had been dressed for the watch when we abandoned ship. I recalled the chaos when their boat had overturned and wondered if, like the tins of food, Drew's heavy gear had been abandoned to the sea as he struggled back on board.

Cornelius Drew felt for the log behind him and sat, perching like an owl.

Joseph stepped forward.

I barely recognised in him the man I had married. The drop of his face seemed unfamiliar and I couldn't find my loving, thoughtful husband in its long lines. My life depended on him and yet I had no inkling of how he would account for himself, so different were our circumstances now from what had gone before. How could it be expected, after our brief courtship and few weeks of married life that this man should now be part of me, and I of him?

We had not been tested, nothing had passed between us to prepare us for this. The others waited, like me, to hear him and to pass judgement: what make of man was he? That was what we needed to know. Would he help or hinder our survival? Desperately, I prayed he would stand strong and tall.

In this company, he wasn't handsome, or tall, or strong. Joseph was thirty-one years old, almost a decade older than me, but his wide mouth and full lips, which I had found so sensual in our marriage bed, here appeared boyish. The healthy sun-blush of his skin was already fading to wan. He had boots, but he'd lost his gully in the wreck and wore its empty sheath strapped to his thigh like a weakness. His shirt hung loose on him. I looked up as he drew in his breath, a lank of dull hair slipping forward.

"Joseph Jewell, miner and able seaman, from Devonshire. My wife, Mary." It seemed he had used up all his words the night before, speaking of my frailty. Or perhaps there was nothing else to be said. He stood for a while more. Then he sat.

I pressed my lips together and swallowed my doubt. I turned away from him and stared into the fire so he wouldn't see the disappointment in my face.

The little Cuban half rose and then sat and then rose again, unsure whether there was more to follow. There was not.

"William Murdoch Sanguily-Garritte," he said, with his hand on his heart and a dip of his head. He straightened as if being presented to the queen. He had a delicate face and his moustache was now curled and shone with seal grease. His chin pointed up and the ruff of my petticoat tickled his throat. "I am American! My godparents send me to Boston for my education and I stay there. It is my choice. My brothers, they stay in Cuba where we are born. They are men of the military."

I didn't know where Cuba was. I imagined a sunny island with fat brown children running through fruit trees, glossy chickens pecking underfoot and basking dogs. I wrapped my arms around myself and moved closer to Joseph but felt no warmth coming from him.

"I sign on with Captain Loughlin in Boston, may God have him in his glory. I work hard and I am strong." Sanguily filled himself up so he appeared not to be looking up to his superiors but standing eye-to-eye. He remained standing until Teer gestured he could sit and Aaron Hayman took his place. He was another sailor who had kicked off his shoes in the sea but stood uncomplaining. He had kept his gully strapped in its sheath, and it was then I realised that unconsciously I had been dividing the men into those who had knives and those who did not.

Hayman was English, going home. He didn't give details but he didn't seem to be hiding, like Allen. I recognised a shy man, a man unaccustomed to sharing himself. A man like Joseph.

Bill Scott was the last to announce himself, though as an able-bodied seaman he ranked above the ordinary seamen and should have been called before the Cuban. Despite his disgrace he swaggered, fists clenched, cheeks dimpled in a smiling sneer as if this life was a game he would punch or charm his way through. His cropped hair was messy above a high forehead.

"William Scott. South Shields on the Tyne," he said. "Butcher by trade, came over in a ship's galley. Did me time in the mines but never had the luck, and as for the life of a sailor ... ach, Jesus, will you look at us? Goddamn, but I'll not go back to sea again." I saw the full brown rounds of his eyes as he pretended surprise. "Jesus, excuse me swearing, Mrs Jewell. I forgot we'd a woman present."

Both Caughey and Ferguson leapt to their feet at the blasphemy and Teer had to put out his hand to stop them taking a swing at Scott. Did they expect I would put my hand to my forehead and faint? I felt like I had just walked into a public bar and silenced the room—men unable to be men with a woman in earshot. I blushed at the attention, heat flooding my face in that cold place and I turned to hide in Joseph's shadow. I was ashamed. Not for the cursing, but for being so easily embarrassed by the goading and by my own feebleness that made me unable to hold up my head. Ashamed of being a woman in this company of men where all our lives depended on the skill and strength and courage offered, and I could offer nothing. I was nothing.

With introductions done, the men rose and stretched in the cold air. They looked down to the beach, back to the huts, away up into the hills. One stoked the fire. We waited for someone to take us forward. It was time to discuss our situation and make plans of how we were to live until a ship came. Mr Brown made no move to take the lead. Once again, it was Teer.

"Will ye not speak, Mr Brown?" Teer said, but the first officer remained silent.

The lost look was back on his face, his hair hung into his eyes and his shoulders slumped. He made no effort to energise us. He had no energy at all.

Mr McClelland crouched down. "Come, Mr Brown. You're the senior officer here. Will you no' lead us?"

I could feel a parting of the men. The sailors stayed by the sagging officer, while the miners turned to Teer. Bill Scott moved around, distancing himself from Mr Brown's weakness.

Teer's eyes narrowed. "I'm calling you to stand up and act like a ship's officer or we'll relieve you of your duty, Mr Brown."

"Give him a bit of time," said Mr McClelland, still by the man's shoulder. "He's grievin'. Show some kindness."

"We need food and an oven, tools, shelter, warmth, signal fires, skins, clothing, soap. Kindness comes later. It'll be earned."

The men waited for Mr Brown to rise up or for another to step forward, but nothing happened.

A gull, hovering overhead, dived to snatch a scrap of discarded blubber from the ground. Without landing, it pumped its silver wings and flew away.

"We need to eat," said Teer.

The impasse broke. Teer turned and strode away down the path to the beach. He had become a force, pulling in the loyalty of the men. He was followed by Caughey, Scott, Ashworth and the others, miners and sailors trailing behind him in a long line. Joseph looked questioningly at me. I said to him "Go, go!"

Teer was right. Kindness could come later. Now we needed food and shelter.

We had our leader and they followed him out onto the rocks. I stayed with Mr Brown and Mr McClelland.

"I can watch over him if you want to go with the others," I told the old sailor, but I noticed the strain on his face and caught the glassy reflection in his eyes. His lashes were crusty and eyes rheumy. He had his head turned as if hearing rather than seeing the men moving off.

"Nay, lass, I'll stay. We'll leave our mate to sit for the now, shall we, while we get Scott's bird boiled up for a broth?"

As we cut the bird and put the pitifully small pieces of flesh and bones into the tins, Mr McClelland asked me if I knew island cabbage.

"Looks like rhubarb," he said. "Big fleshy leaves, with a frilled edge. Some species have little hairs on the stalks."

I shook my head. "I've lived my whole life in cities. I don't know anything about leaves. Can we eat them?"

"Maybe the leaves, at a pinch, but the stalks and roots, aye. When we go to the creek to fill the tins we can look, and for watercress, too," he said. "But listen, do ye hear the birds in the forest?"

I stilled my hands from the scraping. Between us and the beach was a rise of springy turf pocketed with clumps of tussock grass and tangles of sharp bushes in the gullies. Seabirds rose on curling winds. I was becoming immune to their screeching now. But beyond, stretching up to the high hills, was a forest of twisted and gnarled trees, and from their dense cover I heard the trills and clacking of many birds.

"That's the bellbird, that clear piping sound. Like a flute. And that's a tūī: it starts with the same clear notes as the bellbird but ends harsh and garbled. It's hard to tell the difference sometimes. Tūī are excellent mimics. Have you ever been to the countryside in New Zealand, Mrs Jewell?" Again I shook my head. I'd been to Manchester and Melbourne. Hardly ever to the countryside, and certainly never to admire the birds.

"And listen, will ye, that *chitterchitterchitterchip*? Parakeets. Watch out for them for me, would you? You'll see the green flashes through the trees. We may have red-headed parakeets if we're lucky."

I didn't understand how seeing a bird with a red head could possibly add luck to our circumstances or be of any interest to a near-blind man, but I liked the tone of his voice when he spoke of the birds. "Can we eat them? The parrots?"

He looked disappointed. "I wasn't planning to eat them."

There was a squawk behind us and a small dust-coloured bird settled by Mr Brown's feet. It was slightly bigger than a sparrow but a similarly dowdy-looking thing, made prettier by a creamy patch on its belly. It pumped its tail up and down and pecked at a glob of seal fat. "What's that?" said Mr McClelland, "I don't recognise that cry."

Mr Brown was sitting with his head to one side. "That's a pipit," he said.

"Is it? Yes, I believe you're right."

"And I saw yellow-crowned parakeets yesterday, in the forest." Mr Brown had lifted his head up and was looking around. He paused at me and Mr McClelland standing by the fire, then took in the scrub behind us and the miserable huts, the forest inland, the wide expanse of empty coastline and the big white sky. He rubbed his hand over his greying hair. He seemed not to know where he was, who we were, or to realise that all the other men had gone. Surprised to find himself sitting on the ground in the wilderness. I watched him coming back into his body, blinking in pain as the memory returned.

We stood quietly, waiting for him. His face contorted as if he'd swallowed something foul and he rubbed his lips with dirty fingers. But after, he was more focused. He looked at the old sailor.

"David McClelland," he said. A statement, not a question.

"Yes, Mr Brown." He gave the man a minute to look him over, to pull the memory together. "And this is the wife of Joseph Jewell, your able seaman on morning watch."

Mr Brown gazed at me without recognition. I waited as the wheels turned, the patterns reforming in his head. "Mrs Jewell." He said my name quietly. "You helped my wife and her friend Elizabeth Oat in the cabins."

"Yes, Mr Brown."

"They're dead now, you know. Drowned in the water cave."

I dropped my head and clutched my hands together. "I know."

"We have fourteen men and Mrs Jewell to keep safe," said Mr McClelland, more loudly now, willing the mate to stay with us, not to let his mind wander back to the cave. "The men have gone to kill seals. If we intend to stay here as our base, we need to build a good shelter. For us, and for the wood and our fire. We cannot let the fire die."

Mr Brown put his shoulders back and slapped his hands on his thighs. "Well, then. We'd better get on with it."

Mr McClelland helped him to his feet and gave him a brush down. I saw him check the first mate's balance and look closely into his eyes. He grinned.

Mr Brown brushed him aside. "All right, McClelland. I'm fine."

"Are you ready to lead us, Mr Brown?"

"I said I'm fine. Yes. Where are the men? Who leads them now?"

"They are following the Irishman, Teer."

"Are they now. We'll see about that."

When the men returned with a small seal and a few handfuls of limpets in the early dark, the fire was well blazing. There were strips of blubbery meat in the embers and boiled meaty broth in our three tins, though we hadn't found any watercress or cabbage. McClelland and Brown had laid logs bivouac-style against one of the partially collapsed walls of the hut and were thatching the space. It would shelter us until we covered the cavity of the hut.

The temperature had fallen and the sky was so white I feared that Mr McClelland's prediction could be right. Even I thought I could smell snow. I threw handfuls of grass into the bivvy but the floor was damp and it was a miserable place. I dreaded the night. That evening, Mr Brown gathered us together and told us the story of another wreck.

"The *Grafton* was wrecked on these islands a couple of years back. She was a small schooner—fifty-six tons or thereabouts," said Mr Brown. "A whaler, though the men were looking for tin. Some of you will know the story of Captain Musgrave and his adventures. It even made the Boston papers. Lost in January of sixty-four."

Teer, next to him, warmed his hands around the tin of hot water, blowing into the rising steam. They were both big men: one young and rising, the other on the wane. The pair seemed to have come to a truce as the Irishman held his opinions and let the officer speak.

"The *Invercauld* also went down the same year in the north. Her men may have come in here, to Sarah's Bosom." He seemed about to say more, but he paused, chewed on his cheek and said, "I know less about her. But the *Grafton* went ashore down in Carnley Harbour, on the southern side of the main island. Captain Musgrave and his men were there for a year and a half. They salvaged tools and supplies from their ship, built a forge. Eventually Musgrave fixed up his dinghy and sailed with two of his men to New Zealand."

With his words the bones of my back curved until I could no longer support my shoulders. Castaway a year and a half? Surely not. My imagination had gone no further than the next passing ship. In less than eight months I was going to have a baby. I needed to tell them we couldn't possibly wait so long for rescue. And I could not get into a dinghy to sail to New Zealand, back on that grey sea. We needed a ship now. Were not ships passing this way all the time?

But the sailors around our circle nodded, as if these were ideas with weight.

My face crumpled and tears pinched my eyes. Beside me,

Joseph sat steady. I wanted him to hold me, to take my hand and keep me safe and away from these unknown men filling the space around me with their acceptance of such a cold fate. Breathing. Watching. I felt them looking for the weak ones. The frail, who would put them at risk and become a burden. A woman. A child. A woman with child.

The fire burned high and lit our small clearing, shadows dancing around the edges. Mr Brown must have recognised my distraught face.

"Musgrave and his men all survived," he said, hastily. "They reached Stewart Island in the dinghy and sent a rescue mission back for the remaining pair. I heard the rescuers left chickens and pigs on the island for future castaways."

Sanguily leapt to his feet. "Thanks to God!" he cried and he kissed his fingers and waved his hands around in some superstitious blessing. He seemed unable to sit still, to listen. "This blubber, it is disgusting. My stomach can do nothing but vomit and shit. Chickens! Where do we find them?" His eyes darted around, the news making him happy as a farmer in a sunlit yard. His expression was so lively even I lifted my eyes and glanced up. It was a trick. There were no plump chickens pecking grain in the flickering light.

"We will send an expedition to find the camp," said Mr Brown, ignoring Sanguily. I was surprised to hear him speak with such determination, when in the morning he had been in such bad spirits. "Musgrave's rescue mission also left depots with provisions for castaways. There will be signposts clearly marked from the coast."

"Where?" said Sanguily, advancing on Mr Brown. He had tied strips of seaweed around my petticoat to form a shirt, and his feet were wrapped in grass. He looked like some grotesque caricature dressed to frighten children. "Where are they, the depots, the signposts? Here in the harbour? Have you found them? Where are they, these provisions?"

He put his face up close to the mate's, almost spitting on him. "Where have you put them?"

Teer stepped forward and shoved Sanguily. It was a mere push on the shoulder, but it folded the smaller man to the floor. He landed cross-legged, the wind knocked from his voice.

"Don't be stupid. If Mr Brown had found provisions he would have declared them. Shut your mouth and listen."

I wanted to believe in the provisions but it seemed such a far-fetched story. Why should Musgrave leave anything behind once he had rescued his men? I didn't like the thought of sending out expeditions around the island. I didn't want to be left here without the protection of Joseph or Teer. Even though the men had sworn to protect me I had no confidence that they could. Our harbour was sheltered. How could any man think of venturing out along the coast again, where the currents and tides smashed ships against the cliffs? We had no portable food other than the remaining few tins, which we had sworn not to touch, no matches, inadequate clothing, and only eight knives between fifteen of us.

A chilling rain drizzled miserably as we crouched, sodden and shivering, beneath a pitiful shelter. We were in no state to launch an expedition.

But the stronger men—Teer and Patrick Caughey, Ferguson and his friends—all agreed with Mr Brown that a party should be chosen to go back to sea to look for this abandoned camp, and so it was decided. I chewed my lip. I strongly wanted us all to stay together but I had nothing to do with the decision, no experience of living in the wilderness, no place to offer an opinion.

I put my head close to Joseph, and whispered quietly, "I'm frightened."

We were huddled in the middle of the men. We had our

places now. A family, each member with his own favourite chair by the fire. I had been put in the middle on a low log with Joseph beside me but I didn't feel protected. I felt stifled. There was no opportunity to talk privately with Joseph and every man would see if I reached for his hand. Even if I did, I wasn't sure his hand would give me what I needed.

"Don't go with them," I muttered against his collar. "Stay here with me."

He dropped his head close to my shoulder. "Hush, Mary," he said, as if I had asked something unreasonable.

I took a deep, shaky breath. Why should I hush when the men debated who would go on the mission and so determine our fate here? I pinched his arm in my frustration. He leaned in and I felt the pressure of his hand against my arm, steadying, calm, bringing my reason back.

"I won't leave you," he said. Joseph Jewell. The man I married. I shouldn't have pinched him. His voice brought back a flash of a time from before the *General Grant*, the quiet voice that I had married on trust. The thrum of it came from his chest and I remembered the warmth of our bed in Melbourne, the safety I had felt in his arms when he had closed the door and been so gentle with me. I didn't know what the cold had done to my senses to make me lose that. Of course Joseph wouldn't leave me. He had sworn before God to protect his wife and he was here, beside me. I hadn't drowned. We were alive.

Teer was selected to lead the expedition in search of Musgrave's camp. I didn't want to lose him, but of all the men he was the obvious one to send, able to master the boat around the coast to gather whatever could be found and come back to us. I watched his face carefully, committing the broad sweep of him to memory, so I would have something clear in my mind when I prayed for his safe return.

We slept all together in the bivouac against the hut with the damp grass pulled over our clothes, and in the night again I woke to find Bill Scott's hand on my leg. I kicked him off, and he grunted in his sleep and pulled his hand down. I tucked up my legs and pulled closer to Joseph, but sleep didn't return.

SEALS AND STORMS

Preparation for the expedition to Musgrave's camp began the next day and we watched the weather, waiting for the wind to drop. Teer went with the beefy sailors, Ferguson and Morrison, onto the rocks across the harbour and brought back seal pups, soft things still suckling, clubbed lifeless. The men cut the pink and brown flesh off in strips and I was given the task of threading the meat on stinkwood skewers, my fingers drenched in the pups' dark blood. Nicholas Allen took one of the skins for himself and Teer laughed at him, holding the dripping pelt at arm's length, asking if he intended to cure it with his spit.

"Put it back so the men can deal with it," Teer said.

"You have no authority over me, Irishman," said Allen. He looked foolish and clumsy with the heavy thing and I noticed none of the men stood with him.

"You could make a silk purse," said Teer. "Though I'm thinking you already have one of those."

Allen turned his back and rolled the thing into a ball and went off somewhere. I thought of a dog going to bury a bone. A while later he returned to sit where I rested by the fire, far away from the men busy with their knives.

I tried to find the memory I had of him from the ship but I had him confused with another man, very similar, who carried the same look of hollow pride. The memories of those days on the ship were merging and blending, their reality out of reach.

After a while, Allen pulled a woman's purse from his pocket and turned it over and over. I watched his hands the way I watched the grass. Somewhere to put my eyes.

"Look," he said, dipping his fingers into the cloth. With the theatrical act of a conjuror the bag fell away and between his fingers he held something small, the size of a knuckle. Something shining, polished the colour of firelight.

Gold.

I'd seen bigger nuggets. I had three bigger than his sewn into a pocket in my dress and several smaller in my petticoat. But in my heightened state his revealing of the lump to me seemed obscene. He'd taken something that should have remained private on his person and flashed it at me.

"The rest's back there in the wreck."

I didn't get his meaning. My thoughts had gone back to the drowned children. I felt ashamed that, even for a second, I had been distracted by the gold he held up.

"The chests would have gone directly down. We have to go back and recover it."

"Back?" I shook my head at him. "I don't follow your meaning."

He ducked his head then, and pressed his fingers across the bridge of his nose as if the smoke had caught in his eyes. The wood, along with everything else, was wet. I welcomed the smoke. I wanted it to rise so high and black in the sky it could be seen from miles away.

"All those portables," he said, and pressed his knuckles into his eyes. I hadn't seen him hide his gold nugget away, a slip of the wrist and it was gone. His shoulders drooped and he shook. The pathetic man was crying.

I pushed myself slowly to a crouching stand, rocking away the pain in my back. Then I turned away from Allen and returned to skewering seal flesh. After all we had witnessed, the men, women and children we had watched drown, Allen was mourning his gold.

One of the sailors, either Ferguson or Morrison—I was too tired yet to mark all the men—built a drying frame from forked branches, but it rained all afternoon and the meat steamed and smoked and remained raw and revolting. Then the rack caught on fire and the meat tumbled into the ash. Teer cursed as he pulled the fatty stuff out and rebuilt the frame himself.

I followed Joseph into the forest and we stripped bark from trees. It was rough and flaky. We took it back to Teer.

"Kindling for the boat," said Joseph, as he laid the pile at Teer's feet. "It'll keep the fire alive."

Teer nudged it with his foot. "Ironwood," said Teer. "Good man. Thank'ee, Jewell."

Later, Teer selected his men. Sanguily had chattered all day of what they would find at Musgrave's camp, expectations growing from fishing nets to suits of fine clothes hanging on a row of hooks. He wanted to be part of the expedition, but Teer was growing tired of the fidgety Cuban and he selected the more experienced seamen. He took Mr McClelland for his knowledge of rigging, and for strength, both Morrison and Ferguson. Their friend Cornelius Drew was also chosen; he was a soft man but perhaps he had skills. I was no judge of these men. McNevin was the last of the group. Joseph, Teer left with me.

"It's guns they need to find," Joseph said later. We had been sent by Mr Brown to watch the signal fire on the hill. "No point in stocking the island with pigs without leaving guns. Guns and pots and building supplies. Then we can wait in a comfortable hut with bacon in the pan until a ship comes by."

How long was he expecting to wait for rescue? They

were just words to cheer me with nothing behind them and I couldn't bring myself to respond to him. We were not intending to set up a settlement and live here. We'd be away with the first ship.

We were on dog watch—two hours in the early evening—though there were no bells and no way of telling the time. The next watch would replace us when they arrived. We had carried fuel up the hill and stacked the pile, and for a while we wove flax and grass into the frame of our shelter as our eyes adjusted to the darkening night.

While we worked, I waited for the right time to tell Joseph that I carried our baby, chewing the words over, delaying the conversation until he was still.

Finally we rested. Our bellies were full of meat and for the first time since the boats the squeezing pain in my spine relaxed. I sat on the ground with Joseph's arm around me and he breathed into my hair, warming my neck. With warmth came hope. Joseph would save me and take me home. Always I was aware of the life inside me growing and beginning to take form. Now was the time to tell him.

"Joseph," I began.

"We should bury our gold," he said.

I had almost forgotten about the stones I carried, though perhaps they should have been on my mind. My thoughts concentrated in another pocket, beneath my flesh, which was altogether more precious to me. But a quick glance showed Joseph with his brow furrowed and eyes on the future. The stones, which were worth nothing more than a heaviness in my hem on the island, would buy our farmhouse in Devonshire and I must keep them safe.

I fingered the heavy fabric of my dress for the lumps hidden below, guilty for my neglect of them. I had lived in Melbourne long enough to know that gold had a different weight for those who dug it from the ground, and I was always careful when Joseph raised the topic. It was never a matter for casual discussion; words about gold weighed more than normal words.

Even so, I was surprised at his suggestion we bury it rather than keep it hidden in our clothing. When a ship came, we wanted to get aboard without delay.

"Are you afraid I will lose it?"

I thought of the ways the gold I carried could be lost. I could tumble off a cliff. My petticoat seams could tear on the bushes and the stuff tumble out. The men could rip my clothes from me. I could go mad and throw it in the forest. And the worst—which made me shudder in Joseph's arms—I could fall from a boat into deep water and the weight of the stones pull me down.

He put his hands on my shoulders and turned me so he could look at my face. "It's a weight we can set down, for a while." He kissed my forehead, unexpectedly tender. "You already carry burden enough."

It was hard to read his eyes. The firelight shifted and I couldn't be sure what I saw. Did he know the burden I carried—had he guessed?

"We've got an hour before we are relieved," he said. "Unstitch everything. We'll bury it under that tree, there— it's an easy mark. We'll dig it up when we're rescued."

He took his arm away.

"Take off your petticoats," he said, and he untied the tobacco pouch from his belt and laid it down for me to fill.

While he dug between the roots of the twisted tree, with my teeth and my tongue I unpicked the heavy stitching around the lumpy stones in my garments and when he handed me his trousers I did the same for him, pulling the threads I had stitched into the false band of his waist. If our watch replacements had come early they would have found us by the fire with our clothing laid out and assumed that we were just a man and a wife doing what married couples do. But there was a desperation in undressing like that, dried hot by the flames. I was shy of my white legs and couldn't look at Joseph. Nakedness is unattractive out of doors in the wild. The thought of lovemaking was far away.

When David Ashworth came to replace us we were back by the fire, picking the dirt from our fingernails.

"Where's Scott?" he asked, looking around as he came into the light. He sounded suspicious—Scott's theft of the tinned meat had branded him. "He was ahead of me."

Joseph shook his head. "Not seen him," he said. "We'll wait with you if you like, until he comes."

Ashworth checked the wood supply and, happy there was enough for the night, sat with his back against the pile and stretched out his legs. "You go on," he said. "Can't say I'll miss him."

Before long, Mr McClelland's prediction came true. The snow he had smelled came over the hill on the wind and fell in a sleety drizzle. Later when Scott appeared out of the darkness on the track, snow was already gathering, a white dust blowing in to cover the freshly dug earth under the gold tree.

☙

We slept that night in the broken hut, Allen on his fresh pelt that began stinking as his body warmed it. They had propped the fallen roof back to keep out the snow, but though we had found a handful of nails to secure it in the rotten wood of the hut, we had no hammer and no rope. Fierce arguments broke out between Sanguily and McNevin on the best way to wedge the cover in place so it didn't crash down upon us in the night, and it looked so unstable I was reluctant to go inside. Sanguily escorted me in, insisting I stepped in with my right foot first and taking my elbow to make a ceremony of it, but I crouched close to the door unhappily and wouldn't lie down. Eventually Teer arrived from the forest dragging a small tree, which he shoved in the corner as a crutch, propping up a cover.

I had layered more grass and moss on the peaty earth and with the press of fifteen bodies and four walls to protect us we should have been warm, but our skin sucked the chill from the ground. We were sponges for cold. It would be colder still when the men left to find Musgrave's camp.

"Can you sew for our friend a hat, Mrs Jewell?" Sanguily asked me in the morning, indicating Mr McClelland, who had only a drift of grey hair across his bare head. He held out a brittle bit of bloody pelt and a sharp wedge of bone with a needle hole carefully drilled through. But the untreated skin was unworkable and the needle broke. I had helped Mr McClelland wrap strips of slippery skin around his feet as makeshift slippers, but I didn't know how to make a hat from a seal. Besides, I had no thread.

Instead, I waited until Mr McClelland was alone by the fire, and I told him I had a gift for him.

"What's this, a flute?" There was such a lift to his eyes that I knew I had done the right thing. It was something I could give.

I didn't want to carry the whistle anymore. I knew I was never going to put myself forward to play for the men. My music had been with Mam, or a private pleasure to share with the girls, a trifle that belonged in a feminine room. I'd sung for Joseph, but playing was a performance that felt altogether more bold.

"Where in heaven did you magic it from?"

Mr McClelland put the whistle to his lips but my hand darted out to silence him.

"Joseph didn't want me to blow it," I said. "I don't think

he wanted Mr Sanguily to think I had been blowing it on the ship."

"Did he not? That's foolish."

"Does it not bring bad luck?"

"Mrs Jewell, please don't believe you whistled up a wind. Maybe your husband is trying to protect you—sailors have silly superstitions about such things, and Mr Sanguily, I think, may be sillier than most. But a tin flute is for music, not magic."

"I thought you might like to make the bird songs."

He tucked the whistle into a pocket inside his jacket and patted it thoughtfully.

"That I'll do, Mrs Jewell. And perhaps one day you might teach me a tune."

I shook my head but I'm not sure he saw.

Teer brought in another big seal, clubbed between the eyes as it lay fearlessly on the rocks. He butchered it as we watched. Sanguily took a small chunk of the fattest blubber to offer his collection of deities and muttered prayers while the fat spat back, ferocious in the hottest part of the fire. Teer lay the meat on a hearth stone to sizzle and smoke. This was our sustenance: breakfast, dinner and supper, and our stomachs churned with it. We ate and shat and spewed and froze. I was given a skin washed in the stream to put beneath me when I slept but it took a long time to dry and then became rigid as a plank. Even with the grass packed beneath, it did little to keep out the cold.

It was a miserable day when the wind dropped and the expedition set out. The men carried fire in a tin and lumps of cooked seal flesh wrapped in leaves and I noticed every man stepped superstitiously right-footed into the boat. They rowed northeast to the heads across a rain-pocked harbour and I felt a great wrench of loss. Teer was the last to disappear from sight, a black smudge I found hard to let go.

He was a brute of a man, but I didn't know that we could survive without him. It was a brute of an island.

After the boat disappeared into the wet landscape that fringed our world, those remaining breathed out. Once made, we had to assume the decision was the right one. Mr Brown was in charge of our party, but after his brief show of leadership he seemed to sink back into despondency. His moods were mountains and he was on the way down. Without Teer to bully us we slipped into lethargy, spent longer by the fire, lay longer in the hut. Pat Caughey stepped into Teer's big Irish shoes but he was a different fish. He encouraged us to move, and he put food on the fire every day, but he never raised his voice or his fists. He told me he was returning to England to see his mother. He'd been away twelve years and didn't think she'd recognise him now.

"I don't believe that," I said. "A mother will always know. You'll be back in no time, with plenty of stories to tell."

"Ah, stories. What use are stories?"

"Will you tell us one tonight, Mr Caughey?"

"If it's you asking, Mrs Jewell, I'll not refuse you anything."

I tried to laugh at that, just to show I was grateful for the play, but my misery allowed no more than a forced smile. We chewed on three-day-old smoky seal blubber, and a green stew in a tin was passed around. It tasted like boiled leaves. "There's a story coming," I said to Joseph, and indeed there was.

"I'll tell you one about the Melbourne days," said Caughey. The distraction of a story was more welcome than food. He flapped his hands at the circling flies and moved around the fire to the smoky side, close to where I sat with Joseph. It was a choice we made every evening: flies or smoke.

"It'll begin where every good Irish story begins. I was in a bar."

"Surely not!" called Ashworth.

"Hush, you. This is my story and it's true as I'm sitting here. I was in a bar in Melbourne. I was with James Teer, the very man. We'd met, like we've told you before, side by side in the diggings, like we'd been side by side at home. James had made a strike. Not the big one, that came later, but enough for a celebration."

The fact that Teer had been lucky in the mines did not surprise me. Luck sticks to the lucky.

"He's a man with a generous heart, James, and I pride myself on havin' a bit of generosity, too, you know. So when he says, 'Let's go to town for a celebration,' I felt bound to keep him company and drink his good health.

"We had a few drinks and got chatting with the barmaid. Lovely, she was, with a right friendly manner about her and a voice straight from home. Well, blow me down, she says she comes from Newcastle. And James asks her does she know the cottage between the end of Widow's Row and the harbour wall, where the men sit mending the nets, and she says, 'Know it? I lived opposite all my childhood.' And I ask her name and she tells me, 'Mary Caughey, and I'm thinking you're my brother Pat.'

"She was my very own sister, there in the bar of a hotel in Melbourne! I'd not seen here since she was a girl and there we were, sharing craic and memories all the way around the world. She'd married a man called Higgins—they'd immigrated a few years before. We all became the best of friends."

"Lucky you didn't try to kiss her," said Ashworth, and Caughey laughed, embarrassed or delighted it was hard to tell.

"How was I to know?" he said. And then, "Of course she

was the prettiest girl in the bar. She's a Caughey. We're a handsome lot." And he winked at me.

❧

I woke to Joseph's voice, through the thin wall of the hut.

"She can't come with us. I have to stay. I won't leave her on her own."

I looked around to find I had slept late and was alone. There was something disconcerting in the fact that the men had woken around me, risen and stepped out while I was oblivious to them. I trusted that Joseph had remained behind to screen me. Modesty was not something to put down and pick up later and hope to find it unchanged. I'd seen it myself, with the girls at the hotel. Those that unbuttoned themselves to view left smartly and didn't return. "If you drop your modesty," Matron had told us, "the devil takes it away."

And now I slept on the floor with sailors.

"I can't carry a bloody seal on my own, Jewell. She stays alone or comes with us." The voice of Pat Caughey.

"What if Scott comes back early?" And then a mutter I wasn't sure I heard correctly. "He has an unhealthy interest in my wife."

"I don't know. She's not my wife. It's your decision."

I scrambled to my feet and immediately fell on my knees. I was dizzy all the time. Was it hunger? The baby?

Joseph was at the door, stepping forward, reaching his hand under my arm for support.

"I'll come with you," I said.

"No. We're going sealing."

"In the boat?" My courage fell away.

"No, the others have taken the boat. But Caughey has seen some on the beach around the cove—"

"Then I'll come."

My stomach gripped in a spasm and I pressed my lips together, bending over, brushing down my skirt, until it passed.

Joseph looked at me warily, but Caughey was at the door behind him. "Have some soup first, Mrs Jewell." He ran his hand over his hair, trying to push it down. He looked like a haystack. "Well, there's my imagination running away again. Have some hot water and gull bones. It'll warm you up just the same."

Our way led along the rocks but they rolled under my feet and I toppled often onto all fours, the men waiting as I lifted my wet-hemmed skirts and struggled to find a purchase for my feet. I was physically removed now from the gold left buried on the hill, but still felt a burden draped around me, pulling me down. We ran out of beach and pulled ourselves up a steep face, Joseph behind me and Caughey taking my hand in front, and I wished to God I hadn't come, but the alternative meant, perhaps, no meat on the fire that night.

I was about to lie down and tell them to go without me when Caughey called back to us. He had found a line of scrub cut through the trees, the remnants of a path, and we followed it for a few hundred paces to where it turned off, back down to the sandy scrap and rocks where Caughey had seen the seals. We stepped out at the waterline with the beach a half moon before us.

The morning mist had cleared and a pale sun gave no warmth but shot a sparkle of light across the choppy water. I could see the seals farther up the beach, glossy brown curves on the dun-coloured sand. There were two of them, sleeping, the size and heft of large pigs. Other heads popped from the waves, earless and whiskered, close to shore.

"Look, Joseph!" I said as one rolled onto his back and dived beneath the surface. It lifted a flipper as if waving.

"Did you see? Mr Caughey, look, they're in the water, too!"

Caughey stepped cautiously up the sand, turning his back on the frolics of the animals at sea and intent on their complacent brothers on the beach. He had picked up a lump of hardwood, a spiky thing and not at all club-like, and he raised it above his head. Joseph, behind him, had no weapon but held his arms wide as if he intended to scoop the animals up and carry them home. They hadn't been with Teer or the sailors when they had taken seals.

"How do we do this, Jewell?" said Caughey.

"Go for the head," whispered Joseph.

They were ten feet away when the nearest one raised its head and rolled to display his fat belly, looking totally helpless with puny flippers on the body of a long slug. He regarded the men, sad eyes and a mouth turned up in the sweetest of grins. He touched his flippers together in a strangely human gesture, twiddling his thumbs as if wondering whether he would be obliged to get up and do something or whether he might stay and lounge in the sun with his friend. Then he looked past the men to me at the water's edge and, with the slow blinks of a sleepy baby, gazed out to sea. He'd seen Caughey and his club and didn't think much of him.

Caughey hesitated by the seal's side, the man with the club and the animal lying at his feet. Slaughter was meant to follow. A gust of wind came off the sea and rustled the grasses of the hill and still Caughey didn't strike.

"The head," said Joseph again, but the head was smiling in the morning sun and I didn't think Caughey could do it. I saw his shoulders rise with an intake of breath.

When he slashed down with his spiky weapon he aimed for the belly but the useless weapon bounced off thick skin. The seal curled in a smooth, muscular movement to slash with his long teeth at Caughey's leg, not smiling now, but attacking fast. Then, as Caughey stumbled back and Joseph shouted out his warning, both seals flipped like fish and charged past the men, whiskers raised, hunching and springing off fat chests with bounces that drove them directly towards me, faster than ever I could run.

I'd seen dog attacks before. I had no weapon but I knew enough to make myself big. I flapped my arms out and jumped with my legs apart so my dress billowed out and stuck my neck forward.

"Baah!" I screamed at the rushing seals. "*Baaah!*"

And then I cringed and turned my shoulder as they came at me and I felt the bulk of them lumber past, thumping the sand, swerving away from me to slither into the water with just a nudge against my knees, a nudge that sent me flying to lie sprawled on the beach as Joseph and Caughey came stumbling to save me. By the time they arrived I was sitting up. I had already saved myself.

℘

"'Twas a thing of legend," said Caughey to his audience, as he stretched his wounded leg to dry by the fire. "Mrs Jewell standin' there, an absolute picture of woman defiant, and the seals having to run around her. They'll be telling this story for generations. *Mrs Jewell encounters the seals.* Or to be true, it was more like, *The seals encounter Mrs Jewell.* It's a fine story, is it not?"

We had no bandage with which to bind Caughey's leg, but the seal's tooth had merely scratched his calf, and though it had bled all the way home it looked clean. He'd soaked it in icy seawater and Ashworth wrapped it in damp moss and tied it with coarse strips of grass.

"I know a man, he catch spekk-finger from the bite of the seal," said Sanguily, who offered doctoring assistance from over Ashworth's shoulder.

Ashworth batted him off. "Get away with your pointy little fingers," he snarled.

Sanguily stayed at his elbow, offering advice. He had taken to chewing a twig of ironwood that constantly hung from the corner of his mouth like an unlit cigar.

"He get very sick from the bite on finger. It swell and swell, very bad."

He took the stick from his mouth and pointed with it to the grass knots. "Here, you don't want to do that, you want me to tie it here, and you must cross your fingers while I tie it. I show you."

Ashworth pushed the Cuban away with his elbows. "I'll thrash you," he warned.

Sanguily puffed at his imaginary cigar, watching from a distance, visibly straining to keep quiet.

"Mrs Jewell's heroic tale will be our first story, when James and the others return," said Caughey, and he caught my eye through the smoke and smiled at me. I blushed at the attention and turned my cheek into Joseph's shoulder.

"You should have run," Joseph said.

We had nothing for that night's meal other than a couple of shellfish. You should have clubbed the seal, I thought.

The temperature dropped, the rain fell and the winds ran in a gale. The seals went out to sea.

Day after day we found nothing for the pot other than shellfish: pipis burrowed in the sand, limpets from the rock and the fleshy pāua that Mr McClelland beat with a rock before warming them on a fire stone. The pāua were tough and salty and lived far out on the rocks. We collected their shells with the sea-blue swirls and used them as containers but liquid ran out through the holes. Once a fish washed up and we put its bones in the tin with some green stuff, but we were all sick with it the next day. On the rocks at the end of the harbour penguins began to gather and we hoped for eggs, but there were none so we ate the penguins. They tasted of blood.

Birds came to us for our discarded mess, gnawed bones and seal grease, and they were a permanent affront to our ears and horrible to watch. They pattered back and forth snatching and screeching, the little ones crying with their heartbreaking mewing, the same noise that comes from a starving animal.

With the wind the forest groaned and muttered with things rustling and falling, an endless creaking like disappointed voices. The sound of ghosts. I lay at night with my hands over my ears but I couldn't keep out the moaning. For a while I thought the noise was in my head but I noticed even Ashworth, who believed in nothing, lay with his hands covering his ears.

I survived the days. I can't say more than that. Every morning that I woke up in the freezing hut I thanked God that I hadn't died in my sleep, and a day without giving up every vestige of hope felt like a miracle. I still suffered from the cramps I had endured in the long boat and when I bent over to collect wood, sometimes I fell. I wasn't Caughey's heroine who shouted at the seals but something small and afraid.

I don't know what I ate: I chewed anything that was put in my hand and spat the gristly bits out when there was nothing left to suck. Every day I grew weaker and my stomach hollowed and my fear for the life I carried consumed me and made me uncommunicative. I turned my back on the men and stared blankly at Caughey when he told small stories to make me smile. I turned away from Joseph at night.

We waited for the return of Teer's party, wondering what treasures they might bring us, how long they would be away. Whether they would hail a passing ship on their journey. The days passed in wind and rain and still they didn't come. We were in limbo, our eyes always on the end of the harbour. All our hope on that grey patch of water.

Mr Brown continued downhill. Occasionally he went out with the men in the boat, but offered nothing and sat talking to himself.

"I should have sunk with the ship," he said clearly to the gathered company one night. "If I couldn't save her." I don't know if "her" referred to the ship or to his wife.

With the sinking of his courage came a lethargy of his body and spirit. If he roused himself he'd shuffle along the beach at low tide but return with little for the pot, a handful of limpets perhaps. A strip of seaweed. He often forgot where he was. After a while he stopped going out at all and spent what little daylight there was with his head in his hands. Caughey let him be. I don't think Teer would have been so kind.

∽

After the storm blew over, we were visibly thinner.

The relief from the wind was a blessing, the unexpected stillness so quiet I rubbed my ears to check I hadn't gone deaf. It lasted a day, a pocket of tranquillity, and we all sagged gratefully into our own private doldrums. Even the birds stopped their squawking and turned their heads soundlessly, eyes on the sky. By evening the voice of the island returned: a rustle of leaves across the fireplace, the tips of the forest spinning and a shiver in the trees. The waves collected in the wind at sea and flopped on the shore, raking the gravel into a pattern of swirling curves. When we turned in, the hut was creaking its familiar tune of the westerly wind and the ferns scratched the long nails of ghosts over the roof.

Sanguily, Joseph and Hayman finally managed to club a

seal and we had meat on the fire again, but it was hard to keep down and after two meals of dark gamey seal meat it was easier to say no to a third. And a fourth. I forced myself to eat limpets and mussels for breakfast but I knew I would throw them straight back up. Everyone was sick and the fact that I gripped my stomach and crawled away into the undergrowth every morning went unremarked. At first we talked about what we could do to improve our lot but our talk went around in circles and we had no energy to act on our ideas. It was enough that we kept the fire alive. By the end of the week no one had the energy to swing a club or skin a seal. We had not the speed or agility anymore to strike a bird.

The flux made its way through the camp. My bowels ran with blood and my stomach cramped and bloated. I feared for the baby but there was no sign that it had gone. Every day I poked through my disgusting shitty messes but there was no skin and bone, nothing solid. I pictured the baby as a tiny thing, a doll the size of my thumb, perfectly formed, warm in its cave and protected from what we suffered out in the world.

I told Pat Caughey about Mr McClelland's island cabbage and he went up onto the cliffs and found it there. I said we should eat the root, so he pounded it to mush and put it in the tin. Rubbed with blubber it made a paste that was easier to swallow than flesh. Bill Scott, who alternated between ignoring me and positioning himself as my champion, mixed little balls of cabbage root and seal fat which he fried on a stone and tried to feed me with his fingers. He usually fed me when Joseph was asleep or away, but sometimes, deliberately, he did it with Joseph watching. If my husband objected to a man hand-feeding his wife he said nothing. I ignored the discomfort of this—I was ravenous and the foul stuff was all I could take, though I tried to grab it from his fingers and feed myself. I was trying to stay alive.

Nearly two weeks had passed and Teer and his party didn't return.

The snow had gone but sleet came from the south, gusting in blasts down the valley. Hayman, without shoes, had feet red with chilblains. When I had the energy I rubbed them with melted blubber and wrapped them in moss, but he couldn't leave the hut and nor would Mr Brown or Allen. With three men staying behind and Joseph now too shaky to stand, the others found they couldn't go out either, and we had no nourishment but to chew blubber off an old carcass. The weather ran over us, day after day of rain or wind or sleet. We took turns to stagger out and keep the fire alight, and I took my watch with Joseph, although we dragged along on our knees from the wood pile to the fire.

Our stock of wood grew dangerously low and the fire on the headland went out. We had all succumbed to such a weakness that none of us could walk that far. We had taken to shitting behind the hut and the pile of muck steamed and stunk.

I fell on my knees in the pile one night and sat on the damp ground in the rain trying to gather the energy to crawl to the creek to wash the shit off my dress. I thought I could get that far but didn't believe I would make it back, so I simply rolled into the hut and lay beside Joseph on my bed of grass, reeking like a sewer.

With shrieks and rattles and the sound of things falling, the weather enveloped us.

I thought we would all die that night.

I opened my eyes to a cold white light. The world was quiet. Part of the wall of our hut had blown out in the night's wind and I looked out on a snow-white landscape lit with the sun. I moved my head and felt a dagger between my eyes, the pain so sharp I cried out. Joseph, beside me, stirred and reached out to clasp my hand. There were other rustlings in the hut, a mass awakening after a long time asleep.

"Hayman?" said Joseph tentatively, and shook his friend's shoulder. I felt relief when he stirred. I looked around, wondering who was still alive. Caughey lifted himself from the straw. Scott and Allen lay face to face as if plotting something in their sleep, but one and then the other began to twitch and roll. Scott, as had become his habit, lay with his head at my feet and I curled my legs away to perch in the corner. Mr Brown, when prodded, coughed and muttered.

There was no sign of Sanguily. We found him later by the fire. He had relit the beacon on the headland and dragged a stack of driftwood from the beach to revive our camp fire. He smiled, his fresh stick cigar stuck between teeth as white as the snow behind him. He looked no more than a boy.

"Look, my friends! William Murdoch Sanguily, he is not dead!"

It changed our mood to see the sun. Even Mr Brown came from the hut and made some effort; he encouraged Caughey to take anyone who could walk to collect mussels from the rocks.

"And you see, Mrs Jewell," Mr Brown said, with a pitiful smile in an attempt to cheer me, "the flies have left Sarah's Bosom."

Winter had come and the sandflies had gone. It was a small blessing.

When Teer and his party drifted back after the weeks away, emaciated and near exhaustion at their oars, there was food and a fire. But nothing more. We were still fifteen. The exploration had found nothing, and the men returning were in worse shape than we who had remained behind.

THE QUESTION OF GOLD

Slowly things improved and—miraculously—death took no one.

It was Teer who carried us through. He suffered the bloody flux and the weak shivers like the rest of us but he took the boat every day, with his faithful Pat Caughey and sometimes Joseph, occasionally Hayman or Scott. They swung their clubs and left the young seals maimed and crying until the mothers came back, and then they clubbed the mothers, too.

Teer forced us to eat. He held titbits to me and glared until I swallowed them. He killed seabirds with stones and caught fish on hooks made of bone. He dragged seals up the beach and collapsed trembling and spent on the sand. He pushed the blubber at us as well as the flesh, and enough of the greasy muck stayed in our stomachs to give us the strength to stay alive.

It was a few days before I learned their story: that Teer's party had found nothing. The fire had died in the boat almost immediately but they had battled on around the coast in freezing conditions getting weaker and weaker and seeing no sign that any man had stood on those shores before. No marker posts. No pigs. Not even Sanguily asked after the chickens or the stores of warm clothing. They had turned back but the wind was against them.

"It was Teer," said Andrew Morrison in an awed voice, the bulky man touching his hand to his bowed head in reverence. "I've no' seen the like of it. We should all be dead. I've no' got the words to tell ye what he did out there, against the wind and the tide. I owe him my life."

Every day I ran my fingers over the notches on our wooden calendar post and my hand over my belly, wondering when, within my fleshless body, I would feel a swelling. My time came and went again with no show, but I was so thin and my body so wretched and I felt pangs for everything: hunger, thirst, diarrhoea, toothache, twisted muscles, cramp and food sickness. If there was another pain, I hadn't noticed it. Surely, despite everything, a woman would know? When I had asked advice of Mrs Oat it was because I felt there was something *not me* in me. The feeling hadn't gone away. My skirt hung loose on my hips but I didn't know about these things. I counted the notches again. We'd been on the island little more than a month. There would be nothing to see yet, nothing to tell. Perhaps there was nothing there at all. A wish.

Mr McClelland studied the seals, walking around them while the other men clubbed, swinging long-handled knobs onto soft skulls. The ones on our rocks were mothers and pups, he decided, with their shimmering coats and earless pointed faces. Born before the winter and fattening up. It was probably the best time for hunting, with the bulls out at sea, he said, and we should dry and store the meat for lean times. But these were lean times and we ate everything the men brought in.

There were sea lions, too, bigger than seals, and they came onto land on their strange forward-facing flippers, flattening paths in the undergrowth. We'd never caught one. They were surprisingly nimble through the trees. Sometimes I heard them in the bay past the lookout crashing about, and looked for their dark bulk slapping through the trees.

"They were hunted on these islands until there were none left to breed," Mr McClelland said. "We're lucky any survived. I've seen a few fur seals, too, out past Enderby Island. They'll come ashore in summer for whelping."

"If they come ashore," said Teer, still weak and shaky on his feet, "I'll club 'em."

Mr McClelland liked to watch the seals in our cove playing. Even with his poor eyesight he could recognise their movements, but if the opportunity arose he, too, would swing his club between their eyes and bring them to the fire.

Occasionally, in the distance, I heard the sound of Mam's tin whistle, blowing three pure notes like a bellbird or a chattered jumble of notes like a tūī. There was the start of a tune, broken off and repeated. Once Mr McClelland played by the fire in camp, searching out the first few lines of a hornpipe, and Joseph looked around sharply, his face a flash of different emotions, but he didn't say anything to me, never asked why I had given away the only thing I owned. I wondered at this. My husband had lost the habit of talking to me. I supposed I had been with him too short a time to become necessary. We were one in the eyes of God and had been one in flesh, but since we had fallen into the sea separately we didn't seem to have come together again in any way at all.

We got through our days. It was all any of us could do.

Teer remained shaky and weak. As the others grew stronger he sent them out in the boat and remained ashore. Close by me.

We had a pile of skins now and Teer had me scrape and work the pelt until it was thin and pliable. None of the men had been on a sealing ship, but the Irishman knew about skinning land animals, how to stop them going hard as tack as they dried. It was disgusting work but meant I could stay by the fire and not feel useless. I spread the nasty things out over a log and scraped off the flesh, and when Joseph came back he washed them in the sea, handing back clean pelts from blue hands. Afterwards he had to stand a long time by the fire to thaw.

"Then we wring 'em," Teer said, flinging a wet skin over a branch as if it were a silk shirt. He twisted it with his large hands till the thing knotted. "Stretch 'em as they dry, keep 'em moving, keeps the pelt soft. I don't expect you to do it all, Mrs Jewell," he said, as I watched in despair. "We'll get the men to do the heavy work, sure we will. And then we smoke 'em. And there's the trick of it, see you." He held out the edge of the pelt to me, and with my frigid hands I clung as he tugged gently against me. "If you don't smoke 'em after all this, they go hard again if the water hits 'em. Like them shoes you made for Mr McClelland."

He meant the skin rags I had tied around the poor man's feet on their trip away.

"Did they set hard?" I asked.

"As a brick," Teer said, with a twitch of his beard. "But he stuffed 'em with grass and they were better than nothin'. He was grateful to ye." He gathered the pelt back and stretched it out between his fists—a strong man at the circus. "Though they rotted fast, with no tannin'. We'll see if the smokin' helps. And soap would be nice." He screwed up his nose. "You'll agree, they're not pleasant."

David Ashworth, despite his aspect of privilege and his soft white hands, surprised us with his rope-making skills. He was delicate enough with his fingers to pull the thin threads from flax and twist them into cord. Nicholas Allen sometimes sat at his feet looking up, handing him the fibre of the flax strips he had scraped clean with a shell. He got no praise. Ashworth barely noticed him at all.

Ashworth also made quick skin capes for the men without jackets and cut a pair of moccasins, which I stitched for Mr McClelland—a gift that was greeted with tears of joy.

"We will make jackets, Mrs Jewell," Ashworth said. "Boots and hats. Whole suits. We'll be the most fashionable town on the entire island. Who will be our first customer, do you think?"

I thought of the work involved in scraping and stretching the pelts, the bone needles that broke with every stitch, the labour involved in making strong but fine thread.

"Someone very small," I said.

Ashworth laughed and leaned forward as if he and I were conspirators. "Sanguily," he said and I thought of the funny little man's face peeping out from the lace of my petticoat and draped in a sealskin coat. Ashworth lit up with such delight I could feel a smile stretching my face in return. I wasn't used to being included in the men's jokes and it was an odd sensation.

We recruited Mr McClelland for our tailoring, who could see well enough to do close work and was clever with his hands, and Nicholas Allen by default, as it was impossible to get the lazy man to leave the fireside for other work.

"Mrs Jewell can flesh a carcass faster than you," Ashworth said, and pushed his boot out to topple Allen who, again, was resting on his knees in front of a skin after cleaning a meagre patch. "You want to get that stuff off before it dries up. That won't do, you need to scrape it fine."

Nicholas Allen struck Ashworth's boot away and sat back, throwing the scraping shell across the fire pit. "I don't see you on your hands and knees," he said.

"I won't get on my hands and knees for the likes of you," said Ashworth in a silly voice that made me look up. He pushed the bone needle through the skin and dragged the thread up. "I prefer finer pricking."

Allen rubbed his hands and flicked globules of the seal fat away. He sat back on his haunches and regarded Ashworth.

"Women's work, isn't it, that you're doing?" Allen said.

"More suited to you then, I suppose."

Allen narrowed his eyes. "Have you got something to say, Ashworth? Because if you do, let's have it."

Ashworth laid his stitching down on his lap and leered at Allen. He spoke slowly and deliberately. "I said women's work is more suited to you than to me, Mr Allen. I don't know how to speak plainer than that."

Mr McClelland and I were stretching a pelt. I felt the pull go slack. We waited to hear Allen's reply, wondering if this would blow into another brawl. Many of our men threw a punch faster than they would scratch an itch. But Nicholas Allen just held Ashworth's eyes with a smirk on his face and his opponent was the first to look away.

"I think I'll go and wash now," Allen said. He stood and shrugged his coat squarely around his shoulders, nodded a bow to us and to Ashworth, and strolled off to the creek.

Ashworth, frowning, watched the retreating figure for a number of steps before returning to his work.

Despite the new energy among the men and the warm capes, we were still desperately in want. The thought that there might be an abandoned camp and a well-stocked depot around the coast distracted us from the progress we were making and talk turned again to Musgrave's camp.

Mr McClelland rigged a sail from skins and after a month a new party set out again with the wind behind them, a straight swoop down the coast to where Teer's expedition had left off. I was pleased when Mr Brown led the party and took his sailors, Morrison and Ferguson. McNevin and Sanguily made up the party. Teer, still suffering from stomach pains and the runs, stayed behind with us.

The men continued with their stories to break the tedium of the long nights when we lay packed in the damp hut. We had become snuffling, hibernating animals.

Sometimes Mr McClelland took out the whistle and blew a simple tune, or mimicked the pipe of a bird's call in the darkness. I liked it when he played real songs that belonged in a proper place, a place with walls and chairs and teacups and musical instruments. We had enough bird noise already. He asked again if I would teach him songs but I hunched down behind Joseph and hid my face.

"No," I said. "I can't." I hadn't the confidence for such a thing and my tunes were childish. He would find his own songs.

Often the men talked of those last days on the *General Grant*: what had caused her to drift so far off course, whether the captain had intended to pass south of the islands. They argued over the direction of the winds, the sails they had carried, the speed of the ship, the time she had taken to sink. What they thought they had seen in the mist and what they imagined. They argued about where on those long cliffs the ship had struck and the order of what had happened in the days afterwards. They argued about the size of the cave and the events of that night as the masts fell across the deck. How dark it had been.

How dark.

The first land encountered that terrible night had been Disappointment Island—Mr Brown had remembered the name of the place or maybe he had conjured it up, the sight of it being the precursor of such calamity in our lives. I had been below in the cabin of course; I remember hearing the squeal of the yards and the running on deck as we swung away hard. But as I listened to the stories the picture became so clear to me: the shock of the solid mass appearing out of the fog where there should have been nothing but sea all the way to South America.

The men who had been on deck and those below remembered things differently. Even those who had been off watch and should have been asleep claimed to remember the shift, when the captain, thinking the land spied was the main Auckland Island and ourselves then well clear, had swung back to continue on our course. How sharp had been the turn of the helm that time? We had gone due east to hit the mainland coast. Or southeast. Due south, insisted Allen, who wasn't a sailor and no one listened to him. Joseph just stared blankly into his hands and shook his head. Mr McClelland, whose opinion I trusted more than the others, said nothing.

Teer pulled us away from this obsessive talk, insisting, every night, that one man must distract us with entertainment, and though he lay cramped over with pain, he always led us with a story from somewhere: a river journey with the natives in New Zealand; a whale ship stuck on a rock surrounded by whales come to watch; a strange sunset from which a visiting missionary to Greymouth predicted the end of the world and caused all the natives to leave the camp. The Buller River in flood.

"Ashworth," Teer would say when the lassitude left him unable to carry on, "tell us about America."

And Ashworth would spin a yarn about the time his sister Sarah was lost at a fairground and brought back to his mother by a bearded lady, and forever after she planned to grow a beard and run away with a troupe of players. It seemed an unlikely end for any sister of Ashworth's and I guessed entirely fanciful, but we were entertained for an hour. He told us of a stop-off at Cape Town on his trip to Australia, when one of his fellow passengers thought something amiss and discovered the captain had taken all their money from his safe and was about to abscond.

"You threw him overboard, I hope?" asked Scott.

"We put him ashore," said Ashworth. "Though he wasn't walking."

"Joseph Jewell," said Teer, as the rain soaked into our thatch until the whole hut became swollen with it. "You've a story from the hot dust of the mines for us, sure you have."

When we'd lain together those few weeks after the church in Melbourne, Joseph had told me stories filled with poetry. I barely remembered them now—those days in my memory were drowned by what came after. I could not remember lying in a bed beneath clean sheets without the feeling of water filling the bilges and waves crashing on the rocks. He had told me stories and I remembered some of the words: hills and valleys, fishing boats and sandy beaches, but the feelings behind them had sunk.

When pressed by Teer to speak, Joseph would respond with a quiet account of the building technique he and his brother Edwin had used to shore up the mine, or the sail configuration of a ship he knew. He didn't have any stories of people.

"Mr McClelland," said Teer, as the wind gusts slapped against the sides of the hut and we sat in darkness, "tell us about your birds."

I could almost hear the old sailor smile.

"I've always loved birds," he said. And he told us sailors' stories, happy ones, about birds at sea leading a ship to land, and tales he'd heard from the natives of New Zealand about following the birds flying south to find new land. Birds in trees with sunshine, birds on the wing.

He blew a chattering trill on the whistle and I saw them clearly, clusters of brightly coloured birds like those that had charmed us in the Australian trees, screeching in delight as we girls had passed below, arm in arm on our Sunday walks around the Fitzroy Gardens.

"You were in New Zealand?" asked Teer.

"In Dunedin," said Mr McClelland. "Holed up for a winter for ship's repairs. Stayed with a man on the coast, had a bit of the native about him. He lived beneath a colony of albatrosses that he'd studied for sixty years. There was a big ironwood tree that shadowed his house, it grew out over the cliff edge, like the ones on the island here but huge, magnificent. A rātā tree, they call it there. He would climb up into its branches and sit with the birds to talk to his ancestors. Extraordinary fellow. He wanted me to stay for the summer to see the rātā—said the whole thing would be covered in blood-red flowers. It will be something here in summer, will it not, with the whole island blazing red?"

I wasn't listening to his story particularly. I knew why Teer made Mr McClelland talk last—his gentle voice stopped us falling asleep with heads full of despair. I had a picture of Mr McClelland's birds now to keep the rain out and was beginning to doze with the hillside covered in red flowers. In summer.

"We won't still be here in summer," I said, sitting up. "We can't be."

We were cocooned in the hut and I heard the men turning towards me in their beds of rustling grass, wondering at the voice in the dark. Reminded that there was a woman in the nest. I put my hand over my mouth, embarrassed, and Joseph, sitting cross-legged, shuffled slightly in order to tuck me away behind him.

"Of course," said Mr McClelland kindly. "I was merely painting a picture."

I refused to picture a future here. Summer was months away, why speak of it as if we would care? The sailors had a way of talking about tragedy at sea, they entertained themselves with stories of shipwrecks and storms. Imagining the worst was a way to make themselves feel better—pretending disasters happened to other people. But I wouldn't sit by and let them put us in a story, wrecked on an island and not rescued for six months. If Mr McClelland was going to imagine our story it had to be over soon. There must be a ship coming, if not to England then back to Australia. I didn't care which way it was heading. I would get on a whaling ship to New Zealand if it was the first to come in. We wouldn't still be here in summer.

My hair felt tight on my head but I didn't want to shuffle it about and make myself conspicuous. In the hut full of men I put my head back on the ground and lay silent.

"You were telling us about Dunedin?" prompted Teer.

Even McClelland sounded sleepy now. "I heard of you there, Mr Teer," he said, his voice almost lost in the sound of the rain's sudden run across the roof, the drip that began again over Sanguily's place by the door. "At the port they all knew your name. Wasn't a ship going to Hokitika but told to find Teer to take her over the river bar."

"You never came to the West Coast?"

"Och, I've no interest in the yellow madness. Ships and railways, yes. That's progress. And wild landscapes that show the glory of God. But men wallowing in a muddy mine with a pack of thieves?"

"You'd rather be here?" asked Caughey with a laugh.

"Aye. I'd rather be here."

The wind swirled and the rain ran back across the roof.

I pictured a puddle forming outside, a rivulet breaking free, running in a stream through the hut, welling up through my bed of grass, drowning me. "I want to go home, Joseph," I whispered, but I didn't know what I meant by that. I had no picture of home in my head. Joseph and I had no shared place to go back to and I didn't know what lay waiting. Home was anywhere that wasn't here in this hut, on this island. But if Joseph heard me he didn't reply and the water ran through my dreams.

෴

There was not much daylight in the Auckland Islands in July and, like a hibernating animal, I curled up in my corner of the hut to sleep long hours as the rain thrashed the island.

Joseph rowed with Hayman and Caughey to the small island in the channel at the harbour's end and came back with a story of a derelict turf hut and a hanging seal carcass. Had the owner been rescued or had he died on an exposed hillside with his bones picked clean by the gulls? The men discussed this as if one outcome was the same as the other.

On Enderby Island they had found signs of a settlement and retrieved a blunt axe, which we celebrated, and some planks of cut timber, too rotten to be useful. There were some tin scraps, also—the lining of a bread locker. We were all surprised when Scott suggested cutting them into pieces to make playing cards, and even more that Teer should agree to something so frivolous. He even gave Scott two weeks off his chores to make them. It proved a good decision, the playing cards something to take our minds off our struggles. We were all drawn to the careful way Scott cut the tin into fifty-two equal plates and scratched the emblems on, patiently etching clubs, spades, diamonds and hearts on the faces with the Roman numerals standing out in relief in the centre.

"Here, Mrs Jewell," he said, as he finished one plate and handed it up for my inspection. He touched my hand as he passed it. "What do you think that is?" He passed the others around also. The one he gave me was the ten of hearts, the large X breaking the face of the scratched heart.

"You don't recognise what it symbolises?" he said. "I think it's quite clear."

I handed the piece back to him without comment.

His cards, and a crude collection of stone dominoes made shortly afterwards, took the edge off the miserable evenings. I often fell asleep to the sound of these new amusements played late by the fire. But the games became rowdy, the men either gleeful or frustrated by the fall of fate. There were scuffles and arguments and I heard Allen shouting that Ashworth had bet a coin on a game and wouldn't pay and that Sanguily's earring was plate and worthless.

Teer rose from his bed to ban all gambling. He made Allen give up Sanguily's earring with the threat of a punching and pushed Ashworth's complaints away with a growl. The thought of gold changing hands between the men made me uneasy. There should be nothing for sale amongst us, nothing one could buy.

It was only the hard physicality of our labours through the daylight hours that exhausted the men and prevented the arguments turning into full-blown fights.

We were constantly working to improve our camp.

Teer had lashed together a hotchpotch of rain covers that stretched from the trees over the fireplace and took in the wood store. Caughey hung skins over a branch not far from the fire and pinned them to the ground, and this became the sewing room, where we could sit out of the wind for light work. Mostly I was there alone, twisting thread and stitching, leaving the men the more arduous tasks of preparing the skins.

Caughey brought me bones from the birds.

"Too thick for a needle, Mrs Jewell? Can you use it as a punch, perhaps?"

He drilled holes through the bones and sometimes threaded them for me, but the grasses were fine and his fingers big. "Baker's hands," he said, after passing the unthreaded needle to me. "Better for kneading dough than needlework."

"I'm grateful for your efforts, Mr Caughey."

"But look at you there," he said softly. He had a strange fixed smile that, together with his scrappy yellow beard and gaunt frame, made him look like an ancient teddy bear losing his stuffing. "You look like my Katy."

His voice so tender.

"Who is she, then? Katy?"

"Our Kathleen. My smallest sister and everybody's pet. A right darlin'."

Joseph came to sit with a handful of bloody scraps of skin. He began to scrape, and slimy bubbles of fat fell on my boots. He bent down, tiredness showing in the curl of his back and slow movement as he reached forward and wiped my boots clean with his hand.

Caughey was still chatting to me about his sisters when Joseph left us to go to the creek. But with Joseph gone he quickly crouched down before me and held his hand out. In it lay my blue button, the one lost on our first day ashore, when I had felt my modesty so compromised. It gave me a jolt to see it lying on his big hand. I had almost forgotten that I had come undone.

"I found it in the long grass behind the hut," he said.

I held one hand to my exposed throat and reached out with the other but he closed his fist playfully, as if he expected me to snatch for it. I smiled but wasn't about to play games.

"It's worth something surely?" he said.

"Only to me," I said. "It's a welcome present."

"It's a present, for sure, but I may ask something in return, may I not?"

"If you ask something in return then it isn't a present," I

said. "And it really isn't a present because it is mine to begin with. So. If you please."

"A kiss for a button, Mrs Jewell. Fair's fair. It's a handsome button and you're such a pretty girl."

The straw hut and the rain disappeared and we might have been standing at the bar in the hotel, with Caughey a chancer looking for fun and me a flirty barmaid.

He leaned forward and pursed his lips but I turned his face away with my palm quite roughly. It was just a bit of fun, a childish game with no menace behind it, but I wouldn't have liked Joseph to have seen.

"Mr Caughey, don't say such things," I said, disapproving as a matron. But I didn't blush and I wasn't angry. I was more grateful for the compliment than for any number of needles or thread. I was dirty and frayed and a longing to be clean again pulsed through my thin body. I had once been pretty. Not beautiful, not a woman with a handsomely structured face, but comely enough. I hadn't expected to be called pretty again.

"Oh," he said, sitting back on his haunches. "I'll keep it, then."

He put the button back in his pocket.

"Get back to your work, Mr Caughey," I said. "Aren't you meant to be helping Mr Hayman with the thatching? Right now I'd rather a roof than a button."

Joseph returned from the creek and Caughey went back to his thatching. I didn't think he had really expected a kiss. After a while I left my sewing and suggested to my husband that we might bundle the grass for the workers, and we spent the afternoon passing the sheaves to Caughey, who reached up with long arms to lay them on the roof. Hayman, balanced precariously, tied them in.

Afterwards, when we stepped back to admire our work, Caughey slipped his arm behind Joseph's back and took my hand. I felt the press of the button and grabbed it quickly, shaking my hand free.

The next day I came to my sewing station once again buttoned to the collar.

చ

The wind swung southerly and we lost the protection of the high western hills. The snow had gone but the sleet was worse, carried on the wind and pushed into the gaps between clothing, making any journey beyond the fire unbearable. Teer remained crippled with pains and weakness but arranged for parties to go out every day, foraging for food and firewood, searching for any debris from the earlier inhabitants that might be useful. Around the point there were paths through the trees of a previous settlement. Axed tree stumps showed roads and holes of burnt peat marked remnants of hearth fires, but nothing lingered of the men who made them. Any cut wood for the houses had vanished.

Sea lions had dragged themselves around the place, trampling the clearings. Sometimes in the evenings we heard them barking, but when the men went to find them they'd disappeared back into the sea. Ashworth found bits of broken crockery and some sea-polished glass. They were useless other than as scrapers but I treasured them and rubbed them with my fingertips, proof that we were not alone in the world, that civilised people had been here before and would come again. It was Joseph who, one clear day, walked all the way back to our first landing site and found a mark carved on a tree: *Victoria*. Buried below was a bottle.

He brought it back and presented it to Teer. I could see a curl of paper rolled inside.

"Read it to me," Teer said. He was just back from hunting

and lay on his side in the hut with his arms around his stomach, a grim scowl stretching his thin face and his hair dripping into his dirty beard. I brought him a hot stone from the fire and he took it and cradled it. I waited for a moment for him to look up. It seemed important that he recognised that, for everything he had done to keep me alive, I could do this little thing for him. But he wrapped his body around the stone and closed his eyes, oblivious.

Joseph dried his hands by the fire and the men gathered inside the hut. The light was dim, the paper damp and Joseph's eyes were red with sickness and exhaustion.

"*Victoria Steamship, October 1865,*" Joseph read. He traced his finger over the faint writing. It was a short piece. "I think it says rabbits," he said, rubbing his eyes. He went to show me the paper, but passed over me to offer it to Hayman, who shook his head.

Teer coughed deep in his chest and he pulled himself up on his haunches, where his breathing became easier. "The *Grafton* wrecked in January sixty-four and Musgrave sailed for help the following year," said Teer. "If Brown has his facts straight, this is a message from the return ship, then, the one Musgrave summoned to rescue the remaining crew and leave supplies for future castaways."

The slip of paper in Joseph's hand was a meagre find. If it gave instructions to the castaways' depots and chickens it did so in few words.

We waited impatiently for Caughey and Ashworth to return from scavenging, passing the bottle between us, each peering into its hollow depth looking for something else, a secret map perhaps, a folded message. It was dark green—a heavy glass—a thing from another place buried on this godforsaken island to aid the destitute. I wanted to keep it safe, didn't want the men to handle it with their heavy hands and clumsy ways. It was beautiful. A gift. I stoppered it with the cork, lightly, and tucked it out of sight in the folds of my dress, praying the men wouldn't take it from me.

Caughey and Ashworth returned with light steps, unburdened by the weight of a seal carcass. When we heard the rattle of shells dropped into a tin we shouted out: "Here! Come in here! Look! A find!" and the pair raced in.

"They released goats, fowl and rabbits on Enderby Island. That's all it says," said Ashworth, whose initial excitement fell away on reading the paper. "There is no mention of any supplies. No map. No direction to the survival depots. Nothing that might get us home."

He looked around at our faces in the smoky rushlight and tried to smile. "The fowl won't have survived here. But goats and rabbits will make a welcome change, eh? A rabbit-skin muff, Mrs Jewell? If it stays calm I'll take a party across to Enderby tomorrow. What do you say, Teer?" he said, and Teer nodded.

"I'm with 'ee," he said.

"Just nine months ago, they were out there on the island," Caughey said. "They may have left something behind that's useful. And perhaps we can catch a rabbit."

Why would he talk such nonsense? How could he catch a rabbit with his bare hands?

I couldn't help the look on my face. I wanted a ship, not a rabbit. His words *just nine months ago* repeated in my head, as if that was a short time, as if it could be another nine months before we were rescued. Nine months was the time it took a baby to grow. I didn't have nine months. I breathed in a sob before I managed to press my lips together. When I opened my eyes all the men were looking at me.

I was their barometer—my face the glass to show how far we had fallen. Even Teer watched me, his green eyes a queer hue in the dull light. It seemed he wanted something from me but I didn't know what it was.

"Mr Brown will bring good news," Teer said. "He will have found relief at Musgrave's camp. Have heart, Mrs Jewell."

I found myself at the centre of their attention: if only I took heart then all would be well. Scott brought a fresh bundle of grass that had been dried and warmed by the fire and the men did what they could to make me comfortable, layering a newly cured sealskin for my bedding and bringing me steaming bark tea in a tin. They went out to the fire and Joseph stayed with me and we sat quietly in the hut, watching Teer sleeping in the corner. I took his coat that I had been wearing all this while and laid it over him, watching his shallow breathing. I felt his forehead, which was cool, and stroked his hair back from his face. It came away in clumps in my hand. The men might look to me, but Teer was my barometer. All was not well.

The next day Caughey caught a sea lion, clubbed from the boat and dragged ashore, twelve-foot long and needing six men to carry him up the beach. The enormous pelt was set aside to soak and the steaks smoked, rank and oily on the fire. It was a tough old animal. My teeth were painful in my gums as I chewed.

☙

I was alone on the watch point one midday, eyeing the horizon for rescue and for the return of Mr Brown's boat. Waiting for Joseph to come back from a hunt and join me. He didn't like to leave me on my own, worried one of the other men might step in when he wasn't there, but sometimes, with so few men strong enough to row out, it was unavoidable.

I stamped my feet to keep my blood moving and dragged more wood onto the fire. There had been snow for a week and it was getting harder to find wood. We had the blunt axe the men had found on Enderby to chop logs, but most of our fuel still was fallen branches that had to be hauled across the embers. The flames needed constant minding. I pushed some logs to the fire's edge to thaw.

I had replaced Nicholas Allen on watch and he had done nothing. When I arrived he had been asleep.

"Lazy," I had whispered into his ear, hoping my voice would penetrate his dreams. "Lazy, good-for-nothing."

There was still no response.

I gave him a shake on his shoulder but he resisted me.

"Dinner is served in the front room, Mr Allen," I said loudly, and that woke him.

I returned to the neglected fire and blew the flame back in, hot enough to dry the waiting wood. When I turned, Allen had gone.

There is a limit to what needs to be done with a fire, but I stoked and fanned and sorted the wood, the dread of being alone without distraction approaching like a wind down the harbour. Finally, with nothing to do, I sank with the clouds. Despair was never far away.

I had been hungry before, and cold, but never like this. I had been thrashed by my pa, been lonely, been frightened. I had sat by my dead mother's body knowing that she would never kiss me again. I had travelled as an independent woman around the world to find a life I could call my own and I had always saved myself.

But this was different to anything that had gone before, anything I could have imagined. Now, simply looking after myself was not enough. I had a baby growing and I was helpless. I couldn't will a ship to sail by, I couldn't build a boat and row across the ocean. With no ability to change anything, and fearful of how the men would react when they knew I would deliver yet another responsibility, I tried to shut all thoughts of the baby away. But alone, desperation started to build, clouds on clouds.

We might not be rescued in time.

We might not be rescued at all.

The thought that I might give birth here, in such desolation, with no woman to tend me, left me so tight in my throat I struggled to breathe. It was not something I understood and not something I had the words to tell Joseph. He was just one of a group of men my life depended upon, for better or worse, sometimes no more than the one appointed to stand between me and the others.

That wasn't right. We had been married under God.

I prayed.

I asked God why, of all the women, I had been saved. I called His name aloud but felt nothing there, just the sea wind blowing up the cliff in an icy flow. No presence of God. Had He saved me only to save a child and was that my purpose, to carry one child away from the sea cave? And why?

God?

When I blinked I saw images of babies and children. Elizabeth Oat often came to me, her and her little ones. The baby. The girls. I was ashamed to have forgotten the names of the younger ones, but Mary I saw clearly and she came to me without death. Sweet Mary, with her soft hair. A ribbon disappeared as I reached for a shining lock and a warm child. I held up an empty hand, a claw with swollen knuckles and ripped nails.

Something burst then and I found myself on the ground with my face in my hands, crying and crying for the little girl I barely knew. The darling thing, with her hair loosed from her nightcap and floating out in the sea as the churning and thrashing of drowning went on around her. I cried in huge wracking sobs that tore my stomach and caught in my throat, and my eyes stung with the pain of the flooding that erupted from some deep well.

I cried for Mary Oat and her sisters and mother, and for her father left tending the graves of his other dead daughters in Melbourne, waiting for his family's return. I cried for Mrs Brown, the dear woman, and for poor, lost Mr Brown, who wasn't right in the head and couldn't accept that she was gone although she had drowned before his eyes. All the little children with the families, the two children and the baby with the pretty mother and the man who looked like Nicholas Allen. The Reverend, God rest his soul, and the Italian man with his moon-faced baby. Emilia. I would remember her name.

I cried and cried for them all. And I cried for myself, for the burden of being alive when all those souls had perished. For being cast away on a wretched rock in the ocean where we would suffer and die with our bones found later huddled in our hut of death and picked over by a whaling captain of the future. And cradled inside my bones he would see another smaller cluster of collapsed bones, curled eternally in sleep before ever waking up and he would pity me. Was this God's plan?

I wrung myself out with my crying and then I noticed Bill Scott, across the fire, looking into the flames. He raised his hands quickly as if in prayer. "I'm so sorry, Mrs Jewell. I didn't want to intrude. I came to take your watch and once I had stumbled in I couldn't disturb you by leaving. Oh, Mrs Jewell, I wish I had such tears."

He had such a long face and pain in his eyes and I had been crying for so long. I was wretched but it was over. I felt like I had been submerged in a cloud and suddenly broken free. I almost laughed, a half-laugh, a cough and a splutter. I wiped my face with my dirty hands. I wasn't sure why it was Scott who was relieving my watch—I wasn't expecting him—but at that moment coming out of my despair, I was just grateful not to be alone.

"Don't wish for tears, Mr Scott. None of us should wish for tears."

"Your tears are honest. Why did God give us tears if not to release us from terrible pain?"

It felt intimate to be interrupted in my crying and I had a longing for Joseph, the old Joseph, the one I was confident would hold me if I cried. But I recalled the castaway—my changed husband—and wasn't sure if he stood before me that he would give me any comfort at all. He had been sick to the point that a part of him seemed to have died. We had all emptied ourselves in this place.

Bill Scott stayed over his side of the fire, and I was grateful for that.

"Mr McClelland was due to replace me," I said.

"He's not well. He asked me to take his watch." He held up a skin pelt, half cut. "I've come up a bit early hopin' you might show me a tailor's stitch. I want a pocket in my jacket, but I've only got sailor's knots. No dainty stitches."

"I'm sure your sailor's knots will do you very well." I didn't want to sit with him, here on the headland, alone, and teach him sewing. I looked out to the harbour but the cloud had rolled close in to shroud the hilltop. To distract him, I asked, "Do you know if Mr Allen had a brother on the *General Grant*?"

He looked across at me, wary. "I don't think so. Why do you ask?"

I shook my head, clearing the image away. "There was a man, with a pretty wife and children. I'm confusing him with Mr Allen in my memories, that's all. So much of that dreadful time is muddled. How can anyone recollect a shipwreck? The faces, you know. The children. They appear in my head when I'm on my own. All those faces."

He lifted his fur scraps for my appraisal pleadingly but I shook my head. His supplication was too needy and I felt if I allowed him this, even something as honest as sewing, there would be other things, other needs. I don't know why I thought that and tried to put the thought away. I had nothing to accuse him of and he had, after all, proved his loyalty to me before. My life seemed dependent on keeping this man, all these men, at a balanced distance: close enough to remain loyal and not so close to suggest an intimacy. Scott was oddly anxious and eager around me, but I should be grateful for his care. Trying to please was no sin.

I stood up to go and he held up a hand as if begging me to stay.

"This man," he began, so I stopped to let him finish, though a cold feeling came over me that had nothing to do with stepping back from the fire into the snow.

"The man with the wife and children you describe. You are talking about Nicholas Allen."

The snow came over the top of my boots and I felt it against my leg, sharp and bitter.

"His wife was called Rose. She had a babe in arms and two little ones, barely walking."

"That can't be," I replied. "Mr Allen is not married."

"You saw Allen with his wife and daughters."

I didn't want to listen but the memory came sharply before me. Nicholas Allen had slid down the rope into our boat and looked away from the ship, out to sea. Of that I was quite certain.

Scott walked around the fire towards me, cutting me off from the path.

"He saved himself and left them to drown." He stopped a few feet from me. "You look shocked, Mrs Jewell. Won't you sit by the fire?" He held out his hand to take my elbow, moving closer to me.

He said quietly, "You are such a tender one. A right darlin'."

I jerked my elbow away. What had he said? *Darling?* Who was he to speak in that way to me?

Immediately he dropped his head, stood motionless. "My apologies, Mrs Jewell. It wasn't right for me to say that. I was just … I wasn't thinking straight. I assure you it won't happen again."

We both heard it then, heavy steps on the path, a pushing aside of branches. Teer burst into the clearing as Scott jumped back. It was such a quick response that damned him with a guilt that horrified me. I felt compromised, as if, again, I had led Scott into wrong.

Teer's face was green-tinged and sweating and his body gaunt, but his fists were still meaty and tightly clenched.

"What are you doing here, Scott? You nasty little sniff-frock. You've no business with Mrs Jewell."

Scott lifted the half-stitched skin and then dropped it, tried another tack. "I offered to take McClelland's watch, Teer."

I looked at Scott sharply. That was not exactly what he had told me.

"You told McClelland I changed the watches," said Teer.

"He's an old man and he were sick."

Teer tipped his big beard forward. Without taking his eyes off Scott he waved me away. "You are relieved, Mrs Jewell. You may go down. Your husband and Hayman are coming down the harbour with a boat full of seals. You are a lucky woman, Mrs Jewell, to have married such a fine man."

I stumbled past him and fled through the crooked trees. All the way down the hill, it pained me that I ran away, that I hadn't acknowledged the truth. "I know it," I should have said to Teer, and kept his honest eye. I ran as if guilty. "I know it," I said again, as I tripped through the snow and the rain began to fall.

I ran out onto the stones of the beach as Joseph's boat pulled in, laden with fat seals. He leapt ashore and staggered on the stones exhausted, and I was there to greet him. "You are a fine man, Joseph," I told him. "We'll eat well tonight."

No one mentioned the cut and blackened eye that Scott brought, later, to the fire. Joseph and I went down to the shore together, in moonlight scattered through cloud. The temperature had dropped past freezing but there was no snow falling, just a pause as the mist in the sky gathered overnight and waited for the morning to fall as rain.

We didn't go far. I took his hand and pulled him into the shelter of a tree that stretched low over the stones. He stood with me willingly enough and the sky was glimmery enough to see his face, long and pale with shadows where his eyes should have been. We stood on the shifting stones and touched our cold noses, sharing breath rancid from seal flesh but warm with desperation, and I held on to him tightly as I promised we would get home alive.

"And we will have a baby," I whispered. It was time for him to know.

"Ah, Mary," he said. "I know that's what you longed for."

"You do want a baby, Joseph?" I wasn't testing him. We'd agreed before even we were married that our children would come fast and we would be blessed with a dozen. But he said *you*, and *longed* rather than *long*, and I wondered at the mistake.

His face was dark.

"You do, Joseph?"

"How can you think about that now?" He pulled back from me, shaking his head. My husband had disappeared. The castaway stood before me.

He looked down into the dark void to the splash of the waves on the beach, the ceaseless soft heartbeat of the island. "How easily they die," he said.

From the camp we heard shouting and scuffling, and when we walked past the fire to the hut, Teer had Scott by the throat of his jacket and was spitting hard words at him, the others all cheering him on.

I woke the next morning with Bill Scott's hand, again, on my leg.

၎

It was Ashworth who first asked me directly about our gold. We had developed a tacit agreement in the group not to discuss what we had lost. With the death of so many friends it seemed heartless to cry for stones. The gold helped no one, here, now. We couldn't eat it or burn it or wear it. It was better not to mention it.

But Ashworth wanted to know.

"Your man had a leather pouch on his belt when we first washed up," Ashworth said. "A big pouch that he emptied of tobacco. There's no pouch now. And I notice you're stepping more lightly, Mrs Jewell. You have been sensible and put it somewhere safe?"

We were tailoring again. Mr McClelland had gone down to the beach to soak the pelts and had dragged Allen the Lazy with him.

So it was I found myself alone with Ashworth, who had his head down over his stitches but looked up at me through the flop of his hair. All the men were looking increasingly unkempt but Ashworth remained elegant, his posture upright. The growing wildness in his hair and beard increased rather than dimmed his handsome looks.

I didn't answer him when he asked about our gold. I didn't like the way he waited until there was no one else close by, and then asked one question to reveal something else.

"Here, you need to fold the seam over, use the larger bone as a punch." He had long delicate fingers and rubbed the sealskin against a stone to soften it as he worked. His stitches were neat and sure and he knotted the flax thread as he went to stop it coming adrift. I rubbed my hands together vigorously before accepting the bone he held out, and began punching holes.

I was surprised that Mr Ashworth would open such a conversation with me. He would give me instruction if I was at work, sometimes encouragement, but enquiries came through my husband. "Is Mrs Jewell able to take the lookout watch today? Would you ask Mrs Jewell if she would grind the mash while we fish? Can she use a gully safely?" All questions that might have been asked directly of me came through Joseph. Mr Ashworth wasn't unfriendly, but acted as though a woman in a camp of men was a spiky plant to be handled carefully. He was socially a superior man to the others and though he didn't make much of the fact, I was conscious of the differences between us.

Our work stitching together brought the beginning of a more relaxed relationship. He was teaching me a skill that made me useful and I was grateful for that. The day before he had said, "You have a sweet smile, Mrs Jewell. We don't see it often," a comment that had disturbed me at the time, but when I repeated his words to myself I felt, as I had with Caughey, simply grateful to be noticed at all.

Now he was giving me advice on business I thought should be far better directed to my husband.

"You don't want to keep things stitched in your clothing, either. The salt rots the cotton seams. You've found a safe place?"

I kept my mouth closed and my eyes on my stitches.

"I'm asking, Mrs Jewell, have you buried your gold?"

It was a direct question and I didn't see how I could refuse to respond. I wasn't deaf, or stupid, or insufferably meek. I nodded.

"And how much did you carry? Mmm? Your entire savings? There was none in the captain's box?"

He gave me the stern look a man uses on a child or a servant, expecting and obliging me to reply.

"We carried it all. It's for a farm in Clovelly. We've nothing else."

We had been outside the law, of course, in carrying our gold undeclared, but it was a common crime and Ashworth didn't look like a man particularly bothered with the law. I pressed my lips firmly shut then. I wasn't about to tell him how much we had or where it was buried. To turn my back on him would be unthinkable but I would freeze, dumb, until Mr McClelland returned. Ashworth wouldn't take our gold.

"I'm not going to take your gold," he said, as if reading my mind. "God knows I've enough of my own. But there is talk among the men—it's only natural. Now we have our basic needs, of course the next thing on everyone's mind is the gold. Who has it, where is it, how much escaped the ship. What we can salvage."

Rescue, I thought. Now we had a fire and a hut and food, the next thing was rescue. Not gold.

"And your friend on the ship. The lady with the daughters, Mrs Oat. She seemed well placed. Perhaps she was carrying a heavy petticoat home?"

I dropped my work and left him there, with his haughty laugh and shout of apology.

Alerted now, I became aware of conversations among the men. Joseph would join discussions on the day's work and planning, but afterwards we retired to the smoky side of the fire, away from the speculation and calculation of unreachable, sunken riches. Mr McClelland sat with us. He preferred to talk about birds rather than gold. He said birds could migrate for hundreds of miles across the ocean, soaring on high winds. I learned about the grey-headed albatross, the royal albatross, the white-capped and the wandering albatross. Mr McClelland knew them all, but could no longer see well enough to tell them apart. Across the pit, the conversations took a different colour.

"Jewell measured it at twenty-five fathoms," I heard Allen say on numerous occasions. Allen disgusted me so much I couldn't bear to look at him, knowing what I knew. He was a man who had swallowed the shadow of his wife and their three dead babies and now spoke as if he would go back to that place of horror and dive for gold. Why would he believe gold would be waiting on a ledge for him, rather than the bloated bodies of his wife and daughters? I hoped they haunted him. I hoped God would punish him for his cowardice.

"Going on high tide," Ashworth replied.

"There could be a rock," said McNevin, "a shelf."

"Could be sitting there for the taking."

"Calm day, low tide."

Scott joined in. "I'll be having a piece of it, if I'm diving."

"You'll not be having a piece of mine." This was Nicholas Allen.

I watched the men walking, the drape of their pockets, the weight of their coats. Who among us carried gold, small nuggets worked into leatherwear and seams? Not the sailors, but the passengers, yes, probably. How many sovereigns were stitched into the fold of leather that circled Teer's waist, the thick belt he wore night and day? Perhaps they all had a little bit held close, small fortunes slipped around the Customs men.

I asked Joseph. He was aware of the discussion, but kept out of it. "Does no good to talk about it," he said. "Gold riles a man."

"They're saying there were twenty-five hundred ounces of

gold on board, in two bound chests in the captain's cabin."

"Aye, could be. And the passengers carrying half that again."

The Italian man with the rings on his fingers, the bag that he clutched when he put down his baby. I knew the passengers had carried gold. Had seen the pull of it.

I didn't want Joseph going back to the wreck, gold or no gold. "All the gold in the Bank of England won't get us off this island," I said.

"I've told you, Mary, I'll not go back there looking for it." Joseph's voice shook and he looked white-faced. The ghosts of the dead were not haunting just me.

The talk of gold went rumbling on, overheard in the hut or behind my back: who had it on their person, who had buried his, whether it was folded into Teer's belt or sewn into Caughey's pockets. For all I knew they discussed my petticoats.

GHOSTS AND FIGHTS

We had several good skins stretched out when Mr Brown's party returned to Sarah's Bosom the following week. They had been away so long we had begun to imagine a disaster had befallen the boat, but they returned without mishap though the men were exhausted.

Fifteen souls once again fouled the air in our cramped hut, their warmth and moist breathing smothering any sense I had of myself. Mr Brown had a distinctive reek. He struggled during the night buried in the grass on the other side of Joseph and shouted out his nightmares of drowning. Every time he heaved himself over he released his stench into the enclosed space. It was odious, a smell of decay.

They had found Musgrave's campsite far in the south and the hut was more or less intact. The bones of the *Grafton* were still visible on the rocks, but both ship and camp had been stripped and there was little of use among the debris. They laid some few treasures on the sand for us to admire: scraps of sheet iron that might serve as a frying plate, a small cast-iron Dutch oven. A few planks of cut wood and some shredded canvas. No guns, or tools, no maps or information. They had found no depots of warm clothing or other supplies. They'd taken an empty barrel but lost it overboard and it had smashed on the rocks.

"There were pig tracks at the head of the bay," said Mr Brown, as if we could eat pig tracks.

We made an effort to be cheerful and praised their offerings. The oven we put to immediate use that afternoon as a "bath", where we cut a piece of sacking into tiny scraps of rag washcloth and plunged arms and faces into the steaming bowl. I was allowed to go first, and the men drew lots to follow. McNevin was roused to give us a song about the washerwoman from Whitby. He had a pure tenor, a voice that belonged more in the warmth of a church choir than in our frozen wilderness, but his energy did much to lift our spirits. From the way the men looked sidelong at me and laughed, I think he changed the words so I wouldn't be shocked.

"A story from Mr Brown's brave men!" called Teer that night, but the sailors sat surly and folded by the fire, their lidded eyes offering nothing, and none stepped forward to tell of their adventures. We gave them the benefit of the doubt that they were exhausted, but I felt uneasy with their silence.

They were a tight bunch under Mr Brown. When Scott and the others played cards in the evening, they didn't join in. Even Sanguily was uncharacteristically quiet, puffing on his stick and looking at the end with surprise that his cigar had gone out. If asked about their exploration, they repeated what they had said before: they had sailed south to Carnley Harbour, found Musgrave's camp, spent two weeks searching the area to gather what they could and had come back. Their accounts of the trip matched on all points, which was a strange feat among men who could often not agree who had clubbed a seal or pulled the oars. Perhaps the men had discussed the details of their journey so often they had agreed a truth.

It was Sanguily, eventually, who broke the silence.

Joseph and I were on first fire watch, replacing Teer. The others were already in the hut, their snores making soft rips in the still fabric of the night air. Sanguily remained with us, waiting while I finished the belt of a jacket I was making him. The front needed a good overlap.

"You lost weight when you were away, Mr Sanguily," I said, and I tried to make light of it. "I've had to move your ties. It's more fashionable now, with the cross-over front. All the best-dressed men in the Auckland Islands will be wanting this style."

It was a joke wearing thin. Any man wrapped in a skin became a savage.

Sanguily didn't reply. He was away in his head while he waited, arguing with his spirits. He was a Catholic who pleaded with God every day, loudly, with passionate and desperate prayers. Another, wilder faith seemed to live in a deeper part of his soul that surfaced when he was weak, and often I heard him calling to God to keep the voodoo devils away.

Now he fidgeted and shook his head as he muttered to himself. "They thought we come back for them," I heard him say as he looked away from the fire out into the night. "Not real. They are not real."

Teer paused in stoking the fire and I felt Joseph, beside me, stand still.

I asked gently, "Come back for them, Mr Sanguily? Whatever do you mean?"

Sanguily shook his head, biting down on his lip, a wary look distorting his face. The sailors who had been away were holding something back. He twirled the little stick in his fingers.

On instinct, I asked, "Where have you been?" and when

he still didn't reply, I guessed. "You went back in the boat with Mr Brown to find the cave."

Even the fire seemed to quiet while we waited for his reply. I said it as if I already knew. Sanguily nodded, still not looking at me. A man with a secret he'd been told not to share, and troubled by it.

The firelight painted flames across Teer's face with a devil's brush. He pointed his shovel of a beard towards me to go on.

"What did you find there, Mr Sanguily?" I asked.

"Nothing. We find nothing."

"You sailed up the west coast of the island? You went back to the wreck?" Teer's voice was hard and Sanguily drew back into his petticoat collar. He pressed his lips together and shrank.

I spoke soothingly. "I'm just tying this last thread, then you can try your new jacket on. There. Will you lift your arm for me?" I held out the heavy skin. It was fur seal, a pink-grey pelt. For a man who had been obliged to wear a woman's undergarment for weeks, it was compelling enough. He let me fit the garment on him and, rough that it was, the look of gratitude on his face melted me.

"You like it?" I smoothed the shoulders over his little frame, stroked along the arms.

"Oh, Mrs Jewell …"

Even Teer smiled as the Cuban walked on light feet around the fire, running his hands down the warm panels pressed against his skin, feeling the soft weight on his shoulders. The sleeves were long and covered his hands.

"Come, come." I beckoned him to sit beside me. "I'll fix those sleeves. Leave it on. I'll just fold them back, then you can roll them out like mittens when you're not working."

"*El pan de Dios*. You are the bread of God, Mrs Jewell. You are so good. This gift, it is good. Mr Joseph Jewell, I tell you, your wife, she is my saviour, she is a saint, a woman of mercy. Look at what she does, here, such her skill, such her patience, and also that your wife has already peel off the underclothing for me, when I don't know her, and so the petticoat, it is a treasure for me, so forever I am in her debt and your debt, too, for allowing this ..." His words ran on but he sat and held his arm out to me and I fiddled with the sleeve.

"It must have been frightening, seeing those tall cliffs again," I said, when he paused in his praise.

"I don't want to go back there. Is Mr Brown."

"You found our cave?" asked Teer. He spoke less harshly and Sanguily this time didn't flinch from him.

"There are many caves," said Sanguily, watching my hands on his sleeves and sitting with his knees pressed together.

"Did you find it?"

"Is different. We try to remember. Morrison say big as the ship. I remember small, like house-of-a-mouse. McNevin, he remember the roof is pointed. The sound all along the cliffs, the same. *Schlup, boom boom*."

That sound. I'd forgotten. The sucking of the water against the rock and the booming echo back from the caves. We had passed many caves cut into the cliffs as we escaped. I remembered the fear of being swallowed by the island and dragging ourselves out of her wet mouth.

"Did you find the cave?" asked Teer again, but I told him to shush and he glared at me.

"We sail and when the wind goes, we row. We agree, not this cave, not this cave. This too small, this too wide, and Mr Brown, he remember wrong, too. He say he remember the stars there but how do you see stars inside a cave?" Sanguily threw up his hands to discard these crazy ideas. "I think, maybe he dream it. Mr Brown—" He paused, a sailor trained not to speak ill of an officer. He tapped his temple and whistled. We didn't need his words to tell us Mr Brown was mad.

"The cave?" prompted Teer.

"Yes, the cave. We find a big bay, with both sides rock. We see the other island," he shielded his eyes and mimed peering into the far distance. "Maybe six mile. It is Ferguson who say: 'Here is where the stern struck.' "

He drove the tips of his fingers into his thigh. As if we might have forgotten the moment when the *General Grant* struck and the helmsman was speared. My hands flew to my face as I remembered the horror of that dead man and the sound of his body being pulled from the post.

"And there is a cave. Ferguson is right." Sanguily looked around then, perhaps realising he was telling a story not meant to be told, but his companions were asleep, he was warm in his new jacket and he had found something rare: Teer's undivided attention.

"The cave is there. A black hole in the rock, at low tide same height of a ship. It open out to the biggest cave we see."

"That's too far south—" interrupted Teer, but again I motioned for him to *shh* and let Sanguily tell his story.

"The sea is calm. Is different from when we wreck. We row inside and is the same. Huge. Dark."

Joseph, who until that time had been mindlessly flicking leaves into the fire, sat suddenly and put his head in his hands. Joseph was a sensitive man. Of course this would distress him.

Teer was the practical one. "You say it is our cave?" he asked.

"Yes. Our cave," said Sanguily. "For sure."

"What evidence do you have? Scraping on the ceiling, on the walls? Could you see the ship below?"

"It is too deep, too dark, the water. We see nothing." Sanguily stretched his eyes wide. "But I feel it. The dead whispering. All around the boat, in the water. I tell myself they are not real. But I feel them. There is terrible memory there."

Sanguily's hands were swimming in front of him, pushing ghosts aside. "They want us to rescue them, to take them home. But they are already dead, how they calling to me?"

I had my hands to my face as Mrs Oat and her girls floated in front of me, white arms waving in the lamplight, stretched out. Were their spirits still there, as Sanguily described, trapped in the water of the cave?

"Enough," said Teer harshly. "Look to Mrs Jewell now, how dare you talk like that? Look how you're upsettin' her."

"You ask how I know is our cave. I tell you. I feel it."

I hated the way Sanguily covered me in his dread when I didn't believe in such stupid notions, but a little bit of what he said entered into my mind, pretending to be a memory, and it lodged there as my own. I knew that I would never get it free. It wasn't true and I didn't believe it, such stupid superstitions about the living dead and hauntings. These were devil's tales but the picture was so potent and the feeling so fierce in me that I shook my head to try to clear it away.

"And then Mr Brown, he jumps in."

"What?" said Teer.

"The others, they think we go there for gold. That's what Mr Brown tells them, that we go to look for gold. But I know. I know."

I knew, too. The poor man. "He was looking for his wife," I said, and Sanguily nodded.

"He is crazy man. He say nothing. But I know why he want to go there."

"Did you dive in to save him?" I asked, remembering

when the long boat had capsized and Sanguily had plunged under the freezing water like an otter to rescue the pork.

"No. Mr Brown has no stone, no weight. He don't go down. We haul him in."

"And then?"

"We row for our lives."

Sanguily looked over his shoulder to the hut. There were no shadows in the doorway. The men slept. The Cuban pulled his sleeve back from me and patted the folded hem.

"I don't know anything. Mr Brown, he is crazy. You must talk to Mr Brown. We have no food. We row hard. Then it is dark and we row and sleep and row. We eat penguin." His lip curled in disgust, and I could imagine the men, huddled together in the freezing boat, with no fire and sucking on strips of raw meat.

"Why did you not tell us before?" asked Teer. "You circled the island, went back to find the cave, and yet nobody said? Why is that, Sanguily?"

The Cuban stood up, looking taller in his new sealskin jacket, proud. He looked Teer in the eyes. "You must talk to Mr Brown," he said. "I agree I say nothing. He is officer. But he is crazy so I tell you." He wrapped his arms around his jacket, and went to the hut.

℘

The news that Mr Brown and his men had navigated the west coast on calm waters went around the men like fire.

"The weather was right, the opportunity was there, so we took it." Mr Brown, in a rare rational moment, gave the briefest report. "We've confirmed where the *General Grant* sank. There was nothing to salvage."

Confronted with further hostile questioning, he glared the men down and it was clear he felt no obligation to report to anyone.

He said nothing about going back to find the ghost of his wife.

Teer wanted more. He was dismissive of the men's claims. "You say there are hundreds of caves in the cliffs, Mr Brown. I'd suggest we wrecked considerably north of where you're tellin' us. You saw no evidence that it was our cave."

"We found our cave."

"We didn't leave the ship that morning and row six miles past the island," said Teer. "And that first night we spent at the rocks in the channel. You're forgetting."

I had forgotten the rocks. Yes, there had been rocks. But I couldn't remember the island. It had been foggy, how could we know where we were? More than anything I remembered the agony of being cut apart by the rope, but that had been earlier, in the cave, in the water. There had been water in the boat and it had sloshed over me as I lay propped in the bilge with my back against someone's legs, twisted away from an elbow that pumped above me, and the wooden handle of the oar that threatened to punch me with every stroke. I had sat like that for a day and a night and another day, another night. And more.

There had been no sun. We might have been rowing in circles. The other boat had capsized and lost the supplies. I couldn't remember when that had happened.

Ashworth agreed with Mr Brown. "We rowed through the day and didn't reach the island until the evening. We were well south."

"We were pulling against the current. Barely moving those first hours." This was Caughey, but Ashworth shouted him down, said he had the memory of a girl.

"This cave," said Mr McClelland, "I fancy it's grown bigger in our heads. It was a scoop in the rock I remember, more an overhang. In a crevice."

"You remember incorrectly, McClelland," said Mr Brown.

"You remembered seeing stars from the cave," said Sanguily, but he hung his head as the officer glared at him.

"Why didn't you share this information with us immediately?" asked Nicholas Allen. "Perhaps there was something to see. Spilled bullion. I suppose you saw coins, lying on rocks close to the surface?"

"Are you calling me a liar, Allen?" said Mr Brown. "Because if you are I'll show you an honest punch in your face. There'll be truth enough in that."

"There was nothing to see in the cave," said Ferguson, a man who seemed unlikely to have the imagination to make up a story. "There's no light in there and the water is too deep. You measured it, Jewell. You'll confirm that."

"Twenty-five fathoms," said Joseph. "Port side stern."

"Starboard," said Sanguily. "You measured on the starboard side."

"No," said Joseph. "It was port side."

McClelland, who had measured the depth with Joseph, coughed but said nothing. If someone had asked me I wouldn't have remembered which way the ship lay. No one asked me. I remembered the baby. In the shawl. The baby that tumbled from the deck following her sinking father.

"Did you dive in the cave?" This was Scott.

There was a shuffling from the men before McNevin said, "Mr Brown fell in. We weren't diving for gold, I promise you. We took nothing away."

No one doubted McNevin was an honest man and I thought the argument was over. Teer took a party into the forest for firewood and I went with Joseph and others to collect limpets off the rocks.

Behind us I could hear Scott and Drew bickering with Sanguily.

"Tell them to stop," I said to Joseph. "They should be out here getting their feet wet."

"It's the pull of gold," said Joseph. "It's what it does."

It seemed as long as the men breathed the topic would be with us.

"We're going back," Scott announced later, standing to address the gathering with Cornelius Drew shrugged down into his jacket by his side. "We want to see for ourselves. The weather's settled. Who's with us?"

Teer pierced them with his eyes. "We'll not risk a boat on a fool's mission. We stay away from the west coast."

"Mr Brown showed it can be done," said Scott.

"They had a miracle of weather. We've been stranded near ten weeks and that was the first easterly blow. Feel the wind now, you fool. There's a westerly straight onto the cliffs. I say we'll not risk a boat."

"If you don't have the courage—"

"I'll not lose any man, Scott," said Teer. "Not even a dirty screb like you."

Caughey sided with Teer. "What is it you want, Scott? Think you can collect the fortune here you couldn't find in the mines? The gold sank. We cannot dive so deep. It's not bobbing about to be scooped up in a sieve."

"And we have no proof that they even found the site." This was Allen. "No sight of the wreck."

Scott stood with his legs well apart and his hands on his hips and pointed his chin at Caughey. "It's not just the gold I'm thinking of. The *General Grant* had two thousand bales of wool in her hold," he said, and he looked over at me, considering his words. "Maybe it's come free, floated up. We owe it to Mrs Jewell. See her, shivering there. A bale of wool would keep her warm and dry." His voice was pinched and there was an undertone that came with his remark, something not said. It embarrassed me and I turned away.

Drew added quickly, "And wood. Cut timber in the hold, it may have come loose. And who knows, maybe the long boat has been washed ashore." He spoke reasonably but his eyes were dark with greed. I knew these men weren't talking about wood or wool for my comfort, or the stupid suggestion that the capsized boat could be there for the taking.

Scott's next words made my gut turn in on itself. "We all know we've no hope of rescue," he said. "We won't be reported missing for months and no one knows where to look for us. Whalers don't stop here anymore, the sealers have gone. There's nothing here for anyone else. We may be here for years. We need whatever we can salvage."

"Hold your tongue," Teer said. "No need for that talk."

Ashworth, who had been stomping around the outside of the argument, now weighed in. "It's the damn truth he's talking, Teer. We all know it. They brought nothing back from Musgrave's. An old pot. Some iron. If there is flotsam washed up from the *General Grant* we need to find it."

Teer smashed his fist into his hand. "Your mouth moves and says 'flotsam', Ashworth, but I'm hearing 'gold'."

"You don't put words into my mouth."

"You keep your mouth shut, then."

"You don't lead me, Teer. You're an ill-bred, illiterate whore's son with a—" but Teer was on him in a second, striking out with his fists. Ashworth ducked, but too slowly. He took a blow to his shoulder that sent him flying and his legs gave way as all the men began to shout.

"Mr Brown!" cried Bill Scott. "Reprimand him! Teer had no right."

But the officer turned his face away, another part of him crumpling inside.

Nicholas Allen was on his feet now, some unfinished business with Scott. "And what is it to you if there is gold or not?" He shoved his face close to Scott's. "You had no gold apart from the dust you keep in your boot. You'll have no claim at all if trunks of gold bars wash up here on the beach."

"If it's wrecked it belongs to anyone!" Cornelius Drew, who could barely find the energy to build the fire, was roused up now, bright spots on his cheeks, grabbing at McNevin, who tried to prise apart Allen and Scott. The two men had seized each other and were grappling. "Anything salvaged from the *General Grant* belongs to all of us."

McNevin pushed him off, telling him he had no rights to anything, and Sanguily danced around the pair with his fists up, jabbing the beleaguered Scott on the ear. Teer pushed him back. He did not need the little Cuban, or anyone else, to fight his battles. Ashworth had his fists clenched, but would not step forward to take on Teer.

Ferguson was up now, Caughey holding him back.

Joseph and Hayman formed a protective barrier around me and we walked backwards down to the beach. Unnoticed, we waited by the shore at the lowest of tides, where the rocks turned to shingle and sand. We looked back occasionally to see the men wrestling by the fire. They were draining energy they didn't have fighting over sunken gold they couldn't eat.

&

With winds driving surging waves down the harbour all talk of taking a boat beyond its sheltered confines died. But it didn't stop the talk of gold.

Sanguily came up with a story and I wondered how much it grew with the telling. Crouched under cover in the firelight, with his expressive face and moving hands, he began to tell us his secrets.

"We carry extra cargo," he said one night.

He was often shut down by the other men when he began with his disjointed stories full of spirits and superstitions.

They were not kind to him. Sanguily was the youngest, the lowest in rank and we all needed someone to kick. But even Ashworth listened when the Cuban started talking about gold. Sanguily had found his audience.

"It is not on the papers of the ship. But it is true. We carry cargo meant for the *London*." His sombre expression turned comic as his moustache uncurled on one side and flopped down, glistening as the fat melted. "She wrecked, so we take it."

"What was the *London* meant to carry?" asked Ashworth. "What cargo?"

"Iron-bound crates for the Bank of England," Sanguily said, and he rolled the words around in his mouth, savouring them. "But she never arrive in Melbourne. She is lost outbound."

"This is true," said Mr McClelland. "The *London* was a passenger vessel out, cargo back. But she went down in the Bay of Biscay in January. Nineteen survivors. Two hundred and twenty souls lost and—"

"What crates?" asked Ashworth. "Containing what?"

"From the Bank of New South Wales, Mr Ashworth." Sanguily now had the attention of everyone. "Gold bars. Captain Loughlin puts them in the hold."

"And how would you know this? A captain with such a secret would hardly trust his lowest sailor with such confidence."

Sanguily pinched between his eyes and told us in a theatrical whisper, "He was like a father to me. My captain. Always I am the one. He tell me everything."

Ashworth roared with laughter at that but Sanguily pointed to Mr Brown, sitting blank-faced across the embers. "Mr Brown. You tell them. My captain. You know."

"*Hurmph*," said Mr Brown and scratched his armpit. He'd barely spoken during the evening but it appeared he was listening because he nodded his big head. "Strange. But they were friends. Yes, I saw it. Captain Loughlin and the Cuban. Since Boston. He liked the little man. Stood him at the wheel and talked for hours but had barely a word for anyone else. I didn't understand it. A good captain. A fine man. Went down with the ship. There we are."

Ashworth licked his finger and smoothed his moustache and Sanguily, elevated, now stopped his talking. A good storyteller knows how to spin out a tale. Maybe the Cuban did know things. Maybe there were mysteries held back about the *General Grant* and her cargo. But he let the men seek him out, make his friendship. In this place, a story was currency.

∽

In the evening we settled into our grass beds, padding around like cats to get comfortable. We each had a sealskin mat on our pile of straw now; I had the old brittle one below and a thicker pelt on top. It stopped the cold from climbing up into my bones during the night. I lay between Joseph and the leaking wall. On the other side of the wall I could hear one of the men straining his bowels painfully.

Teer, due to replace Scott on watch, wrapped his coat around his shoulders and his big frame blocked the light as he stumbled out into the cold. He stopped at the corner of the hut.

"Don't do your shitting there. Use the jakes in the bush."

"I'm crawling." Scott's voice, wheedling. "I can't make it."

"You'll shit in the bush like everyone else. Tomorrow you'll dig a pit and cover that. We'll not live like pigs."

Teer's heavy tread walked away and a second later Scott scuttled after him, calling, "Give that back."

It was an unusually still night; the constant wind had died and a strange clarity of the air caused the sound to carry. I lay quietly and heard the footsteps, the fire spitting, the voices.

"What's it doing hangin' out your pocket?" asked Teer.

"Give it here. I don't know. Give it to me."

"What it is? Some scrap of lace?"

"It's nowt. Give it here."

"It wouldn't be Mrs Jewell's handkerchief, would it?"

My breath caught in my throat and senses tingled. Listening.

Joseph lay unmoving beside me but we had only just gone down, for sure he was awake. Listening to the men talk.

There was none of the usual rustling in the hut. All the men were holding themselves still. Listening.

"Why would you be carrying Mrs Jewell's handkerchief?" said Teer.

My hand slid slowly across my bodice but I could feel no fold of fabric tucked away. I had lost so much weight that my handkerchief often fell between the layers. Perhaps I had lost it.

"I'll give it back to her," said Scott, his voice strained. "What are you scowling for, Teer? Give it to me. I'll see she gets it. What's bothering you, eh?"

"You tell me why you've got her handkerchief in your pocket and I'll tell you what's bothering me."

"It's not your business, Teer."

I wanted Joseph to stand up then, and go out and stop them talking about my handkerchief. I was disturbed that the scrap of my lace was somehow in Scott's possession and it appeared he treasured it. He pleaded to Teer to give it back. My dirty rag.

I had nothing of my own here. Nothing clean, nothing that gave me any pleasure. My handkerchief was grey and stained and I had wiped my body with it. The thing held my odours. It was not something I wanted any of the men to touch and here were Teer and Scott scrapping over it by the fire. I heard them scuffling, could imagine Teer holding it up and Scott jumping for it. A bit of lace that should be tucked under my breast was in the open and the men were playing with it.

"You want to know if she gave it to me. That's what's bothering you, isn't it, Teer? You're wishing she'd given it to you."

Oh! The vile suggestion. I squeezed my eyes and held my body rigid and I willed with all my mind that Joseph would leap up and go and stop this. There was not a movement in the hut and I imagined every man had an ear uncovered, the better to hear this degrading talk. If I turned to Joseph, if I made any sound, all of their attention would come to me. I flushed hotly.

They were farther away now, with the fire crackling in-between. I strained to hear as Teer said "married woman" and Scott, with a nasty laugh, "As if you've never had a married woman in your bed!"

There was a tumbling and a scuffle and the *ooof* as a man dropped to the ground with the breath punched out of him.

Later, I smelled Scott come into the hut. He climbed across the noiseless bodies and when he dropped down onto his mat at my feet I curled upwards in disgust. Nothing happened. Nobody said a word. Joseph breathed as if asleep. I lay with the shame of the eavesdropper, unable to retaliate against something I should not have heard.

In the morning, the handkerchief was tucked into my boot and I hid it until I could go deep into the forest and bury it. I had to tell myself that the men had slept and heard nothing or the humiliation would have overwhelmed me. Teer looked at me with different eyes after that. As if I had done something shameful.

Teer kept the men busy, some over on Enderby Island for seals, others on the smaller island at the harbour mouth where they'd found the hut. We named it Rabbit Island after Caughey came back with a clutch one day, but the rabbits made dry, difficult eating and the skin was patchy with disease. Mr McClelland became ill after sucking the bones.

Sanguily said the bad luck was because the men had carried the rabbits in the boat, and he suggested we try again with the rabbits tied to an oar that sat over the water. He said superstitious gibberish like this all the time but Caughey did bring back another rabbit that hadn't touched the boat. We all ate it and nobody got sick.

"You see?" said Sanguily, and puffed on his twig with his eyes half closed. In his head he was smoking the finest tobacco and smiled as though he could smell it—odours of the smoking room: men's cologne and furniture polish and wine and whatever food they ate in Cuba or America or wherever it was he claimed to come from. Sometimes I envied him his imagination. I wished I could imagine myself anywhere else.

Bill Scott followed me around. I kept my head down and refused to look at him, but Joseph didn't seem to notice and I didn't want to draw attention. Perhaps my husband hadn't heard Scott suggest I had given him a token. It was only Teer who watched, with a frown on his face. He seemed to be watching me rather than Scott, waiting for some sign that I was loose.

I was given tasks and I did my share, as I was able. I worked the skins and sewed. The Dutch oven we filled with seawater and kept boiling all day for salt. It made pitiful amounts, but I scraped the powdery stuff out and kept a soft pile in a pāua shell. I had to go farther and farther afield along the beach and into the forest for firewood, which I carried up to the headland and laid out at our camp even on the bleakest of days. The day I managed three trips and collapsed exhausted in the evening I felt a real hatred of Nicholas Allen and Ashworth, who piled up more fuel than was needed, fuel it had taken so much effort to carry. It was my labour they burnt so carelessly and I needed all my strength.

I was hungry all the time. I was hiding my growing condition from all of them but I ate whatever I could. Whatever the men brought for the pot was never enough and always nearly inedible. But I kept trying, fighting for my life and the other I held inside me.

The stories about the gold continued, Sanguily drawn to a certain wildness now in the telling, claiming that the captain had entrusted him to hide tons of gold in the ballast.

"That's fatuous balderdash, you wet monkey," said Ashworth. "How are we to believe any of this? Mr Brown, what do you have to say? Did we have tons of gold hidden in the bilges? Secret compartments, perhaps, stuffed with yellow rocks?"

Mr Brown had nothing to say. He sat with his head dropped and hands loose.

"McClelland!" Ashworth cornered the old mate. "You helped with the loading. What was our ballast?"

"Chinese spelter," said Mr McClelland, but he walked on past, hands running over the sharp end of a stick. He was digging new bush jakes and wouldn't stop to gossip. Ashworth followed him.

"Laced with gold?"

"A zinc mix, which I think is a valuable commodity in itself."

"Sanguily tells us there were nine tons of gold with it," Ashworth continued, but he could get no conversation out of Mr McClelland, who was able to appear now both deaf and blind when it suited him.

Nicholas Allen was disgraceful. He suggested Mr Brown and his men were lying about the location of the cave because they didn't want to share the gold, as if the captain's chests were sitting on the bottom of the cave waiting to be fished up with a line. The bodies of Allen's wife and three children were sunk there and he showed no remorse for them. Ashworth told me Allen had escaped with his wife's purse full of gold and had buried it somewhere around the camp. It was the purse he had shown me. He had taken it from his wife and left her to drown.

I didn't think any of us carried gold anymore, it was safer buried. Safer from being accidentally lost, and, perhaps, safer from the greed of men who were slowly going mad. Even Teer had removed his belt and buried it and I was glad for that. A man in a boat shouldn't wear a weighted belt. Teer had made me throw bush flowers out of the boat once because they brought bad luck and yet he had gone out strapped with rocks.

The turn of conversations sometimes went in dark directions and there was a keen look in the eyes of the men that reminded me of the foxes at home along the canal, sharp and wary, waiting for an opportunity to steal a prize. I'd seen gold fever in Melbourne and wanted no part of it. I was glad we had buried Joseph's pouch of gold under the tree up on the headland.

The evenings often ended in fighting. I tried to shield my eyes to the men thrashing on the edge of the fire and looked away up the harbour. Mr Brown, who should have kept discipline, was a sad and forgotten figure. Scott and Sanguily would start something that ended in fists, Mr McClelland would try to break them up, Ferguson would push him aside and McNevin would be in.

"Leave them," Teer told Joseph when he went to interfere. "Let them beat out their frustrations." It was ill advice that served no one. We had become animals.

One evening after a day too choppy to go out, with the men bored and restless, Nicholas Allen began picking on Cornelius Drew. His wheedling voice crawled like a worm into my ears. Allen, the man who took more than his share of everything, accused Drew of laziness and Drew threw back at him that Allen had abandoned his wife and children to drown and we all knew it, and of course Allen started throwing punches and grappling Drew, rolling in the dead ash and the dirt. My breath became shallow and I was sick at the stupidity of it but no one did a thing to stop them.

Then Allen grabbed Drew and pulled the collar of his jacket, a jacket that had taken me days to stitch with freezing hands, and the whole thing came apart, the collar unravelling with a rip. Allen held it aloft as he lay panting on the ground.

I leapt to my feet and tore at him. Never having lifted a finger to anyone before, I swung my boot forward and kicked the nasty little man in the back of the ribs as hard as I could and screamed at him: "You bloody man! Give me that! You bloody, *bloody* man!"

I pulled back and kicked again and Allen rolled to protect himself, hiding behind the curled body of Drew. I kicked Drew, too.

"You will stop it! Right now!" I turned and faced the men who had frozen in poses half raised from their seats, caught red-handed in their base behaviour by the angriest woman in five hundred miles.

I wanted to scream at them that they were not animals and they must not fight. But there was I with my foot raised and foul language on my tongue and I could say nothing to excuse any of it. I quivered with an exhausted rage and felt powerless to do anything to save myself, to save any of them.

"Mary, don't ..." said Joseph, rising carefully, a black shadow against the flames—flames from a fire for which I had spent the day collecting wood so we could all savage each other in its glow. The bloody bastards, bloody bastards, bloody bastards.

I stamped my foot and Drew pulled farther away. Even Joseph waited on my next move. I had nothing more.

I bent down and snatched the ripped collar from Allen's outstretched hand and ran past the fallen men to the hut, where I sat in the corner with a stiff sealskin folded around my cold body and Joseph came and lay before me like a wall. I sat still and angry and watched them come in, one by one, and they saw me watching them and they lay down with bowed heads and turned away, and I went on watching them and made them feel their shame.

In the morning I took Drew's jacket and sewed the collar back on.

AN ANGEL SINGS

Something changed in me with my outburst at the fighting men. I had raised my voice and been heard. I had kicked the scrapping men and I didn't feel at all ashamed.

I threw Drew's mended coat back at him without a word and he accepted it meekly, almost cringing back as if afraid I might strike him again. Part of me thought I might.

Joseph asked me if I was all right and I replied that yes, I was. I was quite all right, in fact. I told him if the men started fighting again I would stop them again, even if I had to thrash them with a stick. My husband looked at me with rounded eyes but made no comment. I was given the first of the bark tea and Teer handed me a skewer of bird breast he had been holding over the fire. He served me and I took it.

I left them to their scavenging and their fishing and walked alone along the coast. The tide was out and I could step easily over the exposed rocks. At the end of a beach I followed what seemed to be a path up a small bluff, a gap in the low trees where feet had stepped before mine. The way led to a ledge of flat boulders above the sea, and the winter sun shone so brightly on the water below that I had to shade my eyes. I sat on some dusty moss and leaned against a rock, feeling, for the first time in so long, almost warm. Across the long arm of the harbour I could see Joseph's boat bobbing close to shore; he and Hayman had woven nets out of flax and were trying to fish the rocks. Mr McClelland's long figure perched at the stern holding the oars steady on the swell. It was the middle of July and I felt a change, knowing that the days would grow longer and winter would release its grasp. My belly rumbled and I thought it was the baby, a little body growing and sharing its heat with me.

It was a girl, I decided, a tiny thing, perhaps four months old. I pictured her curled there, the perfect child now the size of my fist, with her arms wrapped around herself as she slept. She had black hair and a pretty face and chubby arms. I rubbed my hand across my belly and felt a swelling. All of us often had swollen bellies full of wind, but this was different.

For a moment, I was almost happy. I needed to be happy, to be strong. To believe good things might happen. We might be rescued tomorrow. A ship might take us on to England. We might make it to Joseph's home in Clovelly for when the baby came and we would wrap her in a woollen blanket and lay her in the crib that had been Joseph's. And his mother would bake bread. The smell of it came on the wind like hope, and a song came to me, one of Mam's Gaelic folk songs. I sang the first line, softly under my breath, "*Bà bà mo leanabh beag …*"

I felt the pressure of the words, of a song wanting to be released. I sang the line again, louder. I'd always sung with Mam but my father had discouraged singing. With the girls in the hotel I had sung about lovers and partings but only in our room, and quietly, mindful of Matron in the next room. Most songs I knew were lullabies or folk songs.

"*Bà bà mo leanabh beag
Bidh thu mòr, ged tha thu beag
Bà bà mo leanabh beag
Chan urrainn mi gad thàladh …*"

I sang it aloud, singing to Joseph far away across the water, knowing he couldn't hear but wanting him to lift his head, to realise I was singing our baby to sleep.

"Dè a ghaoil a nì mi ruit?
Gun bhainne cìche agam dhut ..."

Verse after verse, words so well remembered they drew me back to a childhood closer than the rocks on which I sat. The distant boat with the fishermen bobbed away around a rocky point and I couldn't see them anymore. Had I really expected Joseph to lift his head, to hear my song over that distance?

I walked back along the shore, picking sticks for the fire as I went. Ahead, Caughey struggled up the beach with his head down, a bird draped from his hand. It was one of the white-capped albatrosses Mr McClelland loved so much, blood smeared down its long neck from a crushed skull. I hoped the thing was plucked and on the fire before the men returned from fishing so he wouldn't know.

When I stepped up to lay down my wood on the pile I saw Caughey had dropped the bird and was standing with Teer, gripping his sleeve, a strange pleading expression on his face. He was not a man easily ruffled; he was young and strong and full of his own resilience. The only time he wore such a serious expression was when he was at prayer. The sight made me uneasy.

"Mr Caughey, whatever is the matter?" I asked, and immediately Teer swung his gaze towards me. Relief swept over his face. His grim expression broke at the corners and he smiled.

"Mrs Jewell. You have been out walking?" he asked, with Caughey still clinging to his arm.

I indicated the wood pile. "Collecting driftwood, as you see." I stepped closer, wondering at Caughey's haunted look.

"Is there any chance," said Teer, and he looked handsome with his strong teeth showing white through the black beard, "that you have been singing? Pat has been startled by the voice of an angel, he says. Around the point at the end of the northern beach. A song so pure he is convinced God on high has sent an angel to him. Oh, you know what we Catholics are like, Mrs Jewell, filling the things we don't understand with God. But here, look you, Pat. I do believe we have found your angel."

I was mortified that I had been overheard with my sentimental crooning and my hands flew up to cover my mouth, but Caughey looked so confused and childlike as he realised how foolish he had been and I felt my eyes crinkling in a smile. I could have hugged Teer then, for bringing the gentle teasing of his friend into something light enough almost to resemble happiness.

Caughey's mouth stretched long and then he began shaking with relieved laughter. "It was you, Mrs Jewell? The voice I heard over on the rocks, back there? That was you, singing as an angel from heaven above? I thought God was calling me. I thought my time had come."

I nodded, embarrassed, but pleased to see smiles on their grim faces. "I am sorry to have alarmed you. I hadn't meant to be heard."

"Perhaps you have talents yet to share," said Teer. He looked at me as if I wasn't a burden and in return I saw not a hard man or a fighter, but just a man, with a heart and soul, same as everybody else.

I felt myself blush, and I turned away, back to my wood pile, where I spread the sticks carefully out to dry.

⁊

We had a song, the next night, by the fire. I had been sitting quietly next to Joseph as Peter McNevin took up a sailor's tune about the high seas around the horn, joined by Ashworth and Mr McClelland adding a harmony blown on the whistle that sounded like the wind. A song together felt like a corner turned. They followed with an English song I didn't know but some of the men sang along. It made a pleasant change from the fighting.

Mr McClelland had a folk song for us, and then he asked me, "Do you know 'The Bonnie Burn', Mrs Jewell?"

And he began a song I loved, about a man who leaves home and all his life is trying to find his way back to the river that flows past his door. I'd never sung it in English, but I knew the Gaelic. I was shy to sing in front of the men, but to my surprise Joseph told me to go ahead and Mr McClelland nodded to me across the fire, so when he began the chorus I joined in with my mother's language, softly. Timidly.

Joseph's eyes gleamed. I thought I might be embarrassed to sing like this, with him watching me perform for the men. Was I sharing too much of myself with them? I didn't look at my husband, kept my eyes on Mr McClelland, who switched tongues and we sang the next verse together in Gaelic.

Later, in the hut, I was sitting up in my corner, waiting for Scott's snore before I lay down to sleep. I'd laid a piece of driftwood between my feet and his head to force him away but sometimes I still felt him creeping up in the night, his fingers reaching over to touch my leg. I told Joseph I had placed the wood there as I was afraid of kicking Scott in the night. If I'd had any hope Joseph would have moved Scott without causing a fuss I would have told him the truth, but I wouldn't draw attention to my vulnerability. More than anything I wanted the men to ignore the fact that a woman slept among them. I waited with my arms wrapped around my knees and dozed, running through the songs again in my head, glad for the fine voices of Peter McNevin and Mr McClelland and the lovely roll of a Highland song. Across the hut, in the darkness, I became aware of another waking breath. I had slept so long in the company of the men that I knew the pulse of their breathing. Someone else was sitting up. A bulk close to the doorway. Teer.

"That's a fine voice you have, Mrs Jewell," he said so softly I wondered if he could tell I was awake in the dark or if he was just talking into the night. "It gave me hope. Hope that, just maybe, you might save us all."

A long while later, when someone between us turned with a grunt and a snore, I slipped down beside Joseph and closed my eyes.

There was a period then, a few days, a week perhaps, when the group was settled, no one was sick and the men worked together. The wind stayed in the west and there was no talk of taking the boats out onto the waves before the cliffs or the stupid dreams of diving for gold.

Joseph, who was good with masonry after his years in the mines, built a proper fireplace to hold the iron plate, and we had flat stones for cooking in the embers and a rack above for drying meat. We collected the bird fat in a pāua shell and used it to rub into our red, swollen fingers. I'm not sure if it helped the pain, but the imagined relief was better than nothing. Mr McClelland attempted to make soap from ash and fat. I'm sure all the men suffered, as I did, from raw skin where the salt encrusted in our clothing rubbed into open sores. I watched the experiments with soap eagerly, but no one had a recipe. Ashworth asked me if I knew how to make soap, but I told him I was a ladies' maid in a hotel not a peasant.

"Shall we bring madam's soap to her when we draw her bath?" He often mocked me, and I scowled back. With his high boots and fine clothes he thought he was a cut above everyone else, but for all his education and gold in the bank he ate with his fingers like the rest of us and I smelled the rot in his gums when he spoke.

Still, every day Ashworth and I worked together on our sewing so every man without shoes should have moccasins. The skins that weren't soft enough to sew we put on the bed piles. I was given two long pelts that Teer had cured for me, thinly scraped and softened by pulling, rubbing with ash and washing in the sea, all together the softest we had yet achieved. He said I was to stitch them into a skirt. He'd stretch me another for a jacket. It was a fine gift and the thought of a new set of clothing kept me stitching long after my fingers went numb.

Teer and Caughey began the restoration of a second hut and their hands bled from the cuts of the tussock grass they used to thatch the roof. McNevin, bundling the tussock to pass to them, would catch in his singing whenever he was sliced.

"See afar yon hill Ardmore
*Beating billows—*yeow!*—wash its shore*
*But—*ach!*—its beauties bloom no more*
*For me now far from Islay—*arrgh!*"*

I watched the building, hoping there would be a space for me where I could live away from the men. I wanted to sleep without the fear of Scott's hands.

Mr Brown sank into some kind of illness that none of us recognised or knew how to cure. I found him collapsed by the creek and called for help to carry him back to the hut. There seemed nothing wrong with him physically but he wouldn't or couldn't see us. He seemed to be living somewhere else, somewhere horrible, seeing other things. It wasn't hard to guess where his mind had gone.

I was given the task of nursing him and I did the best

I could with bark tea and kind words but lacked any medicines or skill. Brandy might have helped. When we were alone I sang lullabies to soothe him and he lay with the glazed eyes of a baby in a cradle. His neck was swollen and face puffy, his eyes bulged, but these ailments afflicted us all and we managed to keep our minds intact. He ate when I put food in front of him and could sit unaided, though he pushed me away when I tried to get him to stand.

We had no one with us who knew anything of medical matters, but Scott and Ferguson diagnosed bad food, or flux, or scurvy, which was stupid as his stomach was fine. It was his mind that was sick.

"He needs lemons and onions," said Scott.

"That's French nonsense about lemons," said Ferguson. "He's eaten tainted meat. One of the rabbits, perhaps."

"We all ate them rabbits. He needs green vegetables."

"Who tells you this? You can't cure a disease with vegetables. It's bad meat he's eaten."

"I'm a feckin' butcher, you don't tell me about bad meat. I skinned and cooked them rabbits and——" but Ferguson knocked him down with a shove and a curse and they continued their argument with their fists.

I ground my teeth at their stupidity. It was no good to talk about lemons and onions and vegetables. But I pounded fried seal meat to a paste, mixed it with fern root and pushed it with a flat stick into the man's quivering mouth, rubbing his beard to force him to swallow. His eyes flickered but he didn't seem to see me.

"I fed you like that, once." I looked up to find Scott leaning in the hut doorway, his arms folded, and looking at me with that way he had. That intensity. I turned my back, crouching to feed Mr Brown, but every touch of his mouth on the spoon now reminded me of the day Scott claimed to have kept me alive with the tinned meat. It was a memory I didn't want and couldn't cut away.

We had all been living so long in such danger that our group fermented in a broth of obligations and duties and cares as we got through each day. All the tensions, each disappointment simmered; we lived so bound to each other and slept all packed together every night. I had no relationship with Scott that wasn't true of any of the men and yet he treated me as if we had a special bond, as if he was entitled to speak to me with an intimacy that he wouldn't have used in front of my husband. He assumed too much.

I wiped the dribbled meat from Mr Brown's beard and stood to leave. Scott blocked the doorway.

I lifted my chin and glared at him, willing him to let me pass.

"Yet thy father were a bricklayer." It sounded like a conversation he was having with himself, had been having with himself for a while. His nose wrinkled as if my standing before him offended him, but I wouldn't step aside. Did he fancy himself above me and bound to order me about? My father managed a brickyard. I was certainly not socially subservient to Scott.

Footsteps crunched the stones on the path coming from the beach.

Scott stepped forward and shoved me against the wall, pressing himself against me with a violence that knocked away my breath. His hands grabbed and lifted my breasts through my dress and he dropped his face down to my bosom, his filthy hair in my face, in my mouth. And then he loosed me and a breath later, when Joseph stood in the doorway, Scott was kneeling beside Mr Brown, lowering him down onto his grassy mat.

"I'll see to him now, Mrs Jewell," he said with his back to me. "Thank you for the meat."

I staggered past Joseph into the daylight and sobbed great gulps of air, spitting the smell and taste of Scott out onto the peaty ground, and then picked up my dirty hem and ran away, past Teer and Caughey at the wood pile, past Mr McClelland and Ashworth at the creek, and out into the dark and tangled bush.

ↈ

The following day, Mr Brown came out of the hut. It was a miserable sleety morning and we were mostly huddled under cover by the fire doing our chores. He said nothing and made no acknowledgement that he had been sick; he just nodded to the party as if everything was normal, rubbed his shaggy hair that was now entirely grey and went off into the bush to do his business. When he joined us by the fire he took the tin of warm tea that Joseph held out for him and helped himself to the handful of shellfish baking on a rock. Cornelius Drew had placed them there, but he made no comment when his officer ate them.

He reeked of sweat and urine.

Teer, whittling sticks for the door of the new hut, paused in his work and watched Mr Brown, his forehead pulled into a frown. "Are ye back with us, Mr Brown?" he asked.

"As you see," said the older man. He looked around with a clear expression as if he hadn't been incapacitated for days, with me feeding him and the men leading him out for his shits. He looked capable enough, physically well.

"For how long do ye plan stayin' this time?" Teer asked.

"I'm on duty now, Teer. When I feel the need to discuss my plans with you, you can be sure I will."

He did seem to be well. He spoke mainly to his crew, with clear, sensible instructions: Ferguson, Drew, Morrison, Hayman and Sanguily took his orders easily. The other sailors, McNevin, Scott and Mr McClelland, seemed unsure, and, along with Joseph, looked to Teer when told to prepare to go out in the boat to set new lines. Teer nodded that they should do as they were told.

As they prepared to leave, Mr Brown beckoned to Scott. "A word, Mr Scott, before you go out with the line." It seemed staged: the men, standing ready, paused to hear the last word of advice. Teer, with his whittled sticks in a bundle to tie to the frame, waited.

It happened that I was standing behind Mr Brown, holding my sewing, waiting to take my seat by the fire.

When Scott approached the older man he was taken by surprise. Mr Brown had lowered his head and Scott stepped close to hear him. I saw Mr Brown take a deep breath and felt what was coming. He lashed out with a strong left hook, a sailor's brawling punch that caught Scott on the side of the face, and I saw him crumple, his nose knocked away as he was lifted off his feet. He came crashing down in the ashes of the fire and Mr Brown stepped forward and stood over him as Scott sat dazed, his hand reaching up to stem the blood that burst from his face.

Mr Brown spoke quietly, so quietly that every man leaned in to hear him. "You touch Mrs Jewell again, Bill Scott, and I will peel off your skin and throw it to the gulls."

And then he turned and strode off to the beach and the boats and the day's work with the men running behind. Scott pulled himself to his feet and, dazed, staggered after them.

I didn't see Joseph until late that afternoon. I had sat all day at my sewing, head down, listening to Teer and Caughey finishing the roof of the new hut and padding the doorframe with grass and peat. What did they imagine had passed between me and Scott, what did Joseph think? At the hotel there was an understanding that if a man had relations with a woman, she must have tempted him to it.

Always I had avoided any accusation of impropriety during my years in service, keeping distant, never alone with any man; the only man I had ever needed to report had been Scott, that one time, and he had been barred from the hotel as a result. Here he had compromised me again, making me look the temptress—an unlikely temptress, surely, with my thin frame, filthy knotted hair and a dress that had survived a shipwreck and been worn day and night since. My face turned sour at the memory of his hands on my breasts.

"It's done, Mrs Jewell." Teer stood before me with his hands clasped. "Pat is moving your pelts and straw across now. Your husband and yourself can have some peace for a couple of nights, then we'll see what is to be done."

His bulk was so powerful I couldn't look up at him. I dropped my head in a jerky nod.

"Mrs Jewell." He crouched then and pinned me with his eyes so I couldn't look away. "I understand how difficult it must be for ye, here. It's a rough place you're sharing with us, all sailors 'n' miners." He tutted, a low clunk as if his very tongue was heavy. "Ye be married, and that's all well and good, but a man will get ideas and you must stop 'em. Do ye understand me?"

I swallowed. I wanted to ask how I was to protect myself against Scott, who touched my legs when I lay sleeping and grabbed me when he thought no one was watching. Teer wasn't telling me not to encourage Scott. He told me to stop him. I had no idea how to do that. I could feel my eyes welling with helpless tears.

"You'll tell me, Mrs Jewell. Anything that happens by any of the men. If they behave in a way that does not respect your married state, you're to tell me. Can ye do that? You trust me, isn't that the way of it?"

I had to rub my cheek with the back of my hand to

stop a tear from falling down onto my work—the sign of a woman's defeat. He still watched me.

I sniffed, set my jaw and looked up at him. "Thank you, Mr Teer. I shall."

He touched my cheek briefly, just the brush of fingers over a tear.

I felt the touch of him long after he stepped away.

My jaw was still set and my head up when the men returned. I gutted the fish they brought and rubbed them with the precious salt from the oven, and if anyone looked at me I returned such a steely stare they turned away quickly. Scott, with his horribly broken nose, stayed as far away from Joseph and me as he could.

That night we were watched as we went to sleep in the new hut, just the two of us, and I felt a surge of panic at the men's eyes on me. In our communal arrangement, Joseph had been a barrier for my modesty between me and the men, but he had been no more than that. There was no intimacy, no inkling of that feeling that in our Melbourne days had him lifting my nightgown in our new marriage bed, and me shivering in anticipation for what was to follow.

Surely he wouldn't expect to resume that here? And all the men knowing what we did and there being no other woman, would they turn that over in their minds? I felt my safety in this camp depended on my keeping my femininity closed down and giving the men no excuse to think that Joseph was enjoying something not available to them.

"All the time," the girls in the hotel had whispered. "Men think about women in that way *all the time*. They just can't help themselves."

Was Joseph thinking it? There was so much I didn't know about him, about men. I didn't know about babies, either, and whether Joseph, should he insist on his husband's rights, might damage it. I needed to know these things and there was no one to advise me.

Joseph closed the door to the men outside. It was the first time we had been alone, inside, in private, since Melbourne. Rather than being relaxed, the feeling between us was strained.

"Do you want to know why Mr Brown knocked down Bill Scott?"

"I am sure you did nothing wrong."

"I did not."

"I believe you. He was punished. I won't let him bother you again." Joseph was pulling the bedding piles together, the skins now side by side.

I wanted to shake him because he missed the point, understanding nothing because he didn't ask me. It wasn't just Scott's grabbing that had hurt me but the suggestions that came with it, the men thinking that I had played him along. Once the men decided I wasn't united with Joseph I was frightened others might try their luck.

"You can take your dress off now," Joseph said, but I wanted to leave my clothing on. I imagined my body underneath: raw from the salt rash and slashed with grazes, stick thin with a swollen belly where the baby grew. My dress had become my skin and I needed its protection.

"I'm too cold."

"I'll warm you." He sighed when I shrunk back. "I'll just hold you, Mary. I'll not do anything else. Take your dress off."

The hut was dark. An orange sheen from the fire flicked through a gap by the roof but gave no light below the ceiling. He wouldn't see my body, but he would feel it. I held my hands against my stomach and the swelling was there, real. I left my dress on and laid down beside him, my head on his outstretched arm and my back nestled into his side.

I wanted him to ask: *What is it? Why are you troubled?* so I could tell him. A baby was an impossible subject to raise without being invited to tell. If he asked me anything, I would tell him. But Joseph didn't ask. He lay there in his heavy state and eventually I fell asleep with his warm body against my back. It was the first deep sleep I had had since landing on the island and I woke warm and rested.

When Joseph and I came out of the hut in the morning, the men cheered. Mortified, I went back inside.

෴

Scott found me the next day working by the fire. Allen and Joseph had been there, but Joseph had stepped into the forest for a moment and when I looked up Allen was nowhere in sight. Scott stood with bowed head and hands clenched before me. I could hear Teer and Caughey on the other side of the huts.

I was on the edge of calling out, but Scott's face was still swollen with Mr Brown's punch and he looked thoroughly miserable. I waited, wary, to hear what he had to say.

"Mrs Jewell, I am so terribly sorry." I had never heard him speak in such a way before, with painful humility. "My behaviour was inexcusable. A form of madness, some will other than my own took control of my senses. I deeply regret what happened. I apologise unreservedly. It will never happen again."

He spoke in one long stream and then was away, walking quickly around the huts to join Teer and Caughey, so when Joseph returned I was staring into space.

"Mary?" Joseph said, and I looked around. For a second I didn't recognise him. I hadn't looked at him properly for weeks. How wretched we had all become. How gaunt.

He sat next to me and reached for my hands, which lay listlessly on my lap, my sewing dropped. His long face was dirty and his hair fell in a tangled sheet into an equally wild beard. There was so little of him to see. But my thoughts were muddled and not on Joseph. Was it true that madness had taken Scott? Why would he grab me in such a way and regret it so? Joseph lifted my hand and bent his head over it. Did Scott's avowed apology mean I was safe from him at last? Joseph kissed my hand. I don't know why he did it. I had to believe Scott was sincere, that there would be no repeat of his grabbing hands. I glanced at Joseph, but decided against telling him. He looked as if he had been crying.

Allen came back and we all picked up our work, but I ran those two things through my head all day—Scott with his apology and Joseph kissing my hand. They were both so unlikely and I couldn't make sense of either.

Mr Brown's mood revival lasted a day or two but then he slowly sank again. This time he didn't take himself back to bed but his despair hung around him all the time; always with the risk of it wrapping around his mind and pulling him down. Mostly he lived in the halfway place, and I couldn't tell if he was seeing the world in front of him or some unreal imagining. When he was lucid, often it was worse. He disagreed with everything Teer suggested as if the challenge to his authority needed to be stamped out, when Teer was only being reasonable and trying to get things done.

"No," he said, when Teer asked if he would make up a party to look for goats.

"Why will you not?"

"I'm taking the men for firewood up the valley."

"We've enough firewood for several days. Meat is more important."

"I said no, Teer." Mr Brown would then select a party of men to go to the forest, always the sailors trained to obey a senior officer. Even they went with him reluctantly.

He argued with Teer over the importance of fish hooks and nets and about sending parties inland for signs of pigs, or out to the island for rabbits and goats.

And then later, when Caughey had cornered and almost captured a kid goat on Enderby, "We should all go to catch it," Teer said to Mr Brown. "A tethered kid will lead to the mother."

"No."

"A milk goat. You'll not object to that?"

But then Mr Brown switched the topic entirely and laid out his new plan for us all.

"I've decided we will all go south, to Musgrave's camp."

My hands were poised above a mound of blubber. Teer had dumped the skinned seal on the flat rock where we processed the meat, leaving me with a gully knife and the carcass, its pale jellied insides bare to the sky. He faced Mr Brown across me, both standing with their hands on hips. I scraped the knife against the whetting stone and made no pretence of ignoring them. If I worked like a man I could listen in to the men's talk.

Teer paused for a while and I didn't like the way his eyes narrowed. "Where's the advantage in that?"

"It's a bigger camp. Sheltered. Seals on the rocks at the end of the bay. Pigs, perhaps." Brown didn't look at Teer when he spoke. He showed his dislike of the big Irishman by such discourtesies.

"No. Our only hope is a passing ship, coming in for water or repair. They'll come in at the north. Musgrave's is too far south."

"Musgrave's is a known location, on the chart."

"Known to be deserted."

"I'm not going to argue with you, Teer. I'm not telling you this for discussion. I've made the decision that we can survive better at Musgrave's. We'll take what we can from here and leave tomorrow, if the sea stays calm."

Teer whistled out a long breath and his fingers rolled into balled fists.

They were butting heads like senseless goats and I wanted to draw my foot back to boot them as I had Allen and Drew.

Teer turned a deliberate look towards me. God knows I looked savage, in my new sealskin skirt and jacket and my hand wrapped around a bloodied knife. Mr Brown followed his gaze slowly and he focused his eyes. It was the first time since punching Scott that he paid me any mind, and his look was so heartbreakingly melancholic I felt ashamed at my anger at him. He was a sad old man, who had been on his last run home with his wife, ready for retirement and a garden and a pipe, and now his life had sunk and left him with this reality: fifteen souls washed ashore on a rock in the bleak Southern Ocean. He had lost more than a hard man like Teer would ever know. There was no coming together between these two men, no stepping back or giving in.

I began to hack at the blubber and tore off large strips that I would later smoke over the fire to preserve.

⁊

I was not surprised when they announced a split the following day. It had been building for a while between Teer and Brown and their factions.

Brown and his sailors would take one boat south to Musgrave's, and Teer's party would remain behind with the second.

I was loath to split the group. We were so few and so desperate. I felt our only chance for survival was to stay together and combine our energy and our skills, look after one another, help each other. If we couldn't manage that common decency, what were we? Surely the threat of death that hung so close over our heads all this time was enough to persuade two stubborn men to find a way to work together to keep us alive?

It wasn't to be. The sailors packed stores of smoked and salted meat into the boat.

Teer asked for the glass bottle that I had hidden all these weeks. I took several breaths before I went to fetch it. It had become a precious thing to me that I would hold and rub when I needed the feeling of something real, something beautiful made by the hands of men.

When I came back Caughey was holding Teer's arm, restraining him, and the pair were arguing.

"Let her keep it, she has little enough," Caughey said and turning to me said, "No, Mrs Jewell, we won't make you part with it. You must have it." And then to Teer, "It's a small thing. Please."

Teer shook his friend's arm off and snatched the bottle from me without looking at either me or Caughey. He gave it to Sanguily to fill and stopper and put in the boat. I knew a bottle of fresh water at sea could save a life. I kept my eyes on the sand and said nothing.

"You cold-hearted, pig-headed, scurfy, bleeding bastard!" shouted Caughey. "Why do you always have to—" but Teer grabbed him by the scruff of his jacket and dragged him in.

"You are one word away from getting in that boat, do ye hear me, Pat? You think I don't see you? Admiring her?"

He pushed his friend away and when a button flew off and bounced across the shingle I stepped between them and bent down to pick it up.

"If you give me your jacket tonight, Mr Caughey," I said, with my back to Teer. "I'll stitch this back on for you."

I wasn't sad to see Morrison throwing his skins into the boat. He was clumsy with his actions and words. Ferguson was a good worker but argumentative. Many fights started with the pair of them. Cornelius Drew was gentler than most but dreamy and one of the least able of the men. Peter McNevin was nimble and intelligent but I'm sure they took him mostly for his singing. He had lifted our spirits on many occasions. But when Mr McClelland walked past, I cried. He had suffered since the first trip down to Musgrave's—his teeth were loose so he ate little, and the weight had dropped off leaving him scarecrow thin. He looked every day of his sixty years. "Must you go, Mr McClelland?" I asked. "I would far rather you stayed here." I wanted to add, *where I can look after you*, but he was no relation and I had no right to him.

He took my hands and shook them gently. "Sweet child. I will pray for you and we'll meet again when a ship comes. You'll watch out for my birds, won't you—parakeets, you remember? Yellow-crowned, please, if you can. And don't let these fools eat any more albatross unless you are starving and your life depends on it. It's terribly bad luck."

He gave my hands a squeeze and turned his clouded eyes away. He climbed into the boat, wincing with the pain of his swollen and disfigured limbs—just a touch of the scurvy, he said. I bore witness to his suffering and there was nothing I could do. He didn't see the smile I tried to send him away with. He couldn't see farther than the ends of the oars.

The final man of the seven was Sanguily, and he went with obvious reluctance, preferring to stay with Teer. I would gladly have swapped him with Allen, who had no love for me. Or Bill Scott, who had perhaps too much. But no one asked my preference and I stood dumbly by Joseph's side.

Sanguily had hollow pools where my ripped petticoat revealed his collarbones and his arms were thin wires, but he lifted his oar as strongly as any of them and had his precious jacket folded under him while he rowed, keeping it safe. "Goodbye, Mrs Jewell," Sanguily called as they pulled away from the shore. "God bless you and keep you safe until we return!"

They rowed up the harbour to became a distant dot, a bird on the water.

It had been decided in a rare agreement between Teer and Mr Brown that no attempt would be made on the wreck of the *General Grant*, and that if no rescue came by the year's end we would reunite and attempt our own rescue. I didn't tell them my lonely secret. Sometime near the new year my baby would arrive. I couldn't birth a baby on my own. Joseph would have to pull it out of me and the thought set me shuddering. He'd need to borrow a gully knife to cut the cord but I had never seen it done. I had heard the words but didn't know what they meant. I dreamt of the thick mooring lines that tied a ship to the pier, and Joseph hacking at them with a blunt knife to set the ship free.

I sat on the gutting rocks with my jacket wrapped across my distended belly and looked down the harbour to the channel to the sea.

Mr Brown's rescue plan was not complicated. We were to fit out one of the boats with sealskin sails and provisions and strike out towards New Zealand, as Musgrave had done. On the open sea. It was as mad as it was simple. Mr Brown was the only one among us who had studied a chart of the Southern Ocean, but when Mr McClelland had asked him the distance and bearing of New Zealand he couldn't remember or had never known.

"If they find one of the castaway depots, there'll likely be a chart," Joseph said, "An experienced mate like Mr Brown won't go to sea without a bearing."

But who knew what Mr Brown might do?

Across the harbour, Enderby Island blocked our view to

the north and the ocean that lay wide open from Australia to Chile and beyond. Even with a chart, what were the chances of finding New Zealand in all that sea? And who would volunteer to go?

SOAP AND A SHIP

With seven men away we were no longer packed into the huts like penned animals. Joseph and I shared the new hut with Allen and Ashworth, leaving Teer, Caughey, Hayman and Scott in the original. Joseph built a screen so he and I had a private space.

We had a bed of sorts, now, to lift us off the ground; it was a knobbly thing built from fallen branches, padded flat with dried grass and covered with skins to stop us freezing as we slept. I was becoming used to my sealskin suit as well, and though it was a clumsy, bulky thing, the warmth more than made up for the weight. We tried to build an indoor fireplace but without a flue the thing smoked and spat dangerously, so we contented ourselves with hot rocks from the fire pit to warm our cot.

I woke one night by a cry from the other side of our screen. Nightmares stalked us all and I listened to Allen writhing in his sleep and hoped it was his wife and daughters haunting the wretched man. Ashworth was talking to him in a low voice and I let it slide, thinking he was calming him. I woke again later to the sound of them struggling. I nudged Joseph who woke slowly. The muffled whimpering had a strange intensity. It was almost—

"Block your ears, Mary," Joseph said, his voice tight and close to my head.

"But they're—"

"I know what they are doing. It's not our business."

Joseph turned me to face him and put his hands over my ears, my head in the curve of his neck. I was shocked at the lack of him, how thin he had become. I tried to block out the thought of what was happening behind the screen, the disgust of it almost gagged me. In the morning I woke with Joseph's rod pressed hard against my thigh, and I pulled my sealskins down over my petticoats and gathered my clothing together as I escaped the hut.

Allen came out first and went straight to the creek but Ashworth, some minutes later, sauntered over to the fire, put his hands on his hips and looked out along the misty stretch of water. He was sleek as a cat, his pelt jacket fitted with panels and a flared waist that sat neatly on his trim figure.

"Pat's gone out to check the lines," said Teer. "Wait ye a while and we may have fish for breakfast."

Ashworth turned to the men around the fire and ran his fingers through his long hair. A week previously he had asked me to cut it for him with his knife but I had refused. "You can ask one of the men," I had said to him and he had teased me back: "But I want your fingers on my scalp, Mrs Jewell."

"You look out of sorts," Ashworth said to me later, after we had eaten our fill of Caughey's fish and sat stitching. The others were just out of earshot, sorting wood. He had rubbed some fat and curled his moustache, a ridiculous affectation that made me despise him even more. I couldn't bear to look at him, knowing what he had done in the night.

"Mrs Jewell?" he said, trying to catch my eye. "You slept well, I trust?"

"You disgust me."

I said it. I didn't care that Joseph would pretend it hadn't happened. What if they did it again? What if it became a nightly occurrence, as Joseph and I lay less than three feet away? I meant it. What he had done was an abomination.

"Ach." He dropped his sewing onto his lap and shifted uncomfortably. "I'm sorry you had to hear it. A man has needs. Allen obviously wasn't my first choice."

"Oh, you are revolting." I wanted to get up and fly away from him but Teer came over and started throwing logs into the fire. I chewed my lip, flaming with embarrassment.

Ashworth turned his head and spat on the ground. "Allen was all right with it," he said. "I paid him."

That night, it was the quiet Hayman who rolled out his pelt next to Allen in our hut and Ashworth was back in the big hut with Teer. I didn't know how the change had come about, but I thanked God I wouldn't have to hear Ashworth and Allen at each other again. Joseph said nothing, and I didn't want to raise the topic with him. I didn't want it discussed at all. I pulled my full costume around me when I lay beside Joseph and he kept his hands to himself. If I felt his thing stirring beside me I pulled away angrily.

"I can do nothing about that," Joseph said. He spoke without passion, as if he no longer belonged to his body, and my anger submerged under a wave of pity for him. Like me, he was now drained of all desire. His marriage—my marriage, our love—had survived such a short time in the light before sinking.

જ

Scott didn't try to catch me alone anymore and I made no indication that I had accepted his apology. The men were too much for him. Joseph, Teer and Caughey placed themselves between us, a dance with no rhythm or music, but which each man seemed to instinctively understand.

So Scott came at me in other ways, trying to catch my

eye, perhaps waiting for a friendliness I wasn't sure I was ready to give. He spoiled me with courtesies. When it was my turn to drink he repacked the green cabbage leaves in the tea. He set aside the choicest bits of meat for me. He turned my bed stone in the fire, though he never did this service for anyone else. All this he did in the open and I couldn't object to any of it. Perhaps no one else noticed. I wanted to snap at him that I could turn my own stone, but such a reaction seemed provocative and I was afraid of what Teer would do. And tender meat was all I could stomach. So I put up with his attentions and pretended not to see, when twilight obscured him, how he gazed at me and softened his shoulders. I was jumpy and uncomfortable, and there were changes in my body that close observation would surely make clear. The signs of my condition were beginning and I hunched over as I sat to hide my swelling belly.

Hayman, after nearly being butted down a cliff, finally managed to catch a milking goat on Enderby and he built a covered pen for her close to the fire. The men treated her as a pet and rubbed her head and her udders, though Hayman was the only one with any milking experience. Ashworth carved a bucket from the knot of a tree and after a few days of goat-coaxing Hayman managed to pull enough milk to fill it. Unfortunately the bucket was a clumsy, leaking thing and we couldn't pour or drink from it without losing most of the fluid.

Our lack of utensils was frustrating. I had attempted to make cups from soil baked in the fire but there was no clay, only sand and grit. Allen mocked my attempts, with good reason as the things simply crumbled as they cooled. Other than the rough cups and platters Ashworth carved we had managed to make very little, scratching around like savages with what was at hand: wood, flax, stone. We had no brick or clay. No copper or iron from which to make tools, and other than the knives and tins carried from the ship and scraps salvaged from Musgrave's, our living was absolutely primitive. We had nothing to work with. Things we had always taken for granted: a spade, a hammer, a saw, a box of nails, needles and thread, fabric, glass, plate—what a difference these miracles of invention would have made to our uncivilised lives.

When storms came through we were mostly confined to one hut or the other, and without indoor fires or windows we lived in miserable captivity. Scott ranted at the storms. He began to provoke me again, saying the storms were my fault because I had been throwing stones in the sea, but he didn't believe that kind of nonsense; he just said such things to try to get a reaction out of Joseph. Teer silenced him with a slap once, but the accusations stuck: I was a woman. A woman was bad luck. They would be better off without me.

Joseph ignored him.

We brought what work we could indoors and Teer kept us busy with tasks to stop us falling into despair. Every time there was a break in the rain he forced the men out hunting or collecting firewood and made us gather together around the fire to work in the evenings, keeping us talking, pressing the men to tell stories.

"Pat, will ye tell us the about the bosun and the shark again?"

"Ashworth, the gambler at the Cross of St George. He had only one arm, you said?"

"Joseph Jewell, you're a quiet man but I'm thinking you've another story in ye. You've a brother, I think. Is he still at the mining?"

And here Joseph, one of Teer's obedient men, answered yes, that he had two brothers, but neither mining now. William, a mariner who remained in Devon, and Edwin, with whom he had mined in Inglenook, outside of

Melbourne. "He's farming now," he said. It was enough but that was the end of it. He wasn't a man to spin a yarn, not anymore. The shutters I had fancied my love had opened were closed tight and nothing went in or out of his heart.

I had a story I could tell. I had lots of stories. I didn't know that they would interest the men but part of me longed to tell them, to be allowed to speak up and be noticed in the same way that the rest of them were. I had always loved words. Mam had left me a gift of stories and with the girls in Melbourne we'd grown new stories of our own. Would the men want to know things that had passed at the hotel?

There was the night the footman had waited in the rain for his master to tap to open the carriage door, but the master was lying dead in the carriage, choked to death on a nutmeg. No one knew where the nutmeg had come from or why he had swallowed it whole. And a girl I worked with called Lizzie, who so wanted to be an exotic dancer that she would practise in the dining room when everyone had gone up, dancing with the chairs and turning somersaults that fanned out her undergarments. Perhaps not that story.

There were the leaping dolphins south of Cape of Good Hope, and a jellyfish as big as a rowing boat. I'd visited a woman in Melbourne and had my fortune told. "A handsome man and a long voyage," she'd said through her painted lips—though the earthy smell of her underarms suggested she might live another life sometimes as a man. "And a seam of gold stretching out from your shoulder as far as the eye can see." I imagined the crone told that same fortune to everyone but the others said no, they'd had nothing about gold and the sea.

My father had told me never to trust a fortune-teller.

But Teer passed me over and asked Hayman for a story from his travels. He told us about a bridge built over a flooded river somewhere out from Sydney. The water had been so high the animals had drowned in the fields. They had tied planks to the bloated bodies of dead horses to cross.

I listened to their stories and held my own.

Mr McClelland's many attempts to make soap with ash and fat had never succeeded and we were all still itching with skin complaints. I told Teer my skin was rubbed raw under my clothing, which embarrassed him, but he then took up the experiments himself, walking inland for harder wood, burning it in a hotter fire, adding piles of mussel shells that disintegrated into a grey powder. He added seaweed for luck. He reduced and filtered the mess to make lye, all of which was mixed with seal oil and boiled. The resulting stuff never solidified and it turned rancid fast, but it did produce a lather with which we could wash ourselves in a clumsy manner.

There was a joy in washing my petticoats that I never would have imagined. They were black with dirt and itchy with the scabs that fell from my skin. I insisted Joseph and I took the night watch so I could dry my undergarments by the fire without attention, but one by one, to my great embarrassment, all of the men found a reason to pass by my washing line in the night.

The soap worked best on the sealskins, which we lathered up in the frothy muck, washing the residue away in the creek. The pelts felt cleaner though it would have been better if we'd had a barrel or cauldron in which to soak them. It was freezing work in the midwinter and Joseph, who often took the washing task, had hands swollen and cracked with the cold. But the pile of skins grew and soon we were all dressed like warm savages.

℮

We'd been five months on the island with no sight of any passing vessel and I began to understand what none of the men had been brave enough to explain to me. Ships did not pass the Auckland Islands.

"A ship won't come in the winter, will it?" I confronted Joseph.

"We must hope."

"The trading and emigrant ships don't pass here, do they? Any captain would give this place a wide berth. A ship coming here would be way off course and heading for disaster. Like the *General Grant*." I didn't mean to sound accusing but my voice was sharp. I was tired and irritable and just wanted the truth.

"I don't know."

"And the whalers and sealers won't come this far south in winter. I heard Mr Ashworth say it again yesterday. Even in summer they won't be coming. This place was abandoned because there is nothing here. No one is going to come."

"They may."

"But it's not a regular fishing ground anymore. They killed all the seals years ago."

"We've seen plenty of seals."

"But we've seen no ships."

He sighed and tried to avoid my eyes but I stood in front of him to make him see me.

"A ship may come in for water," he said. "Or repairs or for shelter."

He said it without conviction, and then he rolled up the fish hooks he had been threading and went out into the rain.

I still hadn't told him about the baby. I thought my belly would be large by now—large enough so my state would be obvious, but I didn't really know how the timing went. Some days there appeared to be a swelling, others not. The men often complained of swollen stomachs. They said it was bad meat. I was constantly hungry and ate whatever I could take but I didn't suffer from the gripes and wind that afflicted the men; on the contrary, I felt strangely strong and energetic. Mrs Oat had told me, after my monthlies stopped, I should count eight months more until the baby came, and of course I hadn't questioned her about what happened then as I had expected to be safe in Clovelly with Joseph's mother.

I was ignorant of the mechanics of growing a baby. I had no sisters or brothers, and big-bellied women had never visited at the hotel. One of the married matrons had left service to have a baby but from memory she was plump when she left and plump when she returned, a few months later, to show us her boy. A fat woman could hide a baby. It seemed unlikely that would happen to me.

I rubbed my hands over the tight skin, waiting to feel something moving.

In early October we were over on Enderby Island when the call rang out, the cry that we had been hearing in our dreams all these long months.

We had set a fire in a rabbit burrow and I was fanning the smoke while Hayman and Joseph waited with clubs at the exit points. Caughey had gone to check the view from the cliff top, and we heard him scream like a man possessed.

"Ship!" He came galloping down the hillside, scattering boulders and scree in such a landslide he threatened to bury us all. "To the boat! Jewell, Scott, Hayman! With me!" The men dropped their rabbits and the flaming brands and raced for the beach.

"Mrs Jewell!" shouted Caughey, his excitement ringing out across the island. "Light the beacon!"

Oh, I ran. I grabbed my flaming brands and pulled myself up the hill. I ran with the energy of a rabbit, bursting through the scrubby bush tearing at my face and clothing, clutching fire like the devil himself was after me.

We had signal fires ready to go on every outcrop of every island and a few days of dry weather had left the Rabbit Island bonfire a pile of ready tinder. I thrust the smoking brands in and pulled twigs and fallen branches, and when the thing roared into life with a whoosh I added handfuls of green grass and stinkwood leaves that turned the pile into a smoke stack that rose a mile into the sky and stank like shit.

Soon my fire was answered by fire on the point above the harbour. Teer, who had remained back at Sarah's Bosom, was sharp-eyed on watch. The plume grew taller and taller as if the whole hillside was alight.

Far away on the blue sea I could see the ship with its full white sails, and I waved and danced and shouted for it to see our signal, to change course, to come into the harbour and make an end to our suffering. Below, pulling out from shore, our men in the boat struck fast through the surf and across the rolling waves, giving chase, and from my high perch I watched them strongly closing and closing on our deliverance. When they were within a couple of miles of the ship they hoisted the sealskin sail—a flag on the bright, clear sea, directly between the ship and the shore where the sailors must see.

I fell to the earth and clasped my hands in prayer. We were saved.

I waited for the ship to turn, for any indication that she had seen our fires and our men. For once there was no mist and the Auckland Islands rose black out of the blue sea, stark in the clear light. We were unmissable, a giant bonfire smoking on an uninhabited island in the middle of a vast stretch of empty ocean. How could they not be looking at the land? What captain, what sailors, would pass such dangerous rocks without a careful and constant watch?

It seemed the answer was this captain, these sailors. They either weren't looking, or didn't see. The third option was too crushing to bear, that they saw us and chose to turn away. Their white sails blew across our horizon and they abandoned us, their journey onward towards Australia or New Zealand undisturbed by the desperation of us, the castaways. The abandoned.

There was no hesitation, no dip of the sails. The ship had gone and I stared at the empty horizon, while our men in the boat bobbed on an empty sea.

Our rescue ship had come and gone and there was no deliverance.

We got back to camp after dark as dejected as we had ever been, and I ached with legs swollen and great scratches and cuts that plagued me as though I had been whipped and trampled. Under my sealskin skirt my rotten petticoats were shredding away.

"We could see them!" cried Caughey. He flung himself on the ground and pummelled the earth. "Men on the watch, men on the shrouds. We were square in the water off the port side in clear daylight."

"Smoke towering like the chimneys of home!" Scott said. "Beacons clear against the sky. Sailors weeks at sea, where would they have been looking but to the island?"

"A curse on her and all those aboard!" roared Teer. "I hope the damn ship breaks her back! Argghh!" His cry was deep and animal and he smashed his fists into a tree, punching and pummelling like a wild thing.

There was no coming around for the men. No suggestion that perhaps the ship would give word of our whereabouts and send a rescue party. We had been seen and not rescued and the men passed their anger around between them like hot rocks. They quarrelled constantly—even the quiet Aaron Hayman and Joseph fell out and turned their backs on each other. They lashed out at the smallest slight and fists were readily clenched. When Scott and Allen began a fight, Teer shouldered them apart like a great bull and sent them both away from the fire and punched Allen when he tried to return. Joseph and I slept back-to-back at night and barely spoke during the day. We were both so miserable that just to look at the other in our pitiful state threw us into despair.

"We'll never leave this island," I said to him one evening when we turned in, and he just stared at me through eyes that went nowhere. I stared into the blank pits and saw nothing. I wanted to hurt him. I wanted to punish him for taking me away from my life in Melbourne and for the great lie of our promised life in his gentle Clovelly. There was nothing gentle about the life he had given me.

"I will give birth to your child on these rocks," I told him, and the look that came over his face was more than I could bear. All my pain was there in his crumpled mouth. The stupid man carried all the suffering I felt and all of his own and still, still, he could do nothing to save me. If he'd rowed faster or harder or hoisted the sail sooner, we might have been rescued. If Teer had been with them they would have caught the ship. Teer would have made the ship turn around. He would never have let it go.

"What child?"

Joseph reached out his arm to me but I shook away and left him there to crawl under the covers on his own. Our last chance, our only chance of rescue, had been lost because Joseph had let the ship sail away. He wasn't a big enough man for the sailors aboard to see.

I couldn't lie down with him.

I went back out to the fire where some of the men still gathered and I sat at Teer's big booted feet.

VIOLENCE

Caughey brought two more live goats back from Enderby Island. They had "A.S." carved into their horns.

"Acclimatisation Society," said Caughey. "James used to poach these from the Zoological Gardens in Melbourne, so he did."

"Once, Pat," said Teer. "One goat. Your stories grow bigger with every telling."

"We should count ourselves lucky that he left a breeding pair behind for us."

"If I recall, you ate that goat with a great deal of happiness."

"Ah," said Caughey. "If I recall, I borrowed some leeks from the good bishop's garden and our Mary made a pie from the seconds."

"With butter in the pastry! I don't remember where we found the butter, but your sister put it to good use. It was a fine pie."

"Aye, that it was."

The image of that fine leek and goat pie with the buttery pastry shimmered before us, and we breathed deeply together in a communion of longing.

We tethered the new animals with the milk goat and their endless bleating became part of our lives. They drove the men to distraction and attracted the flies but to me they were a welcome sound. I could sit on my log by the fire and close my eyes, imagining I sat on a chair by a real hearth with goats in the barn next door. They were kids and no immediate use to us, but they were a store of meat for the future, so we left them chewing a great circle around the cove and they trampled and ate and extended our living space.

Joseph followed me around like one of the goats, chewing at my skirt.

"You can't be having a baby, Mary," he said, over and over, as if it was a topic of discussion I would have with him and a decision I might change. "It's not possible. How do you know, how can you tell? It's been six months since … since Melbourne. You're so thin."

I hated the way his eyes ran over my body, seeing my scrawny neck disappearing into the thick folds of my pelt collar and wondering what lay beneath. He asked me to undress so he could see the truth of it but I never took my clothes off. I even washed beneath my skirts with Teer's sloppy soap, using a scrap of my petticoat for a rag. I had so little modesty left to me that I clung to my clothing as my last protection. I wanted no man there to imagine I took my clothes off, especially that I took my clothes off for my husband.

It wasn't a conversation I wanted to have, but Joseph was persistent, both of us embarrassed. I told him. "There are signs. A woman can tell."

"How can you tell? What signs?"

I shook my head.

"What signs?"

Surely I didn't need to tell him what Mrs Oat had explained to me, about the repercussions of a man and a woman lying together in the marriage bed and what happened to a woman thereafter. The fact that I hadn't had a monthly bleed since Melbourne.

"Your baby will be born at the end of the year," I said. "You have to get me off this island."

"Mary, don't say such things."

Of course there was nothing he could do and it was the cruellest thing, to charge him with a task he could not possibly fulfil. Fly over the sea, I might have said. Chew through the mountain. Tunnel under the earth. These were tasks for a hero.

There was a new feeling in the camp now—I could see it in the faces of all the men. Before the ship we had still believed that our time on the island had a limit, and if we showed patience and forbearance rescue would come. The despondency hit like a wave after those white sails disappeared into the blue. No one seemed to believe, anymore, that rescue was coming; we no longer talked about sealers or whaling ships coming into the harbour. If we held hope that we would be noted as missing when we failed to arrive in England and searches sent for us, it was a terrible hope, as any such rescue would be at least a year coming. By now the *General Grant* would be deemed late, but it would be months before she would be declared lost and even then, what were the chances of a search party being sent out and where would they begin looking? Many ships were lost at sea, most went straight to the bottom, struck by whales or ice and never seen again. There was no one coming for us and in all this time only the one ship had passed.

Of course it was Teer who roused first and pushed us on, tried to bring back some vestige of hope. He was gone for days at a time, taking Scott and Hayman on the oars. On the points of North Harbour where they could be seen from the sea, they built huge rocky cairns, and flagpoles hung with skins. Teer brought back eggs from the seabirds that nested on the western cliffs and kept us fed when we were too pathetic to move and bullied the men into relentless work: keeping the fires stoked, bringing in seals, working the pelts, keeping us busy.

"I have a task for you, Mrs Jewell," he said to me as I sat lethargically by the fire in the afternoon, doing nothing, thinking nothing, aware of a hollowness inside me. The sandflies had returned with a period of calm weather and I listlessly slapped them away. Teer crouched before me and waited until he had my attention. I found it difficult to fix my mind on him. It seemed so long since anyone had looked me in the eye. He had a flat piece of wood, about the length of my arm, and he rubbed his hands over it. It was chipped into the rough shape of a boat.

"You're going to send out a rescue message, Mrs Jewell. D'you think it might work? We'll get Ashworth to scribe some words here. *Help*. Will that do it, do you think? And our ship and location. *Need Relief*, that sounds like what we need here." He had to nudge the piece of wood into my hands and I took it, and with it, perhaps, came a little bit of Teer's hope. "And I want you to carve the words into the wood, you'll use my knife, carefully, I don't want you going cuttin' yourself, but you'll carve out the message. And then we'll row it out and throw it on the tide and let the wind take it to New Zealand, so they know that we are here and want to be rescued."

He stayed crouched there, in front of me, as I held the piece of wood in my hands and turned it over and over.

"Don't you sit here in despair, Mary. You'll break my heart," the last words so quiet that only I could hear, and so faint they drifted away before I caught them and trusted them to be solid. But I saw him then, his eyes wide open in front of me.

"Ashworth!" he called, and turned to the men across the fire. "Mrs Jewell will do the carving, if you'll scribe it out neatly. *Need Relief,* we think will be a fine message to send."

When he stood up he towered over me and I raised my chin along the length of him, and in the shadows of his shaggy mane of hair I saw he was smiling. I felt then that he was the one, the only one who could save us, the only one who could save me. I had saved my baby from the wreckage and carried it all this time and I owed it to the child to be rescued. I blinked slowly and when I opened my eyes Teer was still there.

છ

I took Teer's knife and chiselled out messages on his whittled boats, carefully going over the letters scratched by Ashworth on the wood. I was clumsy with it and one of the men would have done a better job, but Teer had given me the responsibility and I did the best I could.

When I had three made, Joseph took a boat and a crew out to sea and beyond the breakers on the far side of Rabbit Island they dropped them into the outgoing tide. It was a tenuous piece of hope.

Spring approached and the days grew longer, but the thrashing wind and rain continued to curse us and warmth was slow coming. I couldn't settle. My emotions were shivery and I looked at Teer for strength but he never looked back at me. He stood up and busied himself when I came to sit and never put himself in a position where it was just him and me able to talk. I wanted to know what it meant to break his heart.

I was sick again—food flowed through me without sticking to my sides. My swollen belly ached but, God help me, I used a stick to poke through my muck and saw nothing alarming dropped from my straining bowels. I loosened my skirt to ease the pain.

I crouched in discomfort as the light grew stronger and

put my bone needles to work on rabbit skins. The skins we had smoked dry previously were useless, stinking and the fur falling out, but Teer gave Ashworth the job of soaking them in warm salt water and ash for days to kill the smell and then scraping the flesh and membrane off with a mussel shell. It was a nasty job, as the stuff stuck to his hands and went brown and brittle when it dried. Stretched properly, the skins became soft and workable. I still found it difficult to look at Ashworth and remained disgusted by the beast in him, but I was glad for his work on the rabbit skins. God knew, the day was coming when I would need to wrap a baby in one.

Teer piled new carcasses up and the skin and guts were flung about, which made my stomach heave but I kept my place. The alternative was to lie all day on my cot, my mind awash with the calls of drowning children, or fixed on the ship that had come so close and then sailed away. The tasks kept coming and I kept working and I dreaded the end of the day when I put my work down and had nothing to distract me from the images in my head.

At the end of one long day, when we had sat working together, me with my back to him, Ashworth called for my attention and presented me with a pair of skin gloves, soft and flexible. They were beautifully stitched things, not at all savage. Ladies gloves. He meant them as a peace offering. I had barely spoken to him since his attack on Allen in the night.

I rubbed my chapped hands in fat before pulling them on. I accepted them without thanking him. There was no one else they would fit and must have been days in the making. It was inconceivable to waste that effort when we had so little. When I had so little. I wore them to sleep, which gave me much relief. "I am obliged," I told him, when he examined my hands a few days later and saw how the red puffiness had calmed. The look on his face surprised me. He seemed truly gratified to have won back my favour but again I turned my back and got on with my work. Cordiality here was born from necessity. He was a sinning man with an unnatural vice, but I was dependent on Ashworth as I was on all the men here and had no choice but to bite back my disapproval.

⁂

When I felt well enough to resume watch, Teer sent me with Joseph to the lookout. It was a still afternoon with good light. We were to replace Allen and Scott on watch; Teer had decided to go sealing and wanted them back.

We walked to the hill track without talking, both of us slow with the swellings in our legs, and we met Allen coming down, saying he was hungry and Scott had offered to watch alone.

"What if a ship comes?" I asked him as I stepped off the path for him to pass. "One man to build the fire, one to sound the alarm?"

"Ship's not coming," he said, and walked on towards the comfort of the camp.

I turned and watched him go, anger rising like a tide in me, pounding my ears. What sort of man was he that he would do nothing to help us, wouldn't do the thing even the very least of us could do, and that was to watch for a ship? It was the most basic thing, the only thing that mattered. Watch.

One man to watch the sea and the other to sound the alarm. It was a simple rule that Teer impressed on us every day as he set the watch. Without rules we were primitives who would never find our way home.

And Allen had turned his back on the watch because he was hungry.

My anger was uncontainable. I screamed at him, "You lazy, good for nothing sluggard!"

Scooping handfuls of stuff from the path—earth and stones—I threw them after him but they landed with a soft splatter and Allen picked up his pace for a couple of steps. I could hear him laughing. I held a rock in my hand.

Joseph put a hand on my arm. Shook his head. "You have to bear it," he said gently. As if he understood everything.

I threw it anyway, but it fell short.

The track to the lookout was long and arduous and we walked it silently, Joseph leading, me following.

We came quietly to the lookout and startled Bill Scott.

He was digging underneath our gold tree.

I saw him as I came up through the scrub. I was expecting him at the fire or the lookout where he should have been watching for a ship, but he was at the edge of the clearing, squatting under the tree where our gold was buried, with a pile of earth at his feet.

"No!" I cried, dashing forward. I heard Joseph behind me throwing down the logs he had carried. He rushed past me at the crouching Scott, who sprung up guiltily with a digging stick in his hand. He looked around as if contemplating taking off into the bush but Joseph grabbed him and shook him.

Scott swung a punch that connected above Joseph's eye. The fist split the skin and blood spurted. Joseph cried out.

"Get your hands off me," Scott shouted, pushing Joseph away. "Can't a man have a shit without being molested? Damn you, man!"

I looked into the earthy hole. I couldn't see how deep he had dug. There was no sign of Joseph's leather pouch. Now Scott was paddling his hands at his trousers, pretending to pull them up as if he had been crouching at nature's business.

I ignored this charade. He had sent Allen away because he was after our gold. "What are you digging for?" I asked Scott in my sharpest voice. "How did you know? What have you found?"

"Nowt for you here, Mary."

I cringed at his use of my Christian name.

He kicked the dirt back into the hole. Had he been watching us digging, that night when I had taken my petticoats off and removed the gold from the seams? What had he seen?

Scott stepped away, keeping his face towards us. He held up his empty hands but I saw the heavy drag of his jacket on his shoulders, pulled down by a weight at the back.

Joseph held his hand to his face, cupping his eye. He pulled it away and stared at the blood dripping through his fingers. He was always a man for letting things go, waiting for troubles to pass. A man of inaction. Now he rubbed the tacky blood on his fingers.

"He's got a pocket in the back of his jacket," I said. "What's in your pocket, Mr Scott? You've stolen our gold."

Scott took another step away. "You're imagining things, Mary."

Again, that use of my name.

"When I tell Teer you're a thief he'll kill you."

"You'll keep that pretty mouth closed."

"Stop him, Joseph," I said. "He's taken our gold."

"I dug it up from the earth, same way any man finds it," said Scott.

Joseph stepped forward as Scott stepped back, matching him step for step, back towards the fire. Joseph was the slightly taller man with a longer reach but Bill Scott had the tension of taut wire running through him. He was a fighter and Joseph was not.

Scott's jacket pulled with the weight in the back.

"You've taken gold that doesn't belong to you," said Joseph. "And you're being familiar with my wife. Both these things I don't like."

Words that should have been threatening sounded so reasonable from Joseph. If he was leading up to something there was no menace in his voice. He stepped in time with Scott, footfall to footfall, the distance between them closing.

"If something is there for the taking," said Scott. "I take it." His voice was a spring of violence, the tight tone of a dangerous man. "You've got things I want, Jewell. Your gold. Your wife."

I expected Joseph to leap at him for that and smash his smiling face.

Both men stopped but Joseph's hands remained, fingers spread, at his side.

"You won't fight me, Jewell. I can walk away with whatever I want. You're a coward, you are. I saw you when the ship went down. You jumped into the sea to save yourself. Abandoned your post. Left the women and the chi—"

The attack came fast, Joseph closing the gap with a leap. He grabbed Scott by the throat but Scott, a brawler, met him with punch to his ribs that knocked the wind from him. Joseph, mid-shout, crumpled and dragged Scott down with him, and the pair flailed in the embers grasping and struggling as the bonfire roared gold behind.

ల

I cried entreaties and beat at their legs. The sealskin trousers I had stitched for both men dragged across the smouldering earth. I stood and kicked hard at Scott's back and my toe smashed against stone. The bulge dragging his jacket sagged, the seam of knots unravelled, and Joseph's pouch slipped to the ground.

It was the size of a large wrapped handkerchief, brown and drab. Such an unlikely thing to hold our entire future.

Joseph was pulling back from the fire but Scott reached in, fumbling with his hand in the embers, fingers closing around a stick the size of his arm.

I tried to kick him but my balance was gone so I reached for a stick of my own to thrash him with, a spindly thing of wet leaves that bounced off Scott's back as he thrust his burning brand at Joseph, catching him on the chest, sending him flailing back and away, scrabbling insect-like on his back with his knees in the air.

Scott was on his feet. He grabbed the pouch by its strings and swung it at Joseph, who pedalled back and back, ducking the swinging bag as the brand came forward, catching his exposed neck. Joseph screamed. He was on the bluff edge and I could smell him burning. Scott was waving the brand, a vicious smoking poker. Joseph was one push from death.

Scott didn't push.

He stopped. Scott wasn't a killer.

Then the strings on the pouch snapped. As it hit the ground the singed seam burst and the colour spilled bright onto the dark earth: nuggets and flakes and coins. Two handfuls of butter-yellow stones.

With them poured out on the ground between us, our balance changed. I felt then an inkling of what Joseph might have felt in his diggings, amidst the squalor and desperation. Each nugget of gold a reward for the terrible risks, giving it a value not for what it could buy, but for what it had cost. I'd been hearing the noise of gold for years. Had listened, these long months, to the hot excitement in the voices of our wrecked miners. It was for this. This was the prize.

It was men's instinct to fight for it. If the thought of gold lying at the bottom of the sea was enough to make a man risk terrible dangers, what would he risk when stones were laid before him on the ground?

Joseph knelt at the fringe of the bluff, one hand clutching the burn on his neck, the other wrapped around a tuft of scrub. It was a flimsy hold. One more thrust from Scott and he would be over the edge. There was nothing below to save him.

"He fell," said Scott. "And I dug these stones from under the tree."

There was no fault in this logic.

And yet still he didn't push him. Not a killer.

I inched forward, unbalanced on my toes. If I was going to leap, I needed to be closer. He would swing around and I would plunge directly onto the brand. It would give Joseph time to leap forward and save himself.

I wasn't sure of Joseph. Wasn't sure he would leap.

"Get down on your knees."

I did as he said and became helpless as a snail. The tuft of shrub that Joseph clung to was pulling loose at the roots. He lay flat on the edge, spreading his weight.

"It is what you want, isn't it, Mary?" Scott asked. "It's our chance, what we've been waiting for. If he falls. You know I'll look after you better than he does."

I prayed, willing myself to believe any charity I had ever bestowed in my past life would grant me favour with God, now. Please God, help my husband. Strike down Bill Scott and bring my husband back from the cliff.

"He doesn't love you," Scott spat, the fling of spittle landing in a thread on the collar of Joseph's jacket, close to his cheek. "Doesn't even like you, Mary. Never looks at you. Never a kind word. He deserves to fall."

I didn't look at Joseph, didn't want him rising in anger now with me on my knees and unable to help.

"We could start again. And now with such a bright

future ahead." He opened his hand towards the gold at his feet. "This is our opportunity, do you see?"

He is not a killer. I had to repeat it to myself. He's not evil and he's not mad. It's the gold talking. He won't do it.

"What happened in Melbourne, Mary, that's past. I can forgive you that." His voice came from some deep place, echoing and hollow. "The way you led me on. The smiles. Before Jewell came along with his gold-lined pockets and tempted you away." He leaned forward and poked the brand towards Joseph as the breath surged in my body. "You regret your choice now, eh, my love?"

He made no sense. He had recollections of a time that hadn't happened. He was behaving as if someone had blasted a bullet between his ears and filled his memories with smoke.

He lifted his eyebrows and nodded to me as if seeking my agreement to send Joseph tumbling.

"So what's it to be this time, Mary? You get a second chance. Do you choose me, or Joseph Jewell?"

The gold lay in the middle and could go either way.

He wouldn't do it. He was asking my permission because he couldn't do it.

"I need you to say it, Mary," he said.

My voice was tiny. I wanted to shout it out, but was so afraid of what his next move would be. I licked my lips.

"Joseph."

Scott looked incredulous. "What?"

"I choose Joseph."

"But you love me."

"Joseph is my husband."

"I'll push him."

"You can't kill a man," I said, with my husband clinging to the edge of life. "It's not in you, Bill Scott. You are a good man. You are not a killer." I put my hands together, begging. "Please. I want you to let him go."

He raised his eyebrows in comical surprise but I didn't change my plea.

"I know you are a good man, Bill Scott. Hear me. You can't kill a man." Was he hearing me?

Slowly, he withdrew the brand and stepped back. Joseph squirmed forward, a yard, two yards from the edge so he was lying at Scott's feet with the gold between them. The small bag that demanded such attention.

"You're right, Mary. I've never killed a man. You see me. You know me."

The smoke from the brand spiralled upward. Scott crouched. He ran his fingers over the nuggets loose on the earth, waiting to be collected up and pocketed. They had not scattered like ordinary stones but landed in a pile, heavy with the desire of so many men. He picked one, rubbed it, weighing it in his fingers as every man did, always an appreciation for how it was loaded. Like a gun.

The stone was bigger, no doubt, than anything he had come across in all his days in the mines. He picked up a second. Each worth more than a year's wages.

He was chewing his lip and he looked at Joseph, prone before him.

"I'll take these," he said, and put the stones in his pocket.

Two golden nuggets. The price of Joseph's life.

"And leave your wife. Until she comes to me willingly. I can wait."

He ran his fingers across the remaining stones, but took no more. As if we should be grateful.

"That gold doesn't belong to you," Joseph said, but he didn't put out a hand to stop him, to fight for what was his. I wanted him to add that his wife, also, did not belong to Scott, but he had said all he was going to say.

"I just saved your life, Jewell. You nearly fell. I'll take it as payment."

"I will tell—" I began, but he cut across me.

"You won't tell the Irishman." Scott threw his brand onto the fire where it landed point down, quivering in the pile. "A word against me to anyone and I will tell such stories to the men of your tricks in Melbourne, Mary—the promises you made me, the games you played with the men there, the flirting. How you led me on, how I were banned from the hotel for being your lover. Once a whore, always a whore."

"Why are you saying these things?" I cried, but I didn't know what Joseph would think or what the men would believe, because part of it was true: Scott had been banned from the hotel because of me, because I had reported the things he had said to me. I had felt dirty saying them aloud. And now he talked as if I was to blame for it, that I had provoked him. If I had ever done anything to lead him to believe I was receptive to him I was being punished for it now.

"What price your wife's reputation, eh, Jewell? You won't be able to protect her when the men know how willing she is. You won't be able to close your eyes."

Scott was away down the path as Joseph crawled in from the ledge and sat like a whipped dog on the ground.

He picked the ash and dirt from his trousers. Then he gathered the gold up in his hands. I didn't know what he was thinking. He didn't tell me anything.

JOSEPH AND THE BABY

I stood close to Joseph and threw branches into the flames, building it to a frenzy and wasting wood that we had laboured to bring to the point. We had stayed at the lookout after Scott had gone, though I could have followed him and stoned him from above. We were on watch and no matter what befell us and what crisis we endured still our lives depended, more than anything, on sighting a ship and escaping the island.

We sank deep in ourselves: me trying to find the words to tell Joseph how cruel were Scott's accusations, and Joseph … I couldn't say. The silence that came from him didn't sound like a silence where he was struggling for words as I was. His was an emptiness where thoughts didn't form into words.

"Leave it," he said finally, as the fire grew so high it threatened the shelter over the wood pile. He stayed looking into the flames, with a stripe down his face where the blood from his cut eye trickled to meet a swollen lip and the red welt of the burn on his neck.

"It's not true," I said, finally. With all the thoughts racing around in my head, it was all I could come out with. Whatever I might have said to Scott when I served him dinner in the hotel, whether I smiled at him or thanked him for a compliment, whether I had sent him off forcefully enough when he had cornered me in a corridor and suggested I walk out with him, whether, abandoned in this godforsaken place I had accepted more than life-saving aid from him, whether I had taken a piece of fish from his fingers or passed him a tin of tea with a kind word or whether I had given him a *good morning* or looked at him without blinking fast enough or put my arms around his neck when he had lifted me to feed me in that dreadful quarter boat as Joseph lay insensible at my feet. Whatever in these things indicated to Scott my availability to him, the charges against me were not true.

Joseph said nothing. I wondered if he had even heard me.

"I said it is not true."

"What?" Startled, his voice came from somewhere disconnected to where his thoughts had taken him. "Of course it's not true. I know my wife."

Then he was silent again.

"I thought he was going to kill you."

Joseph kicked a bit of ash, nudged it forward. He made me feel I was intruding on his emptiness.

"I would have killed myself," I said quickly. But I wasn't sure of that. Because of the baby. I didn't know to what lengths I would go to keep the baby safe. Did Joseph realise?

"I need to keep the baby safe," I said, confused now about how killing myself fitted into this fact. "You know that, don't you?"

"What?"

I didn't know what was wrong with Joseph. His brows were drawn right down, angry as if I had shaken him awake from a deep sleep. It seemed to slip his mind that, though he couldn't see it, I was carrying a burden and the weight of it grew increasingly frightening as the weeks passed. I needed him to protect me. I needed all of the men to protect me, and I needed to be worthy of protection because I carried the one child we had saved from the wreck. Without me, without her—

"Stop this talk about a baby."

His words slapped me. He was hateful. I wondered what the shipwreck had done to his mind. He had not been stupid in Melbourne.

"She won't go away because you don't want her," I said.

"She? What are you talking about?"

"I'm sure it's a girl. I think, because—"

"There is no baby, Mary."

He said it like a fact. No baby. Not: *This is a bad place to have a baby*, or, *this will be a difficult time for a baby*. Even, *I wish you weren't having a baby*. That would be cruel beyond measure. But to deny her existence ... I didn't know what to say.

He shook his head and looked at me with pity. I crouched down on my haunches and began to cry slippery tears of loneliness, and my unspeaking husband sat beside me, with his arms around his knees. So physically close and so very far away.

Later, we saw the boat going out on the harbour below: Scott with Teer and Caughey and Allen, gone to hunt seals. Ashworth and Hayman were at the settlement fire. There was no one to replace our watch until the hunters came back. The afternoon rode across the sky in rolls of textured cotton clouds, heavy with rain that came on by evening. We sat under the shelter. At one time Joseph said, "I will find a new hiding place for the gold."

Even now, when I was in such turmoil, he was thinking about his gold.

We might have struck up a conversation then, decided a new hiding place, discussed what had happened and the cruelty of Scott's allegations about me. How to get our revenge on him and take back the two stolen nuggets. Made plans for what would happen if rescue didn't come in time for me. Why he felt he had to deny the baby.

But there was no talk from Joseph. No speculation or any way forward through our difficulties. Just the deathly silence of the close-mouthed man.

This man beside me, my husband, Joseph, was a stranger. I didn't think he could save me. I didn't think I could save myself and soon I would be utterly helpless.

I let the fire die right down, wondering when Joseph would notice I had stopped feeding it and step in to take control. We weren't relieved until late in the evening and by then the fire was almost dead.

࿊

Joseph became Scott's shadow, watching were he went and with whom, listening to every word he said.

"Leave it be," I told Joseph, but he gave Scott no space. After a few days of this Scott came to the door of our hut as Joseph and I laid down for the night, stepping over Hayman, who slept on the threshold.

"Back off," Scott said, pointing his finger at Joseph, and then he left.

"Got on the wrong side of Scott?" Hayman called through the divide. "Don't mind him, he's a moody beggar. Takes slight at everything, wants revenge for any insult before you've even thought of insulting him. Ignore him. Goodnight now, you Jewells."

Scott stayed away from us and Joseph kept his watch from a distance. We said nothing about his thieving or his violence, and it seemed he spread no slander about my supposedly wanton ways. No one asked about the burn on Joseph's neck, which bubbled and rubbed bloody against his collar. We all carried cuts and burns that festered and scarred. The two nuggets of gold Scott had stolen from us were hidden, but I didn't count them lost. They were ours and we would find a way to have them back from him.

Scott now got up and left whenever I came to the fire, and he made a point of not going out with any party in which I was included. It got so that his avoidance of me became ridiculous.

I was walking down the beach with Joseph one morning, included in a trip to Rabbit Island, when Scott dropped his oar and got out of the boat.

Caughey asked, "Has Mrs Jewell upset you so much, Scott? She does not bite, you know, and she has good eyes for the rabbits."

Scott went away along the shoreline, saying something about fish.

Caughey, arms folded as he watched the back of Scott, frowned deeply. "D'ye want me to speak to him, Jewell?" he asked. "There's no call for that kind of rudeness."

Joseph lifted me into the boat.

"That's not necessary," he said, but Caughey didn't give up.

"Mrs Jewell, would you like me to speak to him?"

"Leave it," said Joseph, and he placed himself between me and Caughey, so no conversation could pass between us.

"We need to split 'em up," Caughey said to Teer as the men took the oars, and we slipped out onto the calm water. I still didn't like the boat, but I would make the harbour crossing to the island if the wind dropped away. "I'll deal with it if you won't, Teer. Scott's a pest."

I thought Joseph should object to the men discussing his wife, but he and his partner Hayman pulled on the oars and nothing more was said.

We caught no rabbits but noticed clutches of seals gathering on the eastern beaches of Enderby, and on this pretext Teer took Scott away with an exploring work party the next day, leaving me behind at Sarah's Bosom with Joseph and Hayman. We were to keep the fire alive and watch for the return of Mr Brown's group until Teer called for us.

Teer was proposing to move us across the harbour to Enderby Island. As soon as he'd suggested it, the plan had seemed an obvious one. As well as giving us a sea lookout for ships, he said it could sustain us better if some mishap caused us to lose the boat: the island had good numbers of rabbits and goats and there were several seal colonies within reach along the shore. I wondered, though he didn't say, if he felt we had outgrown Sarah's Bosom and needed a change before we all went mad.

It was peaceful without the men's presence, and I felt safe enough to sleep during the day while Joseph and Hayman fished and foraged and we waited for the call to cross the harbour and be industrious in our new settlement. Aaron Hayman was good for Joseph, I thought, a quiet man who didn't find Joseph's silences gloomy and who could stir him to talk occasionally by throwing him a problem to solve.

"We could rub seal bladders in oil," Hayman suggested one long evening as we approached the solstice. They were playing draughts with white and black stones on a board scratched in the dirt.

"Or fill them," said Joseph. "Let them sit so the weight of the oil stretches them and seals the membrane." Joseph moved one stone one pace, an obvious move. I turned back to the view down the harbour, the water darkening before the sky lost its shimmering light, little drifts of blue still refusing to die.

"It would be difficult to clean them after. The water would taste rancid." Hayman reached out to touch a stone, but withdrew to reconsider. There was no hurry to anything we did, a faster game would simply make the evening longer.

"Better bad-tasting water than running out. For a week or two?"

They were talking about the crossing to New Zealand and how to fit the boat out for the men who would make the rescue mission. I prayed a ship would come before we would grow so desperate. And who would select the men to go?

"Will you play, Mrs Jewell?" Mr Hayman asked me when they finished their game but I always refused, preferring to sit and stare down the harbour than play with stones in the dirt.

After a week Teer and Caughey returned for us. We had no news of Mr Brown and his men down in Carnley Harbour and could only hope they fared well at Musgrave's camp. I thought of Mr McClelland and his swollen joints and fading eyes and again wished he had remained behind so I could have cared for him. Teer said he wouldn't risk the boat on a search for them and trusted the sailors would return, as planned, at the year end.

Caughey wrote a message for them in charcoal on a stone, but we guessed they would see our fire on Enderby clearly enough as they rounded the harbour head.

There were no regrets when we abandoned our camp at Sarah's Bosom and rowed to Enderby Island across choppy water—me clutching the goats in the stern who bleated and snapped with their sharp little teeth. I wasn't sorry to go. We left nothing I wanted to take away. Joseph had the pouch of gold tied to his belt. It bulged awkwardly where he hid it under his jacket.

⁂

The island, with only small pockets of the oppressive ironwood forest that covered the mainland, felt lighter and less miserable. There were red dots appearing now on the trees, Mr McClelland's promised rātā bloom, and over the weeks they spread like a flaming rash over the dark forest. We looked back down the harbour across a deep beach with sand above the high water mark, stones at the tide and rock pools covered in limpets at each end. From the top of the tussocky hillside behind we could see out to the widest horizon imaginable. The hill was slashed with rocky gullies and the persistent rain caught in rivulets that ran fresh and cold to the bay. There were penguins on the rocks below the cliffs and slender-winged albatrosses circling above, caught on the updrafts. The sounds were different on the island, less intimate. Bigger waves beat farther away and crying birds wheeled, screeching as they dropped in great circles.

There seemed to be fewer of the biting flies on the island.

"It's the penguins," said Teer when I remarked on this. "They attract them away from us. The sandflies much prefer penguins to people."

I found it hard to believe but he was insistent.

"Carry a penguin with you next time you go for a walk, Mrs Jewell," he told me. "You won't get a bite."

"Mr Teer, I believe you're teasing me."

Whatever the reason, it was a welcome relief to be rid of the sandflies and the attention of Teer warmed me. He went off down the beach laughing.

The initial huts Teer arranged for us were crude hovels thatched with grass, closed on three sides with a fire in front and parakeets cackling from the roofs.

"They'll give us shelter while we build decent huts for the winter," he said, setting the men to cut the sods to bake dry for foundations.

I hated the new straw huts, flimsier even than at our previous camp, and still I was wedged in sleeping with men who were not my husband.

"We're building something stronger," said Joseph when I complained.

"They're straw huts, Joseph," I said, not caring that Hayman was with us and I was wheedling like a child. "I don't want to live in a straw hut. Look at us. We're like little pigs."

Hayman laughed at that and snorted like a pig, but Joseph just turned his sad eyes to me and went on packing straw under my pelts for my bedding.

In the night the wind turned and the smoke blew in through the doorway and if Caughey hadn't been alert on watch we all might have choked or burned to death in our sleep. There were dreadful hands on me in the night shaking and pulling and I woke smothered, hearing the crackling of a fire in the hut, in the walls! Men shouting in my ear with such confusion and someone dragging me towards the fire while I fought them off, tearing myself away to the back of the hut.

"Hut's on fire," shouted a voice in my ear, choked and unrecognisable, and Joseph was grabbing me from behind and lifting me.

"We're going through the fire, Mary. Hold on." But he stumbled and it was other hands upon me, men grabbing at me and lifting me, two or three swinging me between them as they leapt over the fire, my body shouldered like a piece of meat and delivered into the sharp air of the night.

"Where's Joseph?" I cried, searching through the flames that the men were stamping and dowsing now with dirt, looking for a body inside on the floor, but Teer strode through the fire and was back with Joseph in his arms.

"I can stand," shouted my husband, pushing Teer from him, sucking in air like he'd been drowning. "Where's my wife?" He turned, prepared to leap back into the hut. "Where's Mary?"

"Here! Joseph, I'm here." I grabbed him and spun him to see me, both of us soot-covered and strewn with straw like dirty scarecrows and we glared at each other, clutched together, as behind us the hut went up in flames.

By the next night the hut had been re-thatched and the fire moved farther from the door. I thought it too far away to offer any heat but still close enough to set us alight. I asked Joseph why he didn't build us a chimney out of stone. He was a miner. Why leave a fire outside a straw hut? But he just told me to be patient.

I lay all night with my aching eyes wide, watching, listening, smelling. Terrified that after surviving drowning and starvation we all might yet burn in our beds.

Teer was experimenting with Hayman's idea of seal bladders for water containers and floats, and he gave Scott the responsibility of fishing from the new buoys, keeping him out in the channel most of the day and well away from me. I was grateful for Teer understanding this without the need for me to ask.

I was rolling flax one afternoon, my head down and fingers working back and forth, when I noticed Teer's big skin boots had stalled in whatever labour had him walking past. I felt him observing me. I pretended not to notice but he didn't leave. So I lifted my head swiftly, expecting to catch some severe look—I was not rolling as finely as I might have and he wasn't slow to criticise any work that was bad. But his face wasn't angry. Just the opposite. He was soft and relaxed, his chin lowered and eyes crinkling as if under that big black beard there was a smile.

For a moment we each held our gaze. He had green eyes outlined with a darker rim that intensified the colour, and he hooked me. Pulled me. Then, shocked, we both looked away and I fumbled with my twine. When I looked up again, he'd gone.

I had often wondered if James Teer saw me as anything other than a responsibility. I knew he had taken on the sacred duty to keep me alive. But it did give me pleasure to think I didn't disappoint him and that, even for the most fleeting of moments, he was happy with me. That, occasionally at least, I pleased him.

The men built and planned and hunted and I became restless, blooming with an energy I had no use for, wanting to be helpful. Several times I offered to gather firewood but the men had an axe now and my efforts were no longer needed. I went out onto the hills, looking for island cabbage and nettles—any herb we could add to the pot, craving vegetables, but I found little in the slips and gullies that pockmarked the hill; the rabbits on this island also feasted on the soft vegetation. I achieved nothing except an exhaustion that allowed me to collapse by the fire pit in the evening and sit silently, like Joseph, with a blanket over my thoughts.

Joseph told me to stop going out onto the hills.

"It doesn't help," he said as I left the hut one morning, out into the pouring rain. "This wildness. Just stop."

He put out his hand as if to catch me before I went off but I stepped away from him.

"I'm foraging."

"There's no need."

"Mr McClelland said it will help against the scurvy."

"It's just grass, Mary. We're not goats."

"They're herbs."

He shook his head. "Don't go off up the hills today."

"You're going off."

"I'll stay. There's work I can do on the new hut."

There seemed to be energetic and productive work for everyone except me. I felt so flushed and fidgety.

"You can rest—" he said.

"I don't want to rest." But I gave in. There was a frame over the wood pile now so I could remain under cover and steam dry in my skins.

Hayman had settled in to make fish hooks from bird bones, and I tried to help him but had no patience for the fine work of scraping and binding. After I grew frustrated he suggested instead I work flax fibres into thread but even that I couldn't do, my twine bulky and knotted and no use for the light skeins he needed for his lures.

"We can use these you've made for something else," Hayman said kindly, meaning he would undo my twine when I wasn't looking and rework it into finer thread. He took the pile of fibre away from me and looked around for a less pernickety task.

There were scraps of leftover rabbit skins that could be used for lining boots or hats and I idled over these, stitching bits together as a kind of patch rug. I didn't like sitting still, for it sent my mind sliding into the dark caves and cavities that haunted my dreams, so I sent my thoughts elsewhere, back before any of this began, to the small room I'd shared with the girls at the hotel in Melbourne. There I imagined I was sewing something for my corner.

I hadn't appreciated the room at the time: four walls, glass in the window, a door that shut. It had a yellow stain on the white wall that I disliked and I'd imagined being married and never having to live in a room with a stain on the walls again. I would have given anything to be back there. I wouldn't notice the stain but instead the white sheets, the feminine smells and the lace curtain we pulled against the harsh sun. Every day one of us would put off-cuts of the hotel flowers in a glass bottle on the windowsill and there always seemed to be someone in front of the looking glass pouting a kiss or fussing with her hair, pinning on a bonnet. Gossip and laughing and, yes, little jealousies and pinches, but nothing, nothing to prepare a girl for shipwreck and the deaths that followed.

Nothing to suggest that if I stepped away, if I took the man's offered hand and walked away from that room, that all life would dissolve into deep icy depths and I would end up sharing a freezing hut of peat and straw with a group of desperate men.

I looked up uneasily to find Hayman watching me and wondered, my chest so tight, if I had sobbed aloud. Teer was close by at the fire, but he and Caughey were arguing loudly over a pot of lye.

Joseph had gone away down the beach with Ashworth, and even in the distance and under the bulk of his skins he looked thin. It was in the way he walked. In a patch of unusually bright sunlight I saw his shadow as a stick stretching from his shoulder across the sea as far as the eye could see.

His promise to stay with me had lasted not half a day.

"What's that?" Hayman asked, and I looked down into my hands.

I had forgotten my sewing and had been stitching with my hands in a different place from my mind. I found a little doll, a bit of twisted rabbit fur tied with arms and legs into an unmistakable likeness, a part-formed baby with a downy face. I was brushing her hair absentmindedly. I went blank at the shock of finding this thing in my lap. Oh God! I shuddered horribly and flicked it from me, but the skin caught on my fingers like a hand and I jumped up as I shook free of its grip.

It fell in the embers in a puff of white dust, and as soon as I'd loosened it I tried to snatch it back, but in my haste and horror I plunged my fingers into the burning ash.

A stick reached over my hand and lifted the doll out, flicked it to safety, where Teer picked it up carefully, respectfully, as if he held something real.

It was nothing real. It was a twist of rabbit skin that my unfettered imagination had transferred into something else. I rubbed my burnt hand and stared at the fur.

Teer looked at it with his head on his side, with a nostalgic smile, recognising a child's toy. It sat on the flat of his hand and he offered it to me. I pulled back, repulsed. It was a dead thing.

Caughey was singing a snatch of song over his pot of soap, unaware of the distress unfolding. Hayman had his head down with his fish hooks.

"Do you not want it, Mrs Jewell?" asked Teer.

I shook my head to clear the picture of the knot of skin, the soft downy hair.

"Throw it on the fire," I said. But it seemed he could not. Even hard man Teer recognised there was something in the scrap that could not be tossed away into the flame. He hesitated.

Reluctantly he stretched to the flame with the skin doll curled on his palm. I didn't see why it was obviously so difficult for him to throw a piece of fur on the fire, why the crude doll should mean anything more than any other discarded waste. It was just a twist of rabbit skin I had sewn into the shape of a tiny baby that lay in his hand.

"No," I said. "Don't burn her."

I spoke in no more than a whisper, but he heard, and he closed his thumb over the little dead thing and placed it in his pocket. He went back to Caughey and their stirring and when I got my breath back I stood shakily and walked to the edge of the rocks to wait for Joseph.

❧

I slept badly that night and woke several times to a cry of pain that disappeared as I surfaced from whatever hell I had inhabited in my dream, to the waking hell in which I had a husband who had denied the baby that I carried. I had held her in my hand. A scrap of fur and twine.

There is no baby.

And yet I could hear her in my head, half-formed, a dying animal. I didn't know what Teer had done with that scrap of rabbit skin but I tried not to think on it. It held no power; it meant nothing. Superstitions were for the ignorant. God was the truth, and I had no time for people who believed in witchcraft and wives' tales and a magic talisman made of skin.

I said my prayers quietly, my lips moving to release a silent breath. I called on God to protect us all, to save us from sin, to keep us true and honest all the days of our confinement, and to bring us relief soon. I regretted our lack of observance: we had let God go from our lives and kept no day free of labour because without our daily labours we would die. So I whispered prayers as I went about my tasks—the prayers of the Irish—memories of my mam's voice in my head, hearing the words we'd spoken together and feeling her close by me.

Then I lay back and ran my hands down under my deflated breasts and over my stomach. There was a swelling, a tight hard stomach, but I thought it was smaller than it had been the month before and it ached like a pain in the guts.

I must have slept then, deeply, because I didn't hear Joseph or the others rousing and going out. I woke to a feeling of disquiet and a sick dizziness as though I had been fighting demons in the night. There was a tangled black skein of despair that I couldn't touch, something I needed to pick at and unravel, but I didn't want to untangle it because the sense of it would horrify me.

I pulled on my jacket and stepped out into fog and

smoke. Joseph was in the distance along the shore with two others, collecting limpets, the low tide leaving puddles of shiny sand reflecting the white sky. I wanted to make him talk to me, but he was far away.

Hayman appeared to be waiting for me by the fire and he stood up when I appeared, nodding to me politely, and I wondered if Joseph had told him to watch me. My chaperone. Allen was there with a tin and a stick in his hands, as usual, eating more than he gathered. Teer and Caughey had their backs to him, fingers busy, knotting Hayman's clever fish hooks on a line. There was no sign of Scott. They didn't notice me and I stood a long time looking out on the harbour, imagining a white sail coming through the channel, a ship coming in. There were gulls swooping low over the water, and waves. Nothing more.

Thoughts of the skin doll stayed me. I'd dreamt that the rabbit skin was a discarded baby. The whole thing was foolish in the dawn light. I felt a wave of embarrassment as I saw Teer reaching his hand into his pocket. But all he brought out was a sharp shell to scrape against a flax knot.

I shook my head when Hayman offered me nettle tea. Fish soup? Strip of dried seal? He let me walk away and I sat on a flat rock feeling empty, searching for the feeling that was missing now, the knowledge that I carried something else. I could find nothing inside me that wasn't me, and that felt little enough. I bent forward at the waist and felt hollow. I wondered where my baby had gone.

A shining mist rolled in over the hills and the tussock sparkled with it. I didn't know what day it was. I had stopped counting, no longer ran my fingers down the markings on our calendar post. The men kept count though. They talked of Brown's party now overdue, of the days now long and light and how the snow had been gone for many weeks. We were at the year's end. The time had come and gone.

She wasn't coming. I nodded my head and said the words aloud: *She isn't coming. I don't have her.* I had felt a baby so powerfully inside me as we rowed away from the sinking ship. A child. *The one child.* I said that aloud, too. We had saved one child. Only we hadn't. She didn't exist. Perhaps she had never existed.

And I knew it was true. Whatever she had been, if she had been, she had gone. Joseph was right. *Damn him. Damn him to hell.* There was no baby. I had carried no one from the wreck, saved no one.

I pushed off the rock and wrenched myself to my feet and ran away from the fire and our miserable camp, along the wide flat track of the shoreline and into the long grasses that drenched my hem, lifting my skirts to stagger through the wet and running up, always up, until my lungs were aflame, onto the hill where the lush plants pulled at me and tripped me and I fell and tumbled and got up again.

I ran sobbing, and the pounding of my feet was the pounding of my heart, the one heart that beat in me because there was nothing else, just my heart alone because it seemed, after all, that I hadn't saved a soul. There was too much breath in the air in this wide open space, too much for my lungs, but I didn't stop running, up the hill and away back from the harbour, where the uneven rock twisted and tripped me so I went flying, but I picked myself up and ran to a place I knew, across the neck of the island where a steep gully ran to the cliffs, a broken and hollow place that tumbled down to a ledge and on to the sea below, a place of sharp edges and hard rocks where one had to take care, step carefully, watch the crumbling rocks on the escarpment. I ran to the edge with all the speed I had and I threw myself over.

Crying gulls.

The screeching came in great swoops.

Close by in my body and plaintive, far away on the wind.

I woke full of pain and then there was blackness again.

The gulls filled me. Their *mew mew* cries will haunt me forever, hammered into my brain with the pain that overwhelmed me as I washed in and out, gulls circling this island, where everything thrown up on the shore is lost to the world and smashed to bits.

Gulls. Pain. Blackness. Gulls. Teer.

"Mary."

Mew mew.

"Come on, now. Wake up, Mary. I need you." Teer again.

The bulk of him blocked my light with his soft brownsugar Irish words. Keeping the gulls away. Stopping them taking me.

Crying and swooping and the wash of waves of fear and loneliness.

"We can't be losing you. What men are we if we canna keep a woman safe? Mary, beloved. Open your eyes now, girl."

The voice turning burnt and gravelly.

Mew mew, cried the gulls, but I heard Teer talking to me, strong and safe. James Teer chasing the crying birds away. His arms around me, his voice deep in my ear. Murmuring now, words like honey. Murmuring and cajoling, pouring a spoonful of fierce on the words' edges, setting the sound into deep earth, digging inside me, finding rock. I felt the warmth of his breath on my cheek.

He took all the pain in my wretched body and held it in his arms, circling me with such a strong pity that I passed my misery to him to hold as he squeezed me and climbed, sure as a goat on a rocky wall. I surfaced with him but faded again and came back as he rocked and swayed with his long strides, carrying me, stumbling over the tussock.

I felt a gentle dabbing on my forehead, on my brows and I thought he was kissing my face as he spoke, nuzzling me awake.

He walked and muttered until beyond him I felt a distant ache of pain and heard again the birds' great circular cries, as far away now as the crashing sea. I remembered what I had lost and what I had done.

"Ach, child, how could you do this to yourself? I promised to protect you, to keep you alive until we are rescued. My darlin', I didn't see you were slipping away. There will be a ship. You must believe me, Mary, we will be saved." His face close again, I felt the scratch of his beard on my cheek. "But you have to help me here. You canna go throwing yourself away. I saw you. I saw you, Mary, you didn't stop. Why in God's name would you do such a thing?"

I had heard him behind me. He had followed me, calling out my name, shouting for me to stop. He had followed me up the hill. And I hadn't stopped. I had run straight over the gully edge. I had intended to die. But here I was. Again, God had not accepted me. Alive, I lay in Teer's arms. A powerful surge spun around my head like a crashing wave and scraped every previous emotion away leaving me drained. Then a hot flush pumped through me like blood. It felt like relief. I was alive.

The pain hit as I came sharply back in the world, it fired across my body. I moaned, the horrible sound of animal caught in a trap. A pain like a dull knife stabbed my shoulder as we moved and scraped across bone. I cried so loudly that Teer stopped immediately and lowered me to the ground. He laid me out, arms crossed over my chest, like I was a corpse.

And suddenly he was talking to other people. I heard Joseph's voice wrung with emotion, barely recognisable through the piercing blade in my shoulder.

And Teer, calm and decisive. "Slipped on the rocks up in the gully. Chasing a rabbit, I think. Lucky she landed in the bushes but here, now, stand back, I'm going to see to her shoulder. Mrs Jewell, can you hear me now? Better perhaps, if she is not awake for it."

The breath pushed against a biting cramp in my ribs and my ankle twisted on the ground in a vice. I didn't know where the pain was the worst. I felt strong fingers at my neck and across to my shoulder but the pain was blinding sunlight stabbing me in the eyes and it was too much. I let go.

℘

I was a long time asleep.

When I woke I heard gulls.

I felt high.

There was mist in my lungs.

A fire crackled somewhere and there was a flickering of firelight on a rough wall to my left, it was the air that was wrong.

Not open, but not stuffy.

I was outside. I was inside.

I slept again.

Joseph fed me and washed me.

I slept again.

Once, I dreamt I was on the ship, but not the *General Grant*. Not with Joseph. I was with the girls from Liverpool and it was on the journey out and we were leaning over the railings with the air so cold, trying to take in great gulps and swallow the mist. Laughing at the vast sea, the freedom of it all. Sometimes I lay through nights that were as long as a year of pain.

I played a game where I waited until the numbness in my hips became unbearable and then I moved and set off the white burst in my head. Another where I kept my ribs absolutely still, counting the shallowest scoops of air, until my body disobeyed me and filled my lungs to screaming point. One night I managed thirty-two tiny breaths before I had to take the big one. Then the pain made me want to vomit.

There was daylight and there was night.

I was wrapped. With my right hand I felt my left arm tied across my chest. I picked at the knot at the shoulder. I remembered Teer knotting the flax on the fishing lines, scraping the threads with a shell. I remembered his fingers on my shoulder. I wondered if he had tied this knot. I wondered. Teer.

The air was fresh and good.

I looked at the ceiling, not knowing where I was.

Joseph had thrown me into the water but Teer had brought me back.

The gulls cried below.

I woke into bright daylight and realised I was at the lookout hut on Enderby. It had walls on three sides and an overhanging thatched roof but was open in front to the sea and sky. Both inside and outside. Day and night. Cold, but I was warm in a bed of pelts and Joseph was rubbing my feet with some grease.

"That hurts," I said, and he stopped.

He built a wedge frame so I could sit up to eat and drink. The pain in my ribs was excruciating and if I swallowed lying down I choked and the coughing was worse than anything. I was so thirsty.

I accepted a wooden cup from his hand, ate the food he put in my mouth but I couldn't look at him. He wanted to know why I had done it and there was nothing I could put into words. I couldn't blame him for anything.

"You weren't chasing rabbits, were you?" he said, but I looked away.

If he wanted to know if I would do it again, I couldn't tell him.

The day I was well enough to stand up and walk some steps across the shelter, Mr Brown's boat returned from Musgrave's camp in the south. They had been six months away by the calendar we kept and all were well. I thanked God to have them back safely. I'd thought of all the things that could have happened to our men on that stretch of coast and their lonely outpost, imagined them perished already.

Perhaps, after all, we were not all doomed to become washed bones on these islands. Or perhaps death would just visit slowly. Greet us one at a time with long years between.

Mr McClelland was the first to visit me.

Joseph and Hayman were playing foot ball with some rolled twigs outside the shelter and I was propped up on the bed watching them. It was diverting and Hayman seemed to be enjoying himself, bouncing the ball off his knee onto his foot and flicking it neatly to Joseph, who played without joy.

"May I come in, Mrs Jewell?" asked a familiar voice. There was a tap on the outside of the shelter and Mr McClelland's pale head appeared, his tall frame followed and he stooped under the thatch. His hair was white and spare, his face more lined and he was terribly thin, but he fumbled forward and found the log that served as a chair. He peered at me through eyes that looked loose in their sockets. When he found me in his sights his entire face crinkled into a smile.

"What's all this about rabbits?" he asked. "Can I not leave you alone for a minute without you tumbling down a gully?"

He had brought me a gift, a softly carved wooden box,

sand smoothed, with a lid that fitted snuggly. Inside was a shell, a small but perfect blue pāua with tiny holes like hopeful bubbles across its rough back. He rubbed the shiny centre with his finger before laying it beside the box on the bed.

"You'll be finding your own treasures to put in here," he said. "It's just a trifle, but I thought you might like something of your own."

I lifted the lid, fitted it back on again and marvelled at his craft. I think it was the first thing any of us had made with no practical use.

"It's lovely," I said. "Thank you." I didn't ask how long it had taken him to make such a well-turned thing with a broken knife and sand.

"We missed you," he said. "We aren't nearly such good men without a woman's company and I'm glad to be back. We were delayed with those storms that came through at the end of the month. But you'll see when you are up and about again that we've made good use of the debris we found at Musgrave's camp. We have a canvas sail for our boat and she sails well, better than the sealskin. We pulled some nails from the wreck. And we found a cauldron on a beach, so we've brought back quite a supply of salt. We thought you might be starving here, but you've obviously fared well."

I noticed he was missing a tooth now, and those on either side had sagged into the space. Scurvy afflicted us all with swellings and bleedings and loose gums, though we had found some relief from the pain with the spring weather; the cold air had stung like toothache.

"Did you find any of the castaway depots?" I asked, but he shook his head.

"I never really believe they existed until we found a fingerpost washed up on the beach. It seemed to have been in the water some time. It said 'Hut' on it and another word which might have been 'Supplies'. Young Mr Sanguily went wild, of course, and ran off searching every cove for miles, but we never found anything. Probably plundered, though there are curses on men who steal with a ship at their backs."

He took my hand and rubbed my fingers. It was nice to be touched like that, in kindness.

"You're staying up here to get away from them all? I can't say I blame you. Hurt ribs, twisted ankle, shoulder come adrift ... you'll need peace and quiet and that clear sea breeze. Not so many flies, either."

"I can watch the horizon," I said. "There's little else I can manage, but I can do that very well."

"My horizons are so limited. I am thankful your young eyes are keeping our watch."

Joseph went down to the camp and came back within the hour with fish to share and water for tea, and we sat in the evening with Hayman and Mr McClelland crowded into the hut. It felt like a party.

☙

Teer was mending the inside of my shelter in the heavy rain, and I watched him from my bed. Joseph had gone off with the axe to find replacement poles. The rain dripped steadily through the roof in several places and a corner threatened to collapse with the weight of the wet grass. Teer was busy with his hands extended overhead, weaving flax rope and new bundles into the frames. His back was to me and I watched his decisive movements, the firm placing of the thatch, the direction of his energy, no movement wasted. There was a potent line that reached from his outstretched hand to his feet on the ground.

He worked in silence, but I was tired of silent men.

"Tell me about your home, Mr Teer," I said.

He crouched then, gathering a new armful of the tussock grass, pulling the bundles into knots with his teeth, spitting out the ends. There was a drip that fell from his unruly hair onto his forehead and I wanted to brush it off. I had a memory of his face so close his eyes embraced me, gulls crying, pain like a shipwreck in my head, and huge tears that dropped from his lashes and down the line of white scar into his beard.

Had his lips rested on my skin? I thought I had felt them, but I wasn't sure. Other things I had thought true had turned out not to be so. I couldn't remember what I had done but I knew the feeling of it. The reckless joy of leaping over the cliff and abandoning my body, and then the offering up of my pain to James Teer, who absorbed it in the vast consolation of his arms. He'd whispered things to me. I wished I could remember them.

He wiped the drip with the back of his heavy hand and stopped his work, arms on his thighs, looking over at me.

"You're awake then."

"I am. And I want a story."

"A story? What makes you think I've a story for you?"

"You and Mr Caughey always have stories." It was true. But I didn't want one of his journeys through jungles or along coastlines, tales of mining towns on the West Coast of New Zealand, strange people he had met on travels. I wanted to know about his home.

Teer sat back on his haunches now—watching me but looking past the outside skin of me and searching for something more—his eyes holding there long enough to make me feel uncomfortable. He knew what I had forgotten.

"If I tell you about my home, you'll tell me why you jumped over the edge?" He screwed up his eyes and shook his head. "It was a terrible thing to see. I'll tell you any story you like if you promise you'll do nothing like that ever again. What do you say?"

I looked up at the ceiling and breathed in as much as I could before letting out a long sigh. I nodded once, sharply.

"Now talk to me," I said.

It sounded like he chuckled. While his fingers went back to work, bundling and tying, he talked. "I'll tell you a story, then. About my sister, Margaret. We grew up in a fishing community on the edge of the Irish sea. Wee Daniel, too, though Margaret and me we ganged up on him something terrible. Boat rats, we were, all of us. But our sister, she was a wild one when she was a girl. Fine looking, and knife-sharp, too," he said. "Like you."

I lay back and closed my eyes and Teer came to sit on the log next to my bed. He recounted the day his sister had hidden in the locker of their boat as he rowed out into the harbour with Daniel. It was a day of strange light and swirling mist. As the boat rocked he put up his oars and told his young brother stories of drowned sailors and the ghosts that haunted the rocks. Then he tapped the deck three times and Margaret began to wail like a demon unshackled and Daniel had leapt into the water screaming and swum to shore.

I liked the story of Teer relating a more innocent time, of his childhood before his travels had hardened him. And I liked the deep rumble of his voice. He wasn't often in such a soft mood and I cherished the familiarity of having him there all to myself. I believed, given time, I could make him into a gentler man, rub the hardness from him. I wanted to see him smile again.

I wondered if he had ever thought of taking a wife. Children.

"Where is the piece of rabbit fur?" I asked him. "The thing you couldn't throw on the fire?"

His expression changed quickly. A dropped brow. A tightening.

"I don't know, Mary."

I held his eyes.

"You said you didn't want it," he said.

"Do you still have it? You do, don't you?"

"What is it?" he asked, but he reached into his jacket pocket and brought the thing out. He had kept it close to him these weeks, a talisman. It looked like nothing at all, a little scrap of fur with a bunch tied at one end. He ran his finger down the head and tapped at the heart of her. "Does it represent something? Something you lost?"

I didn't know if I wanted to tell him. I imagined if I told him I had carried and lost a baby he would think less of me. But I needed to pay him for the story.

"There were babies on the ship," I said, and as soon as I put it in words I was back there again, with the Oat sisters, and the Italian man pushing his baby into my arms. From the way Teer started I might have summoned their spirits to my bedside.

"Here." He pushed the rabbit skin at me, a superstitious man striking away an encounter with bad spirits. "Here, put it somewhere." And then, as I took it and put it into Mr McClelland's wooden box, he said: "You should bury it, Mary. Does no good to hang on to things like that, magic and such."

"Though you held it all these weeks." I wanted to say his name. James. He had called me Mary. Did he realise? Did he think of me as Mary? I breathed it. James. But I didn't say it aloud. "What magic were you hoping for?"

Joseph came back then. At the sound of his steps Teer stood and lifted his hand to the roof, packing in the last of the thatch as my husband appeared in the entrance with an armful of straight poles.

"I was telling your wife stories about my sister, Margaret," Teer said. The way he said it, so quickly and smoothly like that, he seemed to know he was in the wrong.

Joseph laid down his burden and looked from one of us to the other.

"You should go," he said to Teer. "I can finish up here. No need for you to stay."

I pushed the wooden box under my covers and James Teer left without a look for me. For the rest of the afternoon, the evening, and into the next day, my husband barely said a word.

MAN OVERBOARD

The question that faced us now, the reason for the return of Mr Brown's party, was the resolution the men had agreed before we had split. If we weren't rescued by mid-summer, we were to reunite and select a group of men to attempt our own rescue.

Looking out over the vast ocean—as my broken bones and my mind slowly reassembled into props to carry me through the days—I didn't believe it could be done. On the clearest of those long days the horizon was impossibly far away. To take a boat this way or that, across the vastness of the empty plain seemed a fool's errand. And if they reached the horizon there would be another horizon and they would have to decide again: this way or that?

We had no compass, no chart and no heading. The men knew only that New Zealand lay somewhere to the north, a long narrow stretch of land. No stars pierced the clouds at night. In the days the sea was often smothered in fog. Many days I couldn't see Rabbit Island a mile away—what were the chances of finding north in such conditions? Or spotting a distant island when your horizon was a blanket of white?

What if the land appeared at night—black cliffs towering out of the sea?

I knew the dangers. God knew, I could never forget.

And yet, the men agreed upon this course. The choice now was between Teer and Mr Brown: one to stay and lead the castaways and one to captain the rescue expedition. And two men to go with him.

"Not you," I said to Teer as he lifted me from the fire to take me to my bed in the hut. I was always being lifted and carried: by Joseph when he could manage it, by Hayman, by Teer. Joseph was turning my stone in the fire.

"Not you," I said, my face pressed on Teer's chest. "Please don't leave us."

I was lying across his arms. I felt again how he had absorbed me as he had carried me from the cliffs. I remembered his face, so close, as he had cried over me. I remembered. He had kissed my face. James Teer had kissed me.

His eyes narrowed now and his pace paused, just for a beat.

He put me carefully on the bed, laid a rolled pelt under my ankle, lifted away my frame so I could lie flat. "Your husband will see to your bedding," he said, and his voice was gruff with none of the tenderness I wanted to hear.

"James," I said, but he stepped back, hesitating.

"I'll not leave you, Mary," Teer said, and he nodded to Joseph as they passed on the threshold.

My eyes rested on the empty space where Teer had been. I hardly noticed as my husband placed the warm stone at the end of my bed and pulled the skins up over me. My shoulder was unwrapped now but had set stiffly and I found it painful to drag the heavy pelts. I hated being helpless, didn't want to be a burden. Didn't want to be obliged to him.

"Thank you," I said, unmoving as he put his hand on my hair for a brief moment.

Then he went back out to the fire as the rain began. He did the night watch alone, slept at my side during the day.

We tried not to bother one another.

I asked him, once, whether he wished Scott would be chosen to leave with the rescue mission. We had never mentioned Scott since coming across to Enderby Island, the threats, the stolen gold. Teer controlled the movements of the men and Scott wasn't put on watch at the lookout. I never saw him, but the fear of him didn't leave me. Once or twice, when Joseph had collected firewood to carry down to camp, Scott walked up with Teer and Caughey but he came no closer than the top of the path. It would be a relief to me if he would be one of the men to go.

"You must hate him as much as I do," I said to Joseph.

"It's not my place to hate any man," said Joseph. "My only duty is to keep you safe."

And he did that. He lay on a pallet at my feet and brought me food and water. I never got the feeling that his silences were aimed at me in any way, he wasn't punishing me for anything I had or had not done. Talking seemed not to occur to him.

Sometimes, I made him talk. I asked him about the preparations for the rescue mission and in few words he told me how they had covered the larger boat with sealskins to keep out the sea and stored water in seal gullets. I could see in his face what chance he gave for survival in such a boat, on such a sea. I wondered if anyone believed in it. They were smoking goat and seal strips, he said, and had sent Sanguily scrambling along the cliffs for albatross eggs, which they boiled and stored. They also packed the remaining tins of meat, saved all these months through our times of great desperation.

With the mention of the tins came an uncomfortable silence. Joseph went abruptly back out to the fire and left me twisted in shame for that dreadful day, for lying in Scott's arms and eating meat that Mr Brown might now have packed for his mission. Tinned meat to save a life at sea. I wanted to be rid of that sin, to confess and be forgiven but it wasn't something I dared mention to Joseph. He was unable to hear me. His duty was to keep me safe, not to absolve my sins. The shame and guilt of that day were my companions and not millstones to add to his misery. I was mortified for how I had succumbed so easily and hated how weak it proved me.

Teer was on evening watch for a spell of a week, and I often lay on my bed and looked at him out by the fire, watching the colours fade so slowly until he became black. Sometimes he would step inside the hut and talk to me over the sleeping Joseph on the floor.

"Are you comfortable there, Mrs Jewell?" he would ask. Or, if Joseph was thoroughly snoring: "Can I get you something, Mary?"

He lifted my legs for me one time when they were cramped, and restored a pelt that had slipped. He brought me teas made from herbs that Mr McClelland said were good for the health, but they were mostly bitter and not at all comforting.

"Ah, for a dash of honey to add to the brew, eh, Mary?" said Teer, when my mouth turned down at a particularly nasty concoction.

"What is it you've given me?"

"That's made from flowers, that one."

"Perhaps next time you visit you might bring me just the flowers, without the tea," I said.

It was something said fast and without thought, but it stilled him. His voice came into my head, clear as if he'd spoken: *You're wanting flowers from me? Why is that, Mrs Jewell?*

I should have laughed, turned it into a jest. But I let the suggestion hang and didn't drop my gaze. God knows there are words that can be said with closed lips over the body of a sleeping husband.

He took the cup and went back to his watch. When he came in later to wake Joseph I pretended to be asleep.

ॐ

I felt lighter away from the men. I had been a weight on them, my presence a constraint and a problem. Up on the cliffs and away from their eyes I let the tension drain away from me.

I began to hobble about on a crutch, a forked branch of ironwood with a whipped hand-hold that Teer had made. I stood back from the edge of the cliff, with no desire to step closer. It was another woman who'd had the courage to throw herself over. I'd been taken by a madness then; a hysteria that, if it wasn't dead in me, was now deeply sleeping. Perhaps everyone has some of this madness in them. If it came again I think I would recognise it. I hope I would be able to send it away.

Below the cliffs, the sea swelled and waves broke. The updraft of wind brought the tang of salt and carried with it the sound of drowning: that endless beat of the ocean. I turned my face to find the direction of the wind, listening for when it blew equally past both ears. It was from the north one day, then swung west and kept swinging. The mission needed a southerly blow and calm seas. As summer bloomed the conditions grew better.

Mr Brown often came to sit with me. He brought me the decision.

"I'm to lead the rescue party, Mrs Jewell."

I was fond of Mr Brown. It was an affection wrapped in sympathy. If I felt the loss of his wife as my failure I couldn't imagine how he coped, leaving her clinging to the mast in order to save us. There was nothing that could put that right in his mind, or mine.

Mr McClelland had told me that at Musgrave's camp Mr Brown had plunged often into a despair so deep there was no reaching him, and the men had learned to let him be. It didn't happen as often or last as long as previously, and he was harmless in these absences, though incapable of making decisions.

Nonetheless, it was right that he should lead the rescue attempt. Despite Teer's assumption of the leader's role, he was a civilian. We were survivors of the wreck of the *General Grant* with Mr Brown our senior officer.

"Morrison and McNevin with me."

So the decision was made. Three good men to go, and Scott to remain with us. I kept my face impassive. Life and death. I had no influence over these things.

"You are a valiant man, Mr Brown," I said. "And Morrison and McNevin are skilled sailors." I spoke as if I believed their skill would save them, even though I felt the mission to be hopeless. The men had often repeated the story of Musgrave sailing his dinghy to New Zealand from the island—that was what drove them. And they had to go soon, in the long summer daylight.

I had no part in the decision and no vote. But I did wonder, now we had a better site on Enderby Island and sea lions and fur seals were plentiful on the beaches, if we were so desperate that such a perilous journey was necessary. I asked the question that had been weighing heavily on me. "If you were all men here," I said, "and no woman in the party, would you risk this?"

He didn't give me a direct answer. He patted my hand. "It's the right thing to do."

On the last night, all the men came up to join me at the lookout fire and those leaving on the rescue mission ate their fill. It was a farewell and might almost have felt like a party if not for the desperation of the mission. We talked of our achievements and rejoiced that we had not lost one man through all our trials since the wreck. There was praise for everyone and no one raised a voice or a fist. We discussed, as we had many times, our whole story, with no one trying to apportion blame or make accusations. We teased our drama out between us, agreeing on the way things had been: the wind and the strange calm when we wrecked; the cave; how far we had rowed in quarter boats; when we had found the huts; the first rabbit; the goats. Who had been sick and what had cured them.

Ashworth's wooden cups were applauded, and the time Scott had hooked a shark on one of Hayman's wooden fish hooks. We agreed that we would have been lost without that first match and the oven salvaged from Musgrave's camp to make salt. We cheered Sanguily's goat-like climbing skills to bring us eggs. We had all been constantly sick until we found eggs.

"When I get home I will eat an egg every day," said Sanguily. He pulled the eternal twig cigar from his lips and tapped it with his finger to knock off invisible ash.

"Must it be an albatross egg?" asked Caughey. "You'll be sending a servant out, no doubt?"

"Of course," said the Cuban. "What do you want, that I should be eating an egg from a chicken? The egg of an albatross is for a king."

Sanguily had found a sooty breeding colony on the Rabbit Island cliffs. The albatross eggs were definitely of a royal standard.

"You are King of Rabbit Island," said Caughey.

"Yes," said Sanguily. "That should be recorded. Mr Brown, you will please write this in your log, when you find a pen. And you will tell the rescue ship to make ready to collect a king."

"And when you send the rescue boat for us," said Allen, "make sure it is well liquored. In God's name, send brandy."

"And bread," said Caughey, and we were all quiet for a moment, a yeasty golden loaf rising in our minds. Yes, bread. That was something I craved. It had been so long since I had let myself think of proper food. Bread sprinkled with sugar. Mashed neaps and carrots. Drool pooled in my mouth. We could let ourselves believe, at that moment, that Mr Brown would sail over the horizon to wave down a passing ship and that a basket of bread would be delivered the next day.

"Boots!" shouted McNevin, and our minds switched to our feet, swollen and tied in skins. "With soft stockings. When we get to Invercargill we'll order the biggest pair of boots we can find and send them back for McClelland."

The men laughed theatrically as if this, a joke on the size of the old sailor's feet, was the wittiest remark ever made.

"I'm used to my moccasins now," said Mr McClelland. "Besides, as they were so cleverly stitched for me by the hands of Mrs Jewell I wouldn't change them for the world. You can keep your boots!"

"To the moccasins of Mrs Jewell!" called Sanguily, stretching one of my creations out in front of him to admire, and the men all toasted me as if we were at the finest party and drinking champagne.

"Mrs Jewell's moccasins!" they cried, raising hands empty of glasses, though I noticed that Mr McClelland's moccasins had rotted through again and needed replacing.

A little later, as the cold came down and the daylight stretched into the night hours, we drew closer to the fire and quietened. I didn't know how the men would get up and leave. We needed to mark the moment but there was no man of strong faith among us who could unite us in prayer. Joseph was a good churchman and knew his verses, but he prayed in private now. I was born a Protestant and Joseph and I had married in an Anglican church; Teer and Caughey were Catholic, as was Sanguily, though with a different manner. Mr Brown followed an American, Puritan church. Mostly the sailors seemed ruled by superstition more than the teachings of any particular faith. Any religion we had on the island was not shared though I believe every one of us prayed fervently in private.

Mr McClelland began to recite the sailor's hymn we all knew, but his soft voice faltered after the first verse:

"Eternal Father, strong to save
Whose arm hath bound the restless wave
Who biddest the mighty ocean deep
Its own appointed limits keep
Oh, hear us when we cry to Thee
For those in peril on the sea ..."

It was no longer merely a recitation to unknown sailors but to Mr Brown, Peter McNevin and Andrew Morrison, who we were sending off, likely to their deaths. I felt the tears welling in my eyes, and as Mr McClelland folded his hands in his lap and was silent I saw he, too, was weeping. Teer's eyes were shining and Hayman cried openly. Even Allen, the heartless, who had left his wife and children to drown, had his head down, fingers pinching the bridge of his nose. We had been in peril on the sea and knew it. We had seen our companions die all around us. We had learned that God did not listen to the cries of those in peril on the sea.

The sun was long gone but the twilight lingered and still the men did not depart.

It was McNevin, the good, selfless man, who asked across our quiet circle, "Will you sing me away, Mrs Jewell? Do you know a song for a departing sailor?"

The light waited in balance, not quite tipping into night.

I felt the breathing stilled, the men paused for my reply.

I did know a song. I thought it might do. It had been a long time since I had lifted my voice, so long since Caughey had mistaken me for an angel. When I still believed, perhaps, that an angel had given me a child to save from the wreck. When God might, at a stretch, still be called merciful.

It was a Gaelic song, again one of my mother's. I'd learnt it on visits to my grandmother—not that we were allowed Gaelic in her house—but while Father fixed his mother's tumbling down shack, Mam and I would escape to the estuary to watch the birds. Back when we looked out to sea and sang, without any thought of going farther.

It was afterwards that I learned the meaning of the song: a farewell to a boatman and the woman left behind, wondering if she had been forsaken. *Shall I wait up for you, or close the door?* My mother sang with such sadness. She died before I asked her who the boatman had been. Why she had given up on him and married my father.

> "*Fhir a' bhàta, na hóro eile*
> *Fhir a' bhàta, na hóro eile*
> *Fhir a' bhàta, na hóro eile*
> *Mo shoraidh slàn leat 's gach àit' an téid thu*
>
> *'S tric mi sealltainn on chnoc as àirde*
> *Dh'fheuch am faic mi fear a' bhàta*
> *An tig thu 'n-diugh na 'n tig thu màireach*
> *'S mar tig thu idir gur truagh a ta mi …*"

I intended only to sing a verse. My voice sounded like cobwebs and things trapped. But the men sat enchanted and it seemed here, finally, was something I could do for them, a gift I could make. My voice opened as I sang to the end, all eight verses ending sad and forsaken, and they listened: the departing men wide-eyed, gathering the music to remember on their voyage; Joseph with his mournful eyes looking at me, actually seeing me, for what seemed the first time in so long; Scott weeping; Sanguily with his hands folded in prayer.

Teer stood back from the circle, tall and central, the top point on any compass. His eyes pulled me and I lifted my chin to clear my voice and aim it towards him, so it carried. Was I singing for him? Perhaps I was.

☙

I woke rigid and sore in the early morning, taking many deep breaths before I could move. My mending ribs left a stiffness throughout my body. Teer suggested I should exercise gently to regain my movement; Mr Brown and Joseph said I should lie absolutely still; Mr McClelland said I should do what felt right for me. I moved my legs and lifted my arms over my head as I waited for Joseph, still on night watch, to come in and help me.

He made bark tea and laid out wood. I was to watch the fire and the sea while he went down to camp to see the men off. They would row out on the flood tide through the channel and catch the ebb on the open sea by noon. I would see them from the cliff top.

"You'll manage on your own? I'll bring back water."

"Of course." Once I worked the stiffness out I was moving around reasonably well, but didn't want to make the trek down the hill to camp yet. I had said my goodbyes.

"You sang well last night," he said. "Thank you."

"I sang for the men who were leaving."

"I know that."

It was an acknowledgement I hadn't expected from Joseph and I was grateful for it.

The wind carried a drizzly rain onto the embers and they

spat and smoked. Joseph had made sure I had little to do. Alone, I stood in the entrance to the hut and looked over the headland to the sea below. A light morning mist hung in the air and the sky was painted the usual wet grey, but there was a brightening. The last few mornings had grown from such an unpromising start to clear afternoons and maybe the men would be lucky. Lucky today, lucky tomorrow, and the next day and so on. Lucky not to capsize or lose the sail or run out of water or hit a whale. Lucky in everything in the days or weeks it took to sail into a port on the coast of New Zealand and tie up to a pier. What bravery it took to go back onto the open sea in a small boat. Bravery, or madness.

I filled my lungs cautiously and slowly tried to lift my arms. My right arm rose to shoulder height but my left barely had the strength to leave my body. I massaged my shoulder, shrugged it around. With both arms draping I bent forwards towards my feet and pulled on my hanging arms, feeling the pain in a different part of my shoulder. I remained with my head down and circled my arms slowly. I could feel my back stretch out, and heard a couple of quiet clicks—something falling into place rather than breaking away. My blood flowed to my head and my hair tumbled out of its heavy plait and I was comfortable with my feet firmly planted and my back stretched out.

I put my hands on my knees to push myself up, uncurling like a leaf.

Bill Scott stood in front of me. I put my hand to my ribs as my breath raced in.

"I startled you," he said. And then he stepped into the hut, reached out and touched my shoulder. "How does it feel?"

"Don't touch me," I said, stepping back, deeply unsettled to find him there. His eyes, with their full pupils, were steady and unblinking and he was half smiling, amused at my discomfort perhaps. Knowing Joseph was down at the camp. Had he come alone?

"I can rub that shoulder, if it is giving you pain."

"No. I'm not in pain." I shook my head and stepped to the side but he put his hands on both my shoulders to hold me firm. His fingers played against my injury. There was no sound of anyone else, nothing to see but the cliff top and the sky.

My breath came in shallow dips and I fought for calm. "Why are you here?" My voice was tight and he knew I was afraid. He smiled.

I had been so careful, all this time, never to be alone with Bill Scott. Hadn't seen him for weeks until he'd come the previous night and sat in the group, watching me, taking his chance to brush against me in passing, to offer something so his fingers would touch mine. He sickened me.

"What do you want, Mr Scott?" I asked again, angrily this time. But he just smirked and raised his eyebrows as if I amused him. His hands remained on me, I could feel their weight on my jacket.

"I've come to say goodbye."

"You're going with the men?"

"I thought I might, yes."

"What do you mean, Mr Scott? You thought you might?"

"I can be in New Zealand in a week. Send a boat back for you."

He dropped his hands and just stood there before me, bouncing slightly on the balls of his feet and grinning as if delighted with himself. He, out of us all, didn't look so much changed from the months away. He'd kept his hair cut short. He and Ashworth were the only ones to shave, each trusting the other with the knife. The boyish look remained.

"Oh, come on, Mary! You can wish me well, can't you?"

Could I believe him? He had said nothing the previous night. I stepped back. He followed, holding his hands out as if to dance and suddenly it seemed ridiculous. There was a buoyancy rising in me at the hope, a hope I hadn't allowed myself to believe, that it was true, that the men would find New Zealand as Musgrave and his men had done before them and would send a ship for us within a month. We could dare to believe that relief was within reach. And here was Bill Scott standing before me with his open face and smiles, the man who would save us.

"Good luck to you then, Mr Scott, you and the men. God bless you all."

I stepped back again and again he followed, still with his arms out. I shook my head, thinking if he would take my blessing and leave I would be free to forgive him for all the wrong he had done me.

"Give me a kiss to take with me."

"No."

Teer came to mind, from all those months ago, crouching down before me with such compassion and explaining that a man will get ideas and I must stop him.

James Teer was a fool. What could I do, other than say no?

"Just a kiss, Mary. And then I'll go. I'll carry the kiss with me all the way across the sea to New Zealand and give it to the first old salt I find with a seaworthy tub. We'll be back in no time."

I shook my head. If I kissed him he wouldn't walk away. Of that I was sure.

I could see it happening again, that change that came over Scott when things didn't go his way. There was a flicker and the friendliness disappeared in a puff like a blown match. And now I didn't believe he was planning to leave at all.

I looked at the full dark balls of his eyes. They were wider now, almost full circle. He looked mad.

"Joseph's coming," I said, stepping away again and again, circling to get free of the hut and into the open.

"No. He's loading the boat."

He stepped with me. This was the dance he did, step, step, step, pounce. The way he fought the men, moving his slighter build for advantage, balancing on light feet. He wasn't dancing, though. This was prowling.

"Joseph is coming back," I repeated. My voice no longer sounded so confident.

"Why would he?" said Scott. "He doesn't love you. Doesn't even like you. We all know it. The only man here with a woman and he doesn't want her." He spat it out. "The waste!"

A gleam in his eye set a rising panic fluttering in my throat.

"And your Irishman only loves himself. It's shameful, how you worship him."

He waited for my reaction, his lip curled in distaste. If I praised Teer it would incense him and if I denied Teer it would be something else and if I said nothing—

"Do you think I didn't see you last night? The way you looked at him, sang to him as if he was the only man there, as if you didn't have a poor milksop for a husband sitting at your feet. You'd kiss Teer if you got the chance. So you can kiss me."

The escalating madness had to stop. Scott had grabbed me once before, and I had felt the lust on him before Joseph had arrived to stop him. Now Joseph wasn't coming. Teer had said I must stop a man with ideas, but Teer knew nothing.

Scott's eyes lowered to my body and his mouth fell open with a panting breath and I could think of nothing to do to stop him if he grabbed me again. A kiss wouldn't send the man away. I could smell the heat coming off him and—

He darted forward with his greedy, grabbing hands and I lunged into him, heavy on my damaged ankle and stumbling. It was all I could do. I shoved him away with all my force and found he was light. I had thought him a man as solid as a pig, but he toppled as I roared at him, sent backwards over the footstool with his staring eyes wide, and I grabbed my crutch and ran.

ॐ

It was twenty yards back to the forest and I beat across the tussock to the dark tangle of the ironwood trees, where the light disappeared and the roots and branches reached around to protect me in a knotted barrier of wood. Out in the open I had no chance to outrun Scott but in the forest I could disappear. He would come after me. I knew this. I had seen his madness.

I hauled myself behind a trunk and looked back to the shelter. There was no sign of him.

I knew, even if I could hobble on my crutch ahead of him, I couldn't make it down the hill. I needed to hide until Joseph returned, not too far away that he wouldn't find me, not so close that Scott would. I turned sharply and circled through a thick patch of undergrowth and headed deeper in. We had cleared much of the forest debris for tinder and I now needed that tangle of fern to hide myself.

I feared for what Scott might do if he caught me, cursed Joseph for leaving me and cursed Teer for suggesting that somehow this madness of men was my responsibility.

I was sick of living with the fear of Bill Scott. This time I would have him punished and sent away. Teer would put him on some rock out at sea and he could die there. He was mad. Joseph knew what he was, he had heard the way

Scott talked about me, and yet where was he? Where was my husband when Scott came for me?

I pushed through the trees, stumbling on the uneven ground, not moving fast enough, not making the distance.

I didn't know if my husband liked me or not. Or loved me. This was not something for Scott to judge—he had no right to say such things. But Joseph had sworn to protect me.

In a clump of fern I tripped and went flying. My arm struck the ground and my shoulder wrenched and collapsed under me. I rolled across a lattice of roots, hard and ancient as rock, and each hitting a different rib. Clenching my teeth until the sobs suffocated me I reached around for my crutch, while above me McClelland's parrots screeched and squabbled. I needed to move but my ankle wouldn't support me.

On my knees I crawled forward, across the slippery forest floor, where things rotted and decayed. I crawled until a hand seized my ankle.

It felt like the devil.

His face with the staring eyes.

He looked like the devil.

I twisted and screamed my outrage. One arm was trapped and the other useless and I was caught. It seemed the only thing left to me to fight with was my voice and I roared it at him, Scott, who lay on the ground at my feet, crying my name. I filled my lungs with air and screamed again, the pain in my ribs unbearable but nothing, nothing to the agony of that man's hand on me.

"Be quiet, Mary!" he said. "Stop your screaming. Shhh!"

Slowly he rolled and sat up, away from me, his eyes full of pain and his hands jumping in front of him. When he reached forward to touch me I screamed.

"Shhh! Someone will hear you, Mary. Shhh. Don't be

frightened of me! What did I do? If I upset you I am sorry. I am so very sorry. Why did you run away? Let me help you. Hush. Here, let me help you sit up."

He knelt and reached his open hands to me and I screamed into his face.

"Hush, hush," he said, and I felt him stroking my hair. "Mary. I upset you and I want to apologise. Don't misunderstand me. You've nothing to fear from me."

Every time he said my name I felt him coming closer to what I feared the most. I lifted my head and screamed again. I still had breath and while I had breath I would scream and not submit to him.

"Stop it!" he said, as if I was a silly, frightened girl. "Don't treat me like I'm a monster. It's this place, Mary. It drives us all mad."

I felt mad. There was no sense to being otherwise. Madness had found me in my pain and helplessness. My ribs were folded and shoulder hung pinched and I filled my lungs and screamed again. I was getting weaker. I breathed in. I would scream with no voice.

He tried to hold me then, to rock me in his arms and the intimacy of it disgusted me, the barrier I had held between me and the men all these months had been pulled away and with it any modesty I ever had.

I tipped my head back but the scream was thin and wretched.

"Oh, Mary. I'm sorry." His hands on my face. His face close, his putrid breath. "Shhh. Shhh." His fingers on my lips.

I wrenched my head away and his hand grew tighter.

A bird perched above ran along the branch, its little head pumping up and down. With agitated jumps it screeched a high-pitched *pee-it pee-it* trill. Mr McClelland's pipit was crying my distress for me as my own voice ran dry.

From far away, out where the sun broke through in the world beyond the forest, came a cry.

"Mary!"

Scott tensed. He lifted his face. Had he heard it? Again, the cry from the direction of the shelter, urgent and afraid: "Mary!"

He heard it then.

I pulled in all the air in the forest and screamed it out, ripping the soft part of my throat. In one brutal movement Scott pushed me from him and my scream fell, absorbed into the moss. But still I screamed and I breathed and I screamed. He leapt over me and he fled into the forest.

I screamed again, though I had no voice.

And again.

Joseph found me lying crumpled in a hollow of tree roots.

I felt I had all the shame I could possibly bear.

He didn't move me at once, but sat down in confusion and looked over the scene. I tried to sit with a straight back. God knows I didn't want any more pity.

"Give me my crutch," I said.

"Where is he?"

"Gone. My crutch. I need my crutch." My voice was cackle-dry.

"Mary, I will carry you."

"Help me stand up, Joseph. I can't be lying here." I didn't want to be on the ground. I needed to be on my feet. It seemed vitally important to me that I could stand. I grabbed his arm with my one good hand and pulled myself as we stood together. Joseph didn't try to pick me up or carry me, but helped me to my feet.

"My crutch."

He looked around helplessly. The forest floor was littered with branches. "I can't see it." Still he didn't force me but stood steadily while I pulled my shoulders back and ignored the pain. I put my head up and my hand on his shoulder. I could stand and I could breathe and Bill Scott had gone. At that moment, it seemed enough.

☙

At the shelter, I let Joseph strap my shoulder back into its sling and he righted the stool and helped me sit in the doorway. There was sunshine and it surprised me.

"Lie down, won't you, Mary?" Joseph said, but I didn't want to lie on the bed.

My throat after the screaming was flaming and he brought me water in one of Ashworth's cups. He knelt before me and bound my ankle, his long fingers careful with the soft flax, knowing to keep it firm but not too tight. Careful with me.

"Scott did this?" His voice came through a tight jaw and his hands were shaking as he tied the knot and placed my foot on the ground.

"Yes." And then, because he had to understand, I said, "I didn't let him, Joseph. I fought him off."

"I know you did."

I couldn't imagine what he thought, finding me screaming in the forest like a wounded animal and my attacker gone. It was good to hear him confirm he had seen the truth. That I was not to blame.

"He is mad," I said. "Deluded. He said such things ..."

"I should never have left you. He was below with the men and I turned my back to rig the sail and when I looked again he had gone."

"He must never come up here again," I said, and I meant it. I had a terrible fear of what he would do to me if he ever caught me again. "I want him sent away."

Joseph nodded, his face stretched in an odd grimace. "I

will find him, Mary. I promise." And then he rearranged my skirt where I sat, smoothing the skins down over my legs to cover my ankles.

I saw, under Joseph's feet, a distinctive woven button from Scott's jacket. I pointed to it and Joseph picked it up, his fingers running over the flax.

His fist closed around it. "I will punish him," he said.

I was glad when he said that. I wanted Scott punished. For every time he had touched me and for every situation he had put me in. For every base comment said suggestively in front of the men, putting thoughts into heads that compromised me. And for this, for making me so helpless and afraid. Above everything, for making me afraid.

A voice called from the path. "Hallo!" and again as the caller came closer.

It was Mr McClelland, striding across the tussock. "Mr Jewell!"

Joseph stood.

"Don't tell him how close he came—" I said.

"No one needs to know, Mary. I will deal with it."

They met by the fire outside and I heard an urgency in Mr McClelland's voice. I was surprised when Joseph ran fast away down the track, calling over his shoulder: "Stay with my wife."

I straightened my posture and tried to pull my cap down over my hair, which was bunched and wild. But it made no difference. When Mr McClelland stepped from the bright light to the shelter his eyesight was so bad he couldn't see my face or figure. It was my voice that gave me away.

"Would you stoke the fire?" I asked. "I have neglected it."

Perhaps he guessed something of what had happened. He gave a bow, as if I was a lady and he my manservant, and went back out. He pottered around for a while, running his hands over the wood pile to find larger logs, building the fire, kicking over the embers. Finally I called him in. I asked him to bring me some water.

"What has called Joseph away so urgently?" I said, and kept my voice steady through all the pains: my throat, my ankle, my shoulder and back.

"Something unexpected has happened," said Mr McClelland. He felt for the edge of my bed and sat with his hands in his lap, relaxed in himself but looking at me with great seriousness. "Not long after Joseph left to return to you, Scott appeared at the cove very agitated. He had an oar and his pelts. He's volunteered to join the rescue mission, said they needed another strong oarsman."

"What?"

Mr McClelland nodded. "They've left, rowing out towards the gap with Scott and Morrison at the front, McNevin and Brown behind. They were only too happy to have another volunteer. He's a good sailor."

We sat for a while in silence. So Scott had gone, after all. Had remorse driven him to it, or the thought of the repercussions when Joseph caught him, or if I told Teer what he had done to me?

"We'll not miss him," Mr McClelland added. "You, particularly, I think, may have reasons to want him gone."

"You saw him leave?" I didn't think he could see that far and I wanted certainty.

"I could hear him calling the strokes out in the harbour. I have a good ear, Mrs Jewell. He was on the boat, I promise you. He's gone."

I knew then that the chances of my ever seeing Bill Scott again were remote. I felt such relief I began shaking uncontrollably, my teeth clattering and my hands jumping in my lap. I was free of him. Mr Brown, Morrison and the endlessly cheerful Peter McNevin would make use of Scott and I wished them hard and fast sailing as they took my tormentor away. It was a clean end to Scott's pursual of me and now there was nothing Joseph needed to do. His responsibility ended with Scott's departure and Teer need never know of my final degradation at Scott's hands.

The two stolen nuggets went with him. It was the price we paid to see the back of him.

"I thought Joseph should know he'd gone," said Mr McClelland, and I wondered why he thought it necessary to come after Joseph to tell him Scott had left and why Joseph had raced away. What did it matter now?

The sky had cleared and the day was sharp and blue. The wind, such as it was, came from the southwest. Once through the channel Mr Brown's boat would sail due north, directly below the cliffs.

"Shall we watch them go?" I asked. I found it difficult to stand, but Mr McClelland was patient and made no comment as I took his arm and limped out and around the fireplace. The fire was a beacon and the men were sure to look up as they passed. I wanted Scott to see me there, standing strongly on my feet above him. It felt like defiance.

We waited, basking like seals in the unaccustomed warmth of a sunny day. McClelland found a forked stick for me in the wood pile and shaved it clean for a crutch. It was slightly too small and not as robust as the one Teer made me, but I found, when the boat appeared below, I was able to prop myself up and stand apart, unaided by any man.

⁂

Below us the sail hung limply and the boat crawled along. Soon the tide would turn and take them farther out to catch the wind. I could see four figures in the boat silhouetted against the shimmering sea and I whispered godspeed to the men with whom, for nearly a year, I had been castaway. Companions I would never have chosen to have in my life, but with whom God had placed me during this terrible time, for whatever purpose, and from whom I had gained an understanding of the nature of men.

"Do they have wind in their sail?" asked Mr McClelland and I said no, not yet. Not yet. They still hung between the tides, keeping their energy for the time ahead.

"They're not moving," I said, after watching them glide beneath our lookout and hang. They were close enough that I could make out Scott at the stern pulling strongly on his oar while the others paused, holding back. I was so intent on the figures beneath the sail that I didn't see the second boat until it was almost upon them.

"It's Teer," I said. "In the other boat. He's catching them up. With Caughey and that's Joseph with them. Oh! What are they doing, why don't they let them go?"

The three chasers rowed with ferocious speed and Mr Brown's boat twisted around, one oarsman pulling and the others holding. Scott was desperately now trying to pull away and the others ... I could only imagine the confusion as the lighter and unladen boat pulled alongside.

"They're chasing them?" asked Mr McClelland.

"What good can it possibly do?" I cried. "Oh, why are men so stupid?" I was unbalanced on my crutch and had to grab Mr McClelland to prop me up as I watched the scene unfold before me. The boats pulled alongside and immediately a fight broke out: Teer seizing Scott and dragging him half out of the boat, a bird shaking a worm.

Joseph had told him of my humiliation, then.

No one needs to know, he had promised me and then immediately told Teer and Caughey, and now they were riled up to punish a man who had already sentenced himself to almost certain death. I wanted Scott far away and I was watching him go. Who would it help, now, to give him the beating he deserved? He had already gone.

"Tell me what's happening," said Mr McClelland, and I tried to describe what I saw but the movements were jerky and confusing as the boats rocked violently against the bright light that bounced off the water and tears of frustration and anger blurred my eyes.

I blinked the men back into focus.

"Teer has thrown Scott down and boarded the boat, he's ripping up the covers. I don't know what he's doing. Looking for something? Caughey is holding the boats together."

Teer grappled him over a bundle of skins, fists flying as Morrison held Teer back, McNevin trying hopelessly to wrestle them apart before the big Irishman ripped the boat to pieces. Caughey lost his grip and his boat surged away. Mr Brown brought his oar down on Teer's head, but his balance lurched and the blow bounced off.

Joseph suddenly stood as the boat rose on a swell and I cried out as he leapt across the divide.

"Joseph and Teer are both at Scott now," I said. "Teer is shaking him ... he'll tip him out if he doesn't take care. He's trying to grab a bundle of skins behind Scott and Joseph ..."

Joseph wasn't grabbing at the bundle. I saw Scott raise his hands in defence as Joseph stood over him. Whatever it was Joseph and Teer were doing, they were focused on different things. No one obstructed Joseph and yet I felt there was something happening that needed stopping.

"Stop him," I shouted, but my voice, so wrecked from screaming, dried in my throat. He was insubstantial, my husband, beside these burly men and yet he moved with more deliberate force than any of them.

He reached forward, grabbed Scott by his jacket and lifted him high so the man's legs were dangling and arms waving.

I dashed my hand across my streaming eyes.

Scott had gone.

"What?" said Mr McClelland as I cried out. He shook my arm painfully. "What happened?"

We could hear the shouting then, falling out over the water, as the men grasped the side of the boat and threw their hands out to where a great splash settled.

"Teer's diving," I said.

There was no sign of Scott. Teer had plunged head first into the water. I saw his feet disappear beneath the waves and Caughey was yelling and trying to bring the boat around. The others had their oars out, ready to catch the men when they surfaced. All this I tried to explain to Mr McClelland, who couldn't grasp it.

"Scott's overboard!" I said. "Oh! Joseph was shaking him and no one stopped him. They were all fighting over something else ... and then suddenly Scott wasn't there ... and Teer dived."

"It's the gold," said Mr McClelland.

"Gold?"

I could see no one in the water. There were two boats from which men hung out over the side. Close in by the rocks, penguins dived and surfaced, bobbed and swam. There was no such activity by the boats.

"Scott stole Teer's gold. That's what I told Joseph. It's why Teer went after him."

Still nothing in the water. How long could a man hold his breath? How deep would Teer dive and could he pull back a man heavy with gold?

I had seen this type of sinking before. It seemed my knowledge of things was divided into the time before I knew the weight of gold in water and what I knew now.

Finally he surfaced. Teer. Alone. Right next to the boat, straight down and straight up and he had nothing in the arms he wrapped around the oars that dragged him in. He was hauled onto the boat by every man and even then I thought the streaming mass of him would capsize them.

"Just Teer," I said. "They have him in the boat but he's collapsed. Scott's gone."

I felt the sunlight on my face and my hands. It felt strong enough to burn me. My eyes were stinging from looking at the water's glare.

"Teer's gold was stitched into a belt," said Mr McClelland. "If Scott was fool enough to be wearing that on a boat and to fall in—"

"He didn't fall. It was Joseph, he was lifting him and shaking him and then ... oh, what happened? Mr McClelland! What has he done?"

"Mrs Jewell, I didn't see it. I couldn't say what happened."

The boats below rocked as Caughey brought them together again, and this time the sailors reached out for the ropes. Joseph crossed to the chasing boat and sat in the stern looking as insubstantial as a ghost, thin and lost. I saw Teer rouse himself and together the men pulled apart the bundle of Scott's skins and laid them out on the boards. They didn't find anything. No golden belt was lifted into the sun. Teer put back his head and roared and the sound of it flowed up the cliffs.

Whatever Scott carried had been on his person. Teer's belt with its precious sovereigns, our two nuggets in his pocket and whatever else he may have stolen now lay in the deep water of the bay, wrapped around the body of the drowned Bill Scott.

After all we had seen and with all we knew, the stupid man had gone to sea wrapped in gold.

The crew remained staring into the fold of the sea where Scott had gone down, until several breaths passed and the life was surely gone from him.

"They're shaking hands," I told Mr McClelland. "They have split back into the two boats."

Caughey and Teer grasped the oars and Joseph, always reliable in labour, took his position. It was a while before the boats parted. Perhaps they were reflecting on what had passed. A man in their care had died; it was possible there had been a prayer. Then Mr Brown's boat caught the wind and the sea pulled them away northwards out to sea, the tide finally on the turn.

LOSS

I moved back down to the main camp. There seemed no reason not to. I was still bruised, but escaping Scott had left me no more broken than I already was and I decided it would be easier back with the others than alone with Joseph on the hill. Not so dependent on him. With Scott gone I had nothing to fear; I felt no threat from the other men and it brought me closer to Teer.

There were new huts built now as the hovels had burnt again, and these new buildings were well framed with proper chimneys of salvaged brick and stone. Both were twenty foot by ten, divided for sleeping and living. Joseph and I shared with Ashworth, Hayman and Mr McClelland and the men treated me kindly.

They built a table and chair so I could sit inside and gave me work to keep me occupied: Mr McClelland had me twisting twine, I wove flax curtains with Ashworth and Hayman showed me how his bone fishhooks were chiselled and tied, another skill I failed to master. My hands were strong now, but not so nimble. I watched them fold and twist and tie but they were old woman's hands now, their pretty plumpness gone. I pretended they belonged to someone else.

The men played cards and the tin pack, so beautifully crafted by Scott, was allocated to each hut on alternate days. With our two huts and space to sit where we were not all together, constantly, by the fire, we seemed to have a more peaceable arrangement and the incessant bickering and fighting no longer plagued us.

The men hadn't seen beyond the harbour and knew only that Teer, Caughey and Joseph had chased Scott for the stolen gold and returned empty-handed. No one knew of Scott's advances to me and no one said there was a dead man in the deep water before the cliffs. It was a lie of omission and whatever sin Joseph had committed that day on the boat went unmentioned and unpunished.

The others all referred to the "brave four" who had sailed to save us and it became the accepted truth. Teer's gold, if mentioned at all, was said to be "lost", as if accusing Scott of the theft spoiled the story of the rescue mission.

In a rare moment when Joseph and I were alone together in the hut, I asked him to sit down and I saw the flare of warning cross his face. He had become, if anything, more absent to me since we'd returned to the camp and he rarely spoke to anyone at all. It wasn't that he was surly or uncooperative, for he never shirked his duty and did his share of tasks without complaint. But he volunteered nothing, replying to questions with no more than a nod or single word answer. Even Hayman had given up trying to bring him around and no longer tossed the foot ball to him or dealt him into the card games. On the few evenings we sat communally around the outside fire Joseph looked blankly into the flames while the others told stories and discussed their days around him.

Now he sat on the edge of a stool and I sat opposite, saying nothing, hoping that my stillness and nearness would break something and let a trickle of words come out. He looked out the door, wanting to be away from me.

"I want to know what you did, Joseph," I said when I

finally accepted that nothing would come from him. "I was watching from the cliffs. I saw you with Scott on the boat."

Joseph nodded, still looking away. I didn't know whether this was news to him or not.

"Did you know he was strapped with gold? Were you thinking what that might do to his balance and what would happen if he fell?"

A slight frown crossed his face and I thought he wouldn't reply. Knowingly weighted or not, there had been violence done that had ended in a man's death.

"Tell me, Joseph! Don't just sit there like that. I need to know what you did, what man you are." I couldn't bear the blackness that he carried in his gaunt frame, that big hole in the middle of a man I had known on this island for longer than I had known him on shore. I began to believe he had always been like this, and when we married he had managed to hold the edges of his heart together, just for long enough so I believed he was whole.

"I wasn't thinking about the gold."

Finally I had words from him, but not the outright denial I wanted to hear.

"He had our gold in his pockets, too," I said. "The nuggets."

"And the rest. I hadn't had a chance to rebury it. He had my pouch in his jacket."

It was all gone then. Everything we owned.

I had forgotten about our gold in real terms for so long now. On the island it didn't represent wealth or security; it was just a burden. But it felt unbearable now to have the burden relieved, to know that if rescue ever came we would have nothing to weigh us down. What would happen to us then?

But still Joseph didn't tell me what I wanted to hear.

"You were fighting over gold?"

"I told you. I wasn't thinking about the gold, Mary." He stood up and waited, as if wanting me to dismiss him.

"Don't go." I needed to know what this meant. Teer had gone for his gold, that I understood. Joseph had joined the chase for a man who also had stolen our gold, but the thief—and all the gold—had gone into the sea. I reached out my hand to him.

"He shouldn't have touched you."

He walked out then, picking up a club from the ground, and headed away along the bleak beach to where the penguins gathered on the rocks.

It was just another death, another man drowned off the coast of this abominable island. Bill Scott could have been lost when the *General Grant* went down, drowned fishing in the harbour or tipped from the rescue boat by a wave. But the fact that my husband might have had some hand in his death because of what Scott did to me took away the act of God and made me accountable.

Later that night I lay next to Joseph and listened to his slow breathing. He didn't flinch or twitch, a man beyond nightmares with his emotions too deep to surface even in sleep. I lay awake. Scott was gone, and all our gold gone with him into the sea. Joseph had left nothing with his brother and nothing in the bank and we had nothing left in our marriage. No future. The home in Clovelly, the farmhouse, the children we might have had—all were gone. Our brief love affair was dead. And he was empty.

&

"It's lost is all," said Teer. "Nothing to do about it now. It wasn't your husband's fault. He wasn't to know Scott was wearing his thievings when he overbalanced."

We were threading hooks onto the fishing line, mine and Hayman's. Teer would take each hook and examine it.

They were simple things, sticks and feathers, with sinkers to anchor them in the tide.

"Overbalanced, Mr Teer?"

He paused, balancing a weight in his hand.

"I'll not hold your man accountable for a fall from a boat. I've a feeling there was bad blood at play and he had the red fury on him."

I looked away, embarrassed.

"There is something in what I'm saying? He had good reason for his anger, did he not?" Teer wasn't accusing or angry. Probably he knew Joseph better than I did. I didn't want to answer him and kept my face steady and my hands busy with my work.

"But your gold ..." I said, turning the talk back to easier ground.

"Aye, it was a fair fortune. I'd three hundred sovereigns on that belt. A year's lucky digging lies drowned out in the deep part of the bay. I should have hidden it more carefully." He spoke as if the gold itself meant nothing more to him than a measure of his success, a year well spent. Joseph had hated the diggings, his lucky strike had meant liberation from a life of toil. He was a different man to Teer, who seemed to enjoy labour and gained pleasure from physicality. Teer had no aspirations to give up the working life.

"What will you do when we are rescued, Mr Teer?"

He set aside a hook, one of mine that was unravelling and no use.

"First thing is I'll have a whiskey," he said with a laugh that made him handsome. "An Irish whiskey, mind! Rum if there is no whiskey, at a pinch." He shook his shaggy head. "But I've thought about this question a great deal and I think it really should be Irish whiskey."

I threaded the last of our hooks, and Teer knotted the end. Hayman's hooks were superior to mine, which formed a small pile of rejects. I would try harder to get the twine tight.

"I'll not be digging again, if that's what you're asking. I'm not a man for the mines and digging through the earth. I'll go back to piloting, though I won't have my own boat, which is the pity of it."

"Back on the sea? After this?"

"Ah, look you," he said, and I saw the green of the sea in his eyes as he laughed at me. "Can you not see we're still alive? Does it not make us invincible?"

I shook my head at him, but smiling. I liked the words he used. I thought Teer was invincible.

I wanted something more from him. As a bit of foolishness I thought to ask: *And shall I come with you?* But it was odd how he seemed to know when the current of our conversations turned and he was on his feet and gathering the line.

We went along the shore to the rocks, me placing my feet carefully and walking without the crutch. Caughey took one end of the line and scrambled out to the end of a shelf of rocks and I fed the line through my hands to Teer, who tied the other end closer, leaving the line of hooks in the tide. I listened to the two Irishmen calling out and laughing together. The way they lived in the present moment rather than the torment of the past made them strong. They didn't wallow in misery like Joseph did. They suffered, we all suffered, but then they got up and got on.

With four men down we had single watches, and Joseph often took the cliff-top fire. I didn't go with him. My ankle, I said, wasn't strong enough. But the truth was I liked the camp better when Joseph wasn't there; the men were friendlier to me and included me in their talking. There was optimism in the camp. Sometimes, we sang.

"They'll have reached New Zealand now," one man or

another would say, most evenings. "Might take a few days to get a rescue party together."

"They'll be forty-eight hours drunk first."

"And who's to blame them for it? Not a word against our brave men."

Sanguily counted the days since Mr Brown's departure with a cairn of rocks. He had sailed with the first mate since Boston and claimed a friendship that hadn't been at all apparent when Mr Brown had been with us. "Is very long now, Mrs Jewell," he said as the tower of rocks toppled and became a pile. "Maybe something happen?"

"We must pray, Mr Sanguily."

We were quiet then with our private prayers for the men. Those in peril on the sea.

The warmth of summer, such that it was, left us soon enough. The days grew shorter and temperatures dropped and I was grateful for the fireplaces in our huts and the insulation of walls lined with pelts.

Twice the men made a trip around to North Harbour on the main island where they had seen pigs, and one afternoon they came back with a small, muscular animal that squealed and wrestled with the men in the boat. We tethered the feisty piglet with the goats and fed it up on seal meat and a month later we slaughtered it, but although the savoury smell of roasting pig was heavenly, the taste of the meat was not at all like pork.

"I am trying so hard to delight you, Mrs Jewell!" cried Caughey, as he picked at the dish and his face turned sour. "What must I do?"

I took a piece of meat in my fingers and turned it over in my mouth. It was disgusting, with the texture of pork but a tangy, gamey flavour, salty and rancid. "Apart from the fact that it tastes like seal," I said. "I do believe it is perfect."

All our spare time now was spent devising ways to

capture pigs, and a boat went every week to the harbour to dig pits or set traps, but the animals always escaped. Teer, constantly inventive, heated some of the iron scraps we had collected from the whalers' settlements and turned them into hooks.

"I'll be wanting ropes, Mrs Jewell," he said, and got a laugh from the men.

"You going to catch a pig on a hook like a fish?" asked Sanguily. He threw out his hands, a pantomime of a fisherman, and rolled around in the dirt wrestling an imaginary hog.

"Aye," said Teer. "Boil up some lye for the flax. I'll need about eighteen foot, if you will." They teased him but I made him the rope and over the next week he tempered his iron hooks in boiling oil and attached them to a long pole. He went with Sanguily, Caughey and Ferguson to North Harbour and they were back the next day with a fat black sow and her piglet. She had been hooked in the back by Teer's invention and tied with my rope. We determined to keep them alive as food for the winter, though we agreed they would eat herbs rather than seal meat. Sanguily insisted on making pets of them, so he put a ring of twisted tin through the sow's nose and Ashworth christened her Nellie, and the piglet was Roger. Roger made himself at home and settled into the huts with us.

It was over ten weeks since Mr Brown's boat had left and we looked every day for relief. The men went back and forward to North Harbour, mostly, I thought, to be out on the sea should our rescue ship come by. I don't know when we all gave up hope for Mr Brown. The realisation came to us all in our own time and no one would own it.

We ate every night, our bellies filled with meat. We salted pork and seal for the winter, laying down stores we hoped we wouldn't need. We made rough storage barrels of driftwood lined with flax, preparing enough food and fuel to last if we stayed the whole time indoors. We were determined not to repeat the horrible privations of the previous winter. Mr McClelland, our botanist, dug up cabbage tubers and stored them in shallow pits, though we had to go farther and farther afield to find them.

In May we marked our year since we were wrecked and we did no work that day but thought of those we had lost, in the watery cave and out at sea, and we said our prayers for them, each of us in our own way.

Sanguily took it hard and spent the morning weeping, but I convinced him to come with me around the edge of the island to launch another of our rescue boats: this one not just a carved plank of wood but a proper boat, three foot long, with a keel and an iron stern to keep her steady on her voyage. She had a seal bladder balloon to catch the wind.

Ashworth had carved on her: *Ship Gen. Grant, wrkd Auckland Isles, May 14, 1866—11 survive on Enderby Is, May, 1867. Want relief.*

We watched it go out on the tide and stood for a while, looking north through the mist.

"It's more than three months since Mr Brown and our brave sailors left," Sanguily said. I had been thinking the same thing but knowing, as Sanguily did not, that one sailor had made it no farther than the sea we looked upon.

"There may be a ship on the way for us now," I said.

We stood for a while longer until I realised the Cuban was crying again and I took his hand and squeezed it. "Have heart, Mr Sanguily. I believe you will see your home and your family again."

We walked in silence back to camp, Mr Sanguily less doleful, but I had given any light I had to him and was back with my demons. Every step was like the rocking of a boat.

The sky turned black, the world closed in and I returned to the cold cave, my recurring waking nightmare, as the *General Grant* went down and little Mary Oat's hair floated on the black water.

წ

Winter approached and temperatures plunged. I lay next to Joseph, who gave me no warmth. He was quiet and still. I don't know if he slept or if he dreamed. I could hear the other men turning and breathing but Joseph lay as if dead. In the mornings he rose, pulled on his moccasins and went out.

I wondered what it would be like to lie with Teer. How warm it would be with him in my bed. How he might move. I recalled how frightened I had been of him those first months and the power of his fists as he lashed out, but I had learned that I had no need to be afraid of him. He didn't fight out of recklessness or stupidity. He fought to keep us all alive, to keep the men disciplined and drive us on. I imagined pushing my fingers into the roughness of his beard and pulling his face down to mine, to see how soft were the lips of the hard man. There was appeal in the sheer bulk of him, a man who could protect me from anything, who always saw a way forward and never gave in to misery.

Often in the evenings now when we gathered together I sang, and I liked the way he watched me, his face changing, mellowing.

"Sing it again, Mrs Jewell," he would say in a quiet voice, and when I had finished for a second time he would take himself off to his hut. I let myself believe he was dreaming of me. I felt a frustration of the feelings I used to have for Joseph, feelings now with nowhere to go.

And so, one night, I left Joseph sleeping with his back to me and went out to join Teer by the fire. Caughey was up at the lookout and rain had driven the rest of the men early into the huts to sleep. I could hear the whittling stick. Teer never sat idle. It was near the darkest hour when I found him on his perch under the cover of the woodshed, and he put down his woodwork and knife and rose to his feet when I ducked beneath the frame.

"Mary," he said. He spoke softly, questioning the reality of me.

I didn't have anything planned to say to him. It felt dreamlike, with the rain on the thatch and the fire lighting one side of his face. He was half golden flame and half soot black. I just wanted this moment, to see which face he would turn to me.

He did nothing.

I was close enough for him to reach out and touch me and yet he didn't. I found it impossible to look at him and so I kept my eyes dead ahead, on the wooden button of his jacket. A button he had carved and I had sewn. It was undone but I couldn't see what was beyond and beneath. More animal skin perhaps, before his skin stretched over the ribs that held his heart. Quite a barrier.

His hand lifted forward and I thought the moment had come and I closed my eyes and waited for him to collect me up, but it didn't happen. I heard a movement, as if he had stepped back.

"Are you sleep walkin'?" he asked, which made me open my eyes. I couldn't fathom him. I thought that this was what he wanted. He had his head on the side, questioning. So I smiled.

"I'm not sleep walking, James," I said. He didn't return my smile.

"What are you doing here, in the middle of the night?"

If I had taken his hand then, things might have been different. He looked like a man who so wanted to be touched. But I wasn't that bold.

"I thought you might want the company," I said.

"You offering company, is that it?"

Without thinking much about it, I undid the top button of my jacket. I wanted to be a reflection of him. I wasn't looking at him now, but out towards the fire. I craved warmth.

Teer jerked his hat off his head, threw it down and pushed his hair back from his face. He picked a piece of wood off the pile, but it was forked and tangled and he had to yank it free. Stepping out through the rain, he dropped it on the fire. When he came back he looked sharply awake.

"I need to understand exactly what it is you are offering, Mrs Jewell. You come out here to me at a time when all the men are in their beds and look at me as if ..." He paced the length of the wood pile and back and returned into the half-and-half light. He rubbed his beard, but he wasn't confused. He understood me. "You look as if you want me to take the clothes off you," he said.

I did want that. I didn't care about being cold if Teer would warm me. I had been abandoned and alone and I wanted to be claimed with his big arms. It had always been Teer. He had scooped me out of the sea and poured the water out of me when Joseph had drowned me. He had protected and fought for me, defended me, when Joseph had failed again and again. I wanted to thank him. I wanted to give myself to him as a gift.

"Do you want me here with you?" I asked, knowing the answer was yes.

"Jesus Christ, I'm not saying I don't want you," Teer said. "I'd be made of stone not to feel the urges now. If you're suggesting we hide away in the dark here and I get to poke you and no one any the wiser, that's one thing. But I don't think that's what you're offering."

"I love you, James."

I hadn't planned to say it, but it was the truth. I felt him so intensely, I wanted to crawl inside his jacket and bind myself to him. Since he had pulled me from the sinking ship, I had been his.

But he was having none of it.

"Ach, is it love, is it? There's nothing I can do with your love. This is not the time or the place for that sort of thing. I lead these men, and you are the wife of Joseph Jewell. So what do you think happens when the men find out I'm having his wife?"

"Joseph doesn't care for me."

"Bill Scott might say different. If he could talk."

Teer had pulled the ghost of Scott dripping from the sea and laid him down between us. I would rather a punch from his heavy fists than such a blow.

"I don't know what—"

"Bill Scott had a loose mouth—and I do you the credit of not believing the things he said about you. Jewell did what a man should to defend his wife's honour when he bucked him. That's love."

I stepped forward and put my hand lightly on Teer's arm, trying to bring him back, to stop this talk of Bill Scott, but he shook me off.

"Though he'd no need to throw my feckin' gold with him." He shook his head, his lips tight. There was nothing soft about him at all. I didn't know why I had ever imagined there was.

Teer didn't love me. Was that what he meant? He'd said there was nothing he could do with my love. It wasn't the same thing. He'd told me he couldn't love me, not here, because of Joseph and the men. I wanted to ask what happened if we remained here forever. If the years went by and no one came. Would he change his mind? Give in? Forever. I couldn't bear it.

"Don't go offering yourself around," he said, turning away from me. "We have a fine balance here with the men. Bill Scott nearly smashed the whole thing to bits. But I need you to hold on to your marriage, Mary, or things could get difficult. Do you hear what I'm sayin'?"

I heard him. He wanted me to go on pretending with Joseph. To remain under the protection of a man who had no love for me at all, who could barely look at me. I couldn't do it. It had taken me such courage to come to Teer and I needed him so badly. He was every bit the man that Joseph was not.

"Ah Jesus, don't be looking at me like that, girl, you fair make my blood run hot. You get me all excited, you know I beat myself up at the thought of you. I'd be having you if I could, you know I would." He put his hands into his hair again. He pulled it, as if the pain would distract him from his thoughts. "But you're no' mine. You're married to one o' my men." He stopped abruptly as if he had come to a conclusion. A decision had been made. As with everything and always, it wasn't me that made it.

"You need to stand with your husband. That's your place. With your husband. Don't you be coming out here to me again."

And he sat and picked up his knife and his whittling stick and flicked the blade against the wood, cutting a sharp edge.

I returned to Joseph. I didn't know whether he was awake when I lay beside him, or not.

℘

In the morning, when Joseph rose, I sat up with him.

"Good morning," I said. My voice seemed to startle him.

"Good morning, Mary," he said. Expressionless. I didn't know what to make of him.

We found another old campsite, quite by accident. It was around on an eastern bay where the seals wallowed on the beach with their large pups—fat babies slow to grow up. They cooed, snored and twitched. Barked sometimes, like an old man's laugh. The bull, who had protected the pack through the summer whelping and breeding, had gone out to sea and the females were placid, unaware of any threat. We watched them for a while, selecting our target. It was a mistake to think their stored blubber made them slow, though. We'd learned much about seal hunting since our early days when Caughey took his bite.

I was breathing a fire to life on the bank while Joseph and Ashworth approached a big cow that was apart from the rest, a flopping lump of pale muscle with black circles around her eyes and turned-down mouth that made her appear clown-like and funny. They came at her head on, keeping her attention so the soft part of her skull presented to them. None of her companions gave notice; there were no barks of warning or distress. Her languid sisters dozed, unaware or uncaring that one of their own was in deadly peril. They didn't know enough to fear us, yet. Sanguily walked among them on the beach and they idly lifted their flippers at him. The pups were still feeding and had the lazy carelessness of youth.

At the last moment our girl felt the danger and heaved herself swiftly up, but a swinging blow from one man then the other and she was done. She collapsed onto the sand and the men dragged her away while her sisters barked and rolled and waved at the sun.

We skinned her by the fire and parcelled her up to carry back to camp as the blaze burned away the grass on the bank. We'd found things on this beach before, some bits of flint for fire-starters and scraps of tin, but as we kicked the embers to kill the fire we uncovered a flat pavement of brick and tile, which appeared to be remnants of an old Māori lodging abandoned many years before. Further searching uncovered a garden from which Sanguily pulled some very small potatoes, growing wild. He held out his cupped hands filled with the little nuggets, more precious on that island than gold.

"We can make a garden," he whispered, his face radiant.

We were an animated party that night. The seal's flippers had made a pungent soup and we sat together after the meal and told stories. I perched on my log with my head up defiantly facing Teer and sang a lively English folk song about going home, while the men beat time with slaps against wood. Joseph was quiet but I sat close by his side. Caughey picked up the song on the next verse, and the attention turned away from me except for Teer, who remained watching me as I sat straight-backed beside my husband. He gave me a strange, half smile. "Good girl," he mouthed.

Did he think I had given up?

Sanguily stood and made a ceremony of handing over the potatoes to Mr McClelland.

"You will know how to grow them," he said, and McClelland formally agreed to nurture the little knobbly tubers. He examined them carefully and talked at length about potato growing: sprouting eyes and chipping and preparation of the soil. He told Sanguily he would need to collect a mountain of guano from the cliffs to make a garden ready for spring.

"Not me!" Sanguily cried, holding up his hands in a dramatic protest. "Why always me you give the shitty jobs? Always it is me you tell to dig your holes to bury your shit. Now you want me to collect shit of the birds? I am not Sanguily the shit-raker!"

His youth and rank remained unchanged, but it was

not true he was given the worst jobs anymore—we all had our hands in animal innards and fish muck every day. It was true Sanguily was ordered about jokingly with an expectation of his subservience and true, too, that he'd begun to resist this mistreatment and rebel against any order on principle.

"All right, all right!" said Mr McClelland, laughing as the Cuban got increasingly worked up. "My dear aristocratic Sanguily, I'll give the job of guano collection to someone else. It was a fine task I asked of you, to collect the deposits of these noble birds to work into our soil to make a garden that will nourish and provide for us, but you are excused this duty."

"I don't need to collect the bird shit?"

"No. You don't need to collect bird shit. You can get the goat shit."

Poor Sanguily desperately tried to hold his dignity as the whole party roared with laughter at him. His lip quivered and eyes rolled and he gave one of his performances of a man suffering great injustice, but eventually he, too, saw the funny side of it.

"You are joking, Mr McClelland."

"I am. I am delighted with you more than I can possibly express, my friend, that you have discovered potatoes for a garden in this hostile place and I will ensure, next summer, that you are the first to taste the new crop."

"I will have the first potato?"

"You will. There. I will stake my life on it."

The dark had come swiftly and I was suddenly aware of the cold in my back. It was the way of a rich fire, and perhaps the way of the world: you look in one direction and see a golden blaze while a deathly chill comes creeping in from behind. The next day, Mr McClelland cut his hand on a piece of copper.

We thought Mr McClelland's fever was caused by scurvy.

The scourge, always with us, had hit again hard in the autumn. We couldn't cure it, or a cut hand, or any other affliction. Cornelius Drew's joints were so swollen he couldn't bend his legs to sit. We found old cuts, once healed, now reopening on swollen skin. Ashworth, after a year of dignity in fine leather, had to remove his boots for wider sealskin slippers. He looked humbled, limping about on misshapen feet. His ankles, so long covered up, offered tender skin to the sandflies.

"Damn and blast the little bastards!" he shouted as he hobbled around the camp, slapping at his legs.

Mr McClelland's hand puffed up around the small cut in the fleshy part of his palm. He had bad teeth and swollen knees, too, though not as bad as Drew's, but this wound had an evil look to it.

"It's just the cobblers," Mr McClelland said, when he started getting the fevers. The cut still festered but he discounted its effects on his state. "Laudable pus," he said. "It helps the healing." But he wasn't healing.

Sanguily said he knew a cure for scurvy.

"Lemons and onions?" asked Ashworth, sneering.

"Bah. You talk French nonsense," said Sanguily with his mouth turned down. "Where you going to find lemons?"

"God save us all from this monkey," said Ashworth.

"No, I'll tell you what. You got to bury a man. Up to his head. There is magic in the soil, it take the poison away."

"Where did you hear this?"

"My grandfather. He tell me."

"No one's going to listen to such superstitious sorcery," said Ashworth. "I suppose you dance on the grave with your pig tattoo?"

But Cornelius Drew, swaying with his eyes half closed in pain, said, "I'll try it."

"You see?" said Sanguily to Ashworth. "Here is a man understand the power of the earth, how God puts medicine in the soil to support all his creations."

"You're a blasphemous heathen," said Ashworth.

Drew rolled his eyes and moaned. He appealed to Ashworth: "I'm desperate, man. I'll try anything. You'll join me, McClelland?"

Mr McClelland didn't reply. He sat keeled over slightly, cradling his hand. I didn't think his affliction was the same as Drew's. He had a sheen on his face and a yellow pallor.

"Leave him," I told Drew, when he began pestering the older man. "He's not well."

"Not well?" he said, laughing with a hacking craw. "Not well? Of course he's not well. But Sanguily is going to fix us!"

And so the next day, Teer and Ferguson, the only ones left strong enough to dig, found a patch of sandy earth close to the beach and dug a long trench for Drew and we covered him up to his shoulders. Joseph, also with swollen limbs, looked on suspiciously but I shook my head at him. I wouldn't see him buried.

When the men stood back and we saw Drew with his pinched white face sticking from the earth, he looked already dead. His lips were blue. We waited for something to happen.

"It's freezing," he said quietly.

"You stay just a little bit," said Sanguily, but even he didn't look so confident anymore. Teer shuffled around from one foot to the other.

"Take him out," I said. "This is stupid. He'll die of cold." It was horrible, to bury a man alive, and I felt a terrible premonition descend. I saw us all laid out on the beach like

Drew, in graves, with our heads poking from the soil and Teer at the end, with no one left to bury him.

"Take him out!" I cried. I grabbed the digging stick and began flicking at the soil away but my arms wouldn't move properly and the soil was wet and heavy. I flung myself on the pile and kept digging until Teer lifted me bodily away and dropped me beside Joseph. He took the stick from my hand and when I snatched for it he took Joseph's hand and put it over mine.

"Hold on to your wife, Jewell," he said, and he and Ferguson dug around Drew's body as his spirit seemed to drain out into the soil. If the scurvy was seeping out, it was taking his life with it.

They carried him barely breathing back to the fire, with Sanguily dancing around the bigger men crying that we had witnessed a miracle. Drew very obviously was not cured and we saw no miracles that day or any other.

I took charge of the patients, Drew and Mr McClelland, who lay in the hut and suffered. My care consisted of pushing pulped root between their lips, hot tea and prayer. Mr McClelland asked me to play, and I took the whistle from him but could find no soothing tune. I coaxed such hymns as I knew from it while they wheezed out, moving their pale lips in mumbled praise to God. It didn't help. I thought by now we all knew that God wasn't coming. I flapped a large leaf to keep the flies away. Drew warmed up after a few days and though his swellings were still bad he managed to take himself out and move about. The stupid man asked Sanguily if he would bury him again but Teer put a stop to their absurdity.

Mr McClelland did not improve. The pus from his cut was yellow and stinking and red streaks ran from his hand up his wrist and into his arm. He was too dizzy to stand and his skin sank into the hollows between his bones.

"I can't feel it," he said, when I asked if his hand was giving him pain. "There's a numbness in my arm. The hand doesn't bother me at all, Mrs Jewell." He was chilled and shivering when he said it, though I could feel the heat coming from his forehead like a fire stone. I didn't know whether to heat him up or cool him down. I bathed his head with skin rags soaked in cold water, covered his shaking body with pelts and wrung my hands in worry.

There seemed no end to our hopelessness as we lived in near darkness and the temperatures dropped close to freezing.

Teer came in to observe my sleeping patient. He stood close enough to touch me when he felt Mr McClelland's racing pulse and listened to his fast breathing. I didn't move away but stayed on his wing, drawn to him like a disciple. Teer was nearly twice my size, but his movements were so gentle as he rested his hand on Mr McClelland's head. He asked me what he had eaten, whether there were any signs of improvement, and I answered him quietly so that he was obliged to bend his head towards me to hear.

He turned to poke the fire and I followed him, standing close enough that my skirt pressed against his legs. He straightened and dropped his hands to his side. But he kept his attention on the fire. "Nay, Mary," he said. "I've told you, you're not to do this."

I could so easily have reached up and stroked his face. I wanted so much to touch him. I felt if he would hold his arms out I would be safe. I wanted his warmth and his strength around me. I was so tired.

"I just want—" I began.

"I know what it is you want," he said. "But you can't have it."

He said it to dissuade me, but still he didn't move away. He said one thing but he wanted another. I could feel him reaching out to me as though it had happened, as if his arm had already swept around me and pressed me to his chest. I could smell what he wanted. I stepped into that warmth expecting him to pick me up.

But there was no softening.

I hit the solid wall of him and with his great arms he pushed me away.

It was a hard push, both his hands on my chest, a shove such as he might give a man and I staggered back and fell against Mr McClelland's bed. There was no gentleness in the face that stared down at me, no affection. He was the man I feared, the brutal Teer. I cowered down, frightened that in his flash of temper he would discipline me, stamp me with his fist. Raging across his face was anger and a fierce lust or craving, an unreadable mass of conflict. But not love. There was no love in the man.

"I've told you," he said. "We're not doing this."

I clamped my teeth together and didn't cry until he left. The hut smelled as if animals lived there.

After a while there was a stirring beside me and Mr McClelland's hand, the good hand, the one that still worked, reached over and patted my arm. It just made me cry harder.

"There, now," he said. "There, now."

I was so wretched that I was not even ashamed. What did my degradation matter, when we were all so pitiable? I just cried and let Mr McClelland comfort me, in such misery that I didn't care it was the wrong way around: that he was the one dying and I should be comforting him.

❧

Mr McClelland got worse fast. He could eat nothing and his spare frame disappeared under my hands as I tried to wash the fever off him.

"You're a good girl, Mrs Jewell," he said, lifting his head to take a sip of the horrible bitter tea he had us all drinking, the stuff that tasted of dead grass. "That's fine, that is. You'll see, I'll be getting up tomorrow. We'll plant those potatoes."

But of course, he didn't. His eyesight faded some more until he couldn't recognise who it was sitting beside him.

"It's me, Mr McClelland." I had cool water to wash his face.

"I know. Teer leaves and you come in. It's quite the dance."

Was it so obvious? Did everyone see it? "Teer doesn't like me," I said. I wet the scrap of rabbit skin and dabbed his forehead. He wasn't so hot as he had been the last couple of days.

"It doesn't matter whether he likes you or not. You already have a husband."

I sat back. I was nursing a pitiful dying sailor and the man thought to preach to me, to direct me how I should live my life.

"Joseph doesn't want me anymore," I said, sounding more angry than I intended. "I need to look after myself, Mr McClelland."

He took a deep breath then and sighed a long wheeze out that went on so long and so feebly I thought he was breathing out the last of his life.

"Hey," I nudged him and his eyes flicked open, red rimmed and the pupils all cloudy, but I thought he saw me very well.

"You need to look after your husband," he said.

He had a fur-seal pelt for a cover, one of the early ones that wasn't so soft as we later made them, and when I turned it back to wash him the weight off seemed to relieve him, though he immediately began to shiver. It was warm in the hut, the fire was lit and the doorway covered. He smelled of dead meat. I was so horribly sorry for him that he would die on the island. He knew it. He pretended otherwise to me, perhaps thinking that despite all the death I had seen I was still afraid of the process. We both knew he would never see his home or his family again. I took a scoop of the ash and lye soap mix, and gently washed the sweat off his scrawny chest.

He was still watching me with his sightless eyes.

"When the *General Grant* was sinking, the captain ordered your husband to get the women and the children off the ship, to rig up a rope sling to lower you all into the boats."

I knew it. I didn't know why he should bring it up now. I didn't want to go to that cave in my mind ever again. I had tried so hard to leave it behind. I blinked away the faces at the rail. Remembered the weight of the noose Joseph had tied around my waist before sending me into the sea.

"There were twenty-two women and children on board," he said. His voice didn't sound so weak now.

I threw down the rag, covered him up again. I had finished ministering to him. "I know that, Mr McClelland. I watched them all drown, same as you."

"He failed."

He had no need to tell me that, either. I knew Joseph had failed. I had nearly drowned because of his failure.

"I need you to hear me, Mrs Jewell."

"I don't need to hear you. My husband goes about his days like he's all on his own. He doesn't need anyone. He doesn't even *see* me." I said it again. "He doesn't see me."

"He jumped in to save you." Mr McClelland closed his eyes for a second, and I thought he had finished tormenting me, but he was just gathering his breath. "He abandoned his post."

I sat back.

He still hadn't finished. "To save you."

Fire hissed through damp wood.

"Above everyone else."

Outside I heard Caughey calling for Joseph to bring a bag. It was low tide and they were going for shellfish. I hated the limpets and mussels they gathered. Boiled in the pot or baked in the fire, they were chewy and impossible to break down. I could clench them against the roof of my mouth and suck them but they just tasted like the sea. Sometimes I swallowed them whole. Even the thought of shellfish now made me gag.

"What do you think that might do to a man?" Mr McClelland's hollow eyes filled with tears.

"You should rest, Mr McClelland. I'm going to mash some fish for you in a bit of the goat's milk, do you think you could take some of that?" I knew he wouldn't eat it. The only thing he ever asked for was an egg. But it was winter and the birds had gone. There were no eggs.

"You think on it," he said. And then he closed his eyes and collapsed down into his own skeleton, an exhausted fluttering sleep. I looked at his swollen hand. It was just a small cut that had never healed and now his whole arm was swollen red right up to the shoulder. There was nothing I could do about it.

I went out, but Teer was busy building some contraption by the fire, so I passed by without a word and went down onto the beach to where, in the distance, I could see Joseph and Caughey digging for pipis.

The tidal puddles soon soaked through my moccasins and I had left my gloves behind, but cold was such a habit I didn't acknowledge it. I saw Joseph with his hand deep in the sand, chasing bubbles when a wave went out to extract the burrowing things beneath. He worked methodically: hand into the sand, pipi in the bag. Hand into the sand, pipi in the bag. I couldn't see his face but didn't imagine his expression any different from the one he had worn, constantly, for the last year. Resignation. The look of a man sentenced to hard labour who expected to neither give nor receive any joy. A man in purgatory.

I crouched down a few feet from him and watched the bubbles in the sand. "Hello, Joseph," I said. "I've come to help."

He looked up, but there was no pleasure in my arrival. There was no change of expression at all. "You don't need to be here. You'll get cold."

Both statements were true. I could have turned around and gone back to Teer by the fireside, but I put my hand into the raw sand and felt around for a pipi. There were bubbles, but the shell was too deep to pull out. I tried again. It took me three attempts to catch one of the slippery things and I felt it pulling away as I closed my fingers on the shell. But I pinched it firmly and pulled it out into the light. A small triumph.

Caughey was a dozen paces away towards the rocks but threw me a welcoming smile. "Look, Mrs Jewell!" He reached into his bag and pulled out a crab the size of his stretched hand, heavy and purply red. It clacked its mean pincers at me. Caughey tilted it in the light and it glowed with a pink sheen across its shiny back. It was a complicated thing and I went closer to examine it, wondering why God would go to so much trouble to put such beautiful colours on a thing that scuttled about in the mud.

"There's a lot more meat in this than those hairy crabs Sanguily digs up. Sure they don't usually grow so big. McClelland will like to see this one, have a name for it, no doubt."

The crab waved its strange-looking claws around, searching for mud. Perfectly designed for scrambling over rocks but helpless dangling in the air.

"I'm afraid Mr McClelland won't be able to see him," I said. I felt sorry for the powerless, angry thing. "Why don't you put him back, Mr Caughey? It would be a shame to eat him. He's so handsome."

"Ah, you're a soft one," he said, hesitating with the crab snapping from his fingertips. "But you see, I was thinking, we can roast him in bird fat, shell and all, and then grind him into a paste to mix with the fish. Cook it slow. You can find some of your green stuff. Pinch of salt."

I felt desire as a shot of heat in my mouth. It was a forgotten urge, to eat something tasty, something with a layering of flavours. Something that would make us feel happy for the eating and content afterwards.

Perhaps he could make a dish appealing enough to encourage Mr McClelland to take a mouthful.

When Caughey shoved the thing, alive, into his sack, I made no comment, and when we returned to camp I smothered the crab in bird fat and baked him on a hot stone, just as Caughey had said. Ground up, the crab made a fine soup, but while Mr McClelland enjoyed the smell and the story, he could eat none of it.

He was almost gone.

STORIES AND ENDINGS

"I'm going back to the cave," Teer said a few days later. The late afternoon light was beginning to stretch out as we had gathered for a meal. For the first time in a while the rain had stopped and a weak sun shone through a gauzy high cloud.

This seemed to be a surprise to everyone. Even Caughey, Teer's constant ally, paused in his cooking to take note.

"I want some bearings. When this is all over, I'm coming back with a ship for the gold."

Everyone spoke at once then: who was in the party, who got to share in the gold, what if he smashed into the rocks, how could we survive without the boat?

How could we survive without Teer? I wondered.

"I'll not take the boat. You can leave me at the end of the harbour. I'm going overland, across the hills."

Sanguily began his rapid questioning again, small and combative with hands on his hips and thrusting chest. Teer put his hand on the Cuban's face.

"If I was going for the gold I'd take you with me," said Teer. "I'd tie a rope around your waist and a rock to your feet and throw you to the cave floor."

I felt the familiar wave of nausea. Teer said such a thing in jest and some of the men laughed at the image, but Joseph didn't laugh. I saw the cave shadows in the crevices of his long face, in the hollows of his eyes. He rubbed his thumb across his palm as if remembering the rope he'd tied around me.

"I'll get a reckoning is all. From the cliff tops."

"You'll share it, we'll need your word on that," said Allen, and then to soften the greed in his voice, "Fair shares for all of the survivors. Whatever you find."

A sound rumbled from Teer, muffled by all his layers of bulk, unpleasant and directed at Allen. It was a callous laugh with no humour in it. "Sharing, is it? Do you intend to share that little purse you carry with all of us? The stash you've buried and never mentioned, the precious nuggets you took from your wife's petticoats when the ship went down?"

If Allen had carried a knife I believed he would have used it on Teer then. But he was another of the powerless and could do nothing but attack with narrowed eyes and the deepest scowl. Of course no one rose to defend him. No one liked Allen except Ashworth, and in truth he probably despised him, too.

"I've said I'm going for a bearing," said Teer. "See the place in daylight, chart the lie from Disappointment Island. And I will share my findings with you. There's my promise. I'll keep nothing back. A proper bearing for the cave we all take away with us. And then the race is on. May the best man win."

I reported all this back to Mr McClelland when I sat with him in the evening; though in my voice the salvage plan sounded ridiculous and the poor man seemed distracted. He tried to tell me something, but though his papery lips moved and breath came through, no sound followed.

☙

I lay beside Joseph at night and thought of the last things Mr McClelland had said before he stopped talking, about

Joseph assuming blame for the deaths of all the women and children.

It was folly to think such a thing, of course. The ship had wrecked and the miracle of it was that any of us survived. Such guilt could swallow a man. Drive him mad.

I had also felt a responsibility for those deaths. *If* I had stepped up more boldly, *if* I had leapt cleanly into the boat, *if* I had called out for the women to follow me, *if* I had kept the Italian man's baby in my arms, *if* I had held the hand of Mary Oat. All of that horror had filled every thought in my head until there was not space for anything else. I had escaped all that with the thought of a baby, the growing baby I carried that pushed all other thoughts away. When Joseph, with such cruelty, told me the baby didn't exist, I dropped the burden and became responsible for nothing. I could jump into the gorge to end my life. I became free.

Mary Oat was sometimes the girl playing pat-a-cake with her sister and sometimes the dark hair sinking beneath the water, and that was a dreadful thing that had happened that would haunt me forever, but I no longer believed I was to blame for her death.

I listened to Joseph's breathing beside me, and I tried to go back to before that night on the *General Grant*, even to the day before, when we were sailing through the fog and I had glimpsed Joseph on the rigging and had felt …

… but I couldn't bring that feeling back. Whatever it was I had felt then was so cold in me and sunk so deep I couldn't grasp it.

❧

"A word, Mr Teer," I said, a couple of mornings later, when he rose from the fire and looked out along the calm harbour, ready to load the boat for his expedition. The worst of winter had passed, days were longer and he was eager to set out. He looked suspiciously at me from under his heavy brows but indicated that I might step away from the circle with him.

We went a few paces. "You can't go. Not just yet." I bit my lip.

"What's your reason, Mrs Jewell?" he asked, and was about to say more, but I looked across to the hut where our friend lay and Teer stopped on his drawn breath. "Is it McClelland?"

I nodded. I didn't want to ask anything of Teer and I felt crumpled and wet. But I knew he mustn't leave now. "Today. Tomorrow, maybe. And—"

"I see." He did see. He was always a practical man. "You'll be needing someone to dig a grave."

I was relieved I hadn't had to say the words.

"You go and sit with him," he said. "I'll talk to the men."

"Thank you. I'm grateful." I was grateful. I could sit with Mr McClelland. That I could do. But I could not arrange to dig his grave.

I took my washing things and went to the hut. Mr McClelland was awake. He had a flush on him, and he smiled his old grin when he heard me come in.

"Mrs Jewell," he said. "I've been waiting for you."

"You have ears for eyes today," I said. His energy was unnatural. He looked, of all things, drunk. He patted the bed next to him but the stench was strong and I told him I would wash his wound before any chat. I wanted to tell him that Sanguily had dug the garden bed, and we had fertilised the soil with guano and laid down the potatoes.

"There's no time," he said. "Sit ye down. Never mind the smell, 'twill be gone soon enough."

A waft of cloying pus rose from his weeping hand but I found I could ignore it. There was a vivid colour in his cheeks that couldn't last for long. I took his good hand.

"Has Teer gone looking for the ship?" he asked, and I said no, not yet. I wasn't going to say the men had stayed to dig his grave.

"It's not there."

I patted his hand. "What's not there?" I asked, and his face flashed a cheeky grin of the boy he must have been fifty years before.

"The *General Grant*," he said, in a crumpled whisper. "They've all forgotten."

"Forgotten what, Mr McClelland?"

"I've seen it before, how memory plays tricks. How one person's memory turns into another's and every time a thing is remembered it is bigger. Men's stories at night. Something lost, something changed."

"What do you mean?"

One of his eyes was looking at the ceiling but the other flicked sharply to me. "A cave, was it?"

I nodded. A cave, yes.

"Huge. Black. Frightening," he said.

"Yes. All of those things." I could picture the cave with absolute clarity. And yet ...

"And we rowed for five days before the rocks with no food or water."

That wasn't right. I stumbled over my recollection. "Was it only four days?" I asked. Four days or five, it had been terrible. My suffering had been so great. I couldn't remember the detail.

"And we rowed all the way to Disappointment Island. Against the wind in the mist."

"Yes. That island off the coast. We did, did we not?"

"Do you remember seeing the island?" I had no idea what I had seen. Rocks and waves and cliffs rising from the swell. "And then," he suggested, "we rowed halfway around the mainland."

"I don't know. It seemed so far."

"It's what imagination does with nightmares." His breathing was ragged now, the rawness of his voice and the terror of the story raising a chill across the back of my skull.

I nodded my head because he was dying. It was such a strange idea.

"Doesn't matter. Let them search south."

His eyelids flicked open and shut. When they opened again I thought he was dead and I sat in frozen fear. Then I noticed a tick on the skin in front of his ear, a pulse. He blinked.

"But Sanguily's stories."

My heart slowed. I turned to look through the doorway thinking I had heard a scratch but there was no one nearby, just a bird, pecking at the thatch.

"Yes?" I drew closer to him.

"All his babble about the *London*'s cargo, the crates for the Bank of England, the spelter with gold-laden rock."

"I know. It's just Mr Sanguily's imagination."

"No," he said, speaking slowly and with effort, but more strongly now with the flush upon him. It seemed important I understood. "It's all true. We had more gold than declared. Oh, we had much more."

"It's true?"

"More than even Sanguily imagined. I worked with the carpenters at night. There was bullion loaded into sacks and we packed it into compartments hidden in the ship's hull. Crates of it. They say it's bad luck to take another ship's load, and so it seems."

There was no noise from outside now. I waited while Mr McClelland gathered his breath.

"We built a compartment forward of the chain locker. Big enough to fit a hundred bags of gold coin. We reduced the anchor chain to stow before it. We weren't planning to use the anchor—dock to dock we were." He blinked, his eyelids like moths' wings. "The chain might have saved us. 'Never go aground with your anchor up,' a wise pirate once told me. We couldn't use it, you see, that night."

When he swallowed, his throat took a long time to recover. I tried to give him water but he shook his head. "The same again in the walls below the cabins. We were lined with gold fore and aft. It never went on the manifest and no one was told. Captain Loughlin was afeared of pirates. Or mutiny."

I thought of the way the ship had floundered in the water when she had stopped moving forward. And sluggish, Joseph called her as she was pulled out from the wharves. The whole ship was a treasure chest.

"Don't tell them," he whispered.

"I won't say anything."

"And now Teer's off looking south." Mr McClelland's face lit up with the strange smile again, as if he were going somewhere else that was altogether more pleasant than here and couldn't carry these things with him, the things he was telling me. I held his hand and we grinned at each other and Mr McClelland made a sound that I thought was a death rattle, but as I watched his eyes I realised was a laugh.

"Mrs Jewell?" A sharp voice broke in from the doorway and I swung my head around. Ashworth. He had one foot over the threshold but was poised, not a man on the move but a man who had been listening. I hastily stood up.

"What do you want, Mr Ashworth? You shouldn't come up like that—"

"Like what?"

"Creeping in without announcing yourself. Have you, did you ..." I didn't like the expression on his face. He certainly had the fire in his eyes like a man who had just struck gold. "You shouldn't be—"

"I'm sent to ask you to come out for a moment, if you'd be willing. We want your advice. I'm sure Mr McClelland will allow you leave, it won't be for long. My God, it stinks in here."

He stepped forward into the room, looking past where I still held Mr McClelland's hand and on to the bed. Ashworth frowned, and stepped forward again.

"Come away now, Mrs Jewell," he said gently. "May God have mercy on his soul."

The rattling breathing had stopped. God had come and gone while my back was turned and I was holding a dead man's hand. The flush had gone from his cheeks.

I cried out and pulled the hand I held, wanting to shake the life back into the dear old man, to pour some of my own life force down into his body, but I felt Ashworth's arm around my shoulders, steadying me. He reached out with trembling fingers and enclosed my hand and the lifeless hand of Mr McClelland. Slowly, slowly, he detached me from my friend, and gently, gently we let him go.

Together, Ashworth and I folded Mr McClelland's hands over his chest. I pushed his scant hair back from his forehead.

There was nothing in the sunken face of the dear man who cared about the colours of bird's crests, or the names of the crabs and the trees. Who cared enough about me to tell me truths. The grin was gone and his mouth sagged open. Ashworth stroked the thin skin down over his poor blind eyes and together we went to decide where to lay him to rest.

A SHIP

There were ten of us now, of the eighty-three who had stepped so fearlessly on board the *General Grant* nearly eighteen months before. Mr Brown and his men had been gone more than nine months and no one retained any hope that they had landed in New Zealand and were arranging our rescue. "The four who sacrificed their lives to save us," was a constant refrain until I came to repeat it, too. The image of Scott sailing away in the boat to the horizon as strong in my mind as the image of Joseph throwing him into the sea. In reality, I had seen neither.

I came to these agreements with myself. Once, Scott had fed me meat from a stolen tin. I'd allowed myself to believe that without it I would have died, putting my guilt into a pouch I didn't intend to open. Now, when the men spoke of Scott's great sacrifice, I made no correction in my head and let it settle. He had died at sea and no one needed to carry the blame for that.

I think we all made such pacts with ourselves. If we hadn't we would have gone as mad as Mr Brown. All who had rowed from the cave carried guilt stitched into our seams but we rearranged our memories and carried on.

Drew and Ferguson played a game where they proposed that Mr Brown and his men had made land somewhere and were living as castaways. They dropped names like "the Snares" and "Campbell Island", although they had no knowledge of the position of these near-mythical islands nor any reason to believe our men could have found them in the vastness of the ocean. I believed the men had perished on the sea; I hoped swamped by a wave and quickly drowned rather than the alternative, a topic never mentioned. Every night I prayed for their souls.

But Mr McClelland was the first to die from our hopelessness. He had been the oldest, but of a stronger build than either me or Sanguily. Certainly tougher than Allen. The ailing Cornelius Drew commented often that he thought he would be the first to go, as though we should take it in turns to perish and line up behind him.

We buried Mr McClelland close by and set a cairn over his grave. I wanted him up on the headland by the lookout, his blindness now no impediment to his views of the sea and where his beloved birds could circle around him. But I hadn't walked that far since Scott's attack and neither Drew nor Allen had the strength to climb the hill.

Drew was almost totally crippled, so Caughey took him the few yards on his back—the pale sailor with constantly bewildered eyes crying that he was fading and would be dead before nightfall.

Sanguily took off his earring and slipped it over the tip of the dead man's finger. It was the only piece of gold he owned. I thought perhaps it was to buy Mr McClelland his passage to heaven but Sanguily said no, that the gold earring would improve the dead man's eyesight.

"Oh, Mr Sanguily," I said, and I took his hand and rubbed it. The strange dear man. "If he can feel anything at all on his way it will be your great kindness. His eyes will be open to the glory."

Joseph and Teer had dug the grave and we wrapped Mr McClelland in sealskin—his old one. No one suggested we should give up a new, softer one for a dead man. Before we stitched it shut, I placed the tin whistle beside him. The little wooden box he had carved for me went in his hand together with the rabbit skin within, and all of it went into the grave. Mr McClelland could carry the souls of all the lost babies with him to heaven and play for them when they arrived. Ashworth said the Lord's Prayer. We stayed there a long time to say our goodbyes and every man was crying. Mr McClelland had been a good friend to us all and I found it unbearably sad that his wife and children in Scotland knew nothing of his fate. He was just another sailor who hadn't come home from the sea.

As we walked back down the path I took Joseph's hand and squeezed it.

I was surprised when, ten paces farther on, he squeezed back.

It occurred to me that Joseph had also sat with Mr McClelland during his illness and perhaps received relief from his own demons. Would he, also, try to make a pact with them?

In the morning Teer set off on his expedition to find the cave, taking Hayman and Caughey with him. Joseph and Ferguson rowed them past Sarah's Bosom to the harbour end and saw them off into the tangled forests. They would light our old beacon when they returned and we would send the boat for them.

I said nothing of what Mr McClelland had told me. Let them scramble around on the cliff tops. Maybe they would find the cave of the *General Grant* and maybe they would be searching in the wrong place altogether. It seemed unlikely they would recognise the place after all these months and coming from it over the land.

We had talked about the cave so often. The most vivid picture in my head was of Mr Brown jumping in to find his dead wife, but that was Sanguily's story and I hadn't been there. We had wrecked in the darkest of nights in fog, with the lamplight falling in small pools, and yet my memory of the steep walls of the cave was clear as day. Many times our collective stories had mentioned blazing stars. Perhaps our cave existed more in the story than out there under the cliffs.

"They never going to climb down the cliffs," said Sanguily, as the boat slid away into the rain. "They are a thousand feet high. Two thousand feet. Rocks straight into the ocean and water like thunder. But we already see the cave. I can tell you where she is, Mrs Jewell. I have seen her."

Although I didn't believe him and never wanted to go back, I did want the wreck found. Not for the gold, but for the dead. I hoped one day a ship would bring a man of God to say a prayer for those who had perished. I believed the souls of Mary Oat and her sisters were in heaven, but their earthly remains lay beneath those cliffs. The place should be blessed and made sacred.

၇၁

We were a dispirited party that remained at our Enderby camp. Ashworth had staggered off up the hill to the lookout watch, leaning heavily on a stick and delicate on his swollen ankles. Drew and Allen lay in their hut moaning with their disabilities—though there was little wrong with Allen other than idleness—leaving Sanguily and I to fish, cook, tend the fire and bring them cool pelts to put on their legs to ease their suffering.

"You are the strong one," said Sanguily to me as I carried the heavy bucket of water back from the beach to fill the salt pot, my third trip that day. And it did seem so. At that time I was one of the least afflicted. But I made him laugh by staggering around and moaning, clutching my back.

"I am absolutely decrepit," I said.

"You have a great courage in your body and in your head. I see this. Despite all our torment." Sanguily waved his arms around and pulled a dramatic face. "You are still full of life. You will survive."

I stopped my play acting. It seemed he was serious. I didn't believe in Sanguily's hocus pocus and magic spirits but when he said *You will survive* in another voice, deeper, with a different accent, I felt a warm blow of air.

"Thank you," I said, with sincerity. I felt he had told me something important. Somehow, and for whatever reason, the crazy Sanguily had given me his premonition that I would survive. That I had not come this far to die on this island. I realised I believed him.

"And you, too, Mr Sanguily. One day we will both leave this island and we will have long and happy lives afterwards."

He blinked long lashes over his big brown eyes so theatrically I wanted to laugh, until I realised he was deeply affected. He looked about to cry. "When we are rescued and back in a town, I buy something for you."

"A present?"

"Not a present. Something borrowed and I want to return." He blinked rapidly and, seemingly unable to speak, turned to pick up the axe and left, heading to the forest.

I watched him go, bemused. It was only later I thought of the only thing it could possibly be. He was going to buy me a petticoat.

He had a such sweetness to him, Mr Sanguily, a child too soon a man. He made me smile. I wondered if, under the skin jerkin and jacket I had made for him, he still wore the ragged remains of that old petticoat next to his skin.

I was stretching rabbit skins by the fire when Joseph and Ferguson returned, the flames pulling them like a beacon through the long dusk. Sanguily helped them drag the boat up the beach. They were exhausted from the haul across the harbour, two gaunt men like starving beasts. They ate ravenously, directly from the pot.

Then Ferguson went to his hut to sleep and Joseph, also, turned to go.

"Stay with me a while," I said. Since we had found flints we no longer needed to keep a watch all night, but one person always stayed late at the fire to put the midnight fuel on, none of us wanting to be the one to let it die.

Joseph hesitated. I felt such a stab of disappointment that he so obviously didn't want to be there, alone, with me. He looked around to see what needed to be done and began to stack the wood pile, pulling logs that had tumbled back under cover from the rain that would fall later. I left him to his task and when he had finished he stood silently. He seemed to be waiting for me to dismiss him. I held out a rabbit skin.

"Will you stretch this one?" I asked. "My fingers are going numb."

"They can wait until morning. You go inside now. I'll stoke the night fire."

"No, you're exhausted. Will you not just sit for a while?"

There was no reaching him. I thought of what Mr McClelland had said: that Joseph thought he was guilty of all those deaths because he had saved me. And yet he could hardly bear to look at me. Perhaps he regretted the decision.

"Joseph?"

When we married, if I had said "Joseph?" like that he would have taken my hand, brought his head close, and said, "Yes, Mrs Jewell?"

I waited, but now he said nothing at all.

There were so many questions I could have asked.

Have you realised I am in love with James Teer?

Why can't you see me anymore?

Shall I leave, so you are no longer responsible for me?

Are you haunted by women and children falling into the sea?

Do you want to die?

Are you staying alive just to save me?

These questions, and more, spun through my mind like a wheel of fortune and all the time Joseph stood patiently waiting for me to let him go. I couldn't. He had the look of a man thinking about death. I suppose he thought we would all die, one by one, and then he would be released from his torment. If I died Joseph could give up the struggle, his existence pointless because then he would have saved no one. I knew that emptiness.

But I had decided I wasn't going to die. I wanted to tell him. I would survive.

All these things that might have turned into conversation passed by and weren't said. Still, he waited.

"Oh, Joseph," I said, almost crying with frustration. "Can't you tell me what's wrong?"

He blinked, twice. For a second I saw my drowned husband peering up at me from a deep pool of black water. With a cold clarity, I understood. All this time I had been struggling so hard for my own survival and I had left Joseph alone with no hand reaching down into the waters to pull him out. In the wretched man standing before me, in his haggard face, I saw the man I had loved and abandoned when all he had done was try to save me. *You need to look after your husband*, Mr McClelland had said.

He was telling me that this was more than a man could do on his own. It was my turn now to save Joseph.

It distressed me to watch him straining, unable to put any words around his feelings. I enclosed him in my arms and felt him shaking, twig-thin in his sealskin suit. He let out a distressed cry. I held on tighter. He tried to slip away.

I pulled him into me and wrapped my arms so tightly that I could feel his body pressed against mine through all our layers and I gripped him, imagining I was slowly pulling him from the sea.

He shuddered. It was a beginning.

వు

We saw Teer's signal fire one morning a week later and, when the wind died late in the day, Joseph and Allen set out across the harbour. Before he left I held Joseph's face in my hands until he acknowledged me. It wasn't a smile but it was recognition.

"I'll be back tomorrow, Mary."

"I'll be waiting for you."

I watched the boat disappear into the mist, but he stayed all day on my mind.

He hadn't told me, in so many words, what was wrong with him. The talk was slow coming; it had been so long since he had said any important words aloud. I don't think he could express what he felt, and what use were words anyway: how did it help to say out loud such heavy words as *guilt* and *shame*? I went as far as to tell him I had thought I was drowning beneath the wreck until he dived in to stop me sinking. I didn't tell him that I blamed him for sending me in with my petticoats full of rocks. He wasn't ready, yet, to tell me why he had left his post and followed me in. That would come. And one day I would be able to talk about the baby. If there had ever been a baby. Perhaps there had never been anything there at all. One thing I did know was that a part of my body was dead inside. I could never now carry a baby of my own.

The men were still away in the boat when William Ferguson's bellow came from way up the hill. He came charging down the path screaming for his life.

It wasn't until he burst across the beach that we heard him clearly.

"Ship!" he shouted, waving his hands, rousing us all from our morning stupor. "There's a ship gone behind the island! She's heading east."

Ashworth raced down the beach on his sticks, the bindings on his swollen ankles unravelling and flapping behind. "Where's Teer?" he shouted, but it was misty down the harbour and we could not see our boat returning. "Goddamn!" he swore, and threw down his sticks.

"Fire, Mrs Jewell!" shouted Ferguson as he raced past, and even the crippled Cornelius Drew joined me in throwing everything we had on the fire, which burst like a furnace into a wild flame, but though we fanned it and layered on the driest tinder it was a flat, foggy day and the smoke rose barely as high as the trees before sinking back to sit in the air above us, the colour of fog. The colour of hopelessness.

We stood staring to the east to where the harbour met the ocean, waiting for a sail to come in around the point, coming into the harbour to find us.

"I had a good fire at the lookout, she'd have seen it for sure, she'll be coming around the point to us. Come on, come on!" Ferguson raged as he marched along, stopping every few steps to put his fingers to his lips and whistle three long blasts across the water.

Sanguily had taken a fire-brand and raced along the coast, the fastest runner amongst us, and soon we saw the signal fires lighting up on the headlands, but the mist! The damn mist! The smoke drifted into the cloud and no ship appeared around the point.

"If we had the boat we could chase her!" roared Ferguson. "That bastard Teer off after gold and leaving us without a boat. We could have caught her. We could have gone

- 309 -

through the channel and cut her off, we could—"

"Shut your mouth and listen," said Ashworth and we instantly hushed.

Along the harbour came three whistles. The men were back.

"Chase her! Come on! Put about! Ship ho!"

As the boat pulled in Ferguson and Ashworth leapt aboard and I waded out almost to my waist to throw my weight against her and send her off.

"Chase her!" I cried, and the men set to, falling into the strong rhythmic strokes that showed the best of them, pulling together with the skill forged in their long hours rowing around this cursed island. They raced into the mist and disappeared.

I struggled back to the beach, dropped to my knees and prayed.

Out along the coast Sanguily's fires took hold and set the hillsides ablaze.

The men rowed far out through the channel into the open sea.

℘

They caught no glimpse of the sail.

They came back submerged in misery for which there was no cure. Teer was in the blackest of humours and he frightened me. Ferguson riled him up and blamed him for leaving us without a boat and Teer punched him in the mouth so brutally that Ferguson spat out a tooth. I turned away from him and went inside, disgusted.

Hayman told me later that Teer had marched their party for mercilessly long days across mountains where the snow lay on the ground. They had trailed the bitter edge of the land above the cliffs but recognised nothing. There was mist and wind and rain, and though they often couldn't see the water they could hear it booming below. Teer had turned so wild even Caughey had fought him. They found no way down the cliffs though Teer had pushed them to the very edge. They couldn't agree on anything and brought back no bearings to point to where the ship lay in a cave with her bones and gold.

We sank low that night.

The next day the rain came and, other than to feed the fire, no one left the huts. Sanguily came down from the lookout and Ashworth replaced him. The fire almost went out and the following day it hailed. Caughey went to chop wood.

I was sitting with Joseph on the bed, holding his hands.

"A ship will come," I told him. He nodded, but I wanted him to talk. "What do you wish for? One wish, what would it be?"

He gave me his lopsided half-smile. "A ship," he said.

"Another ship will come," I said.

And that afternoon, it did.

es

It was Caughey who saw her, looking up from his freezing labours with his axe in his hand to find white masts dead ahead in the harbour, and he gave the cry "Ship ho!" And again, jerked alive by the prospect of deliverance, we raced, lurching and stumbling to the beach.

And there she was, a brig sailing from the south, close in against the coast.

A thing crafted, made in a shipyard with iron tools and bellows and proper canvas for her sails and filled with the modern world, where people ate off plate and glass and the blankets were of wool. I became faint at the sight of her. A whaling ship. A vessel to take us home had arrived on the breeze and she was sailing into our harbour.

The able men leapt into the boat and pulled out but there was no need to chase her. Despite the low fire and wind and hail, she had already seen us and was heading straight into our cove. The smoke from Sanguily's wild fires still steamed on the hills.

I stood on the sand at the top of the tide and my heart was as full as the oceans. The cries echoed across the bay, new voices, hearty and strong and calling out to us—"Well met, strangers! On board!"—as they struck sails and came to rest. In the full bluster of a southerly squall I felt the warmth of the most beautiful day.

Cornelius Drew and Nicholas Allen joined me on the shore and we linked arms and cried in the rain. The sailors threw down a ladder to our approaching boat and reached out their arms. One by one I watched our companions climb back into the world of men. Teer swung himself on board first and threw back his head—I thought I heard his huge laugh echoing back over the water, loud with the joy of salvation. Laughing with relief for all of us.

Night fell and my friends and I reluctantly left the beach, knowing the row boat would come back for us in the dawn but finding it difficult to take our eyes from the ship close by in our harbour, well anchored now with sails stowed.

I spent the last night in the hut alone. I hung all my wet skins before the fire and gathered together the things I would put in a bundle to take away and laid them out on the table. There were some tin scraps fashioned into pans and a bowl. My rabbit-skin gloves. A flimsy wooden plate and cup and a long-handled spoon carved from ironwood. There were several bone fishhooks—half made—and some treated flax waiting to be twined. Hanging from the ceiling were rabbit skins in various stages of treatment. One of Teer's pig hooks. Such treasures. And on Hayman's pallet were Scott's tin playing cards, spread out as if the men had been interrupted mid-game to go out and be rescued.

I put the playing cards in my jacket pocket.

They were hard and cold. I hadn't touched the things since Scott had—had what? What had he done and what had become of him?

The words were there but the memory hidden in a swirling fog. He had tainted me, betrayed us all, escaped, been drowned. Been drowned? Was that what had happened? He had been drowned.

Since Scott had gone I had banished him so well from my mind I could barely picture him now.

The cards draped my jacket down like a pocketful of gold and some memory stabbed me, but it passed and I didn't take the cards out. A man had been with us and had been driven mad by this place and had gone away in the boat to look for rescue. I remembered Scott, with his tirelessly strong arms at the oars, a cocksure and handsome young man from Shields. We had been through terrible things and madness had afflicted us all. We hadn't brought it on each other willingly. Guilt hung over our shoulders like so many dead albatrosses.

I would give the cards to Ashworth to take home to Scott's family. There were things we needed to lay down and let rest in peace. The remainder of our treasures I left. I never wanted to eat with a wooden spoon off a driftwood plate again.

Captain Gilroy came ashore to collect me in the morning, and he walked up the beach and across the grass to my hut as if he was an ambassador paying a visit to a resident queen. He gave me an apple and I held it in my hand, proof that the world beyond these rocks still existed. Of course I couldn't bite it and he immediately recognised his mistake and called his mate, a fearsome-looking New Zealander with a tattooed face, to peel and pare it, and they watched me put a slice into my mouth and suck on its sweetness. It felt like the first time in my life I had tasted sugar.

While the men collected the sealskins to take on board and turned our animals out for the benefit of future castaways, Joseph and I showed the captain how we had lived. We took him to our drying frames and the salt store, and the soaking pools in the stream for the skins, and we showed him our vegetable patch—that narrow trough of sandy dirt where the potatoes had yet to sprout. We had become so accustomed to our animal existence that it confused me to see the pity etched on his face.

When we turned our back on the fire for the last time I collapsed, and Joseph had to carry me onto the boat. A team of dark-skinned sailors lifted me on board the *Amherst*. Our salvation, come at last, was a whaling brig out of Invercargill.

ON BOARD THE AMHERST

We sailed with Captain Gilroy around the east coast to Carnley Harbour, where we came upon the ship we had seen two days before, the cutter *Fanny*, which had come to Musgrave's hut and found our messages inside the glass bottle left by Mr Brown. They were setting sail to come and find us. After eighteen months with only one ship sighting we had two rescues in as many days.

The *Fanny's* captain provided what he could for us: clothing and provisions donated by his men to add to what the *Amherst* crew could spare. I was given a sailor's shirt to wear under my seal pelt jacket and the much-worn fabric against my skin was the soft touch of cotton from the mills at home.

I asked for the bottle Mr Brown had left with our rescue message and this time was allowed to keep it. It still felt like treasure.

Teer kept his skins, but the men took him ashore, where they barbered and oiled his hair and trimmed his beard, which presented an entirely different face to me. Uncovered, he lost some of his power. There was a pale line around the edge of his new beard and I wanted to trace it with my fingers, touch the scars on his cheeks and feel his vulnerability. The razor had uncovered the small white scar. I hadn't forgotten it.

Captain Gilroy told us Teer had looked so wild we were lucky to have been rescued at all, that the *Amherst* crew had almost fled when he emerged wet and wild from the sea, shaggy as Neptune himself.

"You look very different, Mr Teer," I told him as we stood out by the *Amherst*'s bowsprit, watching a sea lion bull lumbering ashore amidst a group of waiting females.

He said nothing for a while. And then, in the soft voice that had once made me think I could change him, he said, "I hope it pleases you, Mary. I feel a weight gone. More than the beard." He smiled but he wasn't looking at me. He was looking ahead, across the calming water. "Now we are at sea again, I feel a freer man."

I laughed quietly and watched the play of the animals on the shore, feeling the roll of the ship beneath my feet, the polished wood under my hands. There was singing from men aft and the smell of coffee coming from the galley.

"I think, Mr Teer, now we are back in the world again, that you should call me 'Mrs Jewell'."

I gave him a minute, but he didn't reply. I went off to find Joseph.

We stayed with the *Amherst* as they hunted the islands. It was a strange kind of rescue—we had been lifted off the island but went nowhere. The same rocks, the same crying birds, a growing pile of sealskins. But my heart hammered with the novelty of new faces and strange voices, for the feeling of brass and carved timber under my fingertips, for biscuit and porridge, rice and sugar.

Teer got his rum. Though there was no more than a cupful each, it made the men reel. Drew cried when he drank the stuff, and immediately threw it up over the side. Mr Caughey encouraged me to take a sip of his and I did, to please him, which made me splutter and laugh and all the men cheered. Joseph didn't take any, making him a favourite of the crew, whose sharing of their precious spirits came with some reluctance.

On board the *Amherst* the men lived in cramped and difficult conditions but they treated us with great kindness. They were mostly New Zealand natives and they spoke their own language. At first they were wary of me, and Captain Gilroy explained they were unsettled to have a white woman among them. I watched them go about their tasks and smiled at all the ordinary things they did, coiling ropes and scrubbing the deck. They had rescued me. I felt nothing but love for them all. After a week of observing how familiar I was with my companions, they relaxed and grew friendlier to me. One proud-faced tattooed man had a wooden comb and wanted to untangle my hair and I was shy of him, but Joseph said I should accept the offer and not be afraid. He sat with me while the man teased out the knotted mess and braided my long hair for me as if I was his daughter. We had time to sit and enjoy such a luxury.

"I should have done that for you," Joseph said. "I'm sorry. It never occurred to me."

With my hair tied up and a scrap of cloth for a bonnet, the men regarded me differently and a courtesy returned that we had lost on the island. Ashworth bowed when he greeted me in the morning. Cornelius Drew blinked as though I blinded him and he fumbled his words even more than usual.

It was Patrick Caughey, dear Mr Caughey, who caught me by surprise as we gathered for a song in a rare fine twilight.

"You are beautiful, Mrs Jewell."

They were all staring at me and for once I didn't feel ashamed of my womanhood. I didn't drop my head or try to hide behind Joseph.

He took my hand and bent over it, but he didn't kiss it. I would remember that moment, with the pale light on the sea, the dark island and us, the ten survivors.

"Even in our darkest times, you were always thus."

"Thank you, Mr Caughey," I said, and I meant it. I was thankful that such a moment had come.

The mate gave up his tiny cabin and I bunked with Joseph, tightly packed and forced to sleep with our arms around each other. During those days and nights on the *Amherst* we began to grow back together.

"I thought you would go off with Teer," he said one night as we lay face to face and I ran a finger down his gaunt cheek. I didn't know what to say to that. I hoped I would never have left Joseph, but I wasn't able to tell him it hadn't occurred to me. I realised, now, that my feelings for James Teer had nothing to do with love. It was a switch of allegiance to a man who might save me. How could I tell my husband that I saw death coming like a wave? That his withdrawal had left me to drown and Teer was in the boat, the one pulling me aboard, the only one who could drain the water out of me, cut the rope from my waist?

One day, perhaps, I would tell him. It didn't need to come now, all at once.

A while later he let out a long sigh and then took several quick breaths and I thought he was crying though his eyes were dry. He had his own confessions.

"I think I threw him overboard," he said. "Scott. I have no memory of it. He was there and I wanted to punish him. And then he wasn't. I didn't mean him to drown. I swear, Mary, it was never my intention to throw him."

I held his face but he said no more. "We've both done terrible things, Joseph," I said. I bit my lip. I would hear what he needed to say in time. "These months brought out the worst in us."

"You have survived so much. You are the strongest woman alive."

I looked up at the ceiling, close above our heads.

"I won't ever be able to have a baby," I said. I hadn't said that word aloud in all the months since my fall, but there hadn't been a day I hadn't thought about the children who would never come. The strongest woman alive and unable to have a child. "What sort of woman does that make me?"

"A resilient one, my love. We'll find a way to have a child. I promise."

Joseph went with Hayman, Sanguily and Ferguson to the beaches. They clubbed the newborn seals and their mothers easily, more experienced than any sealer off the ship. Teer and Caughey joined the *Amherst*'s crew and went for the larger sea lions, following the females into the bush, where they went to keep away from the males. On the beach they boiled blubber in huge pots for oil and salted the skins for packing. The *Amherst*'s hold filled.

Allen and Drew stayed aboard, watched, did nothing. Rested and recovered. They had discarded their sealskins and dressed in dirty old clothes from the ship's mushroom locker. They looked as grubby as each other but the men pitied them and no one made them work.

Ashworth took a boatswain's role and overhauled the ship's ropes. He called me to help, understanding my need to prove myself useful. Together we repaired the leech lining of a sail, and stitched up small rips in the canvas. The needles were triangular, with dull corners and points. They didn't shatter with every stitch and a palm thimble protected my hand. We threaded them with a linen twine we hadn't had to make. We took Allen's fur-seal trousers— which he didn't want to keep—and the pelt was still good so we made a hat, which I presented to Captain Gilroy with our thanks for the rescue.

He looked embarrassed. I don't think he realised what the gift meant. You needed to be on the rocks without a ship at your back to understand such a thing. I never saw him wear it.

There was talk, there was always talk, of seeking the wreck of the *General Grant*. "To see where she lies," the men said, by which they meant "to dive for her gold".

So, when her hold was full, on a blustery southerly we sailed around the south of Adam's Island and up the west coast, where the cliffs reared like cathedrals, their great overhangs and arches carved by giants. Waterfalls tumbled and never reached the sea, blown skywards by the great driving wind that hit the cliffs and soared upwards. Around the *Amherst* birds plummeted into the water, coming out of the clouds like thrown spears. Lone rocks sharp as teeth rose snarling from the sea.

The wind changed, veering west, shoving the whole weight of the Southern Ocean to where the cliffs—the ship killers—howled with the cries of a hundred lost souls. The crew held tightly to the wind in the sails.

I knew what would happen if the wind dropped.

"Going about!" cried the captain, pushing the ship around far too close to the rocks, sucked with the current until the sails filled again, and the men pulled and pulled until there was no slack and I thought the sails would shred. We raced south, screaming along the foot of the cliffs.

"We'll wait for better weather," said Captain Gilroy to his terror-stricken crew.

Twice more we tried to come up the west of the island to the point where it curved away to the east and Disappointment Island appeared in the distance, and we looked for a cave in a shambles of smashed coast. Each time the waves breaking high up the cliffs and raging gales forced us back. We saw hundreds of caves.

"She's there," shouted Teer, bound up tightly against the rising wind. "Bring her in closer!"

But Captain Gilroy didn't like our big Irishman commanding his ship and as the wind hit gale force he took us skudding back to shelter in the south.

When a southerly blew through the next morning the captain decided the risk of the venture was too high and pointed his ship north to New Zealand. The *General Grant* and her golden cargo we abandoned to the weather and the tide.

It was a relief to turn our backs. The scab that had sat over the wound all these months peeled away, and underneath I was surprised to find no gaping sore but a scar, already turning silver.

We, the survivors, stood at the *Amherst*'s stern as we sailed until the cliffs disappeared in the mist and only the sea remained. Once clear of the island and sailing north the sky cleared and the sun returned.

"I'm coming back for her," Teer said. "A paddle-tug's the thing. Get us right in under the cliffs." Cornelius Drew, newly stable on his legs after a month of doing nothing, agreed that he, too, was coming back for the *General Grant* and the gold. I didn't imagine they would work together. Sanguily, Ferguson and Caughey determined to take the next ship home to their families, and Aaron Hayman swore when he got ashore he'd never step aboard a ship again. Allen was silent. He had his own demons to face. Ashworth didn't reveal his plans and shot me a warning glance, but I had nothing to say. They could do what they liked when we reached the shore. I wished good luck to them all.

I said a prayer in my head for the lost innocence of Mary Oat and left my love for her on the sun-drenched sea.

I squeezed Joseph's hand and he put his arms around me, pulling me close.

Portrait of Mr and Mrs Jewell dressed in their
sealskin suits, 1868, Melbourne, by Charles Hewitt.

NOTES ON THE STORY

Mrs Jewell and the Wreck of the General Grant is loosely based on a true story. The ship, carrying eighty-three souls, sank in the Auckland Islands on 14 May 1866 and the survivors describe the cave and their escape in detail. The history of what happened on the island comes mainly from the testimonies of three men. We can't know the accuracies of their reports or what was missed. I have made up a story based on what might have happened to people in such a place, after suffering such a trauma. Mrs Jewell is barely mentioned in the events other than a rumour that William Scott had an unhealthy interest in her. Women's stories have been peripheral to much of our recorded history; part of my intent in this is to invent what was never recorded. As far as we know, William Scott was lost at sea with officer Bartholomew Brown and the two other sailors.

James Teer, David Ashworth and Cornelius Drew later all made separate, unsuccessful attempts to locate the wreck of the *General Grant*, hunting for her along the cliffs on the west coast of Auckland Island. Ashworth and his party were lost at sea in their attempt. There have been numerous expeditions to find the wreck since, including two efforts this year alone, and many questions regarding the amount of gold she carried. The cliff is littered with hundreds of caves, there are other wrecks, the weather is wild and the sea ferocious.

The *General Grant* and her gold has yet to be found.

ACKNOWLEDGEMENTS

Whānau and friends, thank you for coming to the ends of the earth with me as I brought dysentery, scurvy and shipwreck to almost every conversation over the last two years. Customary advice is that an author shouldn't discuss current work—I'm sorry I didn't listen to that. Paul, David, Annie and Guy and your gorgeous friends, I owe you so much.

Thanks also to all the passionate people who advised on this book: John McCrystal for his enthusiasm and expert knowledge about all things wrecky and his sharp reading; all the crew on the *Spirit of New Zealand*, particularly ship's engineer David Scott for sailing history, terminology and yarns, and John (JR) Reeve for sea stories; Tanya Ashcroft, for solid support (always) and clever editing suggestions, and to Sandra Jordan for linguistic advice including how to swear like a Cuban sailor.

A special thanks to Bill Day for his thirty-year passion for the *General Grant*, and his generosity in sharing the adventure on that wild sub-Antarctic coastline in February this year. I was a vicarious wreck hunter and it was thrilling.

I acknowledge the songwriters whose songs were being sung at the time of the wreck of the *General Grant*, with the singers often changing the lyrics to suit their circumstances and whim.

Thanks to the marvellous Mary McCallum, my editor and friend, and the rest of the team at The Cuba Press: Sarah Bolland, for the book design and golden cover, and Paul Stewart and Whitireia Publishing student Hypatia Orchard for their input—you are all extraordinary and brilliant and

I have been so lucky, once again, to have your guidance and support. And to Blue Star for the beautiful printing and Creative New Zealand for supporting publication of the book.

And finally, thanks to Jo Torr, artist and fellow sailor on the replica *Endeavour*, who, during starboard watch on the vast Pacific Ocean five miles out from East Cape, turned to me and said: "Do you know about Mrs Jewell and the *General Grant* shipwreck?" And plunged me head first into the story.

ANNA WARD

ABOUT THE AUTHOR

Cristina Sanders grew up in the family's Gateway Bookshop in Wellington and has been a keen reader ever since. She worked in publishing and book marketing and had a career in business before becoming a writer. An obsession with New Zealand colonial history and geography defines her stories for adults and young adults.

The novels *Jerningham* and *Displaced* were both shortlisted for the NZSA Heritage Literary Awards. *Displaced* won the 2020 Storylines Tessa Duder Award and has been shortlisted for the 2022 New Zealand Book Awards for Children and Young Adults.

Cristina lives in Hawke's Bay and is a regular volunteer crew member of the youth training ship *Spirit of New Zealand*, where the sailing and the sailors keep her well supplied with yarns.

www.cristinasanders.me